About the Authors

Annie West has devoted her life to an intensive study of charismatic heroes who cause the best kind of trouble in the lives of their heroines. As a sideline, she researches locations for romance, from vibrant cities to desert encampments and fairytale castles. Annie lives in eastern Australia with her hero husband, between sandy beaches and gorgeous wine country. She finds writing the perfect excuse to postpone housework. To contact her or join her newsletter, visit annie-west.com

Riley Pine is the combined force of two contemporary romance writers as you've never seen them before. Expect delicious, dirty, and scandalous swoons. To stay up to date with all things Riley Pine head on over to rileypine.com, for newsletters, book details, and more!

USA TODAY bestselling author **Catherine Mann** has books in print in more than twenty countries with Mills & Boon Desire, Mills & Boon Heroes, and other imprints. A six-time *RITA®* finalist, she has won both a *RITA®* and *Romantic Times* Reviewer's Choice Award. Mother of four, Catherine lives in South Carolina where she enjoys kayaking, hiking with her dog, and volunteering in animal rescue. FMI, visit: catherinemann.com

Royal Temptation

Royal Temptation:

A Passionate Seduction

ANNIE WEST

RILEY PINE

CATHERINE MANN

MILLS & BOON

First Published in Great Britain 2023
by Mills & Boon, an imprint of HarperCollins*Publishers* Ltd,
1 London Bridge Street, London, SE1 9GF

www.harpercollins.co.uk

HarperCollins*Publishers*
Macken House, 39/40 Mayor Street Upper,
Dublin 1, D01 C9W8, Ireland

ISBN: 978-0-263-31913-2

MIX
Paper | Supporting
responsible forestry
FSC™ C007454

This book is produced from independently certified FSC™ paper
to ensure responsible forest management.

For more information visit: www.harpercollins.co.uk/green

Printed and Bound in the UK using 100% Renewable Electricity
at CPI Group (UK) Ltd, Croydon, CR0 4YY

DEMANDING HIS DESERT QUEEN

ANNIE WEST

For Marianne Knip,
the first of my German readers
I was lucky enough to meet.

Marianne, thank you for your continuing friendship.

Your warmth and your enthusiasm for
my stories are precious to me.

*Ich hoffe, wir begleiten weiterhin gemeinsam viele
Liebespaare auf ihren Weg ins Glück.*

CHAPTER ONE

'THE ANSWER IS NO.'

Karim's voice was harsher than usual, sharp rather than simply firm. The Assaran envoy's suggestion had stunned him. It seemed, despite his actions five years ago, he was still a part of Middle Eastern politics.

Karim stared through the window at the panorama of sapphire lake, verdant foothills and Swiss mountains, yet felt none of the calm the view was supposed to inspire. He spun around, ignoring the quickened beat of his pulse and the clench of his gut.

'But, Your Highness...'

Karim stiffened at the words. 'I no longer use a royal title.'

He watched the envoy absorb that.

'Sir, at least take time to consider. You haven't yet heard the Royal Council's reasoning.'

It was an enormous honour to be asked to take the Assaran throne. Especially since Karim wasn't Assaran. He came from the neighbouring kingdom of Za'daq, where his brother now ruled.

Karim wouldn't accept the Assaran crown. Yet he wondered why the Council was looking beyond its borders for a new sheikh. What about the heir? He knew the recently deceased ruler of Assara had left behind a wife and son.

When Karim realised the direction of his thoughts he

sliced them off. But not quickly enough to dispel the sour tang on his tongue.

'Please, sir.'

The man looked distressed. Karim knew his visitor would be blamed for failing in his mission. If it was discovered he'd been ejected by Karim in mere minutes...

Stifling a sigh, he gestured to the lounge. 'Take a seat. You might as well be comfortable.'

The presidential suite of this exclusive hotel might be comfortable, but sadly it hadn't proved exclusive enough to prevent this unwanted diplomatic delegation. As the hotel's new owner, Karim would change that.

'Thank you, sir.'

Even so, he waited till Karim had taken a seat facing him. Deference towards royalty was ingrained in the man. Even royals who'd renounced their regal claim.

For a mad moment Karim considered revealing the truth and ending this farce. But he'd vowed not to. His brother Ashraf had enough to deal with, imprinting his own stamp on Za'daq. He didn't need full-blown family scandal as well.

Their father had believed Ashraf, the younger brother, was the result of an affair between their mother and the man she'd later run off with. It had only been as the old Sheikh lay dying that they'd discovered Ashraf was legitimate.

Instead Karim, the firstborn, the one groomed from infancy to take the throne, was the cuckoo in the nest.

When, soon after, the old Sheikh had died, Karim had renounced the Za'daqi throne in favour of his brother. No one but the brothers knew the scandalous reason for his decision.

'The Council has given this its deepest consideration since the tragic death of our Sheikh.'

Karim nodded. The Assaran King's death had come out of the blue. 'But surely there's an heir?'

If the envoy noticed Karim's voice had turned to gravel, he didn't show it.

'Yes, but he's far too young to take up the reins of government. If the boy were older…a teenager, perhaps…a regent might be appointed to rule in his stead and help guide him. Given his extreme youth, the Council has decided unanimously that it's better for the country to find a new sheikh.'

'Thus disinheriting the child?' Karim had never met the boy. Intended never to meet him. Yet he felt for the child. His own brother would have been denied his true birthright if disapproving old men had had their way.

'Our constitution is different from yours in Za'daq, sir. In Assara what we propose is quite legitimate. The crown is passed from adult male to adult male.'

Karim nodded. This wasn't his battle to fight. He was only hearing the envoy out so the man could tell his masters he'd done his best.

'Surely there are suitable leaders in Assara? You don't need to go outside your country.'

Especially to a man who'd already turned his back on one sheikhdom.

The envoy pursed his lips, clearly taking time to choose his words. 'I need hardly say, sir, that the Council's deliberations are in strictest confidence.'

'Naturally.' Karim nodded. 'You have my assurance that nothing you say will leave this room.'

It would have been easier to end the meeting and send the man away. But Karim's curiosity was roused. He'd spent years building his investment business in lieu of ruling a country. But some things hadn't died—such as his interest in state affairs.

'Though the Sheikhs of Assara have been from the same family for over a hundred and fifty years, other significant families claim the right to offer a candidate in times where the inheritance is...complicated. Several names have been put forward. The one with the best claim is Hassan Shakroun.'

The visitor paused and Karim knew why. Shakroun was a bully whose idea of negotiation was bluster and intimidation. He was interested in personal aggrandisement and expanding his wealth, not in his nation. No wonder the Assarans were scoping other options for a king.

'I see you know the name.'

'We've met.' Once had been enough.

'Frankly, sir—' The man swallowed, then ploughed on. 'The Council is of the opinion that it's not bloodlines that should determine our next leader so much as personal attributes.'

Karim swallowed a wry smile. They certainly wouldn't get royal bloodlines from him, even if his mother *was* from a powerful family. His real father, as far as he could tell, came from humble stock.

'You're after someone who will do the bidding of the Council?'

It had been the same in Za'daq. Many councillors had been close friends of the previous Sheikh and, influenced by the old man's disdain for Ashraf, had made his succession difficult. Things were better now, but for a while many had sought to bring Karim back and install him on the throne. Which was one of the reasons he'd refused to return to visit his homeland, except for Ashraf's wedding. The other being that he knew it was better to cut all ties rather than pine for what might have been.

'Not at all, sir.' The envoy interrupted his thoughts. 'The Council wants a strong leader capable of taking responsibility. A man who knows diplomacy and statecraft. A man who'll be respected by other rulers in the region. If that man is from outside Assara, then it will short-circuit internal squabbling between rival families with an interest in the throne.'

So he was to be the outsider who united the unsuccessful parties? The Assaran Council had a high opinion of his capabilities, if they believed him able to walk in, calm any fractious rivals and make a success of the role.

Once Karim would have been pleased at such proof of respect from a neighbouring government. He must have impressed them in his years helping his father rule Za'daq, trying to persuade the old man into modernisation.

But that had been then. This was now.

He couldn't accept the offer. Even if the Assarans did want him on merit rather than because of a royal pedigree. He'd built a new life. A life that hadn't been laid out for him because of his supposed lineage.

For thirty years he'd followed a narrow, straight path, putting work first, shouldering responsibility for others. He had been dutiful and decent, a hardworking, honourable prince.

Till his life had crumpled like tissue paper in an iron fist.

For a moment an image swam before him of wide brown eyes. Of a cupid's bow mouth. Of smashed hopes.

His breath hissed between his teeth as he banished the memory.

Karim was responsible for no one now but himself. That was exactly the way he wanted it. He knew the burden of being royal. He had no intention of putting on that yoke again.

'Please pass my compliments and thanks to your Royal Council. I'm deeply honoured that they should consider me for such a noble position.' He paused, watching his guest stiffen. 'However, my answer is still no.'

Safiyah stood in front of the mirror in her suite and tried to still the panic rising from her belly to her throat. She wiped her hands down her thighs, hating that they trembled.

It didn't matter what she wore. Yet she'd tried on every outfit she'd brought to Switzerland, finding fault with each one till all that had been left was this. A western-style dress, beautiful, in a heavy fabric that looked almost black. Until she moved. Then the light caught it and it glowed like deep crimson fire.

She bit her lip, suppressing a bitter laugh. Black and crimson. The colours of mourning and sacrifice. How apt. She'd done her share of both.

Safiyah shook her head, refusing to wallow in self-pity. She was far luckier than most. She had her health, a comfortable home and more money than she needed. Above all she had Tarek.

Life had taught her to set her shoulders and keep going, no matter what problems she encountered. To make the best of things and focus on others, not herself.

That was why she was here. To save someone precious. To save a whole nation if her fears were right.

She swung away, but stopped before the balcony and the spectacular view of lake and mountains. This was her first trip out of the Middle East and she felt like a country bumpkin, gawping at everything. Well, not everything. She knew about luxury, about limousines and discreet security guards. But those mountains! And the green that was so incredibly green! She'd seen photos, of course, but this was different. Even the air through the open window tasted unique, ripe with moisture and growing things.

In other circumstances she'd put on jeans and flat shoes and find a way to slip out of the hotel, away from the bodyguards. She'd stroll through the public gardens, take her time staring into the glittering shop windows, then go to the lake and sit there, soaking up the scenery.

But circumstances weren't different. Circumstances were difficult. Possibly dangerous, if the fears that kept her awake at night proved right and Hassan Shakroun took the throne.

Not surprising that her heart knocked against her ribs like a hammer on stone. Too much hung on this visit. Failure wasn't an option.

Safiyah's hand rose to her breastbone, her fingers touching the base of her throat as if to ease the riotous beat of her heart and the acid searing the back of her mouth.

It's fine to be nervous. That will keep you grounded so you don't get distracted by anything else.

Anything else being *him*—the man she'd travelled here to see. Even so, she'd hoped against hope it wouldn't be necessary. That things would be sorted without her involvement. She'd been appalled to learn nothing had been agreed. That she had to see him after all.

Just thinking of him made her insides clutch as if someone had wrapped a rope around her middle and yanked it mercilessly. Her blood pumped so fast it rushed in her ears.

That's good. The adrenalin will keep you alert. Give you courage.

Safiyah took a deep breath and smoothed her hands once more down her skirt. They were clammy, and her knees shook. But her dress covered her knees, and there'd be no handshake, so no one would know how nervous she was.

No matter what happened, she vowed one thing. She would not reveal weakness to this man.

Not after what he'd done to her before.

Ignoring the cold fingers dancing down her spine, Safiyah swung around and headed for the door.

'Her Highness, the Sheikha of Assara.'

The butler announced her in a slow, impressive tone that helped steady her jittering nerves.

This she could do. For years she'd compartmentalised, leaving the real her—Safiyah—behind and donning the persona expected of a queen, gracious and unruffled.

She lifted her chin, pinned on a calm expression that hid her inner turmoil and stepped into the suite's vast sitting room.

A few steps in and she paused, blinking against the light pouring in from the wall of windows. The butler bowed again and left, closing the door behind him with a quiet snick. It was only then that she made out a tall figure, motionless in the shadow just past the windows.

Even looking into the light, even unable to make out his features against the glare, she'd have known him. That rangy height, the sense of leashed energy. That indefinable shimmer in the air.

Her pulse quickened and her ribcage squeezed her labouring lungs. Fortunately she was old enough and experienced enough to know that this was her body's response to the pressure of her situation. It had nothing to do with feelings she'd once harboured.

'This is…unexpected, *Your Highness*.' His voice was whiplash-sharp as he used her title.

Good. She didn't want him trying his charm on her. Once bitten, twice shy. The thought steadied her nerves and stiffened her knees.

'Is it, Karim?'

Deliberately she used his first name. He might prefer to pretend they were strangers but she refused to rewrite the past to soothe his conscience. If he thought to intimidate, he'd discover she wouldn't yield meekly to a mere hint of displeasure. She'd had years to toughen up since they'd last met.

'I'd assumed, as the hotel owner, you'd be informed of royal guests.'

She stepped further into the room, onto a thick-pile carpet that would have taken a team of master weavers years to produce.

'Ah, but I'm here to conduct important business, not entertain passing acquaintances.'

As if she and her business were by definition unimportant. As if they had been mere acquaintances.

Safiyah had never been more grateful for those hard-learned lessons in self-control as his words ripped through to the small, vulnerable spot deep inside. To the tiny part of her that was still Safiyah, the eager innocent who'd once believed in destiny and happy endings.

Pain bloomed as if from a stabbing dagger. She breathed slowly and rode the hurt, forcing it down. 'My apologies for interrupting your...important business.' Pointedly she raised her eyebrows and glanced about the luxuriously furnished sitting room, as if expecting to see a conference table or a bevy of secretaries.

The voice inside told her not to rile him. She was supposed to persuade, even cajole him. But Safiyah refused to let him think he could brush her off.

'To what do I owe this...pleasure?'

There it was again, that emphasis that made it clear she was uninvited in his private space. Wounded pride made her want to lash out, but she reined in the impulse. She owed it to Tarek to stay calm.

'I need to talk with you.'

'About?'

Even now he didn't move closer. As if he preferred her to be at a disadvantage, unable to see him clearly while she stood in the full light from the windows.

She'd thought better of him.

'May I sit?' Did she imagine that tall body stiffened? She took her time moving to a cluster of chairs around a fireplace, then paused, waiting for an invitation.

'Please.'

Safiyah sank gracefully onto a seat and was glad of it, because when he moved into the light something inside her slipped undone.

Karim was the same, and yet more. The years had given his features a stark edge that accentuated his potent good looks. Once he'd been handsome. Now there was a gravity, an added depth that turned his slanted cheekbones, high-bridged nose and surprisingly sensual mouth into a face that arrested the breath in her lungs.

That black-as-night hair was shorter than before, close-cropped to his skull. That, too, reinforced the startling power of those masculine features. Then there were his eyes, dark moss-green, so intense she feared he saw beneath her façade of calm.

His clothes, dark trousers and a jacket, clearly made to measure, reinforced his aura of command. The snowy shirt emphasised the gold tone of his skin and she had to force herself not to stare at the space where the open top couple of buttons revealed a sliver of flesh.

Her breath snagged and a trickle of something she hadn't felt in years unfurled inside. Heat seared her cheeks. She didn't want to feel it. Would give anything *not* to feel it.

For a frantic moment Safiyah thought of surging to her feet and leaving. Anything rather than face the discomfiting stir of response deep in her feminine core.

This couldn't be happening! For so long she'd told herself her reaction to him all those years ago had been the product of girlish fantasy.

'My condolences on your recent loss.'

Karim's words leached the fiery blush from her face and doused the insidious sizzle of awareness. Shame enveloped her, leaving her hollow and surprisingly weak.

How could she respond like that to the mere sight of Karim when she'd buried her husband just weeks ago?

Abbas might not have been perfect. He might have been cold and demanding. But she owed his memory respect. He'd been her *husband*.

Safiyah looked at her clenched hands, white-knuckled in her lap. Slowly she unknotted them, spreading stiff fingers and composing them in a practised attitude of ease.

She lifted her head to find Karim sitting opposite her, long legs stretched out in a relaxed attitude. Yet his eyes told another story. Their gaze was sharp as a bird of prey's.

'Thank you.'

She said no more. None of the platitudes she'd hidden behind for the past few weeks would protect her from the guilt she harboured within. A guilt she feared Karim, with his unnerving perceptiveness, might somehow guess. Guilt because after the first shock of discovering she was a widow, and learning that Abbas hadn't suffered, she'd felt relief.

Not because she'd wanted her husband dead. Instead it was the relief of a wild animal held in captivity and suddenly given a glimpse of freedom. No matter how hard she tried, she hadn't yet managed to quell that undercurrent of excitement at the idea of taking control of her own life— hers and Tarek's. Of being simply…happy.

But it was too early to dream of freedom. Time enough to do that when she knew Tarek was safe.

'I'm waiting to hear the reason for your visit.'

Safiyah had imagined herself capable of handling most things life threw at her. She was stunned to discover Karim's brusque tone had the power to hurt.

She blinked, reminding herself that to hurt she would have to care about him, and she'd stopped caring long ago. She'd meant nothing to him. All the time he'd pretended to be interested in her he'd had other plans. Plans she hadn't understood and which hadn't included her. At best she'd been a smokescreen, at worst an amusement.

Safiyah lifted her chin and looked him full in the face, determined to get this over as soon as possible.

'I want you to take the Assaran crown.'

CHAPTER TWO

'YOU *WANT* ME to become your Sheikh?'

Karim's brow knitted. Before today he'd have said not much had the power to surprise him.

How wrong he'd been.

He'd assumed only self-interest would have budged Safiyah from the Assaran royal palace at such a time. He'd imagined she'd come here to dissuade him from accepting the sheikhdom.

Surely having him as her King would be the last thing she'd want? Shouldn't she be looking for ways to preserve the crown for her son?

'Yes. That's exactly what I want.'

Karim stared at the poised, beautiful woman before him. The whole day had been surreal, but seeing Safiyah again was the most extraordinary part of it.

The moment she'd walked into the room Karim's blood had thickened, his pulse growing ponderous. As if his body, even his brain, worked in slow motion.

He wasn't surprised that the shy young woman he'd known had disappeared. He'd long since realised her doe-eyed glances and quiet ardour had been ploys to snare his interest. The real Safiyah had been more calculating and pragmatic than he'd given her credit for.

Yet the change in her was remarkable. The way she'd sashayed into the room as if she owned it. The way she'd all but demanded he play by the rules and offer her a seat, as if they were polite strangers, or perhaps old friends about to enjoy a cosy chat.

But then life as an honoured and adored queen would give any woman confidence.

To Karim's chagrin, it wasn't merely her manner that got under his skin. Had her hourglass figure been that stunning when he'd known her? In the old days she'd worn muted colours and loosely fitting clothes, presumably to assure him that she was the 'nice' girl his father had assured him she was. The complete antithesis to the sultry sirens his brother had so scandalously bedded.

Safiyah's dress today might cover her from neck to shin, but the gleam of the fabric encasing those generous curves and tiny waist made it utterly provocative. Even the soft, sibilant *shush* of sound it made when she crossed her legs was suggestive.

Then there was her face. Arresting rather than beautiful. Pure skin, far paler than his. Eyes that looked too big as she stared back at him, as if hanging on his every word. Dark, sleek hair with the tiniest, intriguing hint of auburn. Lips that he'd once—

'Why do you want me to take the throne? Why not fight for your son's right to it?'

'Tarek is too young. Even if the Council could be persuaded to appoint a regent for him, I can't imagine many men would willingly take the role of ruler and then meekly hand it over after fifteen years.'

A man of honour would.

Karim didn't bother voicing the thought.

'Why not leave the decision to the Royal Council? Why interfere? Are you so eager to choose your next husband?'

Safiyah's breath hissed between pearly teeth and her creamy skin turned parchment-pale.

Satisfaction stirred as he saw his jibe hit the mark. For

he hated how she made him feel. She dredged up emotions he'd told himself were dead and buried. He felt them scrape up his gullet, across his skin. The searing hurt and disbelief, the sense of worthlessness and shock as his life had been turned inside out in one short night. At that crisis in his life her faithlessness had burned like acid—the final insult to a man who'd lost everything.

Nevertheless, as Karim watched the convulsive movement of her throat and the sudden appearance of a dimple in her cheek, his satisfaction bled away. Years ago she'd had a habit of biting her cheek when nervous. But Karim doubted nerves had anything to do with Safiyah's response now. Maybe she was trying to garner sympathy.

Yet he felt ashamed. He'd never been so petty as to take satisfaction in another's distress, even if it was feigned. He was better than that.

He opened his mouth to speak, but she beat him to it.

'I'm *not*...' she paused after the word, her chin tilting up as she caught his eye '...looking for a new husband.'

Her voice was low, the words barely above a whisper, yet he heard steel behind them.

Because she'd loved Abbas so deeply?

Karim found himself torn between hoping it was true and wanting to protest that she'd never loved her husband. Because just months before her marriage to the Assaran King she'd supposedly loved Karim.

He gritted his teeth, discomfited by the way feelings undermined his thought processes. He'd been taught to think clearly, to disengage his emotions, not to feel too much. His response to Safiyah's presence was out of character for a man renowned for his even temper, his consideration of others and careful thinking.

'That's not how things are done in Assara,' she added. 'The new Sheikh will be named by the Royal Council.

There is no requirement for him to marry his predecessor's widow.'

Was it his imagination, or had she shivered at the idea? She couldn't have made her disdain more obvious.

Which was tantamount to a lance, piercing Karim's pride. Once she'd welcomed his attentions. But then he'd been first in line to a royal throne of his own. The eldest son of a family proud of its noble lineage.

'What will happen to you when the new Sheikh is crowned?'

'To me?' Her eyes widened, as if she was surprised he'd even ask. 'Tarek and I will leave the palace and live elsewhere.'

Tarek. Her son.

He'd imagined once that she'd give him a son...

Karim slammed a barrier down on such sentimental thoughts. He didn't know what was wrong with him today. It was as if the feelings he'd put away years before hadn't gone away at all, but had festered, waiting to surge up and slap him down when he least expected it.

Deliberately he did what he did best—focused on the problem at hand, ready to find a solution.

'So if you have no personal interest in the next Sheikh, why come all the way here to see me? The Assaran envoy saw me a couple of hours ago. Couldn't you trust him to do the job he was chosen for?'

Karim knew something of Assaran politics. He couldn't believe the previous Sheikh had allowed his wife to play any significant role in matters of state. Whichever way he examined it, Safiyah's behaviour was odd.

'I didn't want to get involved.' Again her voice was low. 'But I felt duty-bound to come, just in case...' She shook her head and looked at a point near his ear. 'The Council is very eager to convince you. It was agreed that I should add my arguments if necessary.'

'And what arguments might those be?'

Karim kept his eyes fixed on her face. He wasn't tacky enough to stare at all the female bounty encased in rustling silk. But perhaps she'd guessed that he was wondering what persuasions she'd try. Colour streaked her cheekbones and her breasts lifted high on a suddenly indrawn breath.

'Assara needs you—'

'In case you haven't noticed, I'm not into a life of public service any more. I work for myself now.'

Her mouth settled in a line that spoke of determination. Had he ever seen her look like that? His memory of Safiyah at twenty-two was that she'd been gentle and eager to go along with whatever he suggested.

But that had been almost five years ago. He couldn't be expected to remember everything about her clearly, even if it felt like he did.

'I could talk about the wealth and honour that will be yours if you take the throne...'

She paused, but he didn't respond. Karim had his own money. He also knew that being Sheikh meant a lifetime of duty and responsibility. Riches and the glamour of a royal title didn't sway him.

Safiyah inclined her head, as if his non-response confirmed what she'd expected. 'Most important of all, you'd make a fine leader. You have the qualities Assara needs. You're honest, fair and hardworking. The political elite respect you. Plus you're interested in the wellbeing of the people. Everyone says it was you who began to make Za'daq better for those who weren't born rich.'

Karim felt his eyebrows climb. He was tempted to think she was trying to flatter him into accepting the position. Except there was nothing toadying about her demeanour.

'The nobles trust you. The people trust you.'

He shook his head. 'That was a long time ago.'

'Your qualities and experience will stand you in good

stead no matter how long it's been. And it's only been a few years.'

Years since he'd left his homeland and turned his back on everything he'd known. He was only now beginning to feel that he'd settled into his new life.

Safiyah leaned forward, and he felt for the first time since she'd arrived that she wasn't conscious of her body language. Earlier she'd seemed very self-aware. Now she was too caught up in their discussion to be guarded. He read animation in her brown eyes and knew, whatever her real reason for being here, that she meant what she said.

Karim canted closer, drawn to her in spite of himself.

'It's what you were born to do and you'd excel at it.'

Abruptly Karim sank back in his seat. Her words had unravelled the spell she'd woven. The moment of connection broke, shattered by a wave of revulsion.

'It doesn't matter what I was *born* to do.' His nostrils flared as he swallowed rising acid. 'I've renounced all that.'

Because he wasn't the man the world thought him. He was the bastard son of an unfaithful queen and her shadowy lover.

'Of course it matters!' Her clasped hands trembled as if with the force of her emotion. 'Assara desperately needs a ruler who can keep the country together—especially now, when rival clans are stirring dissension and jealousy. Each wants their own man on the throne.'

Karim shrugged. 'Why should I bother? One of them will be elected and the others will have to put up with it. Maybe there'll be unrest for a bit, but it will die down.'

'You don't see...'

She paused and looked down at her hands. Karim saw a tiny cleft appear in her cheek and then vanish. She was biting the inside of her mouth again. Absurdly, the sight moved him.

'What aren't you saying, Safiyah?'

It was the first time he'd spoken her name aloud in years. Her chin jerked up and for a moment her gaze clung to his. But he wasn't foolish enough to be beguiled by that haunted look.

See? Already it was gone, replaced by a smooth, composed mask.

'You're the best man for the role, Karim—far better than any of the other contenders. You'd make a real difference in Assara. The country needs a strong, honest leader who'll work for *all* his people.'

Karim digested that. Was she implying that her dead husband hadn't been a good ruler? The idea intrigued him. Or was she just referring to unrest now?

To his annoyance her expression gave little away. The Safiyah he'd once known, or thought he'd known, had been far easier to read. Even more annoying was the fact his interest was aroused by the idea of doing something intrinsically worthwhile. Something more meaningful than merely building his own wealth.

Karim frowned. How had Safiyah guessed such an appeal would tempt him?

He enjoyed the challenge of expanding his business interests. The cut and thrust of negotiation, of locating opportunities ripe for development and capitalising on them. That took skill, dedication and a fine sense of timing. Yet was it as satisfying as the work he'd been trained to do—using his skills to rule a nation?

The thought of Safiyah knowing him so well—better, it seemed, than he knew himself—infuriated him. This was the woman who'd spurned him when she discovered the secret taint of his illegitimacy. He'd believed in her, yet she'd turned her back on him without even the pretence of regret, much less a farewell. It galled him that anything she said could make him doubt even for a second his chosen course.

What was wrong with concentrating on his own life, his

own needs? Let others devote themselves to public service. He'd done his bit. Assara wasn't even his country.

Karim leaned back in his seat, raising his eyebrows. 'But I'm not a contender. I have already made that clear.'

He almost stood then, signifying the interview was over. But something prevented him. Something not at all fine or statesmanlike. An impulse grounded in the hurt he'd felt when she'd abandoned him.

'Unless...'

Satisfaction rose as she leaned closer, avid to hear more, her lush, cherry-red lips parted.

Karim had a sudden disconcerting memory of those lips pressed against his. They'd been devoid of lipstick and petal-soft. Her ardent, slightly clumsy kiss had enchanted and worried him. For, much as he'd wanted her, he had known he shouldn't seduce an innocent, even if they were on the verge of marriage. Especially an innocent who, with her father, was a guest in the royal palace.

Safiyah had been all the things Karim hadn't even known he wanted in a wife: generous, bright, shyly engaging and incredibly sexy. She'd been the reason he'd finally decided to give in to his father's demand that he marry.

'Unless?' Her voice was like honey.

'Unless there was more to the deal...an inducement.'

He leaned forward, and for a moment the space between them was negligible. He was close enough to see the tiny amber flecks in her brown eyes, to reacquaint himself with the creamy perfection of her skin and inhale a teasing drift of scent. A delicate floral perfume, with a warm, enticing undertone, that was unique to Safiyah.

That hint of fragrance hit him like a body-blow, sweeping him back to a time when he'd had everything. He'd been a prince, secure in his position, his place in the world and his family. He'd enjoyed his work, helping his father run Za'daq. He hadn't even regretted giving up his sexual freedom because Safiyah had turned the prospect of marriage from a duty to a pleasure.

'What sort of inducement?' Her voice was steady but her eyes were wary.

Karim told himself to leave it. To walk away. He had no intention of taking this further.

Then he heard his own voice saying, 'Marriage.'

He couldn't mean it.

He wasn't talking about marriage to *her*. Yet a strange shivery feeling rippled down her spine and curled into her belly like large fingers digging deep. Her skin prickled all over and heat eddied in disturbing places.

'I'm sure that will be no problem.' She forced a smile. 'You'll have your pick of eligible women.'

And Karim didn't need a crown or wealth to attract them. He was handsome, urbane and, she knew to her cost, charming. He could coax the birds from the trees if he set his mind to it. No wonder she, so unworldly and inexperienced at twenty-two, had been taken in, thinking his attentions meant something special.

'I don't need to pick when there's one obvious choice.'

His crystalline gaze locked on hers and his voice deepened to a baritone note she felt vibrate through her bones.

'The Queen of Assara.'

His words were clear. Safiyah heard them, and yet she told herself Karim had said something else. He couldn't really mean—

'*You*, Safiyah.'

'Me?' Her voice rose to a wobbly high note.

Once she'd believed he wanted to marry her, that he cared for her. Her father had been sure too. And so had Karim's father. He'd permitted her and her father to stay at the Za'daqi palace even while, as they'd discovered later, he was in the final stages of terminal illness.

But when a family emergency had dragged her and her father back to Assara everything had fallen apart. Karim hadn't farewelled them. Nor had he responded to the note she'd left him. A note she'd written and rewritten. There'd been no attempt to contact her since. Just...nothing. Not a single word. When she'd tried to contact him at the palace she'd been fobbed off.

Then had come the news that Karim's father had died. To everyone's amazement Karim had renounced the throne and left Za'daq. Even then she'd waited, refusing to believe he'd really abandoned her. Days had turned into weeks. Weeks to months. And still no word. And over those months her faith in him had shrivelled and turned into hurt, disbelief and finally anger.

Even at the last moment, when she'd been cornered in a situation she'd never wanted, a small, irrepressible part of her had hoped he'd step in and stop—

'Safiyah?'

She blinked and looked into that dark gaze. Once those eyes had glowed warm and she'd read affection there. Now they gave nothing away. The coldness emanating from him chilled her to the core.

'You want to marry *me*?' Finally she managed to control her vocal cords. The words emerged husky but even.

'Want...?' Forehead crinkling, he tilted his head as if musing on the idea. But the eyes pinioning hers held nothing like desire or pleasure. His expression was calculating.

That was what gave Safiyah the strength to sit up, spine stiff, eyebrows raised, as if his answer was only of mild interest. As if his patent lack of interest in her as a potential wife, a woman and a lover, didn't hurt.

She would *not* let him guess the terrible pain his indifference stirred. Everything inside her shrivelled. Bizarre that, even after his rejection years before, part of her had obstinately clung to the idea that he'd cared.

'You're right. No sensible man would *want* to marry a woman who ran out on him like a thief in the night.'

She gaped at the way he'd twisted the past. How dared he? Hearing the devastating news of her sister's attempted suicide, of *course* Safiyah and her father had gone to her immediately. Her father had made their apologies for the sudden departure, referring to a family emergency. Safiyah had assumed she'd have a chance to explain to Karim personally later.

Except he'd refused to take her calls. He'd led her on to believe he cared, then dumped her, and now he was pretending she'd been the one at fault!

'Now, look here! I—'

'Not that it matters now. The past is dead, not worth discussing.' He sliced the air with a decisive chopping motion, his expression cold. 'As for wanting marriage now... Perhaps *need* is a better word.' He opened those wide shoulders and spread his hands in a fatalistic gesture.

'I can't see your logic.'

Safiyah's voice was clipped, that of a woman ostensibly in control. She wouldn't demean herself by rehashing the past. He was right. It was over. She should count herself lucky she'd discovered Karim's true nature when she had. He hadn't been the paragon she'd believed.

'There's no reason for us to marry.'

'You don't think so?' He shook his head. 'I disagree. Despite what your law says, even the most optimistic supporter couldn't expect me to take the throne of Assara without a ripple. I'm a foreigner, an unknown quantity. You've said yourself that there are political undercurrents and rivalry in the country's ruling elite. To overcome those an incoming ruler would need to show a strong link to Assara and to the throne.'

He paused, watching her reaction. Now, with a sinking heart, Safiyah understood where he was going. And it made a horrible sort of sense.

'What better way of showing my respect for Assara and cultivating a sense of continuity than to marry the current Queen?'

Except said Queen would do just about anything to avoid another marriage. Particularly marriage to *this* man. Call it pride, call it self-preservation, but she'd be mad to agree.

'I disagree. With the Council's backing a newcomer, especially one with your qualities and experience, would be able to establish himself.' He was far, far better than the other alternatives.

Karim steepled his fingertips beneath his chin as if considering. But his response came so quickly she knew he'd immediately discounted her words.

'Besides, if I married you...'

Was it her imagination or did his voice slow on the words?

'Your son wouldn't be disinherited. That would satisfy any elements concerned at him being replaced by a foreigner. It would ensure the long-term continuity of the current dynasty.'

Safiyah sat in stunned silence, thinking through the implications of his words. 'You mean Tarek would be your heir? You'd adopt him?' The idea stunned her.

Emotion flickered across Karim's unreadable expression. 'I'm not a man who'd happily rip away someone's birthright, no matter what the constitution allows.'

There was something in his tone of voice, a peculiar resonance, that piqued her curiosity. Safiyah sensed there was more to his words than there seemed. But what?

She was on the verge of probing, till she read his body language. His hard-set jaw and flared nostrils revealed a man holding in strong emotion. Now wasn't the time to pursue this—not if she wanted him to take the throne.

Which was why she didn't instantly refuse. She needed time to persuade him.

'Are you saying if I agree to marry you…' she paused, fighting to keep her voice even '…you'd take the crown?'

His gaze sharpened. She felt it like an abrasive scrape across her flesh. The grooves bracketing those firm lips deepened, as if hinting at a smile, yet there was no softening in that austere, powerful face.

'I'm saying that if you agree to marry me I'll *consider* changing my mind about accepting the sheikhdom.'

Well, that put her in her place. Safiyah felt the air whoosh from her lungs, her chest crumpling with the force of that outward breath. Even if she agreed to marriage, it might not be enough to persuade him.

She'd never thought herself a particularly proud woman, but she hated that Karim had the power, still, to deflate her. To make her feel she was of no consequence. That incensed her.

For years she'd fought to maintain her self-respect and sense of worth, married to a man who adhered to the traditional view that a wife was merely an extension of her husband's will. Particularly a wife who'd been exalted by marrying a royal sheikh.

Fury surged at Karim's off-hand attitude. How dared he on the one hand ask her to marry him and on the other make it clear that even such a sacrifice on her part might not be enough to sway him?

Not that he'd *asked* her to marry him. He'd put it out there like some clause in a business contract.

Safiyah felt hot blood creep up her throat and into her cheeks. She wanted to let rip. To tell him he was an arrogant jerk, despite his royal blood. Her marriage had taught her that royals were no more perfect than anyone else. If anything, their ability to command not only great wealth, but the obedience of everyone around them, could amplify their character flaws.

But she didn't have the luxury of plain speaking. This wasn't about her. It was about Tarek's future, his safety. As well as the future of their country.

'What do you say, Safiyah? Is your country's wellbeing enough to tempt you into marriage again?' He sat back, relaxed in his chair, as if he didn't care one way or the other.

'There's something else.'

She'd hoped to persuade Karim without telling him of her fears, knowing he might well dismiss them since she had no proof. But what proof could she have till it was too late? The idea curdled her stomach.

'Another important reason for you to accept the throne. Hassan Shakroun—'

Karim cut her off. 'No more! I've already heard everything I need from the official envoy.'

As if *she*, the Queen of Assara, had no insight to offer! Perhaps he believed as Abbas had—that women weren't suited for politics. Or perhaps he was simply impatient that she hadn't leapt at the chance to marry him.

Safiyah was convinced Tarek would be in danger if Shakroun took the throne. She'd never liked the man, but the things she'd learned recently made her blood freeze at the idea of him in the palace. He wouldn't leave a potential rival sheikh with royal blood alive, even if that rival was a mere toddler.

Her throat closed, making her voice husky. 'But you must listen—'

'No.'

Karim didn't raise his voice, but that decisive tone stopped her.

'No more arguments. I don't *have* to listen to anything. You came to me, not the other way around.'

His words stilled her instinctive protest.

'I'm not inclined to accept the throne, but I'll consider it more thoroughly *if* you're willing to marry.'

Safiyah drew a deep breath, frantically searching for a semblance of calm. She couldn't believe the direction this conversation had taken. What had begun simply had become a nightmare.

She was about to ignore his warning and spill out her fears, but the stern lines of his expression stopped her. Karim didn't look like Abbas, but she recognised the pugnacious attitude of a man who'd made up his mind. Not just any man, but one raised to expect unquestioning obedience.

She'd learned with her husband that defiance of his pronouncements, even in the most trivial, unintended way, only made him less likely to listen. Safiyah couldn't afford to have Karim reject the crown.

Carefully she chose her words. 'I need time to consider too.'

Karim raised one supercilious eyebrow, obviously questioning the fact that she hadn't instantly leapt at the chance to marry him.

Except the thought of being tied in marriage to any man, especially Karim, sent a flurry of nervous dread through her.

'*You* need time?'

His tone made it clear he thought it inexplicable. He was right. Any other woman, she was sure, would jump at the chance to marry him.

'It seems we both do.' She held his gaze, refusing to look away. She might be reeling with shock inside, but she refused to betray the fact.

'Very well. We'll meet tomorrow at nine. A lot rides on your answer, Safiyah.'

CHAPTER THREE

'I LIKE IT,' Ashraf said over the phone. 'Accepting the Assaran crown is a perfect solution.'

Karim frowned at his brother's words as he wiped the sweat from his torso. The morning's visits had left him unsettled, and he'd sought to find calm through a workout in the gym, only to be interrupted by Ashraf's call.

'Solution? I don't see that there's a problem to be solved from your perspective—and especially not from mine.'

Yet, if not a problem, Karim sensed there was *something*. He and Ashraf had spoken at the weekend. It was unlike his brother to call again so soon. Unless something important had arisen. They didn't live in each other's pockets, but there was a genuine bond between them, all the more remarkable given the fact they'd been kept apart as much as possible by their father.

The old man had been prejudiced against Ashraf, believing him to be another man's son. He'd neglected the younger boy, fixing all his focus and energy on the elder. Not because he'd cared for Karim—the old tartar had been incapable of love—but because, as the eldest, he was the one to be moulded into a future sheikh.

If it hadn't been so personally painful Karim would have laughed when the truth had been revealed, that the Sheikh had picked the wrong heir. That Ashraf was the true son and Karim the bastard.

'I've no need of a throne, Ashraf. You know that.'

There was a growl in his voice. A morning besieged—first by the envoy from the Assaran Royal Council, and then by the only woman he'd ever seriously thought of marrying—had impaired his mood. The idea that Safiyah believed he still cared enough about her to be coaxed into doing her bidding set his teeth on edge. It would take more than an hour in the gym to ease the anger cramping his belly.

Karim stared through the huge windows, streaming with rain, towards the mountains, now shrouded in cloud. He usually found peace in a long ride. But he had no horses here. And even if he had, he wouldn't have subjected any poor beast to a hard ride in this weather just to shift his bad mood.

'Of course you don't need a throne.' Ashraf's tone was matter-of-fact. 'You've taken to being an independent businessman like a duck to water. Not to mention having the freedom to enjoy lovers without raising expectations that you're looking for a royal life partner.'

Karim's frown deepened. Did his brother miss his old life? Ashraf and Tori had been blissfully wrapped up in each other when he'd seen them last, but... 'What's wrong? Are you pining for your days as a carefree bachelor?'

Ashraf's laugh reassured him. 'Not a bit. I've never been happier.' He paused, his voice dropping to a more serious note. 'Except I'd rather you were here more often.'

It was a familiar argument, but Karim was adamant about not returning to Za'daq long-term. His brother was a fine leader, yet there were still a few powerful men who chafed at the idea of being ruled by a younger son.

His brother sighed at the other end of the line. 'Sorry. I promised myself I wouldn't mention it.'

'Why don't you just get to the point?'

The point being the outlandish suggestion that he,

Karim, should take the Assaran throne. Interestingly, the proposal hadn't been news to Ashraf. Nor did he think it outlandish.

'You rang to persuade me. Why?'

'Pure self-interest.' Ashraf's answer came instantly. 'Life will be much easier and better for our country if there's a stable government in Assara.'

Karim didn't dispute his logic. The two countries shared a border, and what affected one ended up affecting the other.

'If Shakroun becomes Sheikh there'll be stability.' Karim didn't like the man, but that was irrelevant. 'He's strong and he'll hang on to power.'

'That's what I'm afraid of,' his brother murmured.

'What?' Surely Ashraf wouldn't advocate civil unrest.

'You've been away a long time. Certain things have come to light that put a different slant on Shakroun and his activities.'

'I haven't heard anything.'

Despite removing himself from the Middle East, Karim followed press reports from the region. He'd told himself more than once that his interest in matters he'd left behind was a mistake, but though he'd cut so many ties he couldn't conquer his innate interest. He'd been bred to it, after all, had spent a lifetime living and breathing regional politics.

'We're not talking about anything known publicly. But a number of investigations are bearing fruit. Remember that people-smuggling ring that worked out of both countries?'

'How could I forget?'

Za'daq was a peaceable country, but years before the borderland between the two nations had been lawless, controlled by a ruthless criminal called Qadri. Qadri had unofficially run the region through violence and intimidation. One of his most profitable ventures had been people-smuggling from Za'daq into Assara and then to more distant markets. Tori, before she'd become Ashraf's wife, had been kidnapped for the trade, and Qadri had attempted to execute Ashraf himself.

'We don't have enough quite yet to prove it in a court of law, but we know Qadri's partner in the flesh trade was Hassan Shakroun.'

'I see...' The surprising thing was that Karim wasn't surprised. Not that he'd guessed Shakroun was a criminal. He'd just thought him deeply unpleasant and far too fixated on his own prestige and power. 'How sure are you?'

'I'm sure. The evidence is clear. But it will take time till the police are ready to press charges. Since Qadri's death Shakroun has taken over some of his criminal enterprises. They're trying to get an iron-clad case against him on a number of fronts. It's tough getting evidence, because Shakroun gets others to do his dirty work and witnesses are thin on the ground. A couple of people who stirred up trouble for him met with unfortunate "accidents".'

Karim felt an icy prickle across his rapidly cooling flesh. He grabbed a sweatshirt and pulled it one-handed over his head, then shoved his arms through the sleeves.

'That's one of the reasons the Council is searching for someone else to become Sheikh.'

Now it made so much more sense. Did Safiyah know?

Immediately he dragged his thoughts back. Safiyah wasn't the issue. He refused to be swayed by her. Yet the thought of her with her small child in the Assaran palace and Shakroun moving in made his stomach curdle.

'It's also why they're eager for an outsider,' Ashraf added. 'If they choose from within the country Shakroun is the obvious choice. He's from an influential family, and on the face of it would make a better leader than the other contenders. But with you they'd get someone they know and respect, who has a track record of ruling during those years when our father was ill.'

Karim let the words wash over him, ignoring Ashraf's reference to the man who'd raised him as his father. His thoughts were already moving on.

'How many know about this?'

'Very few. It's too early to accuse him publicly—not until the evidence is watertight. But if he becomes Sheikh...'

Karim could imagine. A criminal thug with almost absolute power. It didn't bear thinking about.

He ploughed his hand through his damp hair. 'It's still a matter for the Assarans.'

'And they want *you*, Karim.'

Karim's mouth flattened. His nostrils flared as he dragged in a deep breath. 'I've got a life here.'

He watched the stream of rain down the windows and another chill encompassed him. It didn't matter how long he spent in Europe and North America. He still missed the wide open skies of his homeland. The brilliant, harsh sun, and even the arid heartland where only the hardiest survived.

'I've got a business to run,' he added.

Ashraf didn't respond.

'I'm a private citizen now. I've had my fill of being royal. From the moment I could walk I was moulded into a prince, crammed full of lessons on public responsibility and politics. Now I'm living for myself.'

Not that he expected sympathy.

Finally his brother spoke. 'So you're telling me you'll just turn your back on the situation? Because you're having such a good time answering to no one but yourself?' He didn't hide his scepticism.

'Damn it, Ashraf! Do I look like a hero?'

His brother's voice held no laughter when he answered. 'I always thought so, bro.'

Karim flinched, feeling the twelve-month age difference

between them like a weight on his shoulders. Some hero! He hadn't been able to protect his own brother.

Karim had been a serious, responsible child, his world hemmed in by constant demands that he learn, achieve, excel, work harder and longer. Even so, he'd devoted himself to finding ingenious ways to keep the old Sheikh's attention off his younger brother. When he hadn't succeeded—when the old man had focused his hate on the boy he'd believed a bastard—Ashraf had been bullied and beaten. Karim hadn't been able to protect him all the time.

Ashraf had never blamed him for not looking after him better, but the twist of guilt in Karim's belly was something he'd always carry.

'You don't have to be a hero to become Sheikh,' Ashraf continued, as if he hadn't just shaken Karim to the core. 'Shakroun would have no qualms about taking the throne and there's nothing heroic about *him*. He'd enjoy the perks of the position.'

The words hauled Karim's thoughts out of the past and straight back to Assara. To the idea of Safiyah at the mercy of a man like Shakroun. Hassan Shakroun wouldn't be slow to recognise that tying himself to the previous Sheikh's beautiful widow would cement his position. Karim might not care for Safiyah any more but the thought of her with a thug like Shakroun...

Karim cursed under his breath, long and low. His brother, having made his point, merely said goodbye and left him with his thoughts.

Instinct warned Karim to keep a wide berth from Assara and its troubles. Yet his sense of responsibility nagged. It wasn't helped by the realisation, crystallised during the meeting with Safiyah, that his new life wasn't as fulfilling as he'd like. Yes, he had an aptitude for business and making money. Yes, he enjoyed the freedom to choose for himself, without pondering the impact of his decisions on

millions of others. And Ashraf was right: it was far easier enjoying a discreet affair without the encumbrance of
royalty.

But Karim had spent his life developing the skills to ad-
minister a nation. He'd had a few years of taking on more
responsibility when the old Sheikh's health had faded. He'd
thrived on it. It had been his vocation. Which was why he'd
been so devastated when he'd had to step away. Ashraf had
told him to stay as Sheikh but Karim hadn't been able to do
it. His brother had already been robbed of so much. Karim
had refused to take what was rightfully his.

The idea of making a real difference in Assara, doing
what he was trained for and what he enjoyed, tempted him.
He could do a lot for the place and its people. Assara was a
fine country, but it was behind Za'daq in many ways. He'd
enjoy the challenge.

Yet behind all those considerations was the thought of
Safiyah. Of what would happen to her and her son if Shakroun became Sheikh.

Karim paced the private gym from end to end. Safiyah
was nothing to him—no more important than any other Assaran citizen. He should be able to contemplate her without
any stirring of emotion.

He grimaced. Emotion had lured him into playing out
that scene with her earlier. He'd drawn out the interview
with talk of marriage purely so he could watch her squirm.
It had been a low act. Karim was ashamed of stooping to it.
He couldn't recall ever deliberately lying before. But he'd
lied blatantly today. To salve his pride. And because he
hated the fact that Safiyah could make him feel anything
when she felt nothing. To her he was, as he'd always been,
a means to an end.

But his talk of marriage had backfired mightily.

Because now he couldn't get it out of his head.

Karim was intrigued by her. He kept circling back to the

idea of Safiyah as his lover. Maybe because although they'd once been on the verge of betrothal, they'd never shared more than a few kisses. The night she'd agreed to come to him had been the night his world had been blown apart.

That had to be the reason he felt so unsettled. Safiyah was unfinished business.

Lust speared him, dark and urgent, as he remembered her in the crimson dress that had clung like a lover's hands. The delicate pendant she'd worn, with a single glowing red stone, had drawn his eyes to the pale perfection of her throat. He'd wanted to bury his face where her pulse beat too fast and find out if she was still as sensitive there as he remembered. Or if that too had been a hoax. Like the way she'd pretended to fall for him.

He knew he should walk away.

Safiyah tested his limits more than any woman he'd met. He didn't want to spend his life with a woman he couldn't trust or respect. Even to satisfy his lust.

But what if he did walk away? If he let Shakroun take the throne?

Karim would be in part responsible for what that thug did to Assara. And what he might do to Safiyah and her boy.

Karim stopped pacing and stared at the tall figure reflected in the mirror on the far side of the room. He saw hands clenched into fists, tendons standing taut, a body tensed for action.

He'd been raised to put the welfare of a nation before his own. That conditioning was hard to break.

Surely *that* was what made him hesitate.

He had a major decision to make and it would *not* hinge on Safiyah.

Karim forked his hand through his hair, scraping his fingers along his scalp. The trouble was, the more he thought about it, the more he realised marriage to the Assaran Queen was the best way to ensure he was accepted as Sheikh.

If he chose to take the role.

If he could bring himself to marry the woman who'd once spurned him.

'He's *fine*, Safiyah. Truly. It was just a runny nose and he's okay now. He's bright as anything and he's been playing with the puppies.'

The phone to her ear, Safiyah rolled onto her back on the wide bed, imagining Tarek with a tumble of puppies. He'd be in his element. He loved animals, but Abbas had always said a palace was no place for pets.

'You brought them to the palace on purpose, didn't you, Rana? You're hoping we'll keep one.'

Not that she minded. These last few years she'd missed being around dogs and horses. There was something soothing about their unquestioning love.

'Guilty as charged.'

Her sister's chuckle made Safiyah smile. It was such a carefree sound, and one she still cherished. Rana was happy and settled now—such a tremendous change from a few years ago.

'But you know how hard it can be to find homes for a litter. Especially since they're not pure-bred. What's *one* little puppy…?'

Safiyah laughed at Rana's exaggerated tone of innocence. 'Probably a lot of trouble until it's house-trained and learns not to chew everything in sight. But you're right. A dog would be good company for Tarek.'

Not that her son showed any sign of missing Abbas. He'd rarely seen his father more than once a week, and then only for short periods, usually in the throne room or the royal study.

Those meetings had been formal affairs. Abbas hadn't

been one to cuddle his son, or play games. He'd said that was how royal heirs were raised. They weren't supposed to cling to their parents. And besides, as Sheikh he'd had other things to keep him busy. He'd assured Safiyah that when Tarek was old enough he'd take him in hand and teach him what he needed to know to rule Assara.

That was never going to happen now.

Tarek would grow up without knowing his father.

Nor would he become Sheikh.

A pang of fear pierced her chest. Would her son be allowed to grow up in safety? What would happen if Karim didn't take the crown? He'd looked anything but happy about the idea. But if he didn't and Hassan Shakroun became Sheikh—

'Safiyah? Are you still there?'

'Sorry, Rana. I got distracted.'

'Things didn't go well?'

'I'm sure it will work out just fine.' Safiyah was so used to putting a positive spin on things, protecting her sister as much as possible, that the words emerged automatically.

'Reading between the lines, it doesn't sound like it.' Rana paused, then, 'You *can* talk to me, you know, Safiyah. I'm not as fragile as I used to be.'

'I know that.'

These days Rana seemed a different person entirely from the severely depressed young woman she'd once been. It was habit rather than need that fed Safiyah's protectiveness, yet old ways died hard.

'But there's no news yet—nothing to share.'

Other than the fact Karim had asked her to be his wife.

No, not asked. Demanded. Made it a condition of him even considering accepting the sheikhdom.

She couldn't share that fact. Not till she'd worked out what answer she was going to give.

Marrying Karim seemed impossible. Especially as

there'd been not even a hint of warmth when he spoke of it. Instead he'd looked so cold, so brooding...

She *couldn't* say yes. The very thought of accepting another marriage of convenience when she'd just escaped one sent shivers scudding down her spine.

Naturally they were shivers of distaste. They couldn't be anything else.

But if she said no what would happen to Tarek? She'd do whatever it took to see him safe. Of course she would. Yet surely there was some other way. Surely marriage wasn't essential.

'Well, if you need to talk I'm just here.'

It struck Safiyah how far Rana had come from the troubled girl she'd been. 'Thank you, Rana. I'm so lucky to have you.' Especially as a few short years ago Safiyah had almost lost her. 'To be honest, I—'

A knock on the door interrupted her. 'Sorry, there's someone here. I'll just see who it is.'

Safiyah swung her bare feet off the bed, retying the belt of her long robe. She glanced at the time. Nine o'clock. Too late for a casual visitor, even if she'd known anyone else in Switzerland. And the special envoy who'd accompanied her from Assara would never dream of simply turning up at her door. He'd ring first.

'That's fine. I need to go anyway.'

In the background Safiyah heard yapping. She grinned as she crossed the bedroom and entered the suite's sitting room, flicking on a lamp as she went.

'Okay. Give Tarek a hug and kiss from me and tell him I'll be home soon.'

'I will. And good luck!'

More yapping, this time more frenzied, and Rana hung up.

Safiyah reached the entrance of her suite and peered through the peephole. Her vision was obscured by a large fist, raised to knock. When it lowered she was looking at a broad chest, straight shoulders and the dark gold flesh of a masculine neck and jaw.

Karim!

Safiyah's pulse catapulted against her ribs, taking up a rackety, uneven beat. They'd agreed to meet tomorrow morning. Not tonight. She wasn't prepared.

She glanced down at the silk robe of deep rose-pink. It covered her to her ankles, but abruptly Safiyah became aware that beneath it she wore nothing but an equally thin nightgown.

That hand rose to knock again, and she knew she had no choice but to answer.

She cracked the door open, keeping out of view behind it as much as possible.

'Karim. This is a surprise.' Despite her efforts her voice sounded husky, betraying her lack of calm.

'Safiyah.' He nodded and stepped forward, clearly expecting her to admit him.

She held the door firmly, not budging. 'It's late. I'm afraid it's not convenient to talk now.' Not when she was barefoot and wearing next to nothing. 'Can this wait till the morning?'

By then she'd have some idea of what she was going to say. Hopefully. Plus she'd be dressed. Definitely. Dressed in something that didn't make her feel appallingly feminine and vulnerable just standing close to Karim.

Was she entertaining a lover? The idea flashed into his brain, splintering thoughts of sheikhdoms and politics.

Her cheeks were pink and her hair was a messy dark cloud drifting over her shoulders, as if she'd just climbed out of bed. Her eyes shone like gems and he saw the pulse jitter at the base of her throat, drawing attention both to her elegant neck and her agitation.

Karim's pulse revved as he propped the door open with his shoulder. He heard no noise in the room behind her but that meant nothing.

'I'm afraid this can't wait.'

Wide eyes looked up at him. Still she didn't move. He watched her swallow, the movement convulsive. Karim felt a stab of hunger. He fought the urge to stroke that pale skin and discover if it was as soft as he remembered.

Such weakness only fired his annoyance. Bad enough that his every attempt to think logically about this situation and his future kept swinging back to thoughts of Safiyah. Karim chafed at his unwanted weakness for this woman.

'Surely tomorrow—'

'Not tomorrow. Now.' He bent his head, bringing it closer to hers. 'If I walk away now, Safiyah, don't expect me ever to walk into Assara.'

He didn't mention the sheikhdom. Even in this quiet corridor he was cautious with his words, but she understood. He saw the colour fade from her cheeks and she stepped back, allowing him to enter.

One quick, comprehensive survey revealed that she wore silk and lace. Her robe clung to an hourglass figure that would make any man stare. Especially when she swung round after shutting the door and her full breasts wobbled with the movement, clearly unrestrained by a bra. That wobble shot a dart of pure lust to his tightening groin.

Karim guessed her robe had been put on quickly. It was belted, but gaped open over a low décolletage, over creamy, fragrant flesh and more pink silk. Even the colour of the silk was flagrantly feminine.

A flicker of long-buried memory stirred...of his mother's private courtyard, filled with the heady scent of damask roses, their petals a deep, velvety pink. It had been an oasis of femininity in his father's austere palace. And it had been razed to bare earth when the old man had discovered her sons, at four and three respectively, were pining for her after she'd run off with her lover and had secretly sought solace in her garden.

But memories of the past faded as he took in Safiyah, looking lush and sensual. Outrageously inviting. Especially with that cloud of dark hair spilling around her shoulders, the ends curling around her breasts.

Had some lover been fondling those breasts? Was that why her hard nipples thrust against the silk?

Heat drenched Karim as he flexed his hands and made himself turn from temptation. He strode into the sitting room, giving it a cursory survey before following the light into her bedroom. The bed was still neatly made, but a pile of pillows was propped up on one side. She'd been sitting there alone.

The knowledge smacked him in the chest, stealing both his air and his sense of indignation.

'What are you doing?'

Her voice came from just behind him. It sounded husky, and something drew tight in his groin.

'Nice suite.' He turned and gave her a bland look. 'I hadn't seen it before.' With luck she'd think that as the hotel's new owner he was simply curious about the accommodation.

He walked back into the sitting room and heard the bedroom door snick shut behind him.

Wise woman.

'What is it that can't wait?'

Karim swung round to find her closer than he'd expected. She'd adjusted her robe so barely a sliver of flesh showed beneath the collarbone and she was busily knotting the belt cinching her waist. As if a layer of silk could conceal her seductive body.

'Things are moving quickly.'

That was one thing his deliberations and a second discussion with the Assaran envoy had made clear. If he was going to accept the crown he needed to act fast—before Shakroun got wind of the attempt to bring in an outsider. The man could stir all sorts of trouble.

'I need your answer now.'

'Oh.' She frowned. 'My answer.'

Safiyah looked distracted. As if her mind were elsewhere, rather than on the honour he'd done her by suggesting marriage so she could retain her royal status.

Karim gritted his teeth, fury rising. She acted as if his suggestion they marry was trivial. Not enough to hold her interest when she had more important things on her mind. And this after the insult of her desertion five years before. It was more than his pride could bear.

Something ground through him like desert boulders scraping together, the friction sparking an anger he'd harnessed for so long.

Karim had spent a lifetime being reasonable, honourable, and above all rational. He'd been trained never to act rashly. To weigh his options and consider the implications not only for himself but for others.

Not tonight.

Tonight another man inhabited his skin. A man driven by instincts he'd repressed for years.

'What is it, Safiyah?' He took two paces, stopping only when she had to hike her chin high to hold his eyes. 'You've got something else on your mind? Is it this?'

He cupped one hand around the back of her head, anchoring his fingers in that lush, silky hair.

No protest came. His other arm wrapped around her waist, tugging her close. He had a moment of heady anticipation as her soft form fell against him, her eyes growing huge and dark as pansies.

Then his mouth settled on hers and the years were stripped away.

CHAPTER FOUR

SAFIYAH CLUNG TIGHT, her fingers embedded in the hard biceps that held her to Karim's powerful frame. It was so unexpected she had no time to gather her thoughts. No time to do anything but bend before the force of sensations and emotions that made her sway like a sapling in a strong wind, her body arching back over his steely arm.

To her shame it wasn't outrage that overwhelmed her. It was shocked delight.

Because she'd never been kissed like this.

Never felt like this.

Not even in those heady days when Karim had courted her, for then he'd been considerate and careful not to push her into a compromising position. She'd been innocent and he'd respected that.

Even when she'd married she hadn't felt like this.

Especially when she'd married. She'd felt no passion for Abbas. No desire except the desire to do her duty. And Abbas, though he'd enjoyed her body, hadn't expected anything from her other than acquiescence.

Which made the fire licking her veins unprecedented. Totally new.

Safiyah shivered—not with cold, but with a roaring, instantaneous heat that ignited deep inside and showered through her like sparks from a bonfire, spreading incendiary trails to every part of her body.

This was passion.

This was desire.

It was like the yearning she'd once felt for Karim, multiplied a thousandfold. Like the difference between the heat of a match and the scorch of a lightning strike.

Her mouth opened, accommodating the plunging sweep of his tongue, relearning Karim's darkly addictive taste. It was a flavour she'd made herself forget when she'd told herself to stop pining for the mirage of true love. When she'd given herself in a dutiful arranged marriage.

Because to hold on to those broken dreams would only have destroyed her.

Now, with a force that shook her to the core, Safiyah felt them flood back, in a deluge of sensation to a body starved of affection, much less delight.

Once Safiyah had yearned for Karim with all her virgin heart. Now, time, experience and loss had transformed her once innocent desire into something fierce and elemental. Something utterly unstoppable.

Instead of submitting meekly, or turning away, Safiyah leaned into his hard frame. It felt as natural as smiling. As necessary as breathing.

Her tongue slid the length of his, exploring, tasting, enjoying the rich essence of sandalwood and virile male that filled her senses. She revelled in the feel of his taut frame solid against hers and rose onto her toes to press closer.

A shudder passed through him and his hands tightened possessively, as if her response unleashed something in him that he'd kept locked away. He leaned in, forcing her head back, deepening the kiss, and she went willingly, exulting in the breathtaking intensity of the moment.

Past and future were blotted out. The present consumed her. Her need for this, for him. Nothing else mattered except assuaging that.

Karim's arm slid down her back, his palm curving over

her backside, lifting her towards the drenching heat of his muscled frame. Excitement tore through her, a fierce exhilaration as she read the tension of a man on the brink of losing himself.

Then, with an abruptness that left her swaying, he released her.

Blinking, Safiyah watched him step back. Saw his mouth lengthen in a grimace. Saw him shrug those broad shoulders and straighten his jacket as if brushing off the imprint of her clawing hands. Then he shoved both fists in his pockets and lifted one eyebrow in an expression of cool enquiry.

Flustered, Safiyah felt her heart smash against her ribs, her breasts rising and falling too fast as she tried, unsuccessfully, to get her breathing back to normal.

Her robe had come undone and she knew without looking that her nipples were hard, needy points against the thin fabric of her nightdress. Worse, between her legs was a spill of dampness. Restlessness filled her, and the need to climb up that big body and rub herself against him, chasing the fulfilment that no-holds-barred kiss had promised.

Instead she stood stock-still, feet planted. Mechanically her hands grabbed the sides of her robe and tied it tight. Because, despite the thwarted desire churning through her, Safiyah read the chill in those green eyes surveying her like an insect on a pin. Her skin turned to gooseflesh and the fine hairs at her nape stood on end.

Karim wasn't even breathing heavily. He looked as calm and remote as a stone effigy. And as welcoming.

Looking into those austere features, Safiyah felt all that lush heat dissipate. Instead of his deliciousness she tasted the ashes of passion. She might have been swept away by forces she couldn't control but Karim hadn't.

'Well, that little experiment was instructive.' His voice came from a great distance, like low thunder rolling across the wide Assaran plain. 'It's as well to test these things in advance, isn't it?'

'Test what?' Her voice was husky, but reassuringly even. She'd had years of practice at perfecting a façade that hid her feelings.

Those powerful shoulders shrugged nonchalantly. 'Our physical compatibility.' He paused, his gaze capturing hers as he continued with conscious deliberation, 'Or lack of it.'

Deep, deep inside, in that place where she'd once locked her secret hopes and cravings, something crumpled and withered. There was an instant of shearing pain, like a knife-jab to the abdomen. Then it morphed into an unremitting ache that filled her from scalp to toe.

He'd kissed her like that as an *experiment*?

Safiyah wanted to scream and howl. To pummel that granite-hard chest with her fists. But that would achieve nothing except further embarrassment.

· A new kind of fire bloomed within her and seared her cheeks. *Shame*. Shame that she'd responded to this man who now surveyed her with such detachment. Shame that she'd ever been attracted to him.

Swallowing the tangled knot of emotion clogging her throat was almost impossible. Finally she managed, though it physically hurt.

Pain was good, Safiyah assured herself. Pain would make it easier to strip away the final fragments of feeling she'd harboured for Karim.

She'd repressed her feelings for years, told herself she couldn't possibly still want this man who'd rejected her. Whose abandonment had devastated her and branded her with a bone-deep disdain for him and his callous ways.

Yet once in his arms, once his mouth had met hers, she'd responded with an ardour that had been nothing short of embarrassing.

Even now part of her protested. He *had* responded. He'd

wanted to follow that kiss to its natural conclusion just as she had.

Then her brain began to work. People pretended all the time. Hadn't she pretended enthusiasm for Abbas in her bed even when she'd far rather have slept alone? Just because Karim's kiss had been passionate, it didn't mean he'd felt anything but curiosity.

The inequality of their experience told against her. She'd only kissed two men in her life: Karim and her husband. And no kiss before today had awakened such a powerful response in her. Whereas Karim had had women following him, sighing over him and trying to capture his interest for years. No doubt he'd kissed hundreds of women and could feign sexual interest.

He wasn't interested now.

Safiyah's mouth firmed. '*If* I were to marry you...' her words dripped acid '...it wouldn't be for the pleasure of your company.'

Let him read what he liked into her response. She refused to admit anything. After all, she could claim that, like him, she'd been experimenting, searching but not finding a spark between them.

Except she'd never been a liar. The knowledge of her complete submission to Karim's demanding kiss devastated her. She wanted to turn tail and hide.

'Then why *would* you agree to marry me?'

It was a timely reminder, and it stiffened her wobbly knees. She met Karim's stare head-on. 'For my country and my son. I'm afraid of what might happen to both if Shakroun becomes Sheikh.'

Slowly he nodded. 'I understand. I've been hearing more about him this evening.'

Relief made her shoulders sag. Karim sounded like a man who'd changed his mind. If he took the throne Tarek would be safe.

'But what I've heard only reinforces what I said earlier. He's from a powerful clan. If I became Sheikh I'd need to do everything I could to shore up local support. Like marry you.'

Karim's deep voice and narrowed eyes held nothing soft. His needle-sharp scrutiny grazed her skin and her pride. Safiyah might have let him make a fool of her years ago, and again just now, but no more. Enough was enough.

'*If* I were to marry you…' How the thought appalled. But Safiyah would sacrifice her freedom ten times over for her son's life. 'I'd expect you to take your pleasure outside the marriage bed.' She almost choked on the word 'bed', but forced herself to carry on as if unfazed by that kiss. 'Discreetly, of course.'

'Would you, indeed?' Something dark flashed in Karim's eyes. 'And where would you…take *your* pleasure?'

Safiyah stood as tall as she could, lengthening her neck and calling on all the lessons in dignity she'd learned in the past few years. 'That needn't concern you. Rest assured I won't cause any scandals.'

Because sex with Abbas hadn't left her with a burning desire for more. And the one man who'd had the power to wake her libido was staring at her now as if she were something he'd picked up on the sole of his shoe.

Safiyah blocked the jumble of hurt and indignation writhing within, shoving it away with all the other hurts and disappointments she couldn't afford to think about. Instead she concentrated on playing the part of Queen, as her dead husband had taught her. And instead of her usual composure, she aimed for a touch of Abbas's condescension. Presumably it worked, for Karim's dark eyebrows climbed high.

'And if I want pleasure *within* the marriage bed?'

The silky words drew her up short, made her pulse accelerate wildly.

Karim wanted sex with her?

Or was he just trying to make her squirm?

Her hair brushed her cheeks as she shook her head. 'No.'

'Because you don't want me, Safiyah? Or because you're scared you want me too much?'

'Your ego is monumental, Karim.' Adrenaline shot through her and her jaw tilted imperiously.

He merely shrugged. 'I call it as I see it. From where I stand I suspect you're not as uninterested as you say. But I would never force myself on an unwilling woman.'

Safiyah exhaled slowly, trying to banish that panicky feeling. 'I have your word on that?'

'You do.' He paused to let her absorb the words. 'No sex unless you want it, Safiyah. Does that satisfy you?'

She surveyed him carefully. Surely this was just macho male posturing because she'd said she didn't want him. Karim would soon find some ravishing mistress to keep him occupied.

He might be the man who'd dumped her, but she believed him too proud to break his word. Clearly the Council thought the same. And when it boiled down to it what real choice did she have? She needed to save Tarek.

Finally she nodded. 'Yes.'

'You actually trust my word?' His cool tone and the jut of his jaw spoke of haughty male pride.

'Yes.'

Still his frown lingered.

'After all, I'd be entrusting you with my son's wellbeing.'

Saying it aloud sent a shiver rippling down her spine. Not because Karim would hurt them, but at the idea of tying herself once more to a man who saw her as a mere convenience. But she'd survived that once. She could again.

Safiyah returned his stare with one of her own, trying not to catalogue those spare, attractive features she'd once daydreamed about. She reminded herself that he was arrogant and unfeeling, a man who'd toyed with her.

What had happened to the man she'd fallen for at twenty-two? Had she been completely misled by his charm and apparent kindness? What had made him cold and bitter? The same mysterious thing that had driven him to give up his throne?

It didn't matter. She wasn't about to pry into his past or his character, beyond the fact that he would do the right thing. When it came to his honour, and his work for his people, Karim's record was strong. The Royal Council wouldn't have made its offer if there were doubts. It had deliberated carefully before approaching Karim, investigating not only his years in Za'daq but his recent activities.

Nevertheless...

'If you become Sheikh, what about my son, Tarek? Are you serious about adopting him?'

Karim inclined his head. 'I told you before—I'm not the man to steal your son's birthright. He'll still be in line to become Sheikh eventually.'

It seemed too good to be true. If anyone else had said it Safiyah would have doubted they meant it. But Karim had already walked away from one throne. It was still on the tip of her tongue to ask what had prompted that action, but she kept silent. That didn't matter now. As he'd said earlier, the past was best left alone. All that mattered was Tarek's safety and Assara's.

She clasped her hands at her waist and stood silent, watching him. He couldn't have made it clearer that he saw marriage to her as a necessity, not a pleasure. And she should be used to being viewed as a political expedient.

Yet still it hurt!

Abbas had married her because it had suited him to build an alliance with her clan, so when the time had come for him to marry he'd turned his eyes to her family. At first he'd been interested in her clever younger sister, studying at university in the capital. When that hadn't been possible he'd made do with Safiyah.

To accept a second marriage of convenience, to another man who had no feelings for her, was a terrible thing. So terrible Safiyah wanted to smash something. To tell Karim in scathing detail what he could do with his marriage plans.

But she loved her son too much. She'd do anything to keep him safe. Her happiness meant nothing against that. And as for the dreams she'd once harboured of finding love...

Safiyah shuddered and rubbed her hands up her arms. As a twenty-seven-year-old widow she'd be a fool to believe in romance.

'What are you thinking?'

Karim hadn't come closer, yet his voice curled around her. She stiffened and moved to the window, needing distance from his looming presence. She looked out at the sprinkle of lights in the darkness, where the town bled down the slope towards the lake.

'What if you have children? Wouldn't you want them to inherit? I can't believe you'd put your own flesh and blood second to someone else's.'

Safiyah spun around to find him watching her, his expression intense yet impenetrable. Before she could puzzle over it he spoke.

'Don't worry, Safiyah, I won't foist any bastard children on you.'

His tone cut like a blade and his brow wrinkled into a scowl, making her wonder at the depth of his anger. For anger there was, vibrating through the thickening atmosphere.

Safiyah tried to fathom it. Even when she'd told him he could forget about sharing her bed she hadn't sensed fury like this.

Then, as abruptly as it had surfaced, it disappeared.

'So, you agree to marry me?'

He still didn't approach. Didn't attempt to woo her with soft words or tender caresses.

Safiyah told herself she was grateful.

'I...' The words stuck in her throat. Duty, maternal love, patriotism—all demanded she say yes. Yet it was a struggle to conquer the selfish part of her that wanted something for herself. Finally she nodded. 'Yes. If you take the throne, I'll marry you.'

She hadn't expected a display of strong emotion, but she'd expected *something* to show he appreciated her sacrifice. Even a flicker in that stern expression.

She got nothing.

'Good. We'll travel to Assara tomorrow.'

Karim kept his tone brisk, masking the momentary flash of emotion that struck out of nowhere and lodged like a nail between his ribs.

He inhaled, drawing on a lifetime's training in dismissing inconvenient feelings. He didn't *do* sentiment.

'Tomorrow?'

Her eyes rounded. Almost as if she didn't want this. Didn't want *him*.

'I'll accept the Council's offer in person. Now I've decided there's no time to be lost. There's no point giving Shakroun any opportunity to build more support.'

It would be a long, tough road ahead, establishing himself as Sheikh in a foreign country. Karim was under no illusions about that. But excitement burgeoned at the prospect. It was the work he'd been bred to, the work he'd missed even if he hadn't allowed himself to admit it.

And nor was it just the work he looked forward to.

He watched Safiyah watching him and kept his face studiously blank. It wouldn't do to let her guess that one of the benefits in acting quickly was to secure her.

Purely for political reasons, of course.

Yet Safiyah unsettled him more than she should. Thoughts of her had interfered with his decision-making and he'd kept following her around the room as if his body refused to follow the dictates of his brain. Baser impulses ruled—impulses driven by the organ between his legs and the urgent need to claim what he'd once so desired.

That *had* to be the reason for his current fixation. He'd once been prepared to offer Safiyah everything—his name, his loyalty, his wealth. Now he had the opportunity to claim what he'd been denied.

Relief dribbled through him. It was good to have a sane explanation for this urgent attraction.

A powerful throb of anticipation pulsed through him. That kiss, brief as it had been, had proved the attraction was there, stronger than ever.

'What are you thinking?'

She repeated his own question, her eyes narrowed and her chin lifted, as if she'd read the direction of his thoughts and didn't like it. That surprised Karim. He'd long ago learned to hide his thoughts.

'Just thinking about my priorities when we get to As-sara.' He paused. 'I'll instruct my lawyers to draw up the adoption papers with the marriage contract.'

'Really? I hadn't expected that so soon. Thank you.'

For the first time since they'd met again Safiyah actually approached him. The tight line of her beautiful mouth had softened and her eyes glowed. If Karim had needed any proof that she was motivated by love of her child, here it was.

He watched the slow smile spread across her face and felt a curious niggle inside. What would it be like to have someone—Safiyah, for example—look at him that way.

Not because he was doing something for the one she loved, but because she cared for *him*?

Blood rushed in Karim's ears as he stiffened and pulled back. Such fanciful thoughts were totally foreign. He was a grown man. He didn't need anyone to care for him. It was just curiosity about the loving bond between mother and child. Something he'd never experienced.

As a child he'd convinced himself that his mother loved him. He had fragmentary memories of being held in soft arms and sung to. Of playing with her in that rose-scented courtyard.

But those memories were wishful thinking. If his mother had loved either of her children she wouldn't have deserted them—left them to the mercies of the man who'd raised them. The man he'd thought of as his father had been irascible, impatient, and never satisfied, no matter how hard Karim had tried to live up to his impossible standards.

'Karim? What is it?' Safiyah had lifted her hand as if to touch his arm.

A white-hot blast of longing seared him. Unlooked-for. Unwanted. Because hankering after such things made him weak. He'd almost fallen for that trap once before with Safiyah. But he'd learned his lesson.

'Nothing. Nothing at all.'

He let his mouth turn up in a slow smile. The sort of smile he knew melted a woman's resolve. Safiyah blinked. Twice. Her lips parted and he saw her pulse pound in her throat.

'On the contrary. Everything is perfect.'

CHAPTER FIVE

KARIM LEFT HIS meeting in the Assaran palace torn between satisfaction and frustration. The interminable deliberation over legalities was complete. Agreement had been reached on all the important issues—including the provisions for Tarek and Safiyah.

And if some of the Assaran officials had been surprised that he, the incoming Sheikh, was the one ensuring the little Prince lost nothing as a result of Karim's accession, they'd quickly hidden it.

As for the red tape…

His homeland of Za'daq had its fair share, but Assara outdid it. They'd spent hours longer than necessary on minutiae. But Karim hadn't hurried them. Time enough to streamline processes after he became Sheikh.

But now, after hours hemmed in by nervous officials and nit-picking lawyers, he needed air.

He turned away from the palace's offices, past the broad corridor leading to the state rooms, and headed down towards the main courtyard where he guessed the stables were.

Emerging outside, Karim glanced at the lowering sun dropping towards the distant border with Za'daq. Purple mountains fringed the horizon and even here, on the coast, he registered the unmistakable scent of the desert.

His nostrils twitched and he inhaled deeply, though he

knew he was imagining that elusive scent. The desert was half a day's journey away. Yet the very air seemed familiar here, as it hadn't in Europe and North America. He felt more at home in Assara than he had in years there.

Karim smiled as he sauntered across the yard to the stables. In the couple of days since he'd agreed to come here his certainty had increased. He'd made the right decision.

But his smile faded as he registered the stable's echoing silence. The doors were shut and there was no sign of activity except in a far corner, where part of the stables had been turned into garages. There, a driver was busy polishing a limousine.

'The stables?' he said, when questioned. 'I'm sorry, sir, but they're empty. No one has worked there in years. Not since the last Sheikh's father's time.'

'There are no horses at all?'

Karim couldn't believe it. Assara was known for its pure-bred horses. Surely the Sheikh would have the finest mounts? Plus, Safiyah had virtually been born in the saddle. Riding was a major part of her life.

He remembered the first time he'd seen her. She'd been on horseback, and her fluid grace on that prancing grey, her lithe agility and the way she and the horse had moved as one had snagged his admiration. The sight had momentarily made him forget the reason he was visiting her father's stud farm, the horse he wanted to buy.

'Where does the Sheikha keep *her* horses?'

'The Sheikha, sir? I don't know of her riding or about any horses.'

Karim stared. Safiyah? Not riding? It was impossible. Once there'd been talk of her possible selection for the national equestrian team. He recalled thinking she'd never looked more alive than on horseback. Except when she was in his arms.

The memory curled heat through his belly, increasing his edginess.

Thanking the driver, he turned and entered the palace, heading for the royal suites. It was time he visited Safiyah anyway. The past couple of days had been taken up with meetings and he'd barely seen her.

Five minutes later he was admitted into her apartments. His curiosity rose as he entered. This was the first room he'd seen in the palace that looked both beautiful and comfortable rather than grandiose. The sort of place he could imagine relaxing after a long day. He liked it.

'If you'd like to make yourself comfortable, sir?' The maid gestured to a long sofa. 'I'll tell the Sheikha you're here.' She bobbed a curtsey and headed not further into the apartment, as he'd expected, but through the open doors into a green courtyard.

Instead of taking a seat Karim followed her, emerging into a lush garden full of flowering plants. Pink, white and red blossoms caught his eye. Fragrance filled the air and the swathe of grass curving amongst the shrubs was a deep emerald.

He paused, taking in the vibrancy of the place, so unlike the courtyards elsewhere in the palace, which were all symmetry and formal elegance. This was inviting, but casual, almost mysterious with its thick plantings and meandering paths.

The sound of laughter drew him forward. There was the maid, moving towards someone half hidden from view. Beyond her, on the grass, was a tumble of movement that resolved itself into a floppy-eared pup and a small boy. Giggles filled the air and an excited yapping.

Karim stepped forward and discovered the half-hidden figure was Safiyah, seated on the grass.

His gaze was riveted to his bride-to-be. In Switzerland he'd seen her cool and reserved, then later satisfyingly

breathless in his arms. He'd seen her mutinous and imperious. But he hadn't seen her like this—relaxed and happy,
with laughter curving her red lips.

For a moment something shimmered like golden motes
in the late-afternoon light. A mirage of the past, when
they'd enjoyed each other's company, gradually getting
to know one another. Safiyah had laughed then, the sound
sweet as honey and open as sunshine. Her laughter, her
eager enjoyment of life, had been precious to someone like
him, brought up by a man who had been at best dour, at
worst irate, and always dissatisfied.

'Karim.'

Her eyes widened and the light fled from her expression.
Stupid to mind that the sight of him dulled her brightness.
It wasn't as if he wanted to share her laughter. He wasn't
here for levity.

Safiyah said something and the maid moved towards
the boy as if to scoop him up.

'No. Don't take him away.' Karim turned to Safiyah.
'Don't cut short his playtime because of me.'

It was time for him to meet the boy. Karim had agreed to
be a father to him. The idea still elicited a confusing mixture of feelings and he'd berated himself more than once
for acting as if on a whim where Tarek was concerned.

But it was no whim. The thought of the little Prince at
the mercy of a ruthless man like Shakroun had struck a
chord with Karim. He'd had to act. Nor could he rip the
child's birthright away. Just as he hadn't been able to take
the crown of Za'daq over Ashraf, though he'd been brought
up solely for that purpose.

Besides, Karim knew what it was like growing up with
the burden of royalty. The child needed a role model—one
who understood that there was more to life than court protocol and politics. Karim would be that mentor.

An inner voice whispered that he hadn't been such a

good mentor to his younger brother...hadn't been able to protect him from his father's ire or bring much joy into his world. He vowed to do a better job with Tarek.

Safiyah rose in one graceful movement. Her long dress of deep amethyst slid with a whisper around that delectable body and Karim cursed his hyper-awareness of her. It had been like that since they'd arrived in Assara. No, since that kiss in Switzerland, that had left him fighting to mask his urgent arousal.

Karim drew a slow breath and forced himself to admit the truth. He'd been attuned to her from the moment she'd turned up in his hotel suite. She still had the power to unsettle him.

Safiyah murmured something to the maid, who melted back down the path.

'How kind of you to visit.'

Safiyah clasped her hands at her waist and inclined her head—the gracious Queen greeting a visitor. Except this visitor was the man who was about to save her country and her son. And he was going to become far more to her than a polite stranger, no matter how hard she pretended indifference.

Satisfaction banished his jab of annoyance at her condescension. Soon there'd be no pretence of them being strangers.

'The pleasure is all mine.'

He let his voice deepen caressingly. Her eyes rounded and he smothered a smile. Oh, yes. He was looking forward to a much closer relationship with Safiyah. Her attempts to keep him at a distance only fired his anticipation.

'I thought I'd take a ride, but discovered the stables empty.'

'My husband wasn't a rider.'

Karim watched her refold her hands, one over the other. Her mouth flattened, disguising those lush lips. Curiosity stirred. His nape prickled with the certainty that he'd hit on a subject she didn't want to discuss. Which made Karim determined to discover why.

Was her reaction a response to him or to the mention of her dead husband?

'But you are.'

He wasn't sure why he pressed the point, except that it was sensible to know the woman he was about to marry.

She lifted her shoulders but the gesture was too stiff to be called a shrug. 'I was.'

Karim lifted one eyebrow questioningly.

'I don't ride any more.'

The words were clipped and cool, but he sensed something beneath them. Something that wasn't as calm as the image she projected.

He waited, letting the silence draw out. Concern niggled. Had she had a bad fall? Had she been seriously injured? It would take a lot to keep the woman he'd once known away from her beloved horses.

Finally, with a tiny exhalation that sounded like a huff of exasperation, she spoke. 'Abbas didn't ride and he preferred that I didn't either.'

'Why?'

Karim shoved his hands in his pockets and rocked back on his feet, reinforcing the fact that he had plenty of time. Especially as he sensed Safiyah was reluctant to explain.

Equestrian prowess was a traditional part of a warrior's skills. It was unusual to find a ruler who didn't ride—especially as Assarans were proud of their fabled reputation as horsemen. The country was world-renowned for the horses it bred in the wide fertile valley along its northern border.

Safiyah darted a glance at the little boy and the puppy, now playing a lolloping game of chase. Was she checking they were okay or whether her son was listening?

'When I got pregnant I was advised not to ride. To keep the baby safe.'

Karim nodded. That he understood. But that had been years ago. There was more to this tale.

'And after the birth?'

A wry smile curved her lips. 'Only someone who hasn't gone through childbirth would ask that.'

It was tempting to be side-tracked by that smile, but Karim knew a diversion when he heard it. 'Not immediately, but in the years since your son was born. Why haven't you ridden?' A crazy idea surfaced. 'Did he forbid it?'

Karim knew by the sudden widening of her eyes that he was right. Sheikh Abbas had forbidden his wife to ride. But why?

Safiyah lifted her chin. There was no trace of her smile as she surveyed him with regal hauteur. That was something she'd learned only recently. The woman he'd known had been as fresh and unaffected as they came. Or, he amended, had given that impression...

'If it was known that I rode regularly I'd be expected to ride during royal processions and official gatherings. That was what royals have always done in the past. But...'

'But then you'd show up your husband if you were on horseback and he wasn't?'

A flush climbed her slender throat and she looked away. As if *she* were the one with an embarrassing secret.

'What happened? Did he have a bad fall? Is that what made him afraid to ride?'

The colour had seeped across her cheekbones now. 'It's not important. Abbas was beginning to modernise Assara. He saw no point in clinging to tradition. Travelling by car is quicker and more convenient.'

The words sounded like something she'd learned by heart. No doubt they'd been her husband's.

Karim felt something gnaw at his belly. Dislike.

He'd carefully not allowed himself to dwell on thoughts of Safiyah with her husband. He'd spent enough fruitless hours in the past, fuming over the way she'd dumped him so unceremoniously and then given herself to another bridegroom a mere five months later.

At the time the idea of Safiyah with another man, in his bed, giving him what she'd denied Karim, had been a special sort of poison in his blood.

But now his animosity was directed at Abbas.

Particularly as the possibility now arose that her defence of the dead man might be driven by love.

It hadn't occurred to Karim that Safiyah had *loved* her husband. There'd been no outward sign of it. On the contrary, her response to *him* had told him she didn't carry a torch for Abbas. No, ambition had been behind her first marriage, not love.

'Tradition matters if the people still value it.'

He read the flicker in her expression and knew that to many in Assara seeing their Sheikh on horseback *was* still important.

'And it matters that he stopped you from doing something you love just to save himself embarrassment.'

It was the action of a coward. But Karim kept the thought to himself. He was, after all, talking to the man's widow.

Something dark and bitter curled through his belly. He ignored the sensation, shifting his stance.

Safiyah curved her mouth into a smile that didn't reach her eyes. 'Well, you'll be able to fill the stables if you wish.' Before he could respond she looked at her watch. 'It's getting late. Time for Tarek to go to bed. If you'll excuse me…?'

'Introduce me—' Karim stopped, wondering. Did four-year-olds *do* introductions, or should he just get down on his haunches and say hello?

For the first time since he'd agreed to come here and take

on the kingdom he felt unsure of himself. He ignored his uncertainty and crossed the grass to where the child and dog lay, panting, after their game. The kid registered his presence, looking up, then up again, till a pair of brown eyes met his. Brown flecked with honey, just like his mother's.

Why that should affect Karim he didn't know, but he registered a thump in the vicinity of his ribs as that little face with those wide eyes turned to his.

'Tarek, I want you to meet...' Safiyah paused. Was she wondering how to describe him? Not father...not Sheikh yet.

'Hello. My name is Karim. I've come to live at the palace.'

The boy scrambled to his feet and, after swiping his dirty hands on the back of his shorts, stood straight and extended one hand. 'Hello. I'm Tarek ibn Abbas of Assara. It's a pleasure to meet you.'

Karim closed his palm around the tiny hand and gave it a gentle shake. He stared into the small, serious face regarding him so intently, as if looking for signs of disapproval.

With an audible whoosh of sound in his ears Karim found himself back in time, learning from a courtier the precise grades of greeting and which was suitable for royalty, for members of court, foreign dignitaries and ordinary citizens. He must have been about Tarek's age and he'd mastered the lesson quickly, since the alternative—disappointing his irritable father—hadn't been an option.

'The pleasure is mine, Prince Tarek.' Karim inclined his head over the boy's hand before releasing it.

The child nodded in acknowledgement but his eyes were already flicking back to the puppy chewing at his shoe. Tarek might be a prince but he was above all a little boy. And in that instant Karim was swamped by a determination to achieve at least one thing. To allow Tarek to have a childhood despite being royal.

Something Karim had never had.

He'd grown up with no time for idle play or cuddles. Instead there'd been constricting rules and a strict regimen devised to ensure he became a miniature copy of his father.

Seeing the yearning look on the boy's face as his royal training battled his inclination for fun, Karim smiled and squatted down. 'He's a fine-looking dog.'

In fact the boisterous pup was anything but beautiful. It had the long, silky tail and soft ears of a hunting dog but those short legs and nuggety body belonged to some other breed entirely.

Karim recalled the pure-bred hounds his father had kept, whose pedigree was as important as any other quality. Karim felt a surge of empathy with the mongrel pup and reached out to pat it—only to have it gnaw experimentally on his fingers.

'He likes you!' The last of Prince Tarek's gravity disintegrated as he threw himself down on the ground with his pet. 'He doesn't mean to hurt you,' he added earnestly. 'He bites people he likes.'

'I know. It's what puppies do.'

Karim was rewarded with a wide smile and responded with a grin.

'Do *you* have a dog?' the boy enquired.

Karim shook his head. 'I'm afraid not.'

'You could play with us if you like.'

He was surprised to find himself moved by the child's generosity. How long since he'd done something as simple as play with a dog? Or talk to a child?

'I'd like that, thank you.' He scratched the dog's spotted belly. 'What's his name?'

'Blackie. I picked it.'

Karim nodded. 'You picked well. Is he yours?'

'Yes. But he doesn't sleep with me.' The boy pouted, using rounded cheeks and outthrust lip to full advantage as his gaze slid reproachfully towards his mother. 'He *should* sleep in my bed. So I can look after him if he gets lonely in the night. Don't you think?'

Karim sensed Safiyah standing behind him, yet she said nothing. Was she waiting to see how he responded?

'Dogs need space, just like people do. I'm sure Blackie has a cosy bed of his own.'

'He certainly does,' Safiyah chimed in. 'Just down the hall. He sleeps so well that Tarek has to wake him up to play sometimes. Now, it's time to say goodnight. Tarek and Blackie need to go to bed.'

Karim watched the little boy struggle with the urge to argue. But eventually he got to his feet.

His eyes were on the same level as Karim's as he said, 'I like you. Come and play again.' Then, with a flickering look at his mother he smiled and added, 'Please.'

Tarek's mixture of royal imperiousness and friendliness appealed. Far more than the cautious, almost obsequious approaches Karim usually got from those eager to impress.

'I'd like that. Thank you,' Karim said again. He returned the smile with one of his own.

He'd enjoy spending time with little Tarek. For one thing, it would be a pleasant change. For as long as he could recall he'd been unable to trust that the people who tried to get close to him did so out of affection instead of for personal gain.

Safiyah bent to scoop the tired pup into her arms and take Tarek by the hand. Karim felt that all too familiar clench in his groin as her dress pulled over ripe curves.

Once she'd played up to him because she'd believed he could make her a queen. Now she'd come to him because she needed his protection.

Always because she wanted something from him.

Not because she wanted *him*.

It was a timely reminder. One he wouldn't forget.

But that didn't mean he couldn't enjoy the benefits of having Safiyah as his wife.

Suddenly the tedium and frustrations of the afternoon's long meeting disintegrated. Karim found himself looking forward to embracing his new life.

The vast, circular audience chamber was filled to the brim. Guests even outnumbered the stars of pure gold that decorated the domed ceiling of midnight-blue. The crush of people made Safiyah glad she was on the raised royal dais. Yet her heart still pounded as if she'd had to fight her way through the throng.

As of a few minutes ago, Karim had become Assara's ruler.

Thinking about it made her light-headed—with relief, she told herself, not nerves. Yet she kept her eyes on the crowd, not on the man further along the dais.

She had a perfect view of their faces, the VIPs of Assara, as they took turns to swear fealty to their new Sheikh. There were politicians, clan elders and powerful businessmen. Even the other men who'd hoped to be Sheikh.

Safiyah watched, her breath stalling, as the person before Karim bowed and backed away. Next in line was Hassan Shakroun. Shakroun's lips twisted unpleasantly, but that wasn't unusual. The man rarely looked content.

To her immense relief, when Karim had been proclaimed Sheikh there'd been no protest. Karim's swift acceptance of the crown meant Shakroun had had no time to act against him.

Now Shakroun moved forward and bowed perfunctorily, then backed away.

Safiyah sighed in relief. She'd done right. Shakroun had no reason now to harm Tarek. He was safe. It was Karim who had the power to make or break Tarek's future.

Despite his assurances, it was impossible not to wonder what sort of ruler he'd make, and what sort of father.

What sort of husband?

A jitter of nerves shot through her, churning her stomach. She breathed out slowly, forcing her heartbeat to slow.

As soon as the coronation ceremony was over their marriage would take place, and then Karim's formal adoption of Tarek.

What she'd give for her sister to be here. But, following tradition, there were no females in the room. Except her. Karim had made an exception to past practice by inviting her to attend the ceremony that would make him Sheikh.

Reluctantly she looked again at the centre of the dais. There, surrounded by the leaders of the Council, stood Karim, regal in pure white trimmed with gold. Even the *agal* encircling his headscarf was gold, a symbol of his new status.

He stood a head taller than the older men around him. Confident and commanding. His strong profile was proud, betraying no hint of doubt or weakness.

Tarek would grow up as the adopted son of the Sheikh. And she… She was destined to become once again wife of a sheikh.

Another breath, snatched into lungs that didn't seem to work.

Even the knowledge that this would be a marriage in name only couldn't ease the hammer-beat of her heart or the uneasy feeling that she'd acted against her better judgement.

Her second marriage of convenience. Her second marriage without love or real caring.

Safiyah pressed her palm to her abdomen as pain sheared through her. She'd learned to live with Abbas's indifference. Theirs hadn't been a close relationship, and in some ways there'd been relief in the fact they hadn't spent much time together.

Surely this new marriage would be similar. Karim's distaste had been clear after that kiss in Switzerland. *She'd* been the one swept away. He'd been as unmoved as one of those looming Swiss mountains. Her cheeks flamed at the memory.

And yet, this marriage *wouldn't* be like her one to Abbas. Then she'd been so miserable and lost that even going through the motions of marriage had been just one more burden. Dazed with grief over her father and her broken heart, nothing had mattered but doing her duty.

Now there was nothing to cushion her from the reality of her actions.

Her gaze returned to the arrogantly masculine profile of the new Sheikh. A riot of emotions roiled through her.

This marriage was going to be far worse than her first. She was marrying not a stranger, but the one man she'd ever loved. The man she'd yearned for with all her youthful heart.

She didn't love him any more. The very idea chilled her. Because doing so would make her impossibly vulnerable. But she'd cared for him once and felt sickened by the idea of living a pale imitation of the life she'd once hoped for.

Yet it was worse even than that. For though she didn't love him, and he was indifferent to her, Safiyah still wanted Karim as a woman wanted a man.

She desired him.

How was she to survive this marriage? Ignoring his indifference and the women he'd take into his bed? She didn't—

Suddenly the old men around the Sheikh shuffled back and that bronzed, handsome face turned. Safiyah felt the impact of that stare. It seemed as if his gaze bored straight past her blushing cheeks, past the sumptuous gown and jewels, deep into her aching heart.

The illusion strengthened when his eyes narrowed and

his nostrils flared, as if he sensed her doubts and the urge to flee which she had only just mastered.

But Safiyah was strong. Or she could pretend to be— even if she felt weak-kneed and terrified.

She lifted her chin and held that keen gaze like a queen.

CHAPTER SIX

'SAFIYAH.' KARIM FOUND himself crossing the dais to stand before her instead of simply summoning her with a gesture.

He heard the murmur of voices as people noted his action, and he didn't care. The previous Sheikhs of Assara might have moved for no one, but Karim would rule in his own way. He'd wanted to go to her from the moment she'd paced decorously into the room, like some exquisite medieval illumination come to life.

She glowed in jewel tones, her long dress of gold brocade revealing amber and red depths when she moved. The tiara of old gold and rubies turned the sensual woman he knew into a regal beauty. The matching chandelier earrings drew attention to the delicate line of her slender neck. Her air of shuttered stillness made him want to muss her hair with his hands as he tasted those luscious lips again and brought her to frenzied, rapturous life.

Drawing back from her passionate kiss, pretending to be unmoved by it, had been appallingly difficult. Fortunately pride and his once-bruised ego had come to the rescue.

'Your Majesty.'

She sank into a curtsey so low that the shimmering gown rippled across the floor around her like a molten lake. Head bent, she stayed there, awaiting his pleasure. But despite the profound gesture of obeisance there was an indefinable air of challenge about her.

This woman kept her own counsel and tried to maintain her distance. When he'd spent a little time with her and Tarek he'd been even more aware of the wall she'd built around herself.

He reached down and touched her hand, felt her flinch, and then, as he slid his hand around her wrist, the quick flutter of her pulse.

'You may rise.'

She did, but even so kept her eyes downcast. Anyone observing would see a beautiful queen, modestly showing respect for her new Sheikh. But Karim was close enough to read the swift rise and fall of her breasts and see the tiny tremors that ran through her.

Not so indifferent, my fine beauty, no matter how you try to hide it.

'You look magnificent.' His voice deepened in appreciation.

She lifted her eyes then. The velvety brown looked darker than usual, without the gold highlights he used to admire. They looked soul-deep and...worried? Despite his impatience, the idea disturbed him. What had she to worry about now he'd come to her rescue?

He told himself not to be taken in.

His feelings for her were too confused.

Once he'd been well on the way to being enchanted by Safiyah. He'd believed her gentle, honest and sweet. Then he'd wanted to hate her for deserting him.

Since meeting her again he'd experienced a mixture of distrust, anger, lust and a surprising protectiveness. Whatever else, she'd proved herself courageous when danger threatened her son. Or was she just grasping, scheming to retain her privileged position?

But marriage had been *his* idea, not hers.

He didn't trust her, didn't want to like her, and yet his hunger for her was tempered by reluctant admiration. It took guts for her to face him again, to consent to marry him and carry it off with such panache.

He lifted her hand and kissed it. A whisper of a kiss, yet he felt the resonance of her shock in his own body.

Want. Need. Hunger.

Soon they'd be assuaged.

'Come...' He smiled down at her, not bothering to hide his satisfaction. 'It's time for our wedding.'

Safiyah closed the door to her apartments behind her and sagged back, grateful for the solid wood supporting her spine. She felt drained. The ceremony hadn't taken long, but the celebrations had lasted hours. And that was just the first day. Tomorrow the celebrations continued—and the day after that.

Yet it wasn't the hours in heavy brocade and jewels, performing her royal duties, that had exhausted her. It was stress. The knowledge that she was now Karim's *wife*!

A sob rose and she stifled it, pushing away from the door, making herself walk into her rooms though every limb felt shaky.

It was a paper marriage. It didn't mean anything except that Tarek was safe. And that she'd have to keep on playing the public role of adoring, compliant spouse of a man who didn't give a damn about her.

Again that tangle of emotions rose, almost choking her. She swallowed, blinked back the heat glazing her eyes, and kept walking.

Usually her maid would be there, but Safiyah had known she wouldn't be able to face anyone and had dismissed her for the night. Now she half wished she hadn't. Just unpinning the tiara would take ages. But better to wrestle with it and her overwrought emotions alone.

At least she had practice in doing that. It seemed a lifetime ago that she'd had anyone she could lean on emotionally. Not since her mother had died when Safiyah was in her teens. She'd loved her father, but he'd never fully recovered from the loss of his wife. And her little sister had spent years battling her own demons of anxiety and depression, so Safiyah had supported her rather than the other way around.

As for Abbas...despite their physical intimacy there'd never been any question of sharing her feelings with him. He hadn't been interested. And life at the palace had isolated her from her friends.

She swung around, caught sight of herself in a mirror, all gold and jewels, and grimaced, feeling ashamed. She had so much. She had no right to feel sorry for herself.

Nevertheless, she turned on the music her sister had given her for her last birthday—a compilation of gentle tunes harmonised with wild birdsong and even the occasional sound of water falling. Rana said it helped to relax her and Safiyah had found the same.

She switched on a couple more lamps so the room felt cosy, unhooking the heavy earrings with a sigh of relief and placing them on the waiting tray in her dressing room. Her bangles followed—ornate, old, and incredibly precious heirloom pieces.

With each piece she imagined a little more of the weight lifting from her shoulders.

She lifted her hands to the tiara, turning towards the full-length mirror that took up one wall of the dressing space.

'Would you like help with that?'

The voice, smoky and low, rolled out of the shadows behind her.

Safiyah froze, elbows up, staring at the figure that had stepped into her line of vision in the mirror. Her pulse rocketed and the remnants of distress she'd been battling coalesced into a churning, burning nugget of fire in her abdomen.

Karim looked good—better than good. The traditional robes suited him, accentuating his height, the breadth of his chest and the purity of his strong bone structure that made his stern face so appallingly attractive. He'd discarded his headscarf and for some reason the sight of his close-cropped black hair after the formality of their wedding celebration seemed too...intimate.

As did the fact he was in her private rooms!

'Karim!'

Safiyah swung round, her arms falling to her sides. How long had she held them up? Her hands prickled with pins and needles. Her nape too, and then her whole spine as she met those hooded eyes. His stare was intense, skewering her to the spot and totally at odds with his relaxed stance. He leaned with one shoulder propped against the doorjamb.

Safiyah swallowed, then swiped her dry mouth with her tongue. Karim didn't move a muscle, but she sensed a change in him. The air crackled. The tingling along her backbone drove inwards, filling her belly with a fluttering as if a thousand giant moths flapped there, frantically trying to reach the glowing moon that hung in the night sky.

'What are you doing here, Karim?' Finally she collected herself enough to clasp her hands at her waist to conceal the way they trembled.

'I've come to see you, obviously.' He straightened and crossed towards her, making the room claustrophobically close. 'Turn around.'

'Sorry?' Safiyah gaped up at the face that now hovered far too close.

His expression gave nothing away. 'Turn around so I can help with the pins.'

'I don't need any help.'

Too late. He'd lifted his hands and she found herself encircled by the drape of snowy white fabric, deliciously scented with sandalwood and hot male. *Very* hot male.

Her cheeks flushed and something disturbing rippled through her.

Desire. Memory. The recollection of how she'd lost herself in his kiss.

He plucked at a pin, twisted another. 'Shh...don't fidget. Let me finish this, then we can talk.'

Relief cascaded through her. He wanted to talk. Probably about tomorrow's festivities. She was letting her unguarded responses get the better of her.

When they talked, the first item on her agenda would be to make it clear he couldn't stroll into her rooms whenever he felt like it. But she'd rather make her point when they were out in the sitting room. Having him in this very private space was too unsettling.

Safiyah drew a slow breath and nodded, wincing when his hold on the tiara stopped it moving with her.

'Sorry.'

Her eyes were on a level with his collarbone and she watched, bemused, the play of muscles in his throat. How could something so ordinary look...sexy?

'Wait. I'll turn.' Anything to give her breathing space.

But when she turned she was confronted with a mirror image of him looming behind her, his shoulders too wide, too masculine. Especially when the dance of his fingers in her hair felt like a deliberate caress.

He was surprisingly deft, making her wonder what experience he'd had in unpinning women's hair. Safiyah had no doubt he'd undressed plenty of women in his time. But, to her shock, she discovered having Karim undo her hair felt almost as intimate in its own way as sex had felt with Abbas.

She blinked, stunned at the idea, and found herself looking into a stare that sent fiery shivers trailing to a point deep inside her. That elusive place where, just once or twice, as

Abbas had taken his pleasure with her, there'd been a hint that she too might discover something more—

'There.'

Did she imagine Karim's voice was huskier? He lifted the tiara off with one hand, and Safiyah was about to thank him when he ploughed his fingers through her hair, dragging it down to her shoulders.

His eyes held hers in the mirror as he used his hand like a comb, spreading her hair around her shoulders. Each stroke was a slow, delicious assault on her senses.

Safiyah felt the stiffness ease from her neck and spine... detected an urge to lean into that stroking touch. Horrified, she stepped forward—so fast that her hair snagged on the ancient gold ring that had been placed on his finger at his investiture today. Her head was yanked back, but she welcomed the pain because it broke the spell.

'Sorry.'

He frowned and worked his hand free, during which time she took the tiara from his other hand. Then she moved away, replacing it in the velvet-lined box with the earrings and bangles.

Snapping the lid closed, she spun round. 'Shall we?'

She didn't wait for a response but preceded him out of the dressing room and back to the bedroom. She was on her way towards her sitting room when his words stopped her.

'Here's fine.'

'Here?'

She swung around. Karim stood midway between the dressing room door and the bed. There were no seats in the room apart from a long cushioned sofa.

'We'll be more comfortable in the sitting room.'

'Oh, I doubt that, Safiyah.'

That deliberate tone sent a shot of adrenalin through her already tense body.

Suddenly, as if a curtain had been yanked back, Karim's

expression was no longer impenetrable. She read a glitter in those eyes that was shockingly familiar. Safiyah recognised the look of a man with sex on his mind. She almost fancied she saw the flicker of flames in Karim's dark eyes. The tendons at the base of his neck stood proud, and though he made no move towards her there was a waiting stillness in his tall frame that unnerved her.

Involuntarily, Safiyah backed up a step. To keep him from reaching for her or to stop herself doing something foolish?

In that second of realisation she was torn between dismay and the need to throw herself into Karim's embrace and let him do whatever he wanted.

Because *she* wanted. She'd been on a knife-edge of frustrated desire since that kiss in Switzerland and she despised herself for it.

'No!' She felt her eyes widen as he frowned. 'We're not doing *that*.'

'*That?*' he murmured. 'How coy you are.'

His mouth curled at the corners as if he were amused. Damn him. As if he knew she didn't even want to think about sex with him, much less say it out loud. As if he knew how desperately she fought the desire to do more than talk about it.

Safiyah stiffened her spine. She might not have Karim's no doubt vast experience. But that didn't make her a fool or a push-over.

Her chin hiked up. 'You seem to forget this marriage is for political reasons.'

'So? That doesn't mean we can't enjoy the personal benefits.'

The word 'personal' was a rough burr that rubbed across her skin, making the fine hairs on her arms stand erect.

'Can you honestly tell me you don't want me?'

His words sucked the air from her lungs as she realised

he'd read her secret. Of course he had. He'd had to peel her off him to end that kiss in his hotel suite. The memory mocked her.

Karim crossed his arms over his chest. The gesture emphasised both his powerful frame and that annoying air of arrogance. And, to her consternation, his sheer, unadulterated sex appeal.

She tried to concentrate on his arrogance. Even Abbas at his most regal had never irritated her with just a look. Karim did it with merely a raised eyebrow and the knowing gleam in eyes that looked smoky with intent.

Their marriage wasn't about them as individuals, but he saw no reason to deny himself a little sexual diversion with his new spouse. She was here, he was bored, or he wanted to celebrate, or maybe he just wanted to amuse himself at her expense. In Switzerland he hadn't bothered to hide his disdain.

She planted her hands on her hips and paced a step nearer as hurt, fury and frustration coalesced. 'I'm not a convenience, here for your pleasure, Karim. We established before we married that I won't share my bed with you.'

The lingering hint of a smile on that long mouth stiffened. He shook his head, taking his own step forward so they stood almost toe to toe and she had to tilt her neck to look down her nose at him.

Safiyah knew better than to back away. He'd take advantage of any show of weakness. So she was close enough to read what looked like conflicting emotions as he spoke.

'Believe me, there's nothing *convenient* about this, Safiyah. As for what you said before we married...' he spread his hands wide '...you're allowed to change your mind.'

'You don't really want sex with me, Karim. You're just here to score a point. To amuse yourself. It's a power thing, isn't it?'

He was just reinforcing the fact that *he* was the one in

this marriage who had the power, not her. He might have been kind to Tarek but with her he was ruthless.

'You're not even attracted to me. You made that clear the day you came to my hotel suite.' She refused to let her voice wobble as she recalled his dismissal.

'I did?' His mouth lifted at one side, but it didn't quell the impact of that hungry stare.

The air thickened and her breaths grew shallow as she fought to tug in enough oxygen. Her insides clenched and she pressed her thighs tight together, trying to counteract the bloom of heat at her centre. How could she feel furious and aroused at the same time?

'Don't play games, Karim. You said it was an experiment that proved you weren't interested.'

'An experiment, yes. But the results were obvious. Like a match to bone-dry kindling. If I hadn't stepped away when I did we'd have had sex on the sofa.'

Safiyah was so stunned she couldn't find her voice. She went hot, then cold, as her brain produced an all too vivid image of them naked on that sofa. Those long arms holding her close, that muscular body cradled between her thighs...

A shiver ripped through her and his eyes turned darker when he saw it.

Suddenly Safiyah knew she was in real danger—not from Karim but from herself. How easy it would be to give in and say yes, despite her pride and the way he'd treated her.

'It didn't occur to you that I was experimenting too? That maybe you misread my curiosity for something more?' It was an outright untruth, but it was all she could think of to rebut him. 'If you think I pined for you for years you're wrong. I didn't.'

That, at least, was true. She hadn't let herself pine. She'd tried to excise what she felt for him—like amputating a limb, cutting herself off from emotion. It had been the only

way to survive. Lingering on what might have been would
have destroyed her as depression had almost destroyed her
sister. For five years Safiyah had been emotionally self-con-
tained, her only close relationships with Rana and Tarek.

'Of course you didn't pine for me. You had another
prince to snare.'

The sneer in his tone was like a slap. As if she'd deliberately set out to lure either him or Abbas into marriage!
But before she could snap out a rebuttal he leaned forward,
invading her space, filling her senses with the tang of hot
male skin, with pheromones that made her all but salivate
with longing.

'You wanted me in Switzerland, Safiyah. We both know
it.'

The words ground through her, making her shiver. 'And
you want me now. Every time we get close I read it in your
eyes, in your body.'

His gaze dropped to her aching breasts as if he could
see the hard nipples thrusting towards him even through
the heavy patterned fabric.

Safiyah shook her head. The thick hair he'd undone
slipped around her shoulders. She wished it could conceal
her totally. She wanted to hide where he couldn't find her.
Where she wouldn't have to face the truth about herself.
That she wanted Karim as she'd never wanted any other
man. Still.

'You're imagining things, Karim.' She paused and swallowed hard. 'I don't want you.'

His steady stare should have unnerved her, but she refused to look away. She'd done what she had to in order
to save her son. Now she'd do what she must to save her
sanity. Sex with Karim would be the worst possible idea.

Yet when he took that last tiny step that brought him
flush against her, his feet straddling hers, it wasn't disgust
that made her breath hitch. They were both fully clothed,

yet everywhere they touched—her breasts against his torso, her thighs against his—fire ignited.

'Prove it.'

The words were warm air on her superheated flesh.

'Kiss me and walk away.'

Safiyah's gasp only succeeded in pressing her breasts against him.

'I don't need to prove anything.' Holding that moss-green stare grew harder by the second. In her peripheral vision she saw that firm mouth, like a magnet dragging her gaze.

'One kiss and I'll leave—*if* you want me to.'

'Of course I do. I want…' Her words died as a warm palm cupped her cheek, long fingers channelling through her hair, creating sensations so delicious that despite everything her eyelids grew heavy.

His other hand didn't grab at her, didn't force her close. Instead it settled light as a leaf on her shoulder, then slowly slid down the outside of her arm, and down…down to her hand where her fingers trembled.

He'd promised no coercion and he kept his promise. But the compulsion welling within her to give in to him was almost overwhelming. Safiyah stifled a sob at the strain of withstanding this torture.

He captured her wrist with a surprising gentleness. It was as if he cast a spell that kept her rooted to the spot, breathless. Even when he raised her hand and she felt the press of his lips to her palm, the hot, lavish swipe of his tongue setting off swirling sparks inside her, his compelling gaze and her enthralled brain kept her where she was.

He planted her palm against his cheek. She felt the hot silk of his flesh and the tiniest hint of roughness along his jaw, where by morning he'd need to shave. Under his guidance her hand moved up to his hairline, and of their own volition her fingers channelled through the plush luxury of his hair.

So many sensations to absorb. Not least of which was the fascinating play of light…or was it darkness?… in Karim's eyes in response to her touch.

Safiyah's breath hissed as everything in her tightened. She had to move away, break this illusion of intimacy. Her brain told her that he was toying with her, but it felt so…

'We both want, Safiyah. And it will be good between us, I promise.' Again there was that curve of his mouth on one side, as if the flesh there were drawn too tight. 'Better than good. It will be—'

'Mama! Mama!'

A door banged and a woman's voice came from the next room. Then, before Safiyah could do more than turn her head, a small whirlwind shot through the door and landed against her legs.

'Tarek! What is it?'

She scooped him up and he clung, wrapping his arms and legs around her. He felt hot, and his face was damp as he burrowed against her. Automatically she murmured soothing words, clasping him tight.

'I'm sorry, madam—' Just inside the doorway the nanny jolted to a halt so suddenly she swayed. Her expression grew horrified as she took in Karim's presence and she sank into a deep curtsey. 'Your Majesty. My apologies, I didn't know—'

'No need for apologies,' Karim said. 'Clearly it's an emergency.'

'Just a nightmare, sir. I could have managed, but madam said—'

'You did right,' Safiyah assured her, rubbing a gentle hand over Tarek's skinny back and taking a few steps across to the bed, so she could sit down, holding her son close. 'I gave instructions to bring Tarek here if he needed me.'

It had been liberating, giving that order. When Abbas had been alive he'd demanded the nanny deal with any night-time upset without Safiyah, lest they were interrupted on a night he'd decided to visit his wife's bed.

'It is just a nightmare, isn't it?' Safiyah put her hand to Tarek's forehead as she rocked him in her arms. 'Not a temperature?'

The nanny rose, nodding. 'Just a bad dream, madam, but he kept calling for you.'

'Then he's in the right place now.'

It was Karim who spoke, drawing Safiyah's gaze. He didn't look as if he'd just been interrupted seducing his wife. She saw no impatience or annoyance. In fact he smiled as he told the nanny she could leave.

If it had been Abbas there'd have been cold fury and harsh words. Not because he'd been evil, but because he'd believed he was entitled to have his own way. That the world was ordered to suit *him*. He hadn't been deliberately cruel, but nor had he been sympathetic or used to considering others.

Safiyah looked from the departing maid to Karim, wondering how it was that this man, who'd also been raised to be supreme ruler, could react so differently. Where was the man who'd been so cold and distant in Switzerland?

Rueful eyes met hers and she felt again that pulse of awareness. It hadn't gone. His plans had merely been deferred. The realisation stirred excitement in her belly.

'How is he?'

'Calmer.' Tarek wasn't trembling now, though he still buried his head against her. Soon he'd be ready to talk. 'I'll keep him with me…settle him here.'

She waited for a protest from Karim but there was none. He walked to the bed and placed a large hand on her son's shoulder.

'Everything's going to be all right, Tarek. Your mother and I will make sure of it.'

To Safiyah's surprise Tarek lifted his head, sniffing, and nodded at Karim. Her husband smiled at the boy, then moved away.

'I'll leave you two to rest. Get a good night's sleep. It's going to be a big day tomorrow.'

Karim slanted her a look that made her toes curl. Then he drew a breath that made that impressive chest swell.

'You've had a lot to deal with, Safiyah. We'll discuss this later, when you've had time to adjust. After the wedding. But make no mistake: this is unfinished business.'

Then he turned on his heel and left, closing the door quietly behind him, just as if he hadn't turned her world inside out.

Already Tarek's eyes were closing. It seemed he didn't want to talk, just needed the comfort of a cuddle. Safiyah began singing a soft lullaby, but as she watched her son's eyes close and felt him relax she thought about what Karim had said.

There were two more full days of wedding celebrations. Two more days till Karim expected her to surrender to him. What was she going to do about that?

CHAPTER SEVEN

SAFIYAH EMERGED FROM the bathroom the next morning wrapped in her favourite robe. It was old, but it had been the last gift her mother had given her. The cotton was thin now, but the colour reminded her of the rare pale blue crocuses that grew in the mountains near where she'd grown up.

She hadn't worn it for ages because Abbas had expected her to dress in only the best. But he wasn't here to disapprove now, and in this last week especially Safiyah had found comfort in the memory of her mother.

Life had been turned upside down again and she was reeling from the impact. She hadn't been prepared for the tumult that was Karim's effect on her. She didn't want to trust him, kept remembering how badly he'd hurt her, yet at other times he seemed considerate, even kind. Like last night, when he'd put Tarek's needs before his own desire. It wasn't what she'd come to expect from men...from a husband. Karim confused her and made her feel things she didn't want.

Briskly, she rubbed her hands up and down her arms, banishing that little judder of residual awareness. She smiled at her waiting maid, then stopped abruptly.

'What's that?'

Her gaze fixed on the clothes spread out on the bed. She'd requested her long dress in shades of ochre and amber. Instead the fabric on the bed was an arresting dark lilac, embroidered with gleaming purple and lilac beads.

'Isn't it beautiful? The Sheikh has requested you wear this.'

Safiyah crossed to the bed, leaning down to stroke the fabric. The silk tunic was feather-light, the embroidery exquisite. It would be comfortable as she stood in the open air beside her new husband to receive the greetings of their people. The sunlight would glimmer off the rich decoration with each movement, subtly reinforcing her royal status as consort to the Sheikh.

'Are those trousers?'

Sure enough there was a pair of lightweight, loose-fitting trousers to wear beneath the long tunic. The style was often worn by women in the rural areas of her country, but Abbas had preferred her to wear dresses.

'They are, madam, and I've checked. They're exactly your size.' Her maid slid a sideways glance to her. 'Someone has been very busy making this for you.'

But why? Safiyah was quite capable of choosing her own clothes for royal events, and Karim didn't seem the sort to micromanage such details. But then, this second day of the joint coronation and wedding celebrations was an important one, during which they'd meet the people who had flocked to the capital from every province. Perhaps he was concerned about making the right impression. Wearing clothes that were a nod to the rural traditions of his new people wouldn't hurt.

'Very well.' She shrugged out of her robe.

But as the silk garments settled on her, drifting over her skin like a desert zephyr, Safiyah couldn't help but remember Karim's caress last night. He'd said things would be good, better than good, when she came to him.

If she came to him.

She hadn't agreed.

Yet.

* * *

Safiyah stepped out of the palace and into the main courtyard, only to hesitate on the threshold. There, instead of a gleaming entourage of black limousines, was a bustle she'd never seen within the royal precinct. The scene was alive with movement, the jingle of metal on metal and the clop of hoofs on cobblestones. The rich tang of horse and leather filled her nostrils and something within her lifted like a bird taking flight.

The place was full of riders. Two standard-bearers carrying the turquoise and white flag of Assara were mounted at the head of the line. Behind them, on snorting sidestepping horses, were elders and clan leaders—a who's who of Assara, all looking confident and fiercely proud.

Safiyah thought of Karim's words when he'd learned that Abbas had ditched the equestrian gatherings so loved by his people. It was clever of him to reinstate them, for clearly this was what he'd planned.

'Safiyah.'

As if conjured by her thoughts, there he was, striding towards her, magnificent in pale trousers, boots and a cloak the colour of the desert sands. He had a horseman's thighs, flexing powerfully with each step. The fact she'd noticed sent a tremor through her.

Her stomach dived. How was she supposed to resist him when her body betrayed her this way? Her galloping heartbeat told its own story.

'Karim.'

She saw the gleam of anticipation in his eyes. Clearly he was looking forward to this. Yesterday he'd been solemn and proud, as befitted a newly made monarch. Today his eyes danced.

'You look magnificent.'

His smile was a slow spread of pleasure across his face

that did crazy things to her insides. He took her hand, lifted it and stepped back, as if to get a better view.

For one mad moment she felt that glow of anticipation was for her. Then sense reasserted itself.

Karim had more important things on his mind than the wife he'd married for purely political reasons. Like establishing his mark on the country. Making an impression not only on the great and the good, but on the ordinary people. Which was why he planned to ride out on horseback, as the Sheikhs of Assara had done for centuries.

'That's why you sent the trousers.' Belatedly it dawned on her. 'You want me to ride with you.'

As if on cue a groom led forward two horses. A magnificent grey for Karim and a chestnut mare with liquid dark eyes for her. Safiyah saw the creature and was torn between love at first sight and disappointment that all Karim's excitement was for the success of his plan.

It had been madness to imagine he was pleased to see *her*, personally. She was his convenient wife. Not good enough to marry for her own sake—he'd made that painfully clear years before—but useful to win the people's acceptance.

Safiyah slipped her hand from Karim's, ignoring the twitch of his dark eyebrows at the movement. 'You could have warned me.'

'Warned you?'

'That I'd be riding.' Clearly she wasn't important enough to be informed of his plans. She felt as if she was the last to know. This procession had clearly taken a lot of preparation.

Karim stepped closer, blocking out the stable hand waiting at a discreet distance. 'I thought you'd enjoy the surprise.'

Safiyah's eyes widened. He'd thought about what she'd *enjoy*? She shook her head. This equestrian parade was a PR exercise. Not to please her.

Yet the fact he'd bothered to consider how she'd feel about it was unexpected. Disturbing. She wasn't used to that. What did it mean?

'You don't believe me?' His eyebrows lifted and his chin too, in an expression of hauteur.

'I'm just surprised.' And bewildered.

His expression softened a little. 'Pleasantly so?'

Silent, she nodded.

'Good.'

For a moment Safiyah thought he'd say more. Instead Karim swept her once again with his gaze and it was all she could do not to blush like a virgin. For there was something about his expression that made her think not of the show he was putting on for the populace, but of how he'd stared at her last night. As if he'd wanted to devour her on the spot.

The hubbub died away till all she could hear was the quick pulse of her blood in her ears.

'Mama!'

She swung around as a small figure emerged in the doorway from the palace. Tarek, wearing his finest clothes, hurtled into her arms. Safiyah caught and lifted him, hiding her surprise.

'Did you come to see all the excitement, sweetie?'

He nodded and clung to her.

'He's come to take part in today's festivities,' Karim said. 'I want the people to see that he hasn't been shunted aside.'

That made sense to Safiyah. And it was in Tarek's own interests. It was a clever move that would help both Karim and her son. But, again, she hadn't been consulted.

Although had she really expected that Karim might discuss his plans with her when Abbas never had? Once more she could only obey and play the role demanded of her. It was stupid to feel disappointed that nothing had changed.

'What is it, Safiyah? You look troubled.'

Karim's low voice reminded her how dangerous he was, how much he saw. For she was wearing what she thought of as her 'royal' face. A mask she'd perfected over the years to hide her feelings. It disturbed her to think Karim could see past it.

She shifted Tarek higher. Her son was looking wide-eyed at the horses.

'He's never even seen a horse close up before. He can't ride. It's too much to expect him to be in this procession. It's far too dangerous.'

She refused to let Karim put her boy in danger for the sake of appearances, even if his word *was* law. She'd spent years being seen and not heard, but when it came to Tarek's wellbeing she refused to submit meekly any more.

For a long moment her new husband considered her. When he spoke his words were for her alone. 'You don't think much of me, do you, Safiyah?'

His eyes flashed annoyance. Yet for some reason she wondered if that anger hid something else.

Before she could respond another figure emerged from the palace.

'Rana!' Safiyah couldn't believe her eyes. Her sister... here? Her heart squeezed and her eyes prickled. She opened her mouth to say something but no words emerged.

Safiyah looked up at Karim, who was surveying her from under lowered brows, his crossed arms making him looking particularly unapproachable. As if the man who'd stirred her blood with that one appraising look just moments ago had never been.

Yet he, surely, was the man responsible for her sister's presence. Gratitude and a sudden flood of happiness quenched her indignation.

'Your Majesty.' Rana sank into a deep curtsey and Safiyah watched, stupefied, as Karim took her sister's hand and raised her, bestowing upon her a smile that was all charm.

'It's a pleasure to meet you, Rana. I'm glad you could come to support your sister and your nephew today.'

Safiyah looked from her sister to Karim. What was going on? Assaran royal weddings did *not* include female witnesses, even if the bride had no living male relatives. Safiyah had been the only woman at yesterday's ceremony. Nor were female members of the bride's family invited to the royal events in the days that followed. Safiyah had got through the interminable festivities of her first marriage unsupported except for the maid who'd attended her when she retired to her room.

Before she could ask for an explanation a harassed-looking steward came forward and murmured something to Karim, drawing him away.

'Surprise!' Rana kissed Safiyah on the cheek and Tarek on the forehead, her gentle smile lighting her face. 'Your husband invited me to the capital for the next two days.' Rana dropped her voice. 'You didn't tell me he was so nice. So thoughtful.' She paused, chewing her lip. 'I did wonder if you really wanted this marriage. It's happened so quickly.'

Safiyah could only be grateful that Rana didn't know about the history between her and Karim. Then she'd *really* have her doubts.

'I definitely wanted it, Rana.'

Her sister nodded. 'For Tarek's sake. But...' she paused '...maybe for your own too?'

Safiyah swallowed hard and managed a noncommittal smile. Now wasn't the time for explanations. Karim had already proved himself capable of protecting his new position and his new son. That was all that mattered. His attention to detail today was all geared towards shoring up public approval. Even down to having the Prince accompanied by his aunt instead of a nanny.

Karim was presenting the picture of a united, stable family to the nation.

What other reason could he have for making these arrangements?

'It's wonderful to see you, Rana.' Safiyah leaned in and cuddled her sister with one arm while holding Tarek on her hip. An upsurge of emotions blindsided her, catching at her throat.

She wasn't used to having someone by her side. Strange, too, to realise how much she needed that support. The last days had been a rollercoaster of emotional shocks.

Tarek wriggled in her hold. 'Down, Mama. I want to see the horses.'

'He's a chip off the old block,' Rana said. 'Once he gets a taste for riding you won't be able to keep him away from the stables. Just like you and me.'

Warmth swelled in Safiyah's chest at her sister's smile. They'd both ridden as soon as they could walk, like their father before them.

'Later, Tarek. If you're a good boy you can pat one of the horses later.' For now Karim was striding back towards them and the last of the riders were swinging up onto their mounts. 'It's time for you to go with Auntie Rana.'

But Tarek wasn't placated. He was going to argue. His bottom lip protruded.

'Here. Let me.'

Long arms reached for her boy. Karim's hands brushed against her as he took her son.

She didn't know what stunned her more. The ripple of sensation where Karim's hard hands had touched her arms and, fleetingly, the side of her breast. Or the sight of him holding Tarek. The way a father would.

Safiyah frowned. She couldn't recall the last time Abbas had held his son. For an official photo, most probably.

Karim caught the disapproving scrunch of Safiyah's forehead and turned away, anger flaring.

What was wrong with the woman? Didn't she trust him enough even to hold her precious son?

She trusted him enough to marry him, yet now she was fighting a rearguard action to keep a distance between them.

Karim had taken time to consider how to make these intense days of celebration easier for her. He'd gone out of his way to bring her sister here, and to involve Tarek in the event to shore up the legitimacy of his future claim. He'd even organised that whisper-soft concoction of a riding outfit that made Safiyah look even more beautiful and impossibly seductive.

Had he received any thanks? Only from her sister. From Safiyah—nothing at all. Not even a smile.

So much for gratitude.

But Karim shouldn't have expected gratitude. The woman had abandoned him when she'd discovered the truth of his birth. She only accepted him now because he could salvage her royal position and protect her child.

Wrenching his thoughts away from Safiyah in beaded silk, he focused on the child in his arms. Tarek stared up at him with big brown eyes, his bottom lip quivering.

Maybe Karim shouldn't have swooped in and grabbed the child, but it seemed better to head off a tantrum than have the boy yowling through the parade.

'You want to meet a horse, Tarek?' He smiled encouragingly at the child and felt inordinately pleased when he received a grave nod. 'I'll hold you up high so you can pat one. Would you like that?'

He read the boy's excitement and for a second was

wrenched back to those rare moments in his childhood when he'd managed to steal time out with his little brother. Ashraf's eyes had glowed in just that way.

Karim walked up to the groom holding the reins of his mount and Safiyah's.

Automatically he turned towards the mare, as the smaller and more docile. But Tarek shook his head. 'This one.' He looked up at the dancing grey stallion.

Karim shrugged. The boy had pluck, that was for sure, if this really was the first time he'd got close to a horse. He'd have thought a beginner would be drawn to the mare, standing sedately. But Karim would keep him safe.

'This is Zephyr,' he murmured, and the grey flicked his ears forward, then huffed out a breath through flared nostrils.

Tarek giggled as the horse's warm breath brushed his face and hands. The horse's head reared back and Karim spoke to it in an undertone, reassuring it as he reached up to scratch near its ear.

'You can't be scared of Tarek, surely now? A big strong fellow like you?'

Again Tarek giggled, suddenly lunging forward in Karim's hold, trying to reach the horse.

'Not like that.' Karim hauled the child back. 'Give Zephyr a chance to know you. You have to sit quietly so as not to scare him. Put out your hand like this and let him sniff you.'

'It tickles!'

But to his credit the boy didn't squirm, even when Zephyr, with a sideways look at Karim, pretended to nibble the little Prince's sleeve.

The child gasped at the wet stain. Worried brown eyes met Karim's and once more he was reminded of his kid brother, this time after he'd been summoned before their disapproving father.

'I'm not supposed to get dirty. Papa says—'

'I know, but the rules have changed,' Karim said quickly, ignoring a moment's discomfort.

The child's dead father was beginning to remind him too much of the ever-demanding Sheikh who'd raised him. Karim recalled constant childhood lectures on his appearance, his manners, his attitude and even the way he walked. And that had been before the old man had got started on his studies.

'Don't worry, Tarek. It will dry quickly and no one will notice.' He paused. 'Do you want to know a secret?'

Solemnly the boy nodded.

'It's more important to be happy than to be clean.' Deliberately he looked furtively over his shoulder and pressed his finger to his lips. 'But don't tell anyone I said that. It's a royal secret.'

Tarek giggled, and Karim felt the strangest flutter in response. Even knowing it was the right thing to do, Karim had had qualms about adopting the boy. His experience of kids was limited. He was still learning how to interact with his little nephew on his rare visits to Za'daq. But Karim was determined to do right by Tarek—which meant taking time to build a relationship with the boy.

Finally Zephyr consented to be introduced, bending his head gracefully so the child could rub his palm over the grey's long nose.

'He smells funny.'

'Not *funny*,' Karim amended, watching, bemused, as the most highly strung horse in the city consented to the child's rough pats. Clearly the little Prince had his mother's knack with animals. 'That's how horses smell.'

'I like it.'

Tarek beamed up at him and Karim was surprised at how much he was enjoying the child's pleasure.

Karim caught movement in his peripheral vision and saw the steward scowling at his watch.

'Okay, Tarek. It's time for you to go with your aunt.'

The boy nodded enthusiastically and it was the work of a moment to settle him in the car next to Rana. When Karim turned back towards the waiting horses it was to find Safiyah watching him, her expression serious.

What now? Was she going to complain about him holding her son? She'd have to get used to it. Tarek was officially *his* son now too.

The idea elicited a welter of unfamiliar emotions.

'Ready, Safiyah?' He made to walk past her, heading to where their mounts stood.

'Yes, I...'

Her words trailed off and Karim paused. It was unlike Safiyah to hold back. She said what she thought—particularly when she disapproved. He was sick of her disapproval.

Repressing a sigh, he turned. 'What is it? It's time we started.'

Their route was to take a circuitous route through the city. It would be at least an hour before they arrived at the open-air venue where the celebrations would commence.

Her eyes met his, then swung away. Yet in that instant Karim was surprised to discover not anger but uncertainty. He took in her heightened colour and the dimple in her cheek and realised she was gnawing the inside of her mouth.

She moved closer, her hand hovering for a moment over his before dropping away. His flesh tingled as if from her touch.

'Thank you, Karim. You were so good with Tarek. Not stern or disapproving.' She smiled tentatively. 'It's more than I expected and I appreciate it.'

It was on the tip of his tongue to say of course she should expect people to treat her boy well. Except he recalled what

Tarek had said about his father. And how much he sounded like the man who'd raised Karim. Sometimes common courtesy and kindness to children weren't the norm.

Had that coloured Safiyah's view of Karim? The thought snagged in his brain. Maybe that explained some of the anomalies he'd noted in her behaviour.

It also made him wonder about her relationship with her first husband...

'I told you. I aim to do my best for the boy.'

If his tone was gruff she didn't seem to notice. She nodded, but didn't move. Harnesses jangled nearby yet still Karim waited, knowing there was more.

'I wanted to thank you, too, for bringing Rana here.' The words spilled out in a breathless rush. 'It was the most wonderful surprise. I...' She paused and looked down at her hands, clasped tight before her. 'I can't tell you how much it means to me to have her here.'

Safiyah lifted her head and her gaze met his. Karim experienced that familiar sizzle, but this time her curious expression—a mix of joy and nerves—didn't just ignite the accustomed flare of sexual anticipation. It made some unidentified weight in his chest turn over. The sensation was so definite, so unique, it held him mute.

For a long moment—too long—Karim felt the deep-seated glow of wellbeing he'd known only once in his life. In the days when he'd believed Safiyah to be a sweet, adoring innocent. But, despite her pretty speech of thanks, those days were dead. It was important he remembered that.

He nodded briskly and turned towards the groom, gesturing for him to bring the horses. They'd delayed longer than planned. It was time to ride out.

Suddenly Karim was itching to be gone, to be busy with his new work, his new people. Not second-guessing Safiyah's motives or his own feelings. He didn't have time for feelings—not personal ones. He wasn't here for old times' sake. He was here to rule a nation.

Yet when another groom approached, to help Safiyah into the saddle, Karim shook his head and offered his own clasped hands for her foot, tossing her up into the saddle. It was hardly an intimate caress. Just a fleeting touch of leather on skin. Yet the air between them shimmered and thickened as she looked down from the saddle and those velvet eyes met his. They'd darkened now, all trace of gold highlights disappearing. Her gaze felt intimate and full of promise.

Was it genuine or fake?

Marrying Abbas's widow and adopting his child had never been a straightforward proposition. Yet he hadn't realised how difficult it would be. For, despite years of experience in distancing himself from entanglements, this felt...personal. And complicated.

Karim had walked into a throne but also into a family. Into a place full of feelings and shadowy hints of past relationships that still affected Safiyah and Tarek today.

Suddenly the work of ruling Assara seemed easy compared with playing happy families.

Yet there was one aspect of family life Karim looked forward to with searing anticipation.

Bedding his wife.

CHAPTER EIGHT

'THANK YOU.' SAFIYAH nodded to the maid who was turning down the bed. 'That's all for tonight.'

With a curtsey the woman left. Instantly Safiyah put down her hairbrush and shot to her feet. She was too restless to sit.

Each passing day had fed the awful mix of anticipation and dismay that had taken root inside her. The three days of public celebrations had passed in a whirl of colour, faces and good wishes. At the end of it, almost swaying with exhaustion and nerves, Safiyah had prepared herself for a showdown with Karim.

He'd said he'd come to her when the wedding was over. To claim his marital rights. As if she were his possession, to do with as he wished.

Inevitably the idea had stirred anger. Yet if she were totally honest it wasn't just anger brewing in her belly.

But Karim hadn't come to her room on the final night of the celebrations.

Nor had he in the ten days that had passed since the end of the festivities.

Ten days!

Each night she'd prepared to face him and each night he'd failed to show.

He'd clearly changed his mind about his demand that

she sleep with him. Or maybe he hadn't been serious at all—had just wanted to watch her squirm.

What had she done to make him despise her so much?

Safiyah felt her thoughts tracking down that well-worn trail, but she refused to head there again. Instead she crossed the room, hauling off her robe and nightgown as she went, tossing them onto the bed. Seconds later she'd pulled on trousers and a shirt. Socks and boots.

She'd had enough of being cooped up with her thoughts. Her sister had gone home after the wedding and Safiyah, always careful not to burden Rana, had smiled and sent her off rather than beg her to stay. How she wished she had someone to talk to now.

What she needed was to get out. At least here in the summer palace, just beyond the outskirts of the capital, she had the means to do just that. For her lovely chestnut mare, a wedding gift from Karim, was stabled downstairs.

To anyone who cared to enquire, the Sheikh and Sheikha had begun their delayed honeymoon today. The small, secluded summer palace was close enough to the city for Karim to be on hand should anything significant need his attention, but the location between two idyllic beaches was totally private—perfect for newlyweds.

If the newlyweds had been at all interested in each other!

She hadn't seen Karim since they'd arrived. He'd headed straight to his office, trailed by a couple of secretaries, leaving Safiyah, Tarek and his nanny to settle into their rooms.

With a huff of annoyance Safiyah decided she'd rather be with her horse than stewing over whether Karim would deign to visit her. For ten days she'd been torn between anticipation—wanting to cut through this unbearable tension that ratcheted ever tighter—and dismay that finally she would give in to what she could only think of as her weakness for her necessary husband.

Twenty minutes later she was astride her mare as they

picked their way down the path to a long, white sand beach that shimmered in the early-evening light. Once clear of the palace and the protests of the groom, who had been dismayed that she chose to ride alone and bareback, Safiyah drew in a deep breath. The scent of the sea mingled with the comforting aroma of horse, lightening her spirits.

After all, there were worse things than a husband who didn't want sex and left her completely alone.

Safiyah shuddered, remembering the avid way Hassan Shakroun had eaten her up with his gaze in the days following Abbas's death. The idea of his fleshy paws on her body was almost as horrible as the thought of Tarek's safety being in his control.

Marriage to Karim had been the only sensible option. Tarek was protected and she... Well, she'd survived one loveless marriage and she could do it again. She'd happily live without sex. A marriage on paper only was what she'd stipulated. She should be glad Karim didn't want more.

Safiyah squashed the inner voice that said perhaps there was more to sex than she'd experienced with Abbas. Perhaps with another, more considerate lover, there might even be pleasure.

'Come on, Lamia,' Safiyah whispered to her mount. 'Let's go for a run.'

They were halfway down the beach when the sound of thunder reached her. It rolled along the sand behind her. Safiyah looked up but the sky was filled with bright stars, no sign of clouds. Besides, this noise kept going—a rumbling that didn't stop.

Pulling back on the reins, Safiyah looked over her shoulder. Instantly she tensed. Galloping towards her was a tall figure on a grey horse. An unmistakable horse and an unmistakable man.

Karim.

Together they looked like a centaur—as if Karim were

part of the big animal. Their movements were controlled, perfectly synchronised and beautiful. Yet the urgency of their sprint down the beach snared Safiyah's breath.

A frisson of excitement laced with anxiety raced up her spine to grab at her nape and throat.

There was nothing to fear from Karim. Only from herself and the yearning he ignited in her. Yet she couldn't shake her atavistic response. The instinct to flee was overwhelming. She was desperate to get away from this man she hadn't been able to escape even in her thoughts. He crowded her, confronted her, made her feel things she didn't want to feel. Even after ten days of waiting for him to come to her she found she wasn't ready to face her weakness for him.

Safiyah turned and urged her horse faster, first to a canter and then, as the thunder of hoofbeats closed in, to a gallop. The mare leapt forward and Safiyah leaned low, feeling her hair stream behind her as they raced away, exultation firing her blood.

But they weren't fast enough. Even over the sound of Lamia's hooves and her own heartbeat Safiyah heard the grey close in. Each stride narrowed the gap.

Her breath was snatched in choppy gasps. Her pulse was out of control. Still she sped on, desperate to escape her pursuer and all he represented. The man who threatened her not with violence, but because he'd awoken a need inside her that wouldn't let her rest.

He'd stolen her peace.

She had to get away. To preserve her sanity and the last of her self-respect.

Eyes fixed on the end of the beach, and the narrow ribbon of track that rose from up to the next headland, she wasn't aware of how close he was till a dark shadow blocked the silver of the sea and the thunder was upon her, filling her ears and drumming in her chest.

Even then Safiyah wouldn't give in. If she could get up on to the headland track before him—

It wasn't to be. One long arm snaked out and grabbed her bridle, then they were slowing, her mare easing her pace to match that of the stallion.

Safiyah's heart hammered. Her flesh prickled all over as the fight-or-flight response still racketed through her.

Finally they came to a halt in the shadow of the headland. Safiyah's blood pumped too fast and her breath was laboured. Each sense was heightened. The mingled scents of horse, sea salt and hot male flesh were piquant in her nostrils. The brush of Karim's leg against hers unleashed a storm of prickling response.

She stared at the sinewy strength of Karim's hand and wrist, clamped like steel on her reins. The silence, broken only by the rough breathing of the horses, grew louder.

'What the hell did you think you were doing?' The words sliced like a whip. Karim's eyes glittered diamond-hard even in the gloom.

Safiyah sat straighter, refusing to be intimidated. 'Going for a ride. Alone.' Was he going to take issue with that? After the thrill of being allowed to ride again for the first time in years, it was too much.

'You were heading straight for the rocks.' He sounded as if he was speaking through gritted teeth.

'You think I couldn't see them?' She shook her head, too annoyed to be quelled by the warning jut of his arrogant jaw. 'I was about to take the track up the headland.'

Karim's grip tightened on the reins and her horse sidled, pushing Safiyah closer to the big, glowering form beside her.

'Not at that speed. You'd break your neck.'

Safiyah glanced towards the pale track. This time the route didn't look quite so easy. Yet she refused to explain the urgent impulse to escape at any cost. She knew it would only reveal the fear she'd vowed to hide from Karim. That if she wasn't careful he'd overwhelm her and all her hard-won lessons in self-sufficiency.

She'd learned to cut herself off from the thousand hurts of a casually uncaring husband. She couldn't afford to lose that ability now when she most needed it.

'I'm more than capable of deciding where I ride. I don't need you dictating to me.'

A sound like a low growl emanated from Karim's throat, making the hairs on the back of her neck stand up. She'd never heard anything so feral. Karim had always been the epitome of urbanity, always in control.

'Do you have a death wish? What about Tarek? How would he cope if you broke your neck up there?'

Red flashed behind her eyes. 'Don't you bring Tarek into this!'

How dared he accuse her of being an irresponsible mother? Her mouth stretched into a grimace and her belly hollowed as she thought of the sacrifice she'd made for her son. Giving up her freedom for his sake by yoking herself to a man who disliked her.

Fulminating, Safiyah released the reins and vaulted from her horse.

'Where do you think you're going?'

Safiyah set her jaw and stalked away. Let him work it out for himself.

She'd only taken half a dozen steps when a hard hand captured her wrist, turning her to face him. He towered above her, imposing and, though she hated to admit it, magnificent.

'Don't turn your back on me, Safiyah.'

His voice was soft but ice-cold. It sent a shiver scudding across her skin. Even Abbas at his most imperious hadn't affected her like this.

Karim's hold was unbreakable. She'd look ridiculous

trying to yank her hand free. Instead she chose defiance cloaked in a façade of obedience.

She sank to a low curtsey, head bowed. 'Of course, *Your Majesty*. How remiss of me to forget royal etiquette.'

She heard a huff of exasperation and for a second his hand tightened around hers. Then, abruptly, she was free.

'Don't play with me, Safiyah. It won't work.'

She rose, but found Karim had stepped right into her space. They stood toe to toe, her neck arching so she could look him in the eye. She couldn't fully decipher his expression but saw enough to know she'd pushed him dangerously far.

Good. It was time someone punctured that ego.

'I'll get the horses.'

She made to move but he caught her upper arms. His clasp wasn't tight but for some reason Safiyah couldn't break away.

'Leave them. They won't go anywhere.' He paused. 'Why did you run, Safiyah? You knew it was me.'

She shrugged. 'I wanted a gallop.'

'Don't lie.' Gone was the icy contempt. In its place was a piercing intensity that probed deep.

'I'm not—'

'Was it because of this?'

Before she had time to register Karim's intention he hauled her up onto her toes. His head swooped low and his mouth crashed onto hers. Safiyah felt pressure, tasted impatience and hurt pride.

His anger fuelled hers, made it easier to withstand him. Even so, her body quaked with rampant need from being pressed up against his hard frame.

She just had to hang on a little longer, till he grew tired of this and pushed her away. He was angry. He didn't really want her.

Except even as she thought it everything changed.

Those hands wrapped over her arms turned seductive as they slid around her back. One slipped up into her loose hair, tangling there possessively and cradling her skull as he bent her back. His other hand skimmed her hip bone, then moved to cup her bottom. His fingers tightened as he pulled her up against a ridge of aroused flesh so blatantly virile that she gasped.

That gasp was her mistake. It gave Karim access to her mouth, where he delved deep, evoking shuddery thrills of excitement.

Safiyah told herself she shouldn't want this. Shouldn't want *him*. Not the dark coffee taste of him, not his sea and sandalwood scent, not that honed body. And especially not the tight, spiralling feeling low inside as he pressed against her, his erection a blatant male demand.

Yet there was no escape. Because already her fingers clenched into the soft cotton at his shoulders, digging into taut muscle so she felt the bone beneath. Safiyah tried to make herself let go, but her body acted on instincts that had nothing to do with self-preservation.

Karim murmured something against her lips that might have been her name. She couldn't hear it, just felt it as a vibration in her mouth. Then he kissed her harder, and she clung to him as everything spun away in an explosion of sensual delight.

When she could think again it was to find his hand sliding under her shirt to close over her breast. Her knees wobbled as, instead of a hard, crushing hold, she felt his touch gentle. Her breath hissed out as one finger traced narrowing circles around her silk-covered breast till he reached a nipple pouting with need.

Safiyah trembled at the pleasure of Karim's touch. Even the way he moulded her breast in his hand seemed designed to please her as much as him. The rush of moist heat between her legs surprised her. How could she feel like this when she didn't want him?

But you do, Safiyah. You've wanted him for weeks. For years.

It was the knowledge she'd tried to avoid. But denial was impossible as she shook in his arms. Only the support of his embrace held her upright.

As if reading her thoughts Karim broke the kiss, in the same movement scooping her up into his arms. There was something shocking about being held that way, reliant totally on him, curled against that broad, powerful chest as he strode towards the inky shadows beneath the cliffs.

Her eyes widened as she realised the most shocking part was how much she revelled in it. How the coiling twist of heat between her legs grew to a pulsing, urgent throb.

Safiyah caught a glimpse of their horses grazing at the edge of the beach. Then the world tilted as Karim lowered her to cool sand. He knelt above her, the star-quilted sky behind his head, his shadowed face unreadable.

For a second the idea infiltrated that she should stop this. She'd come here to get away from Karim. But only for a second. This…whatever this was…was unstoppable, like the surge of the tide or the rise of the moon.

Karim's knees were astride her thighs, his heat warming her through her trousers as deft fingers worked the buttons of her shirt undone. Safiyah reached for his shirt, flicking those buttons free with an ease borne of urgency. She was working her way down when he pulled her shirt wide and sank back, imprisoning her legs with his weight.

His eyes glinted like starlight, and he had the stark look of a man about to lose control, his flesh pulled tight over bone.

In one quick, ripping movement he tore his shirt free of his trousers and shrugged it off, leaving her in possession of a view that blew her mind.

She'd felt the solid muscle beneath his shirt, seen the way his wide shoulders and broad chest tapered down towards a narrow waist. But the naked reality stunned her.

Safiyah's throat dried. Karim was built like an ancient sculpture of idealised male athleticism. Dark skin and a dusting of even darker hair covered a muscled torso that drew her like iron to a magnet. Her hands lifted, pale against his bronzed flesh, to settle, fingers splayed, across satiny heat. Intrigued, she let them rove higher, over pectorals weighted with muscle and fuzz that tickled her palm.

Karim's ribs expanded into her palms as he snatched in air. In the soft darkness all she could hear was ragged breathing and the pulse of her blood, louder even than the shush of the waves.

Safiyah let her hands slide down across all that searing heat. She reached his belt, her knuckles grazing his flat belly and the tiny line of hair that disappeared into his trousers. Muscles tautened at the brush of her fingers, the tiny movement incredibly erotic.

'You want me.'

It wasn't a question. How could it be when he could read the need in her touch, in her quickened breathing, in the way she ate him up with her gaze? Yet she felt compelled to reply as he waited for the admission.

He'd challenged her to admit what she'd tried to hide, even from herself.

She swallowed, feeling that, despite their wedding vows last week, this was the real moment of truth between them. The moment of consent. With no witnesses but the vast sea and impervious stars. Where even in the shadows she could no longer hide.

'I want you, Karim.' She watched the quick rise of his chest on another mighty breath as if her words brought relief from pent-up pain. 'And you want me, don't you?'

His teeth gleamed in a smile that looked more like an expression of pain than pleasure.

'Of course.'

He took her hand and dragged it low, pressing it to his trousers. Her hand firmed on his erection and his eyelids lowered, his breath hissing as he pushed forward into her palm, his hand still cupping hers around him.

Heat suffused Safiyah. The sight of Karim half naked, questing after her touch with his head arched back in pleasure, was the most arousing thing she'd ever seen. The pulse between her legs quickened and she squirmed against his solid thighs. The sensations were simultaneously delicious and terrible. She'd wanted him for so long, even as she'd told herself she didn't.

The depth of her desire frightened her with its unfamiliarity. And that gave her the strength to drag her hand away.

Karim made as if to grab her hand, then stopped.

'You didn't come to me.' Her voice was a harsh rasp of fury and hurt as she struggled for breath. 'Ten. Whole. Days. You ignored me.'

How could she be sure he wasn't still playing some cruel game? Making her want, despite her better judgement?

Karim shook his head like a swimmer surfacing, trying to clear water from his eyes. 'You hold that against me?'

Suddenly Safiyah knew this was a bad idea. She lay half naked with a man who'd toyed with her before. Yet here she was, baring if not her soul her desires.

She tried to shift him, but those strong horseman's thighs held her in place.

'I'm sorry.'

Karim's apology froze her in place. Or maybe it was the way he trailed his index finger from her navel over her ribs till he reached her bra. Her nipples pebbled and she couldn't prevent the arch of her back, thrusting her breasts higher. He pressed his thumbs against her nipples and Safiyah gasped as pleasure shot straight to her core.

'I wanted to be with you,' he murmured, his voice low as he bent over her, his breath hot on the bare upper slopes of her breasts. 'But I couldn't. There was too much work to ensure key people were loyal to me, not Shakroun.'

He squeezed her breasts through the lacy bra and everything inside her turned molten.

'I worked day and night to make sure he couldn't mount a challenge.'

His words blurred under the force of her restless hunger but still he spoke.

'To ensure you and Tarek were safe.'

A mighty tremor racked Safiyah from head to toe. Whether from the idea of Karim—of anyone—putting her and her son first, or from the erotic intensity of his touch, she didn't know. But her indignation bled out like water through sand.

Karim reached behind her. Then her bra was undone and he pushed it high. She felt his thighs tighten around her hips. He bent, one hand closing around her bare breast while his mouth locked onto the other. No feather-light caress this time. Karim drew her nipple hard into his mouth and fire shot from her breast to her womb, spilling liquid sparks in a torrent through her blood. His hand kneaded her other breast and she bucked against his constraining legs, trying to shuffle her own legs wider.

Safiyah had never known such urgency, such need. Doubt was forgotten as her fingers dug like talons into his hips. She wanted him to move so she could spread her legs, wanted him to stay where he was and ease the hollow feeling inside her.

He moved, lifting his head and his hand from her body, and Safiyah bit back a cry of loss. Everything in her throbbed, aching for more. She'd felt a weak shadow of something like this in the past, but never so intense.

She was still absorbing that when Karim tugged her boots and socks off, tossing them aside. Then his hands were on the zip of her trousers, wrenching it undone and hauling the fabric down.

Safiyah lifted her hips, helping him drag her trousers and underwear down over her thighs, past her knees, then off. Cool air brushed her skin as she wrestled off her shirt and bra.

But when she'd finished, eager to help Karim undress, he hadn't started. Instead he knelt above her, his gaze like hot treacle, sliding over her bare body.

'You're beautiful.' His voice was hoarse, his hands possessive as they skimmed her trembling flesh.

Safiyah caught his wrists, holding them still as she met his eyes. 'You're slow. Take your clothes off.'

Never had she spoken so. Never had she made sexual demands. But something had altered within her.

Maybe it was that uninhibited race down the beach, unleashing a woman more elemental, less cautious than the one she'd learned to be. Maybe it was the fact that with Karim, for this moment at least, she felt able to admit to desire rather than just submit to another's wishes.

She felt strong as never before, even while his stance, as he loomed over her, was a reminder of his greater physical strength.

Karim laughed, the sound ripe and rich. Then he shifted off her. But instead of stripping his trousers off he moved lower, his hands spreading her bare legs. 'I like a woman who knows her mind.'

Then, before her stunned eyes, he sank onto the sand, his hands on her upper thighs, his dark head between her legs.

Safiyah felt a slow, slick caress that trailed fire. And then another caress, in a way no one had ever touched her

before, and she shuddered, a deep groan lifting up from the
base of her ribs to lock in her throat.

She shook all over, torn between shocked rejection and
utter delight. Her hands locked in that dark hair, clawed at
his scalp. She was going to push him away, because what
he was doing made her feel undone in a way she'd never
known. It scared her and aroused her and demanded too
much of her.

She was about to—

The third caress—slower, harder, more deliberate—
turned into something new. Safiyah opened her mouth to
demand he stop when something slammed into her and she
lost her voice, herself, lost everything in a searing, sparking, exquisitely perfect moment of rapture.

Not a moment but an eternity. It went on and on, rolling
through her taut, trembling, burning body. It went beyond
acute delight to a soul-deep conflagration that catapulted
her into the stars.

Karim gathered her close in his arms as she shuddered and
gasped and clung. He'd expected passion, known there'd
be pleasure, but this...

He stopped trying to catalogue why this was different
and merely held her. Finally Safiyah softened in his embrace and turned into him, nuzzling at his collarbone.

He was smiling in anticipation of entering that satisfac-
tion-softened body when he registered wetness on his skin.
He pulled back just enough to look down at her face. She
watched him with stunned eyes. Silvery streaks tracked
her cheeks.

He frowned. 'Safiyah? You're crying.' He'd had the occasional emotional lover, but the sight of Safiyah weeping
unknotted something in his belly.

'Am I?' She raised a hand and wiped her cheeks. 'I'm

sorry. I just never—' She bit her bottom lip, as if to stop the words tumbling out.

'You never what?'

He waited, but her gaze slid away. He fancied he saw a blush rise in her cheeks, except surely in this light that was impossible. As was the notion her words had planted in his brain. It couldn't be. Could it...?

'Are you saying you've never had an orgasm?'

His voice rose in disbelief and he saw her face shutter. As if he'd accused her of something bad. It confounded him.

'Safiyah, talk to me.'

Five minutes ago it hadn't been conversation he'd wanted. As it was, his groin felt so hard he feared one wrong move might make him spill before he even got his trousers off. Yet he needed answers.

'It's nothing.'

Her mouth curved up in a smile that didn't fit.

Quickly she reached for his belt, starting to unbuckle it. 'I know what you want.'

Yet she didn't sound eager any more. She sounded... dutiful.

Incredibly, Karim felt his hand close on hers, stopping her when she would have pulled the belt undone. She was shaking, fine tremors rippling beneath the skin. The aftermath of her climax or something else?

'What I want is an answer.'

His voice emerged harsh. He felt her flinch and guilt eddied. Curiosity, too, about her relationship with Abbas. For years he hadn't let himself dwell on that. Now he was consumed by the need to know.

'But you haven't even—'

'I can wait.' He couldn't believe he was saying this when desire still rode him so painfully. 'Tell me, Safiyah.'

'It's nothing. I'm just a little...overwhelmed.'

'Because you've never climaxed before?'

The idea battered at him, making it difficult to think. It didn't change anything. So what if Safiyah hadn't found sexual satisfaction with her husband? So what if her eagerness to satisfy him suggested her experience had been about giving rather than receiving pleasure?

But it did matter.

Karim didn't understand why, but it did. He gathered her in and held her close till the last tremors subsided, even though it was torture in his aroused state. When she was warm and pliant in his arms he released her and moved away.

'Where are you going?'

She sounded shocked. As shocked as he felt.

'To get your clothes. We're going back to the palace.' He grimaced, his gait stiff and uncomfortable with his erection.

'Don't you want me?'

Her voice was a whisper, and when he turned she was sitting with her arms wrapped around her knees. Her pale flesh glimmered seductively and it took everything he had not to drop to his knees and continue what they'd begun.

'Of course I want you.' He drew a deep breath, strengthening his resolve. 'But when I take you, Safiyah, I want the first time to be in a comfortable bed—not hot and hard in the sand and over in two seconds.'

Which sounded good in theory, yet Karim wasn't sure how he was going to make it last—bed or no bed.

Why, precisely, the location suddenly mattered, he wasn't sure. Except he suspected Safiyah hadn't been an equal partner in sex before.

Karim didn't want her sharing his bed out of duty. He wanted her as she'd been moments before, full of passion and delight. She deserved more than a quick coupling on the beach.

He wanted to make their first time together special.

Karim refused to dwell on what that meant.

CHAPTER NINE

SAFIYAH LISTENED TO the sound of the shower in the next room and slumped down to sit on the end of the bed. Karim had spoken barely a word on the ride back to the summer palace, or after they'd left the stables for their bedroom.

Their bedroom.

Instead of horrifying her, those words settled in her mind like a comforting blanket. Because she'd given up hiding from the truth. She wanted her new husband and she looked forward to being with him. Even though she knew from previous experience that the actual sex act would be less than satisfying, she still wanted him.

Because he'd been the first man to give her an orgasm?

Her lips curved at the memory.

That would be an easy explanation. But Safiyah refused to settle for anything less than the truth.

She'd never stopped wanting Karim, even after he'd treated her so callously.

Throughout her first marriage she'd compartmentalised, putting her feelings for Karim away in a box marked 'Ancient History', devoting herself to her husband. But now there was nothing holding back those old feelings and they were stronger than ever.

She shifted, trying to ease the ache between her legs— so inexplicable given that stunning climax. Beneath her clothes she felt the abrasive scratch of sand. What she wanted—apart from Karim—was a wash, but he'd stalked straight to the bathroom and she, out of training and habit, was content to wait on her husband's wishes.

Except Safiyah *wasn't* content. She felt edgy and uncomfortable. She wanted a wash and she wanted Karim.

His words kept replaying in her head. He wanted her in a comfortable bed where he could take his time. He didn't want sex to be hot and hard and over in two seconds.

She knew about sex that was over almost before it had begun, and she was accustomed to the listless sense that she'd missed out on something just beyond her reach. Now she knew what she'd missed and she wanted more. How would it feel to reach that pinnacle of bliss with Karim moving inside her?

Safiyah shivered and wrapped her arms around herself, trying to hold in the breathless excitement. An image rose in her head of herself following Karim into the bathroom, stripping off her crumpled sticky clothes and joining him in the shower. Her skin drew tight and her palms dampened as she remembered how good he looked without his shirt.

How would he look totally naked?

Once more she shifted. But nothing could ease that restless ache. Except Karim.

Abbas would have been horrified at her making a sexual advance. He'd always taken the initiative. Not that she'd ever wanted to.

But then he'd never caressed her with his mouth the way Karim had. Never made her fly in ecstasy and never, for that matter, pulled back without taking his own pleasure. Seeing Karim do that tonight had stunned her, making her question what she knew about him.

For years she'd believed him callous, even cruel. Yet he'd adopted her son, made Tarek his heir. There'd been acts of kindness enough to make her think this forced marriage wouldn't be all bad.

Safiyah thought of Karim's very obvious erection as he'd gathered the horses and helped her up, of his grimace as he'd mounted and turned his horse towards the palace. She thought of his ebony head buried in the V between her thighs and the extraordinary experience he'd bestowed upon her.

Karim was a conundrum. But one thing was obvious— he didn't follow Abbas's rules. Whatever rules they followed in this marriage were for her and Karim to decide.

The realisation made her feel suddenly strong.

Toeing off her shoes, Safiyah rose and marched, heart hammering, to the bathroom door. She opened it and slipped in. There was no steam to obscure her husband's naked body. He stood, palms flat on the tiled wall, head bowed beneath the sluicing water that trailed down over wide shoulders and a tapering body to firm, round buttocks and long, muscled legs.

Ignoring the doubts pecking at her determination, Safiyah stripped off her clothes, shivering as the fabric scraped across her hyper-aware flesh. Nervousness almost stopped her, but determination won out. She padded across to the shower, opened the glass door and stepped in.

An arctic chill enveloped her and she yelped as the water sprayed her.

'Safiyah?'

Stunned eyes met hers as she recoiled from the cold water. But when she tried to retreat she found her way barred by one long arm. The other reached for the taps. Seconds later the water turned warm.

'What are you doing here?'

'What are *you* doing standing under cold water?'

One black eyebrow crooked. 'Why do men usually take cold showers?'

Involuntarily she looked down. The cold water had done

its job. He was no longer rampantly erect. But, she realised with a rush of heat, Karim still looked well endowed.

The restless feeling between her legs intensified and she shifted her weight—only to brush up against that brawny arm stretched between her and the exit, reminding her abruptly of her own nakedness.

Her brows knitted. She didn't understand him. 'You don't want sex, then?'

Her stomach plunged. It was like when they'd courted. She'd believed then that Karim cared for her, might even love her. She'd daily expected him to propose. Instead, when she and her father had been called away because Rana had needed them desperately, Karim hadn't even bothered to say goodbye. She'd gone from happiness and breathless expectation to disbelief and hurt in the blink of an eye.

Safiyah reached for the door.

This time he didn't just bar her way—he took her shoulders and turned her to face him. 'Of course I want you. Didn't I tell you so?'

Her heart gave a little shimmy when he said he wanted *her*, not merely sex. Oh, she had it bad. But she couldn't find the energy to worry about that now.

His gaze dropped to her bare breasts and Safiyah saw the spark of masculine appreciation in that look. A pulse ticked at his temple and suddenly she *felt* his stare. His eyes met hers and her breath snagged. Such intensity, all focused on her.

'Then why don't you do something about it?'

His laugh was like a crack of thunder, sharp and short. 'Because I want to make it good for you, not explode the minute I touch you.'

That was the second time he'd said that. She couldn't decide if she felt flattered or frustrated.

'You've already made it good for me.'

Better than she'd ever experienced, though she didn't

say that. It was bad enough that he'd guessed her relative inexperience. She refused to act as if this was a big deal.

Safiyah reached for him, her eyes rounding as she discovered him already growing hard.

Karim's smile was a tight twist of the lips, then he leaned in and whispered, 'There's more to come.'

But instead of turning off the water and opening the shower door Karim crowded her back against the tiled wall. He was all heat and slick muscle and she trembled at the feel of skin sliding against skin, heat against heat. Excitement spiked a fizz of effervescence in her blood.

The flesh in her hand was heavy now, soft skin over rearing steel, his erection larger than she'd expected.

As if reading the scurry of sudden anxiety along her spine Karim stilled, then pulled back so he was no longer pinning her to the wall. 'We'll go back to the bedroom and take things slow.'

He reached out an arm to switch off the taps, but Safiyah wrapped her fingers around his wrist. 'No.' Those remarkable eyes met hers, ripe with question. 'I don't want to wait.'

To reinforce her words she pulled one of his hands towards her, planting it over her breast. Instantly his fingers moulded to her with exquisite pressure and the flesh in her hand swelled as Karim stepped closer and his erection slid against her.

Safiyah bit her cheek against the sudden wash of delight. 'Don't.'

Karim's other hand brushed her cheek, her mouth, pressing her bottom lip till she opened her mouth and tasted him with her tongue.

'Witch!'

Those green eyes seemed to eat her up. A hairy thigh, solid with muscle, insinuated itself between her legs. And a moment later she felt his touch in that most intimate place.

Safiyah's gaze clung to his as he deftly stroked her, evoking a response that made her hand tighten around him.

'You like that, don't you, Safiyah? And you liked it when I kissed you there too. Didn't you?'

She swallowed, trying to find her voice and failing. Instead she nodded, wondering how much longer she could stay on her feet when each deliberate slide of his fingers made her feel weak and trembling.

She loved what he was doing but she didn't want to be weak. She wanted to participate. So she took him in both hands, cupping and stroking, delighted when his eyelids lowered, turning his eyes to gleaming slits.

His nostrils flared and his strong features looked stark and tight. He groaned. 'So much for taking it slow.' Swiftly he moved her hands away, placing them on his shoulders and then lifting her up off the floor. 'Hook your legs over my hips.'

The words emerged as a terse order, but Safiyah read his juddering pulse and the convulsive movement of his throat as he swallowed. Karim was at the edge of his control, just as she'd been on the beach. The thought thrilled her and she complied, wrapping herself around those tight hips, clinging to his wide shoulders.

But there was no time for triumph. Instead she bit back a gasp as he brought them together in one slow, deliberate thrust.

Safiyah's eyes were snared on his and she couldn't look away. She fancied she saw his darken as a second thrust unlocked something deep within her and sensations rushed through her. This felt unfamiliar and a little scary—especially as she was pinned high against his tall frame, not even supporting herself. Yet at the same time she exulted in it when she moved to meet him and felt a shudder rip through him.

'Yes,' he whispered through gritted teeth. 'Like that.'

His big hands held her hips, helping her angle herself to meet him. Instead of feeling used, Safiyah felt powerful. She'd chosen this. Nor was it solely about Karim's pleasure. She craved this with every cell in her body. And, impossibly, the flames she'd felt on the beach were flickering again deep inside her.

Those flames skyrocketed when Karim palmed her belly and pressed his thumb down on that sensitive bud between her legs. Safiyah jerked as lightning sheared through her.

Karim grinned, the picture of male smugness.

She responded by tightening her muscles around him.

His grin solidified and his powerful thrusts turned jerky.

Safiyah saw the bunch of his muscles, the tendons standing proud in his neck and his eyes glazing.

But this wasn't a contest. Nor was it duty. This was what she'd craved for so long. This was Karim and her together, connected in a way that felt almost too profound to be just sex.

Then all thinking stopped as Karim changed the angle of his thrusts. For a moment everything stilled. A second later she was flung into a cataclysm that melded delight and something much more far-reaching.

Safiyah heard a deep shout, felt the hard pump within her and fell into ecstasy, holding Karim tight as he gathered her in.

They lay sprawled sideways across the bed. The pillows had long since disappeared, but no matter. Karim felt as if it would take a tsunami to make him move.

He lay on his back, his bones melting into the mattress, his body limp with satiation. With a supreme effort he slid his hand through the spill of Safiyah's hair, lying like a silken cloud across his chest and shoulder. Predictably, even that simple caress stirred an eagerness for more.

She lay draped over him—a lush, erotic blanket. If he'd

had more energy he'd have devoted himself to exploring that delectable body again. He'd been fascinated by her reactions, a mix of wholehearted responsiveness and shyness. But after a night devoted to carnal pleasure, giving in again and again to the urge for just one more taste of his bride, he'd have to wait to summon some strength.

That didn't stop his mind from working. On the contrary, it was busier than ever, trying to make sense of tonight's events with something that in another man might have come close to panic.

But Karim never panicked. He assessed, reviewed, and determined the logical course of action. It was what he'd been trained to do.

Right now logic wasn't helping.

Sex with Safiyah was phenomenal. Urgent and explosive, yet deeply satisfying. Terribly addictive. The more they shared, the more they wanted.

Karim had been taken aback by the demands of his libido, as if after years of denial he was making up for lost time. As if sex with Safiyah was more real, more satisfying, than with any other lover. Even when they did no more than lie together, body to body, sharing the occasional gentle caress, it felt *different* from previous experiences.

The notion was unsettling. Karim had expected their first night together to be memorable. He'd waited long enough for it, having never quite managed to excise her from his memory. But this was so much more than he'd anticipated.

He thought back over his actions.

The way he'd denied himself instant gratification on the beach because he'd decided on a whim that their first time needed to be memorable. It had been memorable, all right. Harder and hotter and more intense than anything he could recall, with Safiyah's lush breasts jouncing up and down against him, her welcoming body wrapped so tight around him he'd detonated with the force of a rocket.

The way he'd spent so much time denying his own pleasure in order to bring her to climax again and again, despite her pleas and her pouting demands that he take her fully. And his desperation whenever he'd relented and joined her.

He'd taken his fill but he'd done far more. It was as if he'd tried to imprint himself on her consciousness, to make her associate ecstasy with him and only him. As if he'd wanted to obliterate any memory of her first husband.

Was he jealous of a dead man?

Of course not—especially since he'd learned that Abbas hadn't had the sense or generosity to please his wife in bed. The idea of him using Safiyah for his own satisfaction but giving none in return twisted like a drill boring through Karim's gut. He hadn't liked the man but now he despised him.

Yet that didn't explain the other riddle. Why it was that with Safiyah sex seemed more than just an expression of lust and physical pleasure.

He frowned into the darkness, telling himself there was a reasonable explanation. Release after the stress of recent weeks, perhaps?

Safiyah shifted as if to roll away and he stopped her. 'Stay.'

'You're awake?'

'Barely.'

She chuckled, the sound rich and appealing, but it was the way he felt the vibration of her laugh through his body, his hunger to hear more, that threatened to undo him.

Why, he didn't know. Except suddenly there came the certainty that this sense of closeness, of emotional intimacy, was dangerous.

Through the night physical desire had been transformed into the illusion of something more profound. Something akin to what he'd felt when he'd first known Safiyah. When she'd had the power to hurt him—and not just his pride, he finally admitted, but something buried even deeper.

That wouldn't do. No matter how spectacular the sex, Karim needed to remember who he'd married and why. He couldn't allow himself to be lured into thinking this was more than sexual attraction.

'Tell me about Abbas.'

Safiyah stiffened and he heard her indrawn breath. Then she rolled away to lie on her back. Though he'd decided to establish some distance, Karim had to make a conscious effort not to haul her back into his arms.

'Why?'

'Why not?' He turned towards her, pillowing his head on one bent arm.

'You really want to do this *now*?'

He couldn't read her features but the discordant note in her voice sounded defensive.

'Your first marriage is hardly a secret.' He kept his voice even, though it still rankled that she'd gone straight from him to Abbas.

That last night, when she and her father had stayed at the Za'daqi palace, she'd agreed to meet Karim secretly. She'd been his for the taking, though no marriage contract had been drawn up.

Except Ashraf had found him in the secluded garden instead, breaking the news of the medical results that had proved he wasn't the Sheikh's son.

The shocking revelation had pushed everything, even Safiyah, from Karim's head. It hadn't been till later that he'd realised she must have come to their rendezvous and overheard their conversation. After learning he was illegitimate, she'd dumped him for Abbas.

Now she scrabbled for a sheet, dragging it up to cover

herself. 'There's nothing much to tell.' Her voice was brisk. 'He wanted to marry into my clan.'

'Go on.' Was it masochism that made him want to hear more?

'Rana, my sister, caught his eye first. She was studying in the capital and she was…is…intelligent and pretty.'

Her words struck Karim. It sounded almost as if Safiyah believed her sister outshone her.

'But then she got sick. Marriage wasn't possible. And so—'

'And so you jumped at the chance to marry a king?'

For a second she didn't answer. Then, tucking the sheet close around her, she rolled to face him. They were less than an arm's length apart, yet it seemed like more. Even in the darkness he felt the chill in her stare.

'When I was in Za'daq you weren't the only one whose father was unwell. My father had received a terminal diagnosis, though he didn't tell me straight away. He knew he'd be dead within months.'

Karim frowned. He'd never have guessed. Safiyah's father had looked so hale and hearty.

'He was old-fashioned in some ways, and desperate to get Rana and me "safely settled", as he called it, before he died. When Rana got sick…' another pause, '…all his hopes rested on me. He wanted me to marry well—not just for myself, but so Rana would be cared for while she recovered.'

Karim thought of the woman he'd met during the wedding. If she'd been seriously ill it didn't show now.

'So it was all your father's doing?'

On learning of Karim's illegitimacy her father would have pushed her towards another man. But if Safiyah had loved Karim she'd have stuck with him. She wouldn't have let herself be driven into another man's bed. The fact she'd done just that still stuck in his gullet.

'My father suggested it. Abbas agreed and I...consented.'

Karim cursed the darkness that prevented him reading Safiyah. Something in her voice intrigued him. Despite his residual anger he felt reluctant admiration that she'd admitted it had been her choice.

He breathed deep. Time to let this rest. Yet...

'It was a happy marriage?'

Safiyah scanned the dark form before her, trying and failing to read his expression.

A happy marriage?

She almost laughed. She'd believed once that she'd have just that—with Karim, of all people. The absurdity of those dreams tasted like ash on her tongue.

She'd been all but forced into marriage. Technically, she could have said no. But with her father fading before her eyes and both of them worried about Rana, Abbas's offer had been a *fait accompli*. Karim had turned his back on her. Her father's health had been spiralling down as worry increased and they'd struggled to find the care Rana needed after her breakdown.

Abbas had taken care of everything. He'd got Rana immediate entry to an exclusive clinic renowned for its excellence. A clinic which usually had a long waiting list. Safiyah had been so grateful, and in the circumstances what reason could she have given for rejecting him?

'It was a good marriage,' she said finally.

If by *good* she meant that it had conformed to expectations.

Publicly, Abbas had honoured her. Yet otherwise he'd had little to do with her except when he'd wanted sex or needed a hostess. He'd helped her support her sister, and in his own way had been pleased with his son—if disturbingly distant. And if he had been too autocratic for her taste and hadn't loved her—well, he'd been the King and she'd never expected love. She'd done her best to play her royal role.

'A good marriage? Not a happy one?' Karim leaned close, as if intent on her answer.

Safiyah stiffened. Despite the joy Karim had brought her tonight, she didn't have the emotional resources to deal with an autopsy on her first marriage. She'd survived it and that was what mattered. Dredging up the details would only reinforce the fact that, despite tonight's sexual satisfaction, she'd given herself in another loveless marriage.

She swallowed hard, forcing down the metallic taste of despair. Could she really go through this again? Especially when this was a hundred times worse because part of her kept hoping for some sign that Karim cared for her. Even though she *knew* that was impossible.

'That's enough, Karim. I don't ask you about your past. I don't delve into your secrets.'

In the gloom she saw him stiffen as if she'd struck him. Because she'd answered back or because he had secrets he wouldn't share? She was too weary and upset to ask.

'You'll have to forgive my curiosity.' But his voice held no apology. Instead it cut like honed steel. 'I thought it would be useful to know more about you since we've undertaken to spend our lives together.'

He sounded anything but thrilled about that! He made it sound like a prison sentence.

Gone was the passionate lover. Gone the tenderness that had wound itself around her foolish, unthinking heart and made her begin to believe that miracles might be possible.

Karim's haughty tone reminded her exactly why they'd married.

Pragmatism, not love.

Never love.

Safiyah choked back the sob that thickened her voice. Perhaps she was vulnerable after tonight's unprecedented experiences, but suddenly the idea of spending her whole future in a marriage where she'd have to pretend not to crave what she could never have was too much.

'Don't bother about that,' she said. 'A successful royal marriage doesn't require you to know me or I you. In fact, it will work best if we meet as polite strangers.'

She gathered the sheet tight around her and rolled away. 'I'm going to sleep now. I've got a headache.'

CHAPTER TEN

POLITE STRANGERS.

Karim grimaced. The idea was ludicrous, but that was exactly what they were. Even after seven nights away from the capital on their supposed honeymoon.

He swore and shoved his chair back from the desk, swamped by the discontent that hounded him whenever he tried and failed to break through Safiyah's reserve.

Or when he tried to determine why doing that was so important to him.

Every morning and for a couple of hours in the evening Karim worked, grappling with the multitude of matters requiring the new Sheikh's attention. Each day he breakfasted with Tarek and Safiyah, and they spent the afternoons together as a family. For Karim was determined to establish a good relationship with his new son. Not for Tarek a life in which the only male role model was a man he hated spending time with.

To Karim's surprise the boy had accepted him. Not only that but, given the chance, Tarek dogged Karim's footsteps as if fascinated by him.

Or just previously starved of male attention?

The picture Karim had built of Abbas was of a man with little time for his wife or son. A man caught up in the business of ruling, or perhaps a man too wrapped up in himself to care about anyone else.

That possibility stirred indignation in Karim's breast.

His own dysfunctional family had made him impatient with those who didn't appreciate the value of what they had. Which was why he was determined to make this work—for all of them.

Yet between Karim and Safiyah there yawned a void. Safiyah held herself aloof. Each day it was like conversing at a formal banquet with a foreign ambassador—all charm on the surface but with neither letting their guard down.

He'd never met a woman so adept at avoiding discussions about herself. Whenever he pressed for more she lifted her eyebrows as if surprised and deftly changed the subject.

If she'd fobbed him off with trivialities it wouldn't have worked, but Safiyah was a fount of knowledge on Assaran politics. Her shrewd observations on key individuals, on brewing issues and provincial power-plays were informative and incredibly useful to a man shouldering the burden of ruling a new country.

The only time she let her guard slip was in bed. Or in the shower. Or during their midnight swims. Or wherever else they had sex. Then she was a siren who drove him wild with her responsiveness and, increasingly, her demands.

Sometimes he felt as if he was really connecting to the vibrant woman hiding behind the mask of conformable queen and wife. He glimpsed something in her velvety eyes that hinted she was there—the woman he'd once believed her to be. But then, after sex, the barriers came up like steel barricades. Shutting him out.

Karim wasn't emotionally needy. He hadn't been since he was a child and his mother had abandoned him to the mercy of a tyrant. He'd made himself self-sufficient in every way. So it wasn't for his own sake that he wanted to break down the wall between him and Safiyah. It was so they could create a sound footing for a future together, to bring up Tarek and any future children.

His groin tightened and his pulse skipped faster at the idea of fathering Safiyah's children. He'd been semi-aroused all morning, despite the hours dealing with budget papers and plans for law reform. The sea breeze through the window reminded him of their race down the beach that first night here—that fever of need as he'd stripped Safiyah and given her a first taste of rapture.

Karim closed his eyes as a shudder ran through him. Hunger and longing. And regret. Because after the triumphant sex and that incredible sense of closeness she'd said coldly that it was best if they were strangers.

It was what he'd visualised when he'd first imagined this marriage. Keeping her at a distance, using her to secure his standing in this new country and for personal pleasure—not least the satisfaction of having at his mercy the woman who'd spurned him.

But from the start he'd wanted more.

Frowning, Karim shut down his computer and stood, rolling his shoulders.

He'd erred in pushing her for details about Abbas that night in bed. They'd both been exhausted after a sexual marathon that had left them off balance. Yet Karim had been driven by an urgency to establish control over circumstances that had suddenly seemed more complex and fraught than he'd anticipated.

He'd expected great sex, given the constant shimmer of attraction between them. Yet he hadn't expected to *feel* so much when he finally bedded Safiyah. It had been as if the years had peeled away and he still believed she was the one woman for him. As if her happiness was important to him.

His glance strayed to the brilliant blue sky outside the window. It was their last afternoon at the small summer palace. His plans for today would surely help him break down Safiyah's defences.

* * *

'A picnic lunch?'

Safiyah met Karim's glinting eyes. His brows slanted up at her surprise, giving him a saturnine appearance that was both goading and sexy.

It was appalling the way such a little thing made her knees weaken and her insides liquefy. At breakfast today she'd been reduced to wordless yearning just by the crook of Karim's mouth in the hint of a smile.

That half-smile had reminded her of last night, when Karim had teased her mercilessly with his mouth and hands till she'd begged for him to take her. Last night there'd been something in his expression, too. Something she couldn't name and didn't want to, for she feared she'd make a fool of herself, imagining tender emotions when he had none.

She was his convenient bride. Nothing more.

'Yes, a picnic. It's all arranged.'

He made it sound like a typical royal event, with retainers on hand to serve them. She didn't particularly enjoy formality, but if it meant less time alone with Karim that was a good thing. Because it got harder by the day not to be seduced by his charm.

'I'm sure Tarek will like that.'

'Oh, I know he will.'

Was Karim laughing at her? That gleam in those dark eyes—

'He was thrilled when I told him. Ah, here he is.'

Safiyah turned to see Tarek running from his room, not in his usual shorts and T-shirt, but in the trousers and boots he wore for visiting the stables.

'Mama, Mama, we have a surprise for you.'

He stopped beside Karim and looked up at the tall man. Then, to Safiyah's surprise, her son lifted his small hand and Karim's long fingers enfolded it.

A pang pierced her lungs. Could she be jealous of the burgeoning closeness between the two? That would make her pathetic. It was good for Tarek that Karim made time for him and seemed to enjoy his company. Her son had bloomed since coming here, becoming more and more the carefree little boy she'd seen in snatches since Abbas's repressive influence had gone.

'A surprise? How lovely.'

Her boy nodded gravely, then frowned. 'But you need other shoes. For safety.'

He looked up to Karim, who nodded. 'That's right. We don't wear sandals around horses.'

'Horses?'

That explained Tarek's beaming smile. So they were having a picnic in the stables? Despite her attempts to distance herself a little from Karim, she couldn't help smiling at the idea. Tarek was fascinated by horses and she'd promised to teach him to ride.

'That sounds like fun. I'll be right back.'

But when she went to the stables there was no picnic laid out. Instead she found Tarek, grinning from ear to ear, wearing a riding helmet and mounted astride a tubby little pony almost as wide as it was high.

'Surprise!' He threw out his arms, bouncing in the saddle so Karim, holding the pony's leading rope, put out a hand to steady him.

'Easy, Tarek. What have I said about sitting still and not frightening Amin?'

The pony didn't look perturbed—merely shook its head and stood patiently.

Safiyah stopped in her tracks, torn between shock and delight. Tarek looked so enthusiastic, his smile like a beacon. She grinned back at him. He really was coming out of the shell of reserve that had so worried her.

But at the same time she forced down a sliver of something less positive—the feeling that she'd been excluded. *She'd* wanted to teach Tarek to ride, had looked forward to it.

Yet she couldn't be selfish enough to begrudge him his excitement. This was a positive change from Abbas, who'd never made time to be with Tarek, much less encouraged him to learn anything other than court etiquette.

'You're riding? Karim has been teaching you?'

Maybe that explained Tarek's recent willingness to have a nap in the afternoon. Before coming here he'd been adamant he no longer needed a rest. Had he and Karim secretly spent nap time in the stables?

Tarek nodded. 'Brushing Amin and feeding him and learning how to sit.' He chewed his lip. 'But not really *riding*...' He looked up wistfully at Karim.

Karim's eyes met hers. 'We thought you'd like to teach him that.'

His voice was suede brushing across her skin and Safiyah shivered in response.

'You're the expert rider in the family. I've told Tarek how you used to compete.'

Silly how much his words affected her. She drank them in like desert earth sucking in life-giving water. Because it was so long since she'd received praise? Or because it was for something she'd once excelled at?

But even after years of being denied access to the animals she loved she wasn't that needy. This warm feeling came from the way Tarek and Karim looked at her. Tarek with excitement and admiration and Karim with...

Safiyah wrenched her gaze away. Karim was doing what he'd promised—building a bond with Tarek, creating a sense of family so her boy could thrive. So they could present the image of a solid family unit. Karim was pragmatic, that was all. It would be crazy to read more into his actions.

She focused on Tarek. 'You're sitting up nice and straight. I'm impressed. Are you ready to ride out?'

'Can I? Can I really?' He jumped up and down in the saddle, then almost immediately subsided, leaning forward to pat the pony reassuringly. 'Sorry, Amin. I didn't mean to scare you.'

The pony flicked its ear at the sound of his name but otherwise didn't budge.

Safiyah suppressed a smile. 'You found a very calm pony, Karim. I only hope he moves as well as he stands.'

Karim passed her the leading rope. 'Time to find out.'

Amin did, indeed, move. In fact he turned out to be an ideal learner's mount—placid, but not obstinate, content to circle the courtyard again and again while Tarek learned the basics.

'I had no idea what you two were up to,' Safiyah said as they stopped before Karim. Despite her stern self-talk, she found herself smiling into those glinting eyes. 'You kept the secret well.'

He shrugged. 'We kept Amin at the far end of the stable, away from the other horses, so you wouldn't see him. He's only been here a couple of days. I don't think Tarek could have kept the secret any longer.'

Tarek piped up. 'I wanted to tell you, Mama, but I wanted to surprise you with how much I know.' He rattled off information about grooming his pony and even caring for his tack.

Safiyah raised her eyebrows.

'I told Tarek that if he had a pony he had to learn how to look after it.' Karim caught her eye.

'I agree.' She turned to her son. 'You've learned so much. I'm proud of you.'

He grinned. 'Can we go now? Can we?'

'Go?' Safiyah looked from Tarek to Karim.

'Our picnic, remember?' He turned and went into the

stable, emerging with her horse, already saddled. 'Up you get.' When Safiyah hesitated he continued. 'You and Tarek will ride. I'll lead the pony.'

Karim would walk, leaving her and Tarek to ride? She couldn't imagine many men of her acquaintance doing that—especially Abbas, even if he *had* been able to ride. Usually women and children tagged along while the man took precedence.

'Hurry up, Safiyah. I don't know about you, but I'm hungry.'

There was no impatience in Karim's expression, just a twinkle of amusement that she found far too attractive. With one last look at Tarek she took the reins and swung up into the saddle.

They didn't ride far, and not down to the beach—for which she was grateful. Even with Karim holding the leading rope, the track there was steep and would challenge a first-time rider. Instead they went to a sheltered grove a little way along the headland.

The view across the sea was spectacular, but what held Safiyah's eye was the tent erected for their convenience. It was tall enough to stand up in. The floor was covered with carpets and cushions. And she caught the glint of silver from platters, jugs and intricately decorated goblets. Cool boxes stood in one corner, no doubt packed with their picnic meal.

The place looked inviting and, she realised, deserted. The servants who'd set up this temporary camp had clearly returned to the palace. Maybe that accounted for the sense of intimacy here. There was silence but for the snort of the horses, Tarek's chatter and the whisper of the sea below.

She caught Karim's gaze on her. Warmth swarmed through her, climbing to her cheeks. Suddenly the tent with all its rich furnishings looked like the setting for seduction.

She remembered that morning, when Karim had persuaded her to stay in bed, ostensibly by reaching out one hand to stroke her bare body. But it had been the searing hunger in his expression that had held her there. For she'd been consumed by a matching hunger.

How dangerous it was, trying to keep her heart whole while sharing her husband's bed. This wasn't like her marriage to Abbas. Then there'd been no difficulty in maintaining an emotional distance. But with Karim—

'What are you thinking?'

His voice hit that baritone note that never failed to make Safiyah feel weak and wanton.

'I...' Her gaze shifted and she noticed for the first time that one end of the tent was a cosy bower, where a couple of Tarek's toys were propped against fluffy pillows. A kite lay beside them.

Safiyah swallowed, her throat closing convulsively as emotion see-sawed. This looked...felt...like the action of more than a man taking a pragmatic approach. It felt like the action of a man who cared.

'Safiyah?'

Suddenly he was before her, looking down from under sombre brows.

'What's wrong?'

She shook her head, swallowing the reckless words that crammed her mouth. Pushing away the almost overwhelming urge to pretend this was real. Once she'd yearned for love, had believed in it with all her heart. To her dismay it seemed even the hard lessons of the last years hadn't banished that craving.

'Mama! Karim! I'm starving. Aren't you?' Tarek raced into the tent, lifting the lid on one of the cool boxes.

'Nothing's wrong.' She aimed a vague smile in Karim's direction. 'You seem to have thought of everything. Thank you.'

Before he could question further, she hurried after her son. 'Wait, Tarek. You need to wash your hands first.'

Again Karim felt he'd missed his opportunity with Safiyah. In the rare moments when it seemed they were on the brink of something more than sex, or a purely dynastic marriage, the possibility shimmered for an instant and then shattered.

Was it weakness to want more?

He'd told himself he wanted to secure their future. If he and Safiyah knew and trusted each other they'd create a unit that would underpin his new role.

Or did his need for more from Safiyah have another explanation?

Personal experience made him particularly sympathetic to Tarek's situation. A childhood devoid of love had made Karim determined to do better for the boy than his own parents had done.

His mouth twisted in distaste. *His parents.* He didn't know who his father was. His mother had died when he was young and her lover had never lifted a finger to contact Karim.

Maybe that was it. Apart from Ashraf, Karim was alone. Maybe his determination to build a family unit wasn't just for Tarek's sake, but his own.

He scowled. The notion was absurd. He had a plan and he was determined to make it work. That was all. The throb of anticipation now, as he joined Safiyah and Tarek, simply meant he was pleased at his progress so far. No more than that.

Yet a couple of hours later Karim had ceased to think in terms of plans and progress. Relaxed and replete, he found himself enjoying Tarek's amusing chatter and Safiyah's company. Their easy conversation seemed the most natural thing in the world.

How long since he'd done something as simple and fine as enjoying a picnic?

The answer was easy. Never.

His early life had been filled with royal responsibilities. There'd been no lazy afternoons. And since he'd left Za'daq he'd thrown himself into his investment business, needing to fill the huge gap in his world where duty had once been.

Now he stood in the centre of the clearing, one hand on Tarek's shoulder as the boy leaned into him, his head flung back to watch the red kite bobbing above them.

'Look, Karim! Look, Mama! It's flying.'

'I'm looking, sweetie. It's wonderful.'

'Karim can teach you too.' The boy twisted to look up at Karim. 'Can't you?'

'Of course.'

The boy relinquished the kite's string and scampered across to his mother, dragging her back to Karim. 'Here.'

Ignoring Safiyah's rueful smile, Karim stepped closer. Immediately the light perfume of her skin teased him. So instead of merely handing the kite to her he moved behind her, wrapping his arm around her waist. He felt her sudden intake of breath and the silk of her hair against his mouth as he brought his hand to hers, offering her the kite.

For a moment she stood stiffly. Then the wind jerked the kite and she gave an exclamation of surprise and delight.

'Careful. Watch it doesn't dip too low,' he warned.

She tugged, and together they moved to catch the up-draught. It took some manoeuvring, and a near miss, but soon they had it flying high again.

'Thanks. I've never done this before. I didn't know it was so thrilling.'

She smiled up at him over her shoulder and the glow of her pleasure drenched him like sunlight banishing the night's shadows. Gone was the reserve she usually maintained when they weren't having sex.

Karim's chest expanded as pleasure filled him. 'I haven't either. That makes us all novices.'

'You haven't?' She looked astonished. 'I thought you must have learned as a boy.'

Karim shook his head. He was about to explain that there'd been little time for childish pursuits in the Za'daqi royal court when someone entered the clearing. His secretary—looking grim.

'Your Majesty... Madam.'

He bowed deep and Karim saw his shoulders rise as if he were catching his breath. Karim's smile froze. Such an interruption could only mean serious news.

'Sir, may we speak in private?'

Karim felt Safiyah tense and tightened his hold on her. 'You may speak in front of the Sheikha.'

This was more than some scheduling problem. With his staring eyes, the man looked to be in shock. Karim braced himself. *Not Ashraf. Not his brother...*

'Very well, Your Majesty.' He hesitated, then abruptly blurted out, 'There's a report in the media about your... background. Claiming that your father was—'

He stopped, and Karim came to his rescue. 'Not my father?' Weariness mingled with relief that there hadn't been a tragedy. But clearly there was no escaping some secrets.

'Yes, Your Majesty.' The man stepped forward and proffered a tablet.

Karim took it, reading swiftly. The news piece was carefully worded, but it noted that if Karim's father hadn't been the Sheikh of Zad'aq Karim had no claim to the title of Prince. The implication being that without that the Assaran Royal Council wouldn't have considered him a contender for its throne.

Regret surfaced that today's pleasure should be blighted by an old scandal that he'd thought dead and buried. But then Karim squared his shoulders and concentrated on what needed to be done.

* * *

Safiyah read the headline and froze. When Karim dropped his arm from her waist, moving away with his secretary, Safiyah took the tablet from him with numb fingers.

She felt blank inside...except for a creeping chill where Karim's body warmth had been.

'Mama! Look out!'

Safiyah's head jerked up. The line of the kite was slipping and she tightened her grip on it. With an effort she conjured a smile for Tarek, even as her mind whirled at the news story and Karim's matter-of-fact response to it.

It couldn't be true. The very idea was preposterous.

'Here.' She passed Tarek the kite. 'You can have it, but you must stay here where I can see you.'

A glance revealed Karim and his secretary deep in discussion. Karim was showing none of the outrage she'd have expected if the story were false. Her husband looked stern but calm.

Her husband.

But who was he if he wasn't the son of the Sheikh of Za'daq?

It felt as if the ground beneath her feet had buckled.

Slowly she moved into the shade of one of the trees fringing the clearing. Intent on answers, yet excluded from the terse conversation going on metres away, she turned back to the article. Reaching the end, she went back to the beginning and read it again, astounded.

It was an outrageous allegation, and no definitive proof was provided, though there was mention of a medical technician willing to swear to it. The story claimed Karim's mother had been unfaithful to her husband before deserting him and that the old Sheikh had only learned Karim wasn't his just before his death.

The report insinuated that Karim had then been banished by his younger half-brother, Ashraf, who'd threat-

ened to proclaim the truth if he didn't renounce his claim
to the Za'daqi throne. Yet when Safiyah had seen Karim
and Ashraf together at the coronation they'd seemed on the
best of terms. And Karim had been full of smiles for his
sister-in-law, Tori.

'Seen enough?'

Karim stood before her, eyes narrowed to gleaming slits,
hands clenched at his sides, in a wide stance that was pure
male challenge. Out of the corner of her eye she saw the
secretary hurry back towards the palace. Tarek scampered
around, ignoring them all, watching the kite.

'Is it true?' Her voice sounded unfamiliar.

Karim's mouth tightened, his jaw jutting aggressively.
'Don't play games, Safiyah. You know it is.'

'How could I?' She frowned up at him. 'You're saying
this...' she gestured to the article '...isn't a hoax?'

Karim surveyed his wife, his annoyance giving way to
dawning disbelief. Her skin had paled as if she'd received
a shock. That, surely, wasn't something she could feign.

Gently he took the tablet and put it down.

'Karim? What's going on? Why would anyone print
such a story?'

He watched the throb of Safiyah's pulse in her throat.
Surely only a consummate actress could pretend to be so
stunned? Yet this *couldn't* be a surprise to her.

'You know it's the truth. You heard it five years ago.'

'Five years ago?' She frowned.

'When you came to meet me in the palace courtyard
that night.'

The night he'd been torn between lust and the determination to do no more than kiss her lest he take advantage
of an innocent under his roof.

She blinked, her eyes round. 'I didn't go to the courtyard. That was the evening we heard Rana was sick. Father

and I packed up and went home that same night. He left a formal apology and I wrote you a note.'

Karim's lips curled. 'A note that said only that you were sorry you'd had to leave so quickly. That something urgent had come up.' A brush-off, in fact.

Safiyah shook her head like someone surfacing from deep water. 'I thought I'd have a chance to explain the details later, in person.'

When he didn't respond, she switched back to the news story. 'You're saying your father wasn't the Sheikh of Za'daq? *Really?*'

Karim stared into those velvet-brown eyes he knew so well and felt the earth tilt off its axis.

She hadn't known. She really hadn't known.

All this time he'd believed Safiyah had snubbed him when she'd discovered the truth of his birth. For one golden illuminated second joy rose. She hadn't spurned him after all.

But she would now. Nothing surer. She'd be horrified at the scandal. And then there was the way he'd treated her. Believing she'd dumped him, he'd refused to take her calls, deleted her messages. And, more recently, he'd forced her into marriage.

Karim reeled as the truth sank in.

He'd thought she'd understood who she was marrying.

This news threatened both his crown and the relationship he and Safiyah were building. It could yank both from his grasp.

He looked at his wife and a wave of regret crashed through him.

Suddenly Karim knew fear. Bonedeep fear.

CHAPTER ELEVEN

'WHO WAS YOUR FATHER, then?' Safiyah could barely take it in.

Karim shrugged wide shoulders. 'I don't know.'

'Don't *know*?'

Karim wasn't a man to live with doubt.

'Presumably the man my mother ran off with.' His voice was bitter. 'Though that's pure assumption. Maybe she had several lovers.'

'You didn't ask her?' It didn't seem possible that he hadn't pressed to find out.

'She died of pneumonia when I was a child. There was no one else to ask.'

Except her lover—the man who might be his father.

What must it be like, not knowing who your parent was?

She frowned. It would be worse for Karim, since his mother hadn't been around for much of his childhood. The only parent he'd had was the irascible old Sheikh—a man she'd found daunting and her father had described as arrogant with a mean streak.

'I'm sorry, Karim.'

Another tiny lift of the shoulders but his expression didn't lighten. Instead his gaze drilled into her.

'Surely the rest isn't true? You and your brother seem to be good friends. He didn't really banish you?'

Karim snorted. 'That's nonsense. I decided to step

aside from the crown. I actually had to persuade Ashraf to take it.'

'So,' she said slowly, 'it was your decision to leave Za'daq?'

He nodded. 'The last thing my brother needs is me hanging around. He's a good man—a fine leader. But there are conservative elements in Za'daq who'd prefer me to be on the throne because I'm the elder.' He laughed, but the sound was devoid of amusement. 'Though they won't feel that way now the truth is out.'

Safiyah disagreed. From what she could tell, most of the support for Karim had been because, while supporting his father, he'd proved himself an able statesman, fair and honest. He'd worked hard and achieved respect. The truth of his birth would be a shock, but it didn't change his record.

Safiyah wrapped her arms around her middle, torn between sympathy for Karim and hurt that he hadn't trusted her enough to tell her this before. But why would he? They didn't have that kind of relationship. Their closeness was only in bed.

She looked up to find his gaze fixed on her so intently she almost felt it scrape past her flesh to her innermost self. She looked away. That was nonsense—a product of sexual intimacy. But more and more she found herself stunned by how *close* she felt to Karim. As if with a little effort all those romantic dreams she'd once held could come true.

Except when reality intervened, reminding her they didn't have that sort of relationship.

'You thought I knew all this?'

Karim's expression was hard to read, yet she could have sworn he looked uncomfortable.

'That evening we were supposed to meet...'

He paused, giving her time to recall her excitement and trepidation at the plan to meet him alone. She'd been so in love, so sure of his affection—though he'd never come right out and said the words—that she'd been persuaded to break every rule.

She'd thought the night would end in his bed. Instead it had ended with her romantic daydreams smashed.

'Yes?'

'I was waiting for you when Ashraf arrived instead. He had the results of some medical tests. We'd been looking for bone marrow donors to extend the Sheikh's life.' Karim's mouth twisted. 'The old man had always believed Ashraf wasn't his son, but Ashraf was tested anyway— out of sheer bravado, I think. One test led to another and the results proved just the opposite. I was the illegitimate one—not Ashraf.'

Safiyah wondered how she'd been so blithely unaware of the undercurrents at the Za'daqi court. But then she'd been lost in the romance of first love—only love.

'I still don't see how—'

'Later I discovered you and your father had disappeared in the night with an excuse about a family problem. I assumed you'd overheard our conversation since it took place where we were supposed to meet.' His chin lifted as if challenging her to deny it.

Reading the pride in that harshly beautiful face, Safiyah guessed what a blow the news of his birth had been to a man raised as a royal, with every expectation of inheriting a throne. She breathed deep, imagining what it was like to have your world turned on its head.

She didn't have to imagine too hard. She'd had her life snatched off course not once but twice, her own hopes and goals destroyed when she'd been forced into marriages she didn't want.

'I see,' she said, when she finally found her voice. 'You thought I hid in the shadows and eavesdropped.' Safiyah felt something heavy in her chest—pressure building behind her ribs and rising up towards her throat. 'Then persuaded my father to make up some excuse to leave? As if he wasn't a man who prided himself on his honesty?'

She'd hated the subsequent marriage her father had pushed her into but he'd done it for what he'd believed to be good reasons. He'd been a proud, decent man.

'As if *I*...'

The stifling sensation intensified, threatening to choke her breathing. She forced herself to continue, her chin hiking higher so she could fix Karim with a laser stare.

'You thought I abandoned you when I discovered you weren't going to be Sheikh. That all I cared about was marrying a king? That I didn't have the decency to meet you and tell you to your face?'

Safiyah choked on a tangle of emotions. Disappointment, pain, distress. How could he have believed it of her? He knew nothing about her at all! She'd been in love, willing to risk everything for a night alone with him, and he'd believed *that* of her.

She swung away, fighting for breath. Through a haze she saw Tarek, running in circles, trailing his precious kite.

'You have to admit the timing fitted,' said Karim.

Yes, the timing fitted. Drearily, Safiyah thought of how fate had yanked happiness away from her. But Karim hadn't loved her. If he had, he'd have at least stopped to question his awful assumptions.

She turned to him, seeing not the man she'd once adored, nor the passionate lover who'd introduced her to a world of pleasure. Instead she viewed the man who'd thought the worst of her—and her family. Who'd refused to give them the benefit of the doubt, treated them with contempt.

No wonder he hadn't returned any of the increasingly desperate messages she'd left all those years ago. He'd excised her from his life with ruthless precision.

The choking sensation evaporated and Safiyah dragged in lungsful of clean sea air. They felt like the first full breaths she'd taken in years. For too long she'd lived with regret over the past. She'd hidden it away, pretended the pain wasn't there while she tried to make the best of life. Now, like glass shattering, regret fell away. With clear eyes she faced the man who'd overshadowed her emotions for too long.

'Yes, it was a coincidence. But, believe it or not, the world doesn't revolve solely around you and the Za'daqi royal family.'

'Safiyah, I—'

She raised her hand and, remarkably, he stopped. It was as if he sensed the change in her. The tide not of regret and hurt, but of cold, cleansing disdain. For the first time she could remember Safiyah looked at Karim and felt no yearning, felt nothing except profound disappointment.

'The night you heard you were illegitimate my father and I discovered Rana needed us.' A quiver of ancient emotion coursed through her, that dreadful fear that had stalked her too long. 'She'd tried to kill herself.'

'Safiyah!'

Karim stepped closer, as if to put his arms around her, but she moved back and he halted. Deep grooves bracketed his mouth and furrowed his brow and Safiyah read genuine concern.

'I had no idea.'

'No—because you never gave me a chance to explain.'

He recoiled as if slapped, his face leached of colour. Strange that Safiyah felt no satisfaction.

'Tell me?' he said eventually.

'Rana was living in the city, studying to become a vet. But university life didn't suit her, and she found the city challenging after being brought up in the country. Plus, although we didn't know at the time, she was being stalked by another student. There had been harassment and she felt isolated, afraid to go out. She became anxious and depressed. I knew something wasn't right, but on the phone she sounded...' Safiyah swallowed. 'She overdosed on tablets.'

'I'm sorry, Safiyah. Truly sorry.'

Karim's face was sombre, and she knew he wasn't just referring to her sister, but to all his assumptions about Safiyah's character and actions.

It was easier to focus on Rana. She didn't want to talk about herself. 'I think the shock hastened my father's death. He went downhill fast after that.'

The speed of his illness and his desperation to see at least one of his daughters settled had broken down her resistance to marrying Abbas.

'My husband arranged for Rana to have excellent support. She's doing well now. She enjoys working on a horse stud and she's even talking about doing part-time study.'

Karim was reeling. His feet were planted on the ground but he felt as stable as Tarek's kite, swooping too low towards a bush. All this time...

What must it have been like for Safiyah, watching her father die, worrying about her sister and facing the blank wall he'd erected to prevent any contact between them?

He swallowed hard and it felt as if rusty nails lined his throat. He'd failed her when she'd most needed him.

He winced, remembering how she'd said her husband had arranged support for Rana. Her husband Abbas. Karim had felt jealous of Abbas, and at the same time triumphant that Safiyah's passionate nature hadn't been awoken till he, Karim, married her. But there was more to being a husband than orgasms. Whatever his faults, Abbas had been there for her. She still thought of him as her husband.

How did she think of him?

As the man who'd shunned her? The man who'd blackmailed her into a marriage she didn't want?

He could argue that he was protecting her son, but should her body and her life be forfeit because of that?

Karim considered himself honourable.

Today he realised how far short he fell of that ideal.

'What now?'

Karim dragged his gaze back to Safiyah. Suddenly she looked so small. Minutes ago, as she'd sparked with indignation, she hadn't seemed so diminutive. Now her arms were wrapped tight around her slender body as if she were holding out the world. Or holding in hurt.

Guilt scored pain through his belly.

Most of the time her presence, her vitality, made Safiyah seem larger than life. Now he saw her vulnerability, her hurt. He wanted to protect her, to haul her close and repeat his apology till she forgave him and looked at him again with stars in her eyes.

Fat chance of that.

She hated him.

He'd abused her trust and, because he'd grown up in a world where distrust and double-dealing were the norm, he'd believed the worst of her.

Yet, despite his mistakes, the idea of letting her go was impossible.

'Karim? What are you going to do now the story is out?'

He raised his eyebrows. Did she think he might cower here?

'Go back to the capital. Consult with the Council. Write a press release, then get on with the job of ruling.'

Except it might not be his job for long. Now that he was Sheikh the Council couldn't oust him. Yet Karim didn't want to rule a country that didn't want him. That bitter truth, like the knowledge of how he'd failed Safiyah in the past, curdled his gut. He'd offer the Council his abdication if that were the case.

When he'd been offered the role of Sheikh he'd been

assured it was because of his character and his record as a statesman, not his supposedly royal lineage. What if it wasn't true? What if the stain of his birth was too much for his new country to stomach?

Karim inhaled slowly, deliberately filling his lungs. He'd suffered the fallout of his illegitimacy once, with devastating effect. If he had to do it again, no matter. He had a full and interesting life to return to.

Except that was a lie. Even after a mere couple of weeks Karim knew that *this* was the life he craved. He thrived on the challenges and rewards of his new role. Including his newfound family. Would Safiyah stick with him if he left Assara? Could he ask it of her?

'You're not concerned about a swing of support away from you?'

Had she read his mind?

'To Shakroun, you mean?'

Karim guessed Shakroun was behind this press story. His rival hadn't had the numbers to mount a public challenge, but trying to tarnish Karim's reputation by backhand methods seemed like the man's style.

'Don't worry, Safiyah, whatever happens I'll protect you and Tarek from him.' Shakroun would get his hands on them only over Karim's dead body.

Safiyah surveyed him sombrely, her expression drawn and her eyes dark with shadows.

Reading that look, Karim felt a fist lodge in his ribs and his lungs heaved. 'What do *you* think about it?'

'I think you need to see the Council as soon as possible. Lobby key people and sound them out—'

'I meant what do you think about my birth? About the fact I wasn't really a prince of Za'daq?'

She'd thought him an aristocrat. In reality he was nothing of the sort. Karim swallowed and pain ground through him. His station in life would have an obvious impact on his wife. Pity he hadn't thought of that before.

Safiyah's features drew in on themselves. Her eyes narrowed, her skin tightened across her cheekbones and her generous mouth tucked in at the corners. Her nostrils flared in an expression of disdain.

'You do it so well, Karim. I have to wonder if it's a natural talent or whether you have to work at it.'

'At what?' Karim drew himself up, ready to fight however he must to hold on to what was his.

'At insulting me.'

The words smashed against him, making him blink.

'You didn't have a high opinion of me all those years ago and it seems nothing has changed.'

Safiyah pushed her shoulders back and lifted her chin, and abruptly she seemed to grow in stature. Less crumpled and disillusioned lover and more imperious queen. Despite the fire flashing in her glare, Karim felt relief eddy deep inside him. He preferred her fiery to defeated and hurt.

'It was a simple question. I have a right to know what you think.'

Her fine eyebrows arched. 'Do you, indeed? When the only reason I know the truth is because someone else broke the story? When *you* didn't trust me with it!' She prodded his chest with her hand then quickly withdrew, as if she couldn't even bear to touch him.

'I apologise. I thought you already knew.'

Safiyah sighed. 'What I think doesn't matter, does it? We're stuck with each other.' She lifted her hand to her forehead as if trying to rub away an ache.

'Safiyah...' He stepped closer. He had to know.

For years he hadn't cared what others might think if they knew the truth of his birth. But he cared what Safiyah thought. More than he'd believed possible.

Her hand dropped and her eyes flashed. 'Yes, it's a surprise, but I don't care if your father was a sheikh or a vagrant. What I care about is whether I can trust the man I married. Right now I have my doubts.'

She spun away and gathered up Tarek. Her actions were decisive and distancing. They made Karim feel the way he had as a kid, when he'd tried and failed to please the Sheikh, who had expected nothing short of perfection.

Karim set his jaw. He mightn't be perfect. He might be as flawed as the next man. But he'd be damned if he'd allow anyone to wrench away what was his.

And that included his wife and child.

CHAPTER TWELVE

'It's almost time, Your Majesty. Just a few minutes.' The technician nodded encouragingly, as if Karim were a stranger to microphones and cameras.

Karim glanced at the notes before him on the vast desk and pushed them aside, ignoring a stifled protest from one of his secretaries. He preferred to speak direct to the camera since the broadcast would be live to the people of Assara. He had no need of prompts.

What he needed, or at least wanted, was to know where Safiyah was. Since they'd returned to the capital he'd barely seen her. Every time he went to talk to her she was missing. 'Out', the staff said.

Because she couldn't bear to be with him?

The idea fed the hollow sensation inside him. His wife found him wanting not due to his birth, but because of the way he'd treated her.

To a man who prided himself on doing the right thing, the knowledge ate like acid, eviscerating him.

The door opened to whispered urgent voices. Then he caught a flash of red and a high, childish voice. He pushed back his chair and stood. 'Let them in.' It was Safiyah—and Tarek too.

Karim's heart hammered his ribs, climbing to his throat as he took her in. She sailed towards him, ignoring the minders who would have kept her out. She looked magnificent and beautiful in a dress of glowing crimson. Her hair was piled high and she wore no jewellery apart from her ruby and diamond wedding ring and matching earrings that swayed against her neck as she walked, emphasising the purity of her slender throat.

Their gazes meshed. She was here for him. To offer her support despite the chasm between them.

Karim's chest tightened, filled with a swelling bundle of sensations. He swallowed roughly.

His wife. His Queen.

She was regal, and stunning—and, he realised, the only woman ever to have power over him.

Just watching her approach battered him with competing emotions. Desire, pride and fear that he'd irrevocably destroyed any softer feelings she might once have harboured. For those eyes locked on him were coolly guarded, giving nothing away.

He'd given up pretending that it didn't matter. The news that he'd been wrong about her all this time had stripped all pretence away. He wanted his wife in every way. Not just her sexy body but her admiration, her kindness and her gentle humour.

Beside her marched Tarek, wearing fine clothes and a slight frown, as if he were concentrating hard. Karim felt a pang at the sight of him, remembering how it had felt as a young child, trying to be the perfect little Prince everyone expected.

'Safiyah.'

Karim started forward. But instead of taking his outstretched hand she sank into a curtsey, clearly for the benefit of their audience. Beside her Tarek bowed—a deep, formal, courtly bow.

Karim saw the Councillors on the other side of the room note the gestures of respect and nod to each other, as if approving this confirmation of the Sheikha's loyalty.

When she straightened Karim took her hand and pulled her to him, Tarek too. 'Where have you been?' His tone was sharper than he'd intended, but he'd felt stymied, not being able to find her.

Safiyah's eyes flashed, but she said evenly, 'In the city.' As if that explained everything.

The technician approached, hovering uncertainly. Safiyah nodded to the man and smiled, then turned to Karim. Her voice was low, for his ears alone. 'I thought it might help if we were beside you, Tarek and me, when you do your broadcast.'

'As a show of solidarity?' Karim felt his eyebrows rise. It wasn't a bad idea, politically speaking. Beyond her he saw senior government ministers, nodding in approval at the family group they made.

Before she could answer he shook his head. 'I appreciate your support, Safiyah, and yours too, Tarek.' He smiled at the boy, who was looking far too solemn, and ruffled his hair. The kid relaxed a little then and smiled back, leaning towards his mother. 'But this is something I need to do alone. I won't have anyone accuse me of hiding behind my wife's skirts, beautiful as they are.'

Safiyah stared up into stunning eyes and felt a flurry of emotion ripple through her. She saw pride there, and determination.

He took her hand, raised it slowly and kissed it.

Safiyah's knees almost buckled.

This was the man she'd fallen in love with all those years ago. The man she'd given her heart to. Who, if he only knew, still held that floundering organ in his keeping.

Fear settled in her bones. For though he smiled there was no softness in his expression. He was focused beyond her, on the challenge ahead. On the sheikhdom.

That was what mattered to Karim.

She, as a convenient wife, came a poor second.

Nothing had changed.

Except she'd discovered, faced with this crisis, that she *did* care for him. Had never given up caring. It was a burden she must learn to bear. A secret she'd have to live with.

She moved closer, leaning up to whisper in his ear. 'You haven't changed your mind, have you? You're not going to abdicate?'

'No.' He paused, then added, 'I want this too much to throw in the towel. But, no matter what happens, believe that I'll keep you and Tarek safe.'

She believed him. He would keep his word.

Karim looked past her, then to the technician. 'You and Tarek had better take a seat over there.' He gestured to some chairs clustered on the far side of the room.

And so it came to be that Safiyah was there for Karim's momentous broadcast. She ignored the questioning glances of politicians unused to having a woman present when government matters were being discussed. She hung on every word, and as she did so her respect for Karim grew.

His readiness to misjudge her in the past still rankled, but with time to cool down she'd acknowledged that the stress he had been under must have contributed to his actions.

Now, hearing him talk with simple honesty about his birth and his vision for Assara, Safiyah felt again a once familiar respect and pride.

He acknowledged the truth of the story about his heritage, and said that he'd told the Royal Council he would abdicate if the circumstances of his birth were considered an insurmountable problem. He also took time to sketch his plans for the nation if he were to stay as Sheikh, and ended by promising a final announcement in the near future.

When the broadcast ended Karim looked around the silent room at the powerful men, regarding him solemnly.

It was clear they hadn't yet made a decision on whether to support their new Sheikh. Thinking of the alternative, of Shakroun taking the throne, Safiyah shivered. How could they even consider letting that man into the palace?

Holding Tarek's hand, she made for the door, leaving Karim to deal with the politicians. She had her own priorities. Women might not have an overt role in Assaran politics, but that didn't mean they didn't have their own networks, or that they didn't have any influence at all. Safiyah had already been busy accessing those networks on Karim's behalf.

He was the best man for the position. More, he was the man she loved.

She would stand by him no matter what.

In the days after the public broadcast Karim followed his schedule of regional visits just as if there wasn't an axe poised to fall on his neck if the Council decided his illegitimacy overrode his merits.

Another man—Shakroun, for instance—would have clung to his position, since constitutionally the Sheikh, once crowned, had absolute power. Karim wasn't that sort of man. Call it humility, or perhaps excessive pride, but he needed his new country to *want* him.

Meanwhile he got on with the job he was there to do. Listening to the people, solving problems and planning new directions. And at his side, day and evening, was Safiyah.

She was a revelation. He'd seen her performing her part at the wedding celebrations, and the way she'd stood up for him on the day of his broadcast had filled him with pride and gratitude. But his wife was far more than a beautiful face to adorn a royal event.

Safiyah charmed both the public and VIPs alike, her manner almost unobtrusive but incredibly effective at helping people relax in the royal presence. Time and again

Karim found her leading people forward so their concerns could be heard or their achievements noted. Nor did he miss the way she drew apart from the official entourage on site visits to listen to knots of women who gathered on the fringes of the VIP parties.

Had she supported Abbas in this way?

Karim's mind slewed away from the thought. She was *his* now, through thick and thin. He had no intention of letting her go.

Since returning to the palace he'd slept alone—partly because of the crazy hours he worked, but mainly because of the hurt in her eyes when she'd discovered how he'd mistrusted her. The bitterness in her voice as she'd recommended they keep their distance.

Tonight, surely, they could put all that behind them.

He grinned and knocked on her door, anticipation humming in his veins.

'Karim!' Her velvet eyes widened in surprise and he vowed that tonight he'd smash through the barriers that separated them.

'Aren't you going to let me in?'

She clutched her pale blue robe closed with one hand as she pulled the door wider. He stepped in and watched as she took her time closing the door. Her robe was plain, but on her it looked incredible. Karim devoured the sight of those bounteous curves, the spill of lustrous dark hair. Arousal stirred, thickening his veins and drawing his body tight.

She turned towards him, automatically raising her chin.

Safiyah might be soft and feminine but she was no pushover. He liked that, he realised.

'You've had news? From the Council?'

'Just now. The vote was unanimous. They want me to stay.'

For a second she shut her eyes and he saw a shudder run

through her. It was a reminder that it wasn't just Karim whose future had hung in the balance. Safiyah's had—and Tarek's.

'It's all over now,' he reassured her. 'I'll make a public announcement in the morning.'

She nodded and he watched her swallow convulsively. She'd hidden her fear well but clearly she'd been worried.

Karim smiled. 'I have to thank you, Safiyah. Not every woman would have stood by me the way you have. And you've done more than that. I appreciate the way you've worked to help me, both in public and behind the scenes.'

Her eyebrows lifted. Had she thought he hadn't been aware of her networking on his behalf? His staff had informed him of much he hadn't seen personally. It was one of the reasons he knew he could bridge the gap between himself and his wife.

He moved closer, but then she spoke. 'What choice did I have? You're my husband. My son's fate rests with you.'

It wasn't the words alone that stopped him. It was her tone—flat and bitter. As if she regretted being married to him. As if she had no personal interest in his fate.

For a second, and he didn't know why, he thought of his mother. Had she been bitter about marrying the man her family had approved for her? Had she wished from the beginning that she could escape?

But Safiyah wasn't like his mother, running away and leaving her children. Safiyah had done everything she could for Tarek—even accepting a marriage she didn't want.

Karim's pulse dipped at the thought. Things would be better between them now. He'd make sure of it.

He watched her wrap her arms around her slender waist, her mouth a flat line. Her body sent an unmistakable message of rejection, but he persisted.

'I know I hurt you, Safiyah, and I'm sorry for it. But I also know there was more to your actions than necessity.'

There had to be. Once he'd taken for granted that she cared for him. Lately, learning that she'd never betrayed him as he'd believed, Karim had found himself yearning again for that devotion. Strange to realise how empty his world had felt without it. He'd told himself during those years in exile that he'd been like a rudderless ship, because he'd been cut off from the life he knew. Now he realised it was this woman he'd missed—Safiyah he'd wanted as his anchor.

Her arms tightened, pulling the fabric over luscious breasts. Karim felt a kick of masculine response in his belly.

'What more could there be?' Her eyes were dull with denial.

Karim rocked back on his feet. He'd thought it would be simple. He'd apologised for hurting her and now, with this news, they could start afresh.

But Safiyah wasn't ready to move on. His chest clogged. Pain circled his ribs. She hadn't forgiven him. The tenderness she'd once felt had drained away. She had just helped him because they were legally tied.

He felt a fool. He'd imagined she'd worked tirelessly on his behalf, *their* behalf, because she cared about him—about them. Now it turned out there was nothing personal about what she'd done.

Hurt vied with anger. And with a dawning sense of loss so vast it threatened to engulf him.

'Safiyah. Don't talk like that. You know you want—'

'There's nothing I want, Karim. Not now I know your position is secure and Tarek is safe.' She hefted a deep breath. 'I'll see you in the morning.'

As if he were a servant to be dismissed!

Karim's jaw clenched, his body stiffening.

And yet Safiyah's body betrayed her. Karim saw her

nipples peak against tight fabric, the out-of-control flutter of her pulse.

A hint of musky feminine arousal tantalised his nostrils. His body quivered in response.

She might be trying to hurry him out through the door, but still she wanted him. He lifted his hand to stroke one finger down her cheek. Her eyelids fluttered, then she jerked her face away, staring back with dislike.

Yet she couldn't disguise the glow of amber heat in her eyes—a sure sign, he'd learned, of sexual arousal.

Heat punched his belly. Triumph surged. Safiyah might not want to want him, but in this at least they were still partners, each caught in the same tangle of desire.

'Don't lie, *wife*. You want me.' A heartbeat pounded through him, a second, a third. Her expression gave the confirmation he needed. 'And I'll happily take what's on offer.'

Even if his soul craved far more.

He wrapped his fingers around the back of her skull and stepped in close, lowering his mouth to hers with a slow deliberation that, since it gave her time to pull away, proved his point.

She was his, and she wanted to be his, at least in this.

Wife, he'd snarled at her, reminding her that she was his possession. His words held no tenderness and anguish arced through her from where his fingers cradled her head down to the very soles of her feet.

She longed for so much more—which was why she'd cut him off abruptly when he'd pressed her, almost as if he knew her secret weakness.

When he'd *thanked* her for her help everything inside her had rebelled. She didn't want Karim's gratitude. She wanted so much more. She craved his love.

Which illustrated how mismatched they were. She

couldn't afford to let him know how she felt. He already had too much power in this relationship. She had to stand strong against him.

Except when his lips met hers shock jolted through her. His mouth wasn't harshly impatient. It coaxed gently...a slow brush that tempted then moved on to her cheek, her throat, then back to linger and tease. Strong teeth nipped at her lower lip and fire shafted to her nipples then drove low into her body. Her knees trembled and she found herself grasping his upper arms.

With a muffled sound of approval he wrapped those strong arms around her, enfolding her in searing heat. Hard muscle bound her, and despite her intention to resist Safiyah melted closer.

A sob rose in her throat that she should be so weak. But the pleasure Karim offered was too much, even though she knew it was purely physical. This sense of rare connection was illusory, the product of wishful thinking.

He deepened the kiss, drawing her up against him and delving into her mouth as if he couldn't get enough of the taste of her. As if his need matched hers.

This didn't feel heartless. It felt like everything she craved. And, with a sigh that shuddered right to her heart, Safiyah gave herself up to him.

When he swept her high in his arms she didn't protest. Instead she leaned against his chest, her hand pressed to the place where his heart pounded like a jackhammer.

When he laid her on the bed and stripped her, his eyes glittering like priceless gems from the royal treasury, Safiyah arched her body to help him peel off her clothes.

When he came to her, naked, proud and virile, she closed her eyes rather than search for tenderness in his gaze. She could pretend for this short time that the brush of his hands across her bare flesh was loving.

And when finally Karim stroked into her, deep and

strong, and she shattered convulsively, she steadfastly refused to think or yearn or hope. She took the pleasure he gave and told herself it was enough.

It had to be. For it was all he could give.

CHAPTER THIRTEEN

SAFIYAH OPENED THE window and leaned out, inhaling the fresh morning air, trying to dispel her anxiety.

She reminded herself of how much she had to be thankful for.

Tarek was safe. Not only that, but after only a few months living with Karim he was thriving. The nervous little boy who had expected only brusque orders from Abbas was learning to relax under his adoptive father's encouragement.

Rana was well and happy, actually excited at the prospect of studying again.

Meanwhile, Hassan Shakroun, the man she'd so feared, was on trial with a number of his associates for kidnap, bribing officials and conspiring to murder. Safiyah shuddered.

It truly had been a lucky day when Karim had agreed to take the sheikhdom. Everything was working out so well.

And yet...

Her heart beat high in her throat as she turned to look at the pregnancy test on the bathroom's marble counter. She didn't want to see the result.

The chances of a baby were slim. She'd begun taking contraception as soon as she'd realised theirs wasn't going to be a paper marriage. Yet since then Safiyah hadn't had a normal period. She'd ascribed that to stress, upsetting her cycle. Until yesterday, when she'd folded her arms and noticed her breasts were tender.

Safiyah bit her lip and breathed deep, chastising herself for her fear. Forcing herself closer, she picked up the stick and read the result.

Pregnant.

The indicator blurred before her eyes as her hand shook. She was having Karim's child.

Safiyah groped for the counter-top, grabbed it as she swayed.

She shook her head. Why was she shocked? Hadn't she known in her heart of hearts that there was a child? There'd been mornings where she hadn't been able to face breakfast, and that underlying sense that something was different.

She opened her eyes and stared into the mirror, taking in the too pale features of the woman peering back.

The fact was she'd made herself pretend pregnancy wasn't possible even though she knew no contraceptive was foolproof. Even though she and Karim had a highly charged sex-life. He spent every night with her, and she couldn't remember a night when one or the other hadn't instituted sex.

Her mouth twisted grimly. At least she had the terminology right. It wasn't making love as far as Karim was concerned. It was just sex. Convenient, explosive and satisfying. And she was so weak, so needy when it came to Karim, that far from repulsing him she was greedy for his touch.

Her hand smoothed over her flat belly.

There was nothing convenient about this child. Yet, despite the circumstances, she wanted this baby. Warmth spread through her as she contemplated this new, precious life. She'd do everything in her power to protect and nurture it. No doubt Karim, too, already so good with his adopted son, would love his own child to bits.

Her fears weren't for the baby, who would grow up cared for by both parents. Her concern was for herself.

She sucked in a breath that was half a sob.

Bringing another child into this world, even knowing it would be loved and cared for, revealed the stark contrast with her own situation. Unloved. Unwanted except as a convenience. As a means of propping up Karim's claim to the throne and to breed him heirs.

Pain sheared through her as the ugly truth hit her full force.

She was pregnant *again* by a man who didn't love her. Who'd *never* love her.

Her place in his life was cemented fast—sex object, for as long as his passion lasted, royal hostess and brood mare.

And what would she do about it? What *could* she do? *Demand* he love her?

A bitter laugh escaped, scoring her throat as if with gravel shards. That would only reveal her feelings for him, when the one thing she had left was her pride. She intended to salvage that, at least.

There was no question of her deserting him. She had Tarek to consider, and this new child. She *had* to stay for their sakes.

She drew a slow, fortifying breath, feeling the accustomed weight of responsibility and duty cloak her shoulders. This time it seemed harder than ever to push those shoulders back and stand tall.

It didn't matter that she'd once had romantic dreams, or that she still yearned with all her secret inner self for Karim's love. She had his respect and his gratitude. For the moment she had his passion too.

Time to do what she'd had so much practice at doing—bundle up unwanted yearnings and bury them deep, in a dark recess where they'd no longer tease her.

'Safiyah?'

She spun round. Karim filled the doorway with his broad shoulders and loose-hipped stance. Instantly her insides plunged. The sight of him reinforced her fatal weakness.

Who was she kidding? It wasn't just duty that kept her in this marriage. She didn't have the strength to walk away from the man she loved.

'What is it?' He crossed the room in a couple of strides, grabbing her hands in his. 'You look pale as milk.'

'I'm fine.' Practice allowed her to stiffen her drooping spine. 'What are you doing here?'

He frowned down at her, clearly not convinced by her words. 'I knew you'd planned to ride this morning and I rearranged a meeting so I could ride with you. But you didn't show.'

Bittersweet regret filled her. She'd have enjoyed riding with him. Enjoyed even more the fact that he'd changed his diary to make time for her.

Because you'll take any crumbs you can get from him and be grateful, won't you?

The snarky inner voice hit low and hard, making her press a hand to her churning belly.

Karim looked down. 'What's that?'

Safiyah fought the impulse to whip her hand behind her back. She'd barely had time to take in the test result herself. But what was the point? Karim had to know at some point.

Silently she lifted her hand so he could read the result.

'Pregnant?'

His voice was stretched out of all recognition.

Pregnant!

Karim's head jerked back as emotion punched him. So much emotion. A jumble of feelings such as he'd never known. Pride. Excitement. Tenderness. Fear.

'You're having our child?' His voice wasn't his own.

He'd wondered about the possibility, then set the idea

aside. But now... Safiyah carried his flesh and blood inside her.

Karim dragged in a rough breath, trying and failing to fill his lungs. He didn't know how he felt about passing on genes from his unknown father to another generation. About creating a new life. Far better to concentrate on Safiyah.

'Are you sick?' His hold tightened on her wrists. She looked pale. No, not just pale. Drawn. 'Come on. You need to sit down and rest.'

His heart pounded at double speed as he watched her draw a slow breath. But instead of assenting she drew back, pulling out of his hold, putting her hands behind her as if afraid he'd touch her again.

Karim's stomach dropped. The way she stood there—shoulders back, eyes focussed on a point near his ear—returned him to the early days of their marriage. To a time when Safiyah had been unhappy.

Karim had begun to hope they'd got past that. She'd seemed more content, more at ease with him since the crisis when his illegitimacy had been broadcast. Increasingly he'd basked in Safiyah's gentle smiles, revelled in her ease with him—not just in bed, but at other times. He'd told himself the marriage was working.

He was taking things slowly, not pushing, content to let her set the pace, knowing that after his earlier mistakes he needed to move cautiously in building their relationship. Even if he chafed for more.

He didn't expect miracles, and knew he had a lot to make up for, but surely he hadn't been mistaken? He *knew* she enjoyed being with him. Surely her tenderness hadn't been a lie.

'Safiyah?'

The sound of her name seemed to jerk her out of her thoughts and she turned away, preceding him silently from the bathroom. She didn't stop in their bedroom but kept going to the sitting room, choosing an armchair rather than sitting on the comfortable sofa.

Karim told himself not to read too much into that, even though he wanted to hold her close. He poured a glass of sparkling water and handed it to her, noting that her fingers felt cool to the touch.

Shock?

'You don't seem happy about the news.'

Whereas he, after that initial blast of surprise, felt a glow of satisfaction he had to work hard to contain. Safiyah... pregnant with their child. His whole body seemed to throb with a new vibrancy at the prospect. Even those lingering doubts about his ability to be a decent father were scattered in the face of triumphant excitement.

He watched her swallow a sip of water and then turn to put the glass down, her movements slow and deliberate as if she feared she'd drop it.

He tried again. 'I know we didn't discuss another child, but—'

'It's all right, Karim.'

Her eyes lifted to his and he was stunned to read the blankness there. A terrible nothingness that settled like a shroud over his excitement, instantly suffocating his burgeoning joy.

'I know my duty. That's why you married me, after all. I knew you'd want a child. I just hadn't expected it so soon.'

'Safiyah...?' His flesh prickled at the eerie coolness of her voice. Where was the passionate woman he knew? The caring mother, the warm-hearted Queen, the seductive red-blooded wife? 'Do you mean you don't want our child?'

Karim heard the unsteadiness in his voice and didn't care. He felt as if an unseen fist had lodged in his gut. Hunkering before her, he took her hand.

She blinked and shook her head. 'Of course I want it.'

But she sounded choked, her voice husky as if she fought back tears. 'I just...'

Safiyah looked away.

Karim had had enough of barriers and distance. He lifted his other hand to her chin, turning her to face him.

'Tell me.' His voice was soft but commanding.

For a second her eyes glowed bright, then she looked down. 'I just need time, Karim. Bringing a child into a marriage like ours...' She shrugged and looked up again, her mouth twisting wryly. 'Ignore me. It's just pregnancy hormones.'

'No.' He leaned closer, into her space, sensing for the first time that they teetered on the brink of the indefinable problem that still lingered between them. 'What were you going to say?'

Safiyah's lips thinned as if she was holding back the words by physical force, but eventually they slipped out. 'It's what women do in arranged marriages—breed heirs. It's just that sometimes it feels...lacking.'

Lacking! Karim sank back on his heels, his heart racing and a dreadful queasy sensation rolling through his gut. His hand tightened on hers, as if to reinforce their connection. His other hand cupped her cheek, his thumb brushing across her mouth till it lost its prim flatness and softened against the pad of his finger. He felt the warm humidity of her breath against his flesh and awareness rippled all the way up his arm to his shoulders and neck.

Yet his stomach hollowed. He felt gutted, and a dreadful tight ache seared through his belly as her words penetrated.

He'd felt bereft the night he'd learned of his parentage. But this was worse. This was Safiyah—*his* Safiyah—saying that what they had wasn't enough.

The edges of his vision blackened. This time it was Safiyah who grabbed his hand, steadying him. So much for his careful plan to give her time to grow accustomed to them as a couple.

'Don't talk like that!'

'Why not? It's the truth.' She breathed deeply, as if marshalling her thoughts. 'You're a good man, Karim. A fine ruler. And you've been wonderful with Tarek. Better than I dared hope for. Don't worry. I'll accustom myself in time.'

Accustom herself! As if it were a state of affairs she couldn't avoid. A royal obligation.

Which it was.

Safiyah had married him for Tarek's sake and to save her nation. She'd married dutifully and at first that had suited Karim completely.

But not now.

Karim exploded to his feet on a surge of restive energy. He marched the length of the room, spun on his heel and marched back.

Initially he'd told himself that Safiyah deserved no better. Then, later, when he'd understood the truth about her, he'd believed that if he worked hard enough he could make her care for him again as she once had, despite his mistakes. Yet it was only now, as he looked into her wan face and set features, that the full realisation of her sacrifice slammed into him.

Karim couldn't bear that she saw what they had as a necessity rather than a gift. Not when to him it was so much more.

He skidded to his knees before her, gathering her hands and drawing them against his thudding heart. He couldn't simply ignore her words about an arranged marriage, let them hang as if they meant nothing. Even if the alternative meant risking everything.

It would be the biggest gamble of his life, but he refused to imagine failing. Besides, he'd only held back because he hadn't wanted to put pressure on her.

'Our marriage is much more than that, Safiyah.'

She nodded, firming her mouth. Yet still she didn't meet his gaze. 'Yes, it's for the best. For Tarek and—'

'Much as I care for Tarek,' he murmured, 'this isn't about him. Or even about the little one you're carrying now.'

Karim felt a fillip of excitement, just speaking of their unborn baby, yet he couldn't allow himself to be distracted.

'Yes, there's also Assara. You're doing a wonderful job—'

'Not Assara, either.'

At his words her head jerked up, wide eyes catching his. How often he'd watched those velvety eyes haze with delight as he took her to rapture. How often he'd watched them dance with pleasure as they rode, or when they played with Tarek.

Karim turned her hands, pressing her palms to his chest where his heart thundered, letting her feel how she affected him.

'I want this marriage, Safiyah. I want *you*. I always have. Even when I pretended I didn't.'

Now the moment of truth was here Karim found it easier than he'd believed possible. He'd been taught to avoid discussing emotions, as if the mere mention of them would weaken his masculinity. What a crock that was. He'd never felt stronger or more determined.

Clamping her palms with one hand, he lifted the other to her face, feeling the dewy softness of her delicate flesh. 'I love you, Safiyah. I love you with every fibre of my being, with every thought and every breath I take.'

He paused and hefted air into his overworked lungs, watching emotions flicker across her features.

'Don't! Please don't!'

Safiyah tried to free her hands but he held them fast. She looked up at him with over-bright eyes. 'I'd rather you were honest with me than have you say what you think I want to hear.'

Her mouth crumpled, and with it something inside Karim's chest. He couldn't bear to see her hurting so.

It took a moment only for him to slide his arms around her and lift her high against his chest as he rose to his feet. From this angle he could see the wild throb of her pulse in her throat and her convulsive swallow.

Because he'd hurt her. Not just today but over years.

'I *am* being honest, Safiyah. For the first time ever I'm sharing how I really feel.' He paused, willing her to believe him. 'I don't know if I can ever make up for the mess I've made of things. When I believed the worst of you. When I never even followed up to make sure you were okay all those years ago.'

He strode to the long sofa and sank there, cradling her on his lap. It felt right, holding her like this, soft and warm in his arms. He never wanted to let her go. Surely it was a good sign that she didn't struggle to get away?

'I was hurting so much, Safiyah, because I loved you even though I hadn't admitted it to myself. But that's no excuse. You needed me and I turned my back on you.'

His voice cracked as he thought of her, scared for her sister, grieving for her father, faced with the prospect of marrying a stranger.

Dark eyes locked on his as she tipped her head back, and for once Karim didn't try to mask his feelings as he'd been trained to. His love for her swelled and filled him till he thought he might burst.

'Karim...?'

Her eyes, pansy-dark yet flecked with amber, held his so intently he felt raw inside, with everything he felt, every secret, laid bare. It was like facing his conscience.

'It's true, my love.'

He lifted her palm and pressed his mouth to it, scattering fervent kisses there. But not for long. This had to be said.

He held her wondering eyes. 'I was a proud, arrogant prince, used to attracting women, used to people pandering to my whims. I saw that you cared for me and I took that as my due, never bothering to question my own feelings. If I had I'd have realised that what I felt for you was unique. I'd never cared for any other woman the way I cared for you, Safiyah. After you'd gone I felt like I'd been torn in two, but I blamed that on my changed circumstances.'

He shook his head, amazed at his obtuseness.

'I couldn't bear to think of you—especially when I heard you were to marry Abbas. Because it hurt too much. I pretended it was fury I felt, hurt pride that you'd duped me into believing you cared.'

'I *did* care, Karim.'

Her hand curled around his, the first tiny positive sign from her. It made his heart contract. She'd cared for him once. But now...?

'When you came to me in Switzerland I behaved like a spoiled brat, trying to hurt you.'

'You succeeded.' Her mouth twisted, but her voice was stronger and her eyes shone. Hope rose.

'I've been so blind, my love.' He shook his head. 'So slow to realise *you* were the reason I came to Assara. Not because I wanted the crown but because I wanted to be with you. Become your husband.'

His words ran out and Karim was left listening to the sound of his heart throbbing out a frenetic pulse, looking for some sign he wasn't alone in this.

'You came here because of *me*?'

He nodded. The words had poured out of him—a torrent smashed free from a dam wall. Now he was spent. The rest was up to her. Would she believe him?

'Because you loved me?'

'*Love.* I love you.'

As Karim watched, her eyes filled with tears that spilled down pale cheeks.

'Ah, *habibti.* Please don't. I can't bear to see you so sad.'

He wiped her tears with his thumb but they kept falling. The sight broke him. Was it possible he'd destroyed all the feelings she'd once had for him?

A soft hand cupped his jaw. 'Silly man. I'm crying because I'm happy.'

'Happy?' Karim stared into her lovely face and saw that crooked mouth curve up in a smile that made his heart lift.

'Yes, happy.' Her smile widened. 'You really do have a lot to learn about women.'

Karim didn't argue. He was the first to admit his previous experience had been limited to casual encounters. Nothing that compared to this.

'Tell me,' he demanded, capturing her hand and kissing it.

'That I'm happy?'

Mischief danced in Safiyah's eyes, and for the first time the band constricting Karim's chest eased. He grazed his teeth along the fleshy part of her palm and she jumped, then leaned closer.

Her expression grew serious. 'I loved you all those years ago, Karim, and I never stopped.'

She swallowed hard and he felt the shadow of her pain.

'And now?' He didn't deserve her love, but he needed it. He'd never needed anything more. 'I can live without a crown, Safiyah. Without courtiers and honours. But I can't live without you.'

'Hush.' Her fingers pressed his lips. 'You don't need to. We have each other now.' She leaned close, wrapping her arms around his neck. 'I love you. Always have and always will.'

Karim opened his mouth to reply. To say something

meaningful and memorable. But for the first time ever words failed him. He drew his beloved wife up into his arms and kissed her with a tender ardour that told her better than words how he felt.

He vowed he'd show her every day of their lives together exactly how much she meant to him.

EPILOGUE

SAFIYAH STEPPED INTO the room and pulled up abruptly, seeing Karim alone by the window. It had been a risk, arranging this meeting, but one she'd believed worth taking.

Karim was a changed man—happy and positive and oh-so-loving, unafraid to express his emotions. Especially since their daughter Amira's birth. He doted on their little girl, while his relationship with Tarek grew stronger by the day. And with Safiyah he was everything she'd ever longed for.

But she knew the past cast long shadows. She couldn't change Karim's loveless childhood, but she hoped at least to ease the pain of his not knowing his parents. Which was why she'd tracked down the man Karim's mother had run away to. The man who might be Karim's father.

Seeing her husband's preternatural stillness, the air of barely contained energy vibrating from those broad shoulders, she guessed the meeting hadn't gone well.

Her hopes nosedived.

'You're alone?'

He swung to face her and her heart rocked against her ribcage when she read his expression. In a rush she closed in on him, wrapping her arms tight around his powerful frame.

'I'm sorry, Karim. I thought—'

'I know what you thought, *habibti*.' His mouth crooked

up at one corner in a tight smile. 'That it was time I made peace with the man who might be my father. And you were right.'

He gathered her in, then turned to look out the window. There, just emerging from the palace, was a rangy figure, shoulders straight and gait familiar. He paused, as if sensing their regard, and looked over his shoulder. Karim inclined his head and the man reciprocated, then walked away.

'Yet he's leaving?'

Was it crazy to have hoped the two might begin to build a tenuous relationship?

'No, just stretching his legs. We both need a little time to process things. He's accepted my offer to stay in the palace for a visit. To meet the family.'

No mistaking the pride in Karim's voice.

'He has?' Safiyah stared up at her husband, stunned.

His half-smile broadened into a grin that made her heart flutter. 'What you mean is you're stunned I invited him to stay. But then he *is* my father.'

'Oh, I *knew* it! You have the same walk…and the angle of your jaw…' She paused, searching his face. 'And you're all right with that?'

Karim raked a hand through his hair. 'They didn't know about me.'

'Sorry?'

Safiyah looked up at him with those lustrous eyes and he pulled her even closer. It had been a morning of revelations and powerful emotion. He found he needed the concrete reality of his darling wife to anchor him.

'When my mother ran away with him she had no idea that I was his son. He swears that if they'd realised she'd never have left me with the Sheikh.'

Karim believed him. His father wasn't what he'd expected. A proud yet gentle man, he was a schoolteacher in a remote mountain valley, devoted to the children he looked on as his own, never knowing till recently he had a son.

'He and my mother were deeply in love, but her family ignored that and arranged her marriage with the Sheikh. A lowly trainee schoolteacher wasn't considered good enough for her. They were only together once before the wedding—one night of secret passion before a loveless marriage.'

Karim's thoughts strayed inevitably to Safiyah's dutiful marriage to Abbas. How desperate must she have felt, knowing there was no escape, giving herself as a convenient wife?

Safiyah had given him a whole new perspective on his mother. A new sympathy for a woman caught in an unwanted, unhappy marriage.

'When I was born my mother believed I was the Sheikh's son.' Karim drew a slow breath. 'According to my father...' He paused on the word, testing its newness but liking it. 'She finally left the Sheikh because her marriage broke down. Emotional abuse turned into physical abuse and she feared for her safety. But she always believed he wouldn't lay a hand on me or Ashraf as his precious heirs.'

'Oh, Karim...' Safiyah gripped him tight.

'My father didn't even know she'd run away from the palace till she came to him and they fled together over the border. They only had a year together before she died.'

'That's so sad.'

He looked down into her soft eyes. 'At least they had that.'

'You're turning into a romantic, Karim.'

He smiled, and looked at Safiyah as the shadows inside eased. 'How could I not be when I have you, *habibti*? It's all your influence.'

'And in all those years he never took another wife?'

Karim shook his head. 'Another thing my father and I have in common. It appears we're one-woman men.'

'Sweet talker.'

He pulled his beloved close and stroked his hands over the gossamer-fine silk of her dress. It shimmered, indigo blue, over her delectable curves. Inevitably he felt the familiar tug of desire and satisfaction. This woman was his life, his home—everything he wanted.

'Just stating the truth.' He moved his hands more purposefully and heard Safiyah's breath snare. Anticipation quickened his pulse. 'But they say actions speak louder than words. Perhaps I should demonstrate my feelings.'

He backed her towards the long divan by the window.

'We've got an official lunch in half an hour and—'

'Some things are more important than royal duty, my love.'

Safiyah shook her head, but she was laughing as he lowered her onto the cushions. 'You're right, Karim. Some things are.'

Then she reached for him, using those supple, clever hands so effectively that Karim forgot everything but the need to show his wife just how he felt about her.

* * * * *

MY ROYAL TEMPTATION

RILEY PINE

CHAPTER ONE

Nikolai

IT'S NEVER IDEAL to wake up after a one-night stand to find a European boxing champion glaring at your bare ass. It's worse if the pissed-off guy in question happens to be a childhood best friend.

Scratch that…former best friend.

"Top of the morning." I wryly yank the hotel's satin sheet over my waist. A red thong is bunched on top of the unmade covers, right where I removed it with my teeth around midnight.

If looks could kill, Christian Wurtzer, Baron of Rosegate, would smite me faster than a lightning bolt hurled by an avenging god.

"You really are a first-rate bastard, aren't you, Nikolai?" He balled his hands into meaty fists, a useless gesture, because here in the Kingdom of Edenvale, it's illegal to strike a member of the royal family.

And as Prince Nikolai, third of his name, Duke of Westcraven, heir to the throne of Edenvale and our country's eminent blue-blooded bad boy, I fall square into the "no hitting allowed" category. Rules are often a nuisance in my world, but that particular clause has proved beneficial since reaching my maturity, especially in predicaments regarding the opposite sex.

"Bastard?" I scrub the morning scruff prickling my jaw with a yawn. "But I'm the mirror image of my dear sovereign father, and don't forget that my poor queen mother was forced to squeeze me out in front of an official court representative to ensure my legitimacy." There is a sharp localized pain in the vicinity of my heart; the twinge always accompanies a mention of my long-dead mother. She died bringing my youngest brother, Damien, into the world, the first life that banished asshole ever took.

"You've gone too far this time." Christian's warning growl yanks my attention back to the present moment. "This was my sister. You compromised her virtue."

Not the optimal moment to observe that he could give the ferocious bear stamped on his family crest a run for its money. Once our people were great hunters, the best swordsmen in Europe, as feared as the Vikings of old. Edenvale might be a small, landlocked kingdom, but we harbored a reputation as ruthless, lethal warriors. These days we're better known for luxury casinos, discreet banks and glamorous mountain hideaways. Edenvale is a high-altitude playground for the rich, the famous and those aspiring to the same.

"What will I tell my parents?" He rakes a hand through his blond hair, pacing the plush carpet. "Catriona is ruined. Her prospects for a marriage alliance are now non-existent."

"Come, come. Ask any trust-fund baby in Ibiza. It's common knowledge that your precious little sister gave up her virtue well before I sunk my flag." If his family schemed to marry Cat off as a virgin, they lost that

chance years ago. Typical Rosegate sentiment to at-
tach significance to such an inconsequential thing as a
hymen. But they are an old-fashioned people. The regional characteristic might be charming if their morals
weren't so fucking medieval.

Catriona Wurtzer stirs, snoring lightly, her pink lips
crooked into a satiated half smile. A hot pulse of lust
spreads through my sac. That luscious mouth pouts
from the cover of three different high-fashion magazines this month alone, and last night it worked over
my cock with such deep-throated skill that the interlude
nearly distracted me from this morning's royal duty.

I roll out of bed and slip on my tuxedo pants—
commando—and shrug into my dress shirt, not bothering with the twenty-four-karat-gold cuff links on the
nightstand. Catriona likes it rough, and the room was
trashed during our sleepover. Those expensive baubles
will serve as a more-than-adequate housekeeping tip.
It's time for me to return to the castle.

My father, the king, and my hag of a stepmother,
the current queen, have summoned me for a private
audience this morning at nine thirty sharp. This rare
audience doesn't mean anything good, which is why I
guzzled three-thousand-dollar-a-bottle champagne at
a gala benefit before burying myself balls deep into
the supermodel who happens to be my best friend's
little sister.

"Your family have been loyal subjects for over two
centuries. Based on this valued relationship, I shall issue
a royal decree. Huzzah, huzzah. All hail Catriona, the
realm's newest countess." I can't resist a smirk as I tack
on, "A new title for her trouble." As if bedding me was

a hardship. Which it wasn't. But what the hell? Let her add a castle to her four orgasms. I'm in a generous mood.

"Too kind, Highness." Christian nearly chokes on his words. He wants to beat my ass into Luxembourg, but the microstate of Rosegate has long been a disputed territory with Nightgardin, the country to the north and our ancient foe. The powerful Wurtzer family has been allied to mine for generations, and he knows—without reminder—three salient facts:

I'm an asshole, a leopard can't change his spots, and Edenvale's small but lethal military is the only thing protecting Rosegate against a Nightgardin power grab.

Revenge is a bitch.

Christian and I attended Swiss boarding school together and shared a dormitory room for five years. I love the guy like family, but he recently racked up too many gambling debts playing high-stakes blackjack. My sources say he decided to pay for them by selling titillating gossip about me to the tabloids. I'm not saying banging his hot sister is payback for his betrayal.

But I'm not saying it isn't, either.

A muscle twitches deep in his jaw, the same tic that would act up back when he'd pour over his calculus lessons during late-night study sessions. I'm sure he'd love to order me to "do the right thing" and stick a ring on his sister's finger. But alas, only one of us carries an invitation-only Black Amex card with no preset limits.

Limits are for those who need them. I am no such man.

People can think I'm an arrogant ass all they want. They're right. But at least I'm a consistent asshole. Fuck with me and I fuck back. No hard feelings. It's how the people on top stay on top. And I can make it good.

Or I can make it hurt.

For those who beg nicely—I can make it both.

Got to say, being a prince is full of perks in all ways but one—I still answer to the king. It's not my throne...yet.

I glance in the gilded mirror on my way out the door. Yep, still me. Bed-rumpled jet-black hair, a roguish mouth and gunmetal gray eyes. I clock in at six foot four and possess stamina for days. Last year I came in number one on a list of the world's sexiest royals. The only thing surprising was that it was the first year it happened. Way I see it, Prince Harry over in jolly old England can eat his ginger heart out.

"For Christ's sake. Wake up, Catriona," Christian orders his sister as I exit the room. I outpace the unfolding drama and stride down the hotel hallway, hitting the button on the penthouse's private elevator. My bodyguard, X, waits in the Rolls. He's been idling there all night. He's used to it.

I slide into the back seat without a word.

A language lesson plays on the sound system—Mandarin Chinese. X collects languages like he does medieval knives. Not my first choice for fun, but to each his own.

"To the castle, Sire?" he asks over the intercom, turning off the stereo. I remove my sunglasses from my pocket. Daylight reflects from the snow on the high mountain peaks. My growing headache isn't in the mood for good weather.

"Home sweet home." I slather sarcasm on my affirmative and slide on the shades to avoid the summer sun.

As X starts the engine, I reach into the minibar and

pluck out a handful of miniature cognac bottles. By the time we cross the moat, I toss the fifth empty on the pile by my feet. But the liquor does jack shit to dull the sharp pain in my gut.

Fine. It was an unforgivable move to fuck my best friend's little sister—revenge or no—but I'm sure as shit no Prince Charming.

Kate

I spread my hands across my pleated skirt, then think better of it and rest them atop the leather folder that sits on the table. If I wanted to, I could relax, even luxuriate in the high-backed, cushioned chair, no doubt made of the same buttery leather as the folder in front of me. But it's not exactly easy when you're sitting at a twenty-foot-long mahogany table in one of many rooms at the Palace Edenvale.

It wasn't like I hadn't been here before, but I don't think a prep-school tour counts the same as an invitation that came hand-delivered by a royal herald. The envelope was even closed with one of those fancy wax seals.

Dear Miss Katherine Winter,
Your presence is requested at Palace Edenvale at 9:30 a.m. tomorrow morning. Please come unattended and plan on clearing your schedule for the remainder of the day. Your audience with the king and queen must be kept private. Tell no one where you are going, and after you've been, tell no one what transpires within the palace walls until—should they request your ser-

vices further—the king, queen and yourself enter into contract.

The royal family appreciates you honoring your duty and complying with the above requests.

I huff out a laugh, which echoes in the empty room. *Requests.* As if I had any choice once I broke the royal seal. Sure, Your Highnesses, I'll clear my day. Of course, my illustrious rulers, I'll keep my visit to the palace a secret. Not because of any damned duty, though. If there is one thing I value, it's my business and my independence. I am determined to keep the former and as much of the latter as possible, and if that means zipping my lips about my *royal audience*, fine by me.

There better at least be some sort of monetary compensation for this—this—*request*. God knows my sister and I need it. Our savings account has dipped into the red with Gran's mounting medical bills, which has sent my internal stress thermometer in the exact opposite direction.

I glance at the thin gold bracelet on my wrist, an eighteenth-birthday gift from my beloved grandmother, back in happier times. Back when she still remembered my name.

I swallow the threat of tears. This is hardly the time or the place to wallow in my personal woes.

"We won't lose the apartment." The words are a mantra. "And we'll still be able to take care of Gran."

I figure if I say the words enough, they'll be true. So I open my mouth once more to repeat the statements, but the conference-room doors part with a whoosh, and my worry fades into the distance as the same formal-looking man who delivered my invitation steps over the threshold and announces my small country's rulers in a booming voice.

"All rise for His Highness, King Nikolai of Edenvale, and Her Eminence, Queen Adele."

The herald proclaims the royal couple as if they are entering an arena, and I, of course, shoot to my feet. My first instinct is to bow or curtsy, but neither one of them spares me so much as a passing glance. Yet I'm the only one in the room. I've been requested for a private audience with the *monarchy*, and they don't even deign to look at me.

Still, I wait for the attendants who trail behind the pair to pull out two chairs at the head of the table. I wait some more as they lower themselves into the plush leather seats. And as I'm about to do the same, a man wearing half a tuxedo bursts through the doors still tucking in his wrinkled dress shirt.

He winks in my direction, flashing a knavish grin before turning his attention to the king and queen.

"Sorry I'm late," he says, checking a nonexistent watch on his wrist. Then he kisses the queen on the cheek while the king, a salt-and-pepper version of the young man, simply gives his son—Prince Nikolai— a pointed look.

While his parents—make that father and stepmother— take residence at the far head of the table, the prince sits across from me and flips open the embossed folder in front of him.

"So," he says, sprawling in his chair and thumbing through the folder's contents, "what fire are we putting out this morning?"

He runs a hand through his black hair, and I squirm

involuntarily in my seat. Sure, I've seen photos of him before. Prince Nikolai's image has graced the front page of the tabloids almost weekly since he came of age. But that sort of sensationalism has never been my thing. I wasn't the preteen with pictures of the teen heartthrob prince on my wall. I didn't wallpaper my computer's desktop with his devil-may-care smile, no matter how gorgeous he was.

And he *was*. Even then.

But he was also a grade-A asshole. Even then.

And from the looks of things—from the colorful headlines that always seem to feature Prince Nikolai's name—it doesn't seem like anything is changing soon.

Still, when those slate-colored eyes look up from the folder and meet mine, I squirm again. He was handsome in photos and the few times I've seen him on television. Not that I watch much of that celebrity crap that's thrown in the public's face on a daily basis. But I'm not prepared for my reaction to the prince in the flesh.

He is nothing short of dazzling.

My lungs revolt, unable to take a deep breath even though I need air badly.

And as if it isn't enough that he has some sort of superpower effect between my legs, I feel my nipples stand at attention against the lace of my bra. Thank God I'd had the forethought to keep my suit jacket buttoned.

"Nikolai—" the queen begins, but the prince holds up a finger as he returns to scanning the contents of the folder—the one I have been waiting for permission to examine myself. Apparently, the rumors are true—

stepmother and stepson do not get on as they should. That explains the blatant disrespect.

His shuttered gaze roams the first page, then the second, and several more after that. I watch as his father crosses his arms and humors his son with a look that says no matter what antics the prince displays, the king will have the final word.

Prince Nikolai slams the folder closed and lets out a raucous laugh.

"Please, Nikolai," the king says, steepling his fingers in front of him. "Do tell us what you find so amusing."

The queen rests a hand on her husband's forearm, but the man's icy gaze remains directed at his son. All I do is stare, my head bobbing like I'm watching a tennis match in slow motion.

The prince narrows his eyes, pinning them on me, and my core tightens in disobedient response.

He takes his sweet time scrutinizing me, the corner of his mouth quirked in a crooked grin. Then he splays his hands on the table, leaning forward so that he's close enough for me to smell the tang of alcohol on his breath.

"I find it hilarious," the prince says with an edge to his words, "that you not only expect me to marry but that you think Little Miss Matchmaker-Dot-Com is the one to take care of the job. I mean, why not open me a royal Tinder account and be done with it?"

He has the nerve to sneer at me and my career? Oh, hell no.

Red-hot anger replaces that sensual tightening in my core.

The prince pushes from the table and smooths out

his wrinkled shirt. "Father. Stepmother. As always, it's a pleasure to see you both." He doesn't hide his sarcasm.

On instinct, I stand as he rounds the table, my cheeks blazing with repressed fury.

"I—I am not some dot-com organization. My matches are personal, well thought out…" I sputter as it sinks in not only what I've been called here to do but that my client is anything but willing.

"Save it, sweetheart," he says. "I'd sooner fuck you than let you arrange my nuptials."

The queen gasps, and King Nikolai slams his fist on the table.

"Enough," the older man says, the finality of his authority dripping from the word. "Benedict is entering the priesthood. Damien is banished. If you do not marry with the intent to produce an heir, the throne falls out of the immediate family and to your cousin Ingrid. You will not fault on your duty."

The muscle in the prince's jaw pulses. "That's right, Father. I've had enough." His penetrating stare, though, stays on me the whole time. That's when he leans in, hot breath on my cheek. "And you'd enjoy every goddamn second of it," he whispers. "The word *enough* won't even exist in your vocabulary."

He bows toward his visibly shaken parents before making his dramatic exit.

I give myself a mental pat on the back for at least believing the stories.

The prince *is* a grade-A asshole.

My soaked panties, on the other hand, apparently did not receive the memo.

Perhaps they're waiting for one with the royal seal.

CHAPTER TWO

Nikolai

"MARRIAGE? THAT'S IT, Father has lost his goddamn mind," I mutter, ducking into the unobtrusive staircase, the quickest escape route out of the palace. Two floors down a young servant in a black dress and white apron takes one look at me and nearly drops the silver tray she carries, one laden with teapots, fine china and six different cakes. My mood is so foul that I ignore her alarmed squeal and don't even smooth the situation over with a flirtatious wink.

She must have been assigned catering duty for the ambush upstairs, the one where my father invoked the ancient laws of our realm.

Sweat breaks out on my hairline. A sour taste fills my mouth.

My twenty-ninth birthday is just around the corner.

I am the heir to the crown.

The Royal Marriage Decree of 1674 declared that the Edenvale heir must wed before sundown on his or her twenty-ninth birthday or their claim is null and void. Plus, an Edenvale heir had to marry someone of aristocratic blood. My future bride doesn't have to be a citizen of my country, but she does need to be nobility. Other than that, the requirements are simple: free consent.

Sounds easy enough. Except for the part where I'm not the marrying kind.

I reach the bottom of the stairs and draw a lung-searing breath before pushing through the exit that leads to the castle grounds.

Of course I know about the marriage decree. I memorized Edenvale proclamations and laws alongside my ABCs. But this is the twenty-first century. I never dared believe that Father would enforce that arcane law any more than he would the one about how no high ministers could enter the palace wearing purple, or how hunting on royal lands was a hangable offense.

Don't even get me started on the decree prohibiting anal sex.

Hell, I tapped the back door of a hotel heiress in the castle's highest tower last week. Not something I normally do, but she offered, and I sure as shit wasn't going to turn it down. Not my favorite position, but sex is like pizza in Naples. Even if it's not great, it's still damn good.

The castle grounds are perfectly manicured with hedges cut into topiaries of rabbits and swans. Father enjoys indulging his whimsical side.

The morning sun scalds my neck.

"Sire, Sire, please, wait!" a woman cries behind me. Then she mutters under her breath how hard it is to run in heels.

My molars grind with enough force that it's a miracle they don't shatter. I've heard that lilting voice before—the auburn-haired woman from the match-making service that my father hired.

Marriage decree aside, this situation—them hiring a matchmaking service—is the biggest insult of all. As if I need any goddamn help finding a willing woman.

"Sire!"

I should wait. Chivalry and all that. But remember the part about how I'm no Prince Charming?

I veer into the maze, kicking at stones in the gravel path. Fuck being a gentleman. I turn left, then right, then left again. The walls surrounding me are twelve feet high and covered in leaves. This maze might be the largest in Europe, but it was my childhood playground. I always know the way out. Time to ditch this tenacious matchmaker and figure out a plan to avoid getting tied in unholy matrimony.

That's when I hear it.

A snap, quickly followed by a sound like someone trying not to cry out.

Shit.

She's fallen over.

Not a surprise. I caught a glimpse of her precarious five-inch stilettos when she crossed her legs upstairs in the castle hall and this path is rocky and uneven.

I also caught an eyeful of a toned calf that connected to a perfectly curving thigh. That was the best part of the meeting. Before I glanced at the folder on the table and read the gold-embossed title: Happy Endings Matchmaking Services: Making Dreams a Reality.

A cool mountain breeze brushes my face. I pause. Debating. I want to keep going. I even take a step. It's not like I asked her to give chase. She saw that I didn't need her advice. That I didn't want her professional services. Yet she insisted on pursuing me of her own free will. This is her own fault. I owe the woman—a total stranger—nothing.

The image of that exquisite creamy thigh flashes behind my eyes, this time draped over my shoulder.

Okay. Correction. I don't want her in a *professional* capacity.

My shoulders slump. No matter what my instincts demand, I can't abandon an injured woman alone in the maze.

Before I know it, I'm backtracking. It takes less than thirty seconds to find her.

She's kicked off that lethal-looking shoe and sits rubbing a swelling ankle. Her toes are painted a glossy classic red.

Okay, damn. I like that.

Her lips are flawless, painted in exactly the same shade.

I like that even better.

I'd like it best streaking my shaft.

My cock twitches in agreement.

Fuck. This matchmaker—and maddeningly sexy woman—is the enemy. But try telling that to my ass-hole dick. Sometimes an overactive libido comes with serious drawbacks.

Then her gaze fixes on my face, and with one look at those tear-filled baby blues, my brain fucking flatlines.

Kate

It takes everything for me to hold my prince's fixed stare, not to wince at the white-hot pain in my ankle.

But there is no way I'm letting this guy—prince or otherwise—get the best of me.

"You okay?" he asks.

"Of course not." I glance at my ivory skirt, the side slit ripped even higher. I'm also sure my ass is one big grass stain. And let's not even discuss the hair. I'd gone for professional with the French twist, but now my auburn waves hang in my face, which is probably for the best. His steely gaze is too close.

"Just—show me the way out," I say, attempting to push myself up, but as soon as I put pressure on my bare foot, my knees buckle and I almost hit the ground again.

Almost. Because Nikolai Lorentz, Prince of Edenvale and heir to the throne, catches me.

"Shit," he hisses. "You *are* hurt."

"And you smell like you hit a limousine minibar," I say, trying to cover my reaction to his hands on me with disdain.

But my breath still quickens. He carries me with a concern I can feel in every nerve of my body.

"It was a Rolls, but you're very perceptive, Miss—"

"Winter," I say, having no choice but to throw my arms around his neck for purchase, my broken shoe still dangling from my fingers.

"Aha," he says, that devilish grin taking over his features. "Have you read *Romeo and Juliet*? Doesn't Juliet ask what's in a name?" He begins to walk.

My cheeks grow hot, and the tips of his fingers— his palm where it touches the bare skin of my thigh— sends sparks right through me.

I clear my throat. "You read Shakespeare?" I ask, though it's obvious.

"You're as icy as your name implies."

I huff out a breath and push as far from him as I can while the rogue still has me in his arms.

"I'm no such thing! *You—you're* the one who likened my services to a dating website. My work is nuanced and relies on personal metrics and psychology, thank you very much. You're also the one who just cost me a day's work. So pardon me if I'm not exactly warming to your famous *charm*."

He stops dead in his tracks. We're still in the maze, and I can't tell if we're any closer to making it out of here or if he's taken us deeper.

His eyes dart in every direction, as if he's checking for intruders, before they land on mine. Stone gray and burning with intent, I can't look away if I try.

"I *will not* marry," he says, his voice cool and even. "Is that understood?"

I nod. "And I will *not* walk away from this job."

"Then I guess we're at an impasse."

The air between us is warm, charged with the mingling of our breaths. His skin against mine sizzles. My head tells me that everything I'm feeling is wrong, but the physical need brewing inside me throbs at my core.

I haven't been with a man since my fiancé, Jean-Luc, died BASE jumping in Alaska. He was the love of my life, but he loved the thrill of adrenaline more than me. Afterward, I joined my big sister Madeline's business to devote my life to what I was denied: a happy ending.

It had been two long, careful years of self-denial and occasionally my own hand. Before that it had only ever been Jean-Luc.

But the hand against me now is big, strong and unfamiliar. All it would take is his fingers sliding an inch more, and he'd *feel* that need, wet and pulsing.

He swallows, and I watch his Adam's apple bob. That's all it takes to let me know that whatever this is, it's not only me.

Maybe this is what it feels like to live in the moment, take a risk, something I never let myself do because I had to be careful for both of us. I had to move in with Madeline to save on rent. Never have I let myself simply *want*.

But this stranger's hands on me are warm. Strong. And for a second I imagine what they could do. It's intoxicating, this growing need and the possibility of satisfying it right here and now. I feel drunk and squirm in his grasp, hoping he'll simply think I'm readjusting myself in his arms, but I miscalculate and my lips brush against his.

He sucks in a breath, and this makes me grin.

"I *don't* like you," I say. Truer words have never been spoken.

"Likewise," he answers, his voice low and rough.

All my life I've played it safe, and where did it get me? Lost and alone. But this man exudes raw power, a power that draws me into his orbit, a pull stronger than gravity. I feel myself inching toward some sort of internal cliff, and the woman I thought I was relinquishes control.

"You said you'd sooner fuck me than let me arrange your nuptials."

He nods. "I certainly did."

I lean close to his ear, nip at his lobe, and step across the line of comfort I've hidden behind for far too long and whisper, "It's *sooner*."

I expect a savage response, but instead I feel him adjust his hands, and then I gasp as his thumb hits the crease of my panties.

That's all it takes. I leap off the cliff with a whimper of need and straight into pure pleasure.

He growls.

"You're fucking soaked." He drops to his knees, still holding me like I'm precious cargo, and lays me gently on the grass. "And I want to drink every last sweet drop."

Without another word, he hikes my skirt up and slides my panties down my thighs, over my knees and then off. I feel them snag on the heel of my remaining shoe but don't care. He shoves them in the pocket of his pants, and I know I'm not getting them back. The thought makes me giddy, and I writhe under his gaze.

"Now, Nikolai," I say, and he levels me with his grin.

The next thing I know, my hands are tangled in that jet-black hair as he licks the length of my folds from bottom to top until his tongue swirls around my swollen clit.

I moan and buck against him as he sucks me between his lips. I relish the feel of his stubble against my thighs, the slight pain only heightening my pleasure.

"Use fingers," I command, and he obeys immediately.

One finger plunges deep while he continues to take his fill with his mouth. Then a second joins the first, and my vision clouds with stars. My body bucks with shivers of reaction.

"God, I wish you could fuck me," I say, daring to voice what I long for—what I've gone without for what seems like an eternity. I try and fail not to whimper as he reaches a spot inside me that almost makes me black out.

Two years. It's been two freaking years since a man has touched me. The thought—coupled with his hands on me, in me—threatens to unleash something more than just the adrenaline rush, but I swallow the impending wave of emotion. Because that's not what this is about. These feelings aren't for the prince.

He peeks from between my legs and slides his fingers from my aching pussy. He takes care in licking each one clean.

"You said it was sooner, sweetheart, and I'm *always* prepared for sooner." From the pocket that does not hold my ruined panties, he pulls a foil packet and holds it up for me to see. "Your wish is my command."

CHAPTER THREE

Nikolai

HER TASTE IS ADDICTIVE—honey, salt and rainwater. I hate the idea of matchmaking. But matchmakers? I take my time drinking in the woman panting on the grass, her conservative blouse opened a button too far, exposing delicate white lace, creamy skin and lush, womanly curves.

Yes. I believe I could learn to like matchmakers.

"Sire. Hurry." She stares through a fringe of dark, thick lashes. Her red lipstick is smudging off her plump lower lip. I'm responsible for that, and the fact draws my balls tight against my engorged cock, clearly outlined through the panel of my tux pants. My muscles ripple with suppressed need.

I fold my arms, making an elaborate show of regarding the condom foil, and set my face into my trademark arrogant sneer. It's my mask. The one the public expects a prince to wear, especially a prince with the world at his feet. It comes easy as instinct, which is good because I am not used to being unsettled. And this woman is—*unsettling.*

"Interesting business you run." I lower my voice to a sensual drawl.

"No, not mine. I mean… I am not… It's not mine… um… It's my sister's…her business," she babbles, skimming one hand over the ragged tear in her prim skirt, the one currently offering me an eyeful of the thighs I'd feasted on. Her eyes darken, pupils dilating at my blatant appraisal.

"And do you provide these *services*—" I clear my throat and raise an insinuating eyebrow "—to every client?"

A dusky rose color flushes the skin of her throat as she catches my insinuation. She's pissed. Angry and turned on, my favorite combination in a woman. Hate fucking has all of the fun and none of the responsibility.

"Of course not," she snaps.

I dip a finger between my lips and give it a long lazy suck. The muscles in my neck cord. It still tastes like her. My mouth waters. "Mmm-hmm. Methinks the lady doth protest too much."

"Damn it." A tear spills from the corner of one gorgeous eye, trickles along her high cheekbone. "I don't know what came over me."

My hands twitch to comfort her. Christ. I did not see that response coming. I should regroup, charm her thighs open and plunge into her from behind, working her fancy hairdo and composure loose in brutal doggy-style strokes. Bet it would make her bum ankle feel a lot better than two ibuprofens and an ice pack.

So why am I pocketing the condom? Or brushing a wayward lock of hair on her forehead.

"Look. It's been…" She flinches from my touch with a bitter laugh. "A while. And you…well, you're royal

sex on a stick. It's a lot for a normal person to take in."
She closes the gaping button on her shirt. "An error in
judgment that won't happen again."

Looks like I'm not the only one who slaps on a
mask when the going gets tough. In a blink of an eye
my feisty sex kitten has retracted her claws and is now
back to Miss Prim and Proper.

"Pity," I rumble, trying not to appear disconcerted.
"Errors in judgment happen to be my specialty." I take
my time adjusting my cock, the proud, hard length
straining inside my pants.

The point of her pink tongue makes a quick appearance, dabs her lower lip. The kitten reemerges for a
second. "You do seem quite…specialized."

"And you have once again proven my long-tested
theory correct."

"Which is?"

I tap the tip of her nose with my index finger. "Inside every good girl is a bad girl waiting to get out."

She fingers her pearl choker. "I'm not going to argue
with you there." Her laugh is high-pitched—nervous.
"I've always been the good girl. Oral in a royal maze
is a first and so, *so* not me."

I believe her. She looks like an angel. I might have
sucked her sweet clit, but those doe-like eyes speak to
nothing but innocence. That's when I'm slammed by a
vision of a woman naked in my bed, long legs spread
wide, hiding nothing, each pink honeyed fold exposed
for my pleasure. Her delicate wrists and ankles bound
by thick ropes of pearl.

I blink. My shoulders go rigid. I've never invited a
woman into my royal bed. The west wing of the palace is my personal sanctuary. No one is welcome there

save for my brother Benedict. Not my dalliances. And not my father or stepmother. It's the only place that is just for me. Where I can be—*me*.

The world gets my dick. No one has a right to my soul.

"This was obviously a mistake," she murmurs to herself before rising unsteadily. "We got off on the wrong foot."

"*You* got off on the wrong foot." I nod at her bare right foot, the one on which she can barely place any weight, and I offer her my arm. She takes it, but not before rolling her eyes. "We got off on more than that," I add. My cock jumps like a dog hungry for a treat. "At least *you* did."

She sniffs. Who'd imagine this ice queen could melt into such a passionate, bright, fiery lover?

Interesting.

She limps but is able to hold her own now. I like to think it has something to do with my talent between her legs, that my skillful tongue has a healing effect. I guide her out of the maze. Grass stains mar her perfectly tailored ivory skirt, a visible reminder of what we just did, and just like that, I'm hard as a rock again.

"From the tabloids," she says, "it sounds like you won't suffer for long. Tell me, how long has it been since you were inside a woman?"

I shrug with studied nonchalance. "Mouth or pussy?"

She gasps as my words sink in.

I pretend to count my fingers. "Six hours for pussy. Seven for her mouth. Give or take fifteen minutes. And if her brother hadn't barged in on us this morning, I'm guessing those numbers would be significantly smaller."

"You're a pig." Her brows slam together. "A rutting, depraved boar."

"No. I'm a prince." I draw myself to full height. "*Your* prince."

"And I'm here in service to my king." She juts out her jaw, gaze unbowed, refusing to cave at my power play. "Sire, you are my client. It's been royally commanded by your father and my liege lord, which means we need to get to work. I will return tomorrow to do your personality profile."

"My what?"

"It's protocol for all our clients." There is a note of finality in her clipped tone. She means business.

I click my tongue, half annoyed and half impressed. "You'll never marry me off, sweetheart."

"Tell that to my matchmaking success rate of 100%." She offers a smug smile. "See you tomorrow, Highness."

Once out of the maze, she releases my arm and continues alone. But she's still injured, so her haughty exit falls flat, even as she takes off her other shoe. I bite back a laugh before realizing the joke is on me. Because guess who still has a hard-on the size of the Matterhorn?

Still, I should follow her to the castle lest she goes to the tabloids with some trumped-up story about how poorly she was treated on palace property.

"I am fine to proceed alone," she says, reading my thoughts. An unsettling experience.

"I'm afraid I must insist," I say, taking the few steps needed to catch up to her.

"Please." Her composure slips a notch. The mask

not fully secure. "I—I need a moment alone." A sign this unexpected dalliance affected her, as well.

She turns and makes her way toward the palace gates, clutching her heels, only the slightest limp still evident. Miss Winter has spunk. I'll give her that.

A woman like this could bring a less controlled man to his knees. Good thing that I'm no such man. This angel is more dangerous than any devil.

Kate

I don't care if it hurts to walk. Nothing is more important than distance. And by distance I mean space between me and Nikolai Lorentz.

The only problem? When I slip through the gates onto the main grounds, I can't get to the front of the castle without swimming the moat.

Good Lord. He lives in a palace. With a moat. And I almost slept with him in a freaking maze. I begged the prince of our realm to *fuck me* as I lay in the grass with my skirt hiked up over my hips. What the hell is wrong with me? I don't *fuck* anybody. I have lovely, meaningful sex with men who love and care for me—and who put a ring on it. At least, I did have that once.

As I contemplate my next move, an older man—probably in his late thirties—approaches me from a nearby garden.

"Pardon me, Miss Winter, but I have been instructed to take you home."

I shake my head. "No, thank you. That won't be necessary. If you could point me toward the most direct route to the main road, I'm sure I can get a taxi."

I look behind me, expecting to see Nikolai approaching, but he's nowhere to be found.

"Miss, there is no direct route to the main road other than through the palace." He looks me up and down. "And I am assuming you'd like to make a discreet exit?"

I sigh and cling to the last shred of my dignity, holding my head high even as my just-been-finger-fucked hair falls into my face.

"I'm quite content walking through the palace..." But I trail off as I note myself gesturing with my shoes in my hands—as threads from my torn skirt tickle my thigh—and I immediately deflate.

"So...you were instructed to take me home?"

The man nods, the hints of silver in his dark hair glinting in the sun, and it's only now that I realize his impeccably tailored suit, his straightened spine and hands clasped in front of his hips. His jaw is chiseled and his brown eyes are dark and knowing. He is not royalty. I can tell that much. But he exudes an undisputable authority nonetheless.

"Yes, Miss. His Royal Highness the Prince texted me with the order to see you home safely. I can lead you through the kitchen and out the servants' exit to avoid any unpleasant encounters upon your departure."

I hold out my arms, shoes dangling from my index fingers. "I guess I'm not in any shape to run into the king and queen again, especially if I want to keep this job."

The man doesn't even crack a smile but instead offers me a single nod.

"This way, Miss." He motions toward the garden from which he came.

I limp in his direction, trying not to read into the prince's gesture of making sure I get home safely. There is no way Nikolai Lorentz cares what happens between us from here on out other than him opposing my very being here.

"You can call me Kate," I say, once I reach his side and he holds out an arm. I grab both of my shoes with my right hand and take his arm with my left—not because I need to but because it would seem rude to decline.

I breathe in sharply as my hand grips muscle so tight and corded that I can feel it through his suit.

"As you wish, Miss Kate," he says, and I roll my eyes.

"Maybe you could drop the *Miss* altogether? Makes me sound like a prim-and-proper governess." I let out a nervous laugh. What just transpired between me and the heir apparent was *not* behavior becoming of a governess. Or the me I thought I knew, for that matter.

"As you wish, *Kate*," he says, his voice devoid of any hint of emotion.

"You got a name?" I ask as he pushes open a door hidden in the brick of the palace's side wall.

"His Highness calls me X," he says, ushering me inside a small corridor. The servants' quarters, no doubt.

"What do your friends and family call you?" I ask.

He clears his throat. "I have neither, Miss—my apologies—*Kate*."

My stomach sinks at the thought as he leads me through a white six-panel door. But I forget the heartbreaking answer just as quickly as we enter an enormous kitchen and my senses are assaulted in the best possible way. The aroma of garlic wafts in our direction, and my mouth immediately waters. I skipped breakfast this morning because—hello—I was ordered to the palace. Who can eat with that kind of pressure? And now that I'd been satiated in a whole other way entirely, I was famished. There's also something sweet in the air, a richness I can almost taste.

"Would you like one for the road, Miss?" A woman covered in a white apron spins from where she's plating macarons from a baking pan onto a three-tiered plate.

I swallow before I start to drool. "Please," I say, and she grabs a small saucer from beneath the island where she works and serves me *five* of the delicious-looking confections.

"Our secret," she says with a wink and a smile, handing my bounty to X. The man simply nods and continues piloting me toward the exit.

The next thing I know, I'm sitting in the luxury of a Rolls-Royce, a plate of macarons in my lap, and an ice pack on my ankle—also, according to X, ordered by the prince. But the older man speaks no more as he pulls free of the palace gates, out onto the main thoroughfare and toward the apartment I share with my sister in the heart of town.

As I sit here, the breeze of the car's open windows hits me right up the bottom of my skirt, and I'm reminded of the fact that not only am I going commando, but also my underwear is bunched in the Prince of Edenvale's pocket.

Just swallow me up, world, because I am too much of a cliché to exist. I can see the tabloid headline now:

Royal Touch Wakes Celibate Woman's Libido

It isn't that I've ignored the whole libido thing. I have an active imagination and a pretty stellar showerhead. It's not like I've gone completely without. But the first time I go *with* is not supposed to be with my future king, and it certainly isn't supposed to unleash a torrent of pent-up emotion, not when a pint of chocolate gelato is nowhere in sight.

I close my eyes and try to erase the image of him grinning before he went down on me, but it turns out that eyes open, closed, crossed or whatever still draw the same picture—Nikolai Lorentz pleasuring me and taking pleasure in doing so.

And then when I'd called our little maze dalliance a mistake, he'd ordered his driver to take care of me—right down to a ride in his private car and the cool pack soothing the throb in my twisted ankle.

Maybe I am a cliché, something I never thought I'd be. But then again, maybe Prince Nikolai, Duke of Westcraven, isn't what I'd had in mind, either.

I pop a golden lemon macaron into my mouth and moan with pleasure.

Nope. Not what I had in mind at all.

CHAPTER FOUR

Nikolai

NOTHING LIKE A scalding hot shower after a night of rough sex with your former best friend's little sister, followed by impromptu cunnilingus in the palace maze with the matchmaker bankrolled by your father to find your future queen.

It's been a strange twenty-four hours.

I rock my head back. Forget a standard shower-head. I custom designed my own personal waterfall. My groan bounces off the slate tiles as my tense muscles relax in the spray. Shit yeah. This feels good. Almost as good as it did to be on my knees between Miss Winter's sweet thighs. I chuckle to myself. Me. On my knees before a woman. Can't remember the last time that happened.

A visceral memory flies in from the outer reaches of my subconscious and slams my gut with the intensity of an earth-ending meteor.

There once had been a woman who brought me to my knees. But I wasn't much past a boy then. Now I'm all man with a kingdom that's mine for the taking.

I grab a bottle of my favorite Tom Ford body wash

and pour a generous dollop in my palm. There's one thing that will relax me. Using the wash as lube, I thrust my cock into my hand in slow, lazy strokes before upgrading to my tried-and-true fist-over-fist technique, my length enough that one hand can never do the job. My ass clenches as I give over to the build.

Here's a fact. No woman, no matter how expert a lover, can touch a guy better than he touches himself. I'm captain of my own fucking ship. Yet here I am, imagining innocent, angel-faced Kate and her beautiful hands—small, delicate, manicured. I picture her grabbing me at the root, and I let out a guttural groan. What is it about this stranger that drives me crazy enough for her to invade my thoughts like this? Every nerve ending in my shaft is ready to burst into flames.

That's when I remember.

I still have her panties in my pocket. I step out of the shower, not giving two shits about getting the floor wet, and yank them from my tuxedo pants. The delicate ivory is pale in my tanned hand. On instinct, I lift them to my face and inhale the elegant French lace. My eyes roll. Beguiling. I'm a goddam pussy connoisseur, and this is the equivalent to uncorking a bottle of Château Mouton Rothschild 1945. I keep a case in my wine cellar, each bottle valued at twenty-five thousand euros.

I clutch the matchmaker's panties in one hand and step back in the shower, working over my cock with increased urgency as her scent overpowers my senses. Sweat breaks out across my chest and is washed away in a torrent of steamy water.

There are those who get intimidated by winery tasting rooms, but it's simple. A good vintage is composed of four things: fruits, acids, tannins and sugars. Young tannins can make the mouth pucker, leave your tongue dry. Left over time it increases in complexity, covering your palate with a signature silkiness. My palate is exceptional, able to identify a vintage by the subtle yet complex notes of coffee, chocolate, blackberry and spice.

Women are much the same. Each with her own nuances. And Kate Winter is in a class all her own. Fruity, with a hint of cherry, but also darker, more intriguing notes, such as to be found in a rich forest floor. She is the fruit of the earth, and I'm starving for the harvest.

A few more strokes and I'm poised on the edge, and then I pitch over, shattering into the most mind-numbing orgasm in a decade. For a moment, I wonder if I'm struck blind. Then the world returns, and I wash my hands, turn off the spray and grab a towel for my waist.

It takes me five minutes to regain my breath. After an intense, almost holy, experience like that, there is only one place to go—my brother, the saint.

Benedict will enter the priesthood. As a virgin.

Fucking crazy, right? My father bursts with pride at the fact he has a son destined for the priesthood and St. Egbert Abbey. To me, it's a fate worse than hell, and besides, it's more pressure. Benedict's put our bloodline at risk given that I'm the heir and he's the spare. My youngest brother, Damien, doesn't factor into the equation as he is banished and thereby removed from the line of succession. If I screw up here, the kingdom could pass from my family to my cousin Ingrid. She is a nice enough girl, and I don't mean that dismissively. She is ten years old.

I shove on a pair of sweatpants, lace up my running

shoes and catch my reflection in the window. I look like a debauched lord of the underworld.

Reflections on my banished brother Damien spiral me into a brooding darkness. The latest rumors claim that he resides half-time in London and the rest over in America. He could build a hermetically sealed tower in Madagascar for all I care, and it would still be too goddamn close. My family is like the setup to a bad joke: a commitment-phobic heir to the throne, a virgin almost-priest, and a black sheep all walk into a bar…

I jog through the quiet palace, past row after row of ancient ancestors appraising me from gilded frames. Do they wonder if I'll ever measure up? If I'll fulfill my legacy? Damn these black thoughts to hell. I get outside and run until my lungs are near bursting. On the edge of the grounds, near the Royal River, is the tower where my brother lives. He calls it his sanctuary, and he's not wrong. Poor bastard might not use his cock, but he has peace. And he deserves it because I don't say bastard lightly.

There isn't conclusive proof, but there are many rumors that my mother took a brief liking to the head of her secret-service detail while my father was at a UN summit. The only evidence? My brother's piercing green eyes—neither my mother's nor my father's.

I try the door.

"It's locked, Sir," a formal male voice calls out.

I turn to find X there, watching me with his usual impenetrable expression. One would think that after years of him appearing by my side without setting off so much as a floorboard creak, I would be used to his stealth. But it still unnerves me every time.

"I'm afraid Mr. Benedict was called away on urgent business."

"Where to?" I ask.

"Vatican City."

I laugh without humor. "Of course."

Benedict is the only person that I count a true friend, one I can trust without question unlike recent experiences with Christian. And as far as I'm concerned, Benedict is my *only* brother. If I ever were to cross paths with Damien again, I know Benedict would pass me the knife to gut him.

One happy family.

Looks like I'm not going to be able to get any advice tonight. The only thing I can do is pop an Ambien and hope for a dreamless sleep.

Because tomorrow morning, I'll be facing Kate Winter again. And this time she won't be spreading her legs and offering me a sample of her nectar. She'll be presenting me with a dossier of potential wives.

Kate

It's déjà vu the next morning when I look out my apartment window to find X and the Rolls-Royce waiting against the curb. Maddie peers over my shoulder.

"I still don't get it," she says, and I can hear the disappointment lacing her tone. "Why did they specifically ask for you rather than me? It's *my* agency, after all."

Now that the contract has been signed, I can tell my sister everything. Which is good because that whole secrecy thing won't fly when I'm getting picked up by a Rolls with a license plate that reads *Royal*. Besides,

I'd accepted the job—after the king and queen agreed to double my fee for working with such a reluctant client. Well, it was the queen's suggestion. Turns out that despite the business being Maddie's baby, my recent success at facilitating what I thought had been a few discreet celebrity matches had not flown under the radar of the royal family.

"Come on, Mads," I say. "It's a gold star for the business regardless of whether it's you or me facilitating the matches. Plus, you're my partner in crime, so it's not like we can't work on Nikolai's profile together." In fact, the only thing I cannot disclose to anyone other than Maddie is the list of potential candidates.

She is obviously still pouting, but as much as I love my big sister and her flair for business, I am the one with the perfect match record—fifteen happy couples in just the past six months alone. It's all in the interviews. One face-to-face conversation with each potential partner—separately, of course—and I can either feel their chemistry…or not. That, coupled with my limited celebrity experience, I'm sure is why they asked for me, but I don't rub it in. While I'm proud I've taken so well to the business these past two years, what does it say that I can find happy endings for everyone—except myself?

Then I'm reminded that I risked my heart once, and the payoff was total devastation. No, thank you. I'm good with focusing on everything and anything other than that.

I wave to X and hold up a finger, letting him know I'll be right there. Then I turn to face my sister, staring into icy blue eyes that mirror my own.

"Remember, Maddie, we need this fee. We are almost due for another quarterly payment at Silver Maples." Gran's been deteriorating, her Alzheimer's getting worse almost by the week. We're her sole financial support. Actually, we're her sole *everything*. As much as it kills us not to have her at home, caring for her like she did raising us, her condition has declined too much. Silver Maples is a top-rated facility, one of the best in Europe. And it's priced accordingly. It's just out of our financial means at the moment, but I intend to change that.

I don't mention the part about receiving *no* fee at all if I don't get Nikolai down the aisle—if he is my first and *only* fail. I also may have omitted that despite my vow to find him a suitable queen, I already know what it feels like for his stubble to chafe my thighs, for his tongue to swirl around my swollen clit. Or to know that despite the matches that are perfect for Nikolai Lorentz on paper, the only chemistry I'm sure of at this point is whatever happened in that garden maze between myself and our future king.

"Shit," I mutter under my breath and slip past her. I need to stop thinking myself into climax before I've even had my first sip of espresso. "I'm late." I grab my dossier off our small kitchen table and reach for the small cup that should have three shots of my morning wake-up medicine when I realize the espresso machine is unplugged. I never forget my morning shot. Ugh. I am way off my game, which is not an auspicious beginning to day one with my most important client. *"Shit,"* I say louder and then groan my acceptance at another morning with an empty belly. I kiss my sister on the cheek. "Love you!" And then I dart out the door before she has a chance to respond.

Not that I'm expecting a repeat performance of what happened yesterday, but I wear my auburn waves loose today—in case of any mishaps. Better to have my hair down and unfettered than to attempt the whole conservative look only to wind up disheveled and unkempt. Because I much prefer *kempt*.

X holds open the car door, and I enter to find a veritable feast waiting for me on a small table attached to the wall that separates the rear of the vehicle from the front. There's a bowl of the reddest strawberries I've ever seen, a small basket of scones and a stainless-steel travel mug of what I assume is coffee.

My eyes widen as I lower myself into my seat, and I glance at X before he closes the door. He offers me a small bow, and I blush, embarrassed at the royal treatment when my upbringing is probably more common than he can imagine.

"Compliments of His Royal Highness, Prince Nikolai."

While I'm sure my fresh breakfast probably cost him no more than a few seconds of his time, a quick royal order via text, I can't fight the warmth spreading through my veins that he thought of me at all.

"Thank you, X," I say with a smile I'm unable to suppress, and he nods before closing the door.

I settle into the plush leather of my seat, pulling a napkin that's folded in the shape of a swan from the table before me. A pang of guilt rests in my chest for whoever created this small masterpiece only to have me stain it with berry juice or dripped coffee. Yet I shake it out, a swan no more, and lay it across my lap as X pulls smoothly from the curb.

I opted for pants today—a cropped black pair with

a green silk blouse. And flats. I'd pretty much taken every precaution to avoid a repeat performance with the prince, and I smile smugly to myself at how easy it will be to keep my panties on today.

I unlock the lid to the mug and breathe in the rich aroma, biting back a moan as I do. Whatever brand of coffee is in there, it's miles above the quality of the espresso I buy on sale at the corner market.

I knock on the window that separates me from X, and instead of him lowering it, his voice pipes through a speaker to my left.

"Can I help you, Miss Kate?"

I roll my eyes at his insistence on formality but decide not to give him a hard time.

"It's kind of lonely here," I tell him. "Can we talk without the intercom?"

I hear him clear his throat. "As you wish, Miss Kate."

The window lowers, and I pop a strawberry into my mouth before leaning toward the open space between us. But the expanse is too wide for my torso, and I end up falling to my knees, a dribble of berry juice on my chin. I wipe it clean and scoot the rest of the way to the window frame, leaning through it so X's strong profile is in view.

"Did you make the swan?" I ask.

His eyes remain on the road as he replies. "No, Miss."

"Did you make the coffee?"

"No, Miss."

"Would you like a strawberry?"

At this I see the faintest tug on the corner of his mouth, and I decide that along with making sure I send

Nikolai Lorentz down the aisle, I'm going to make X smile.

"No, Miss," he says, and my shoulders sag.

I follow his eyes to the road ahead and realize we're not headed in the direction of the palace. For a second my heart stutters in my chest.

"Okay, you're not going to ply me with strawberries and scones only to dump me in the river with a backpack full of stones, right?"

Again that twitch of his lip, but it doesn't go beyond that.

"We *are* heading to the river," he says. "But His Highness said nothing about a backpack."

I narrow my eyes even though he won't look in my direction. Despite heading toward the body of water I've avoided most of my living years, I decide to trust my life is not in danger and slide back to my seat, this time bringing a warm blueberry scone with me. Seriously? How is it still warm?

Just as I relax and bring the pastry to my lips, we roll to a stop. X, however, does not leave his seat. Before I can ask him if we've reached our destination, my door opens, and I see the prince—not in a rumpled dress shirt and tuxedo pants but in a fitted black T-shirt and dark washed jeans. I know what I said about not being a preteen fangirl, but holy hell. This man in the flesh is a vision to behold.

He extends his arms wide as if he's brought the world to my doorstep, and based on the breakfast alone, it feels like he has.

"We can't possibly be expected to work indoors on a day like today," he says, his gray eyes shimmering silver in the sun.

He offers me a hand, and I take it, grabbing the dossier with my other as he pulls me into the fresh morning air.

"No," I say, trying to convince myself that the smoldering heat in my core is from the coffee I leave behind in the car. "I guess we can't."

CHAPTER FIVE

Nikolai

"THANKS FOR BREAKFAST." Kate regards me uncertainly.

"Seems only fair, Miss Winter. Especially after the delicious feast you offered me yesterday." Here's hoping that my wolfish smile covers any sincerity that might poke through my veneer. "Nice pants, by the way." They fit slim against her shape, hugging the soft swell of her thighs, tapering at her small waist. I take my time drinking her in for two reasons. One: she looks even better than she did in my dreams last night. Two: it's time to scare her off.

I don't care a whit about ancient marriage requirements. But my father is the king, and Edenvale is a strict monarchy. No constitution. No parliament. His word is absolute law.

But despite his decree, I cannot marry. I *will* not. My heart hasn't been whole for years. To subject a woman to a lifetime of darkness—to a love I cannot give—is anything but fair. I may not play by the rules in my day-to-day—or night-by-night—affairs, but I am straightforward. Each beauty I bed knows full well

I have nothing to offer the morning after other than burying my cock in her one more time.

I do like a proper goodbye, after all.

And I also like to be clear that I will not share my future crown.

Father has to be bluffing about this twenty-ninth birthday bullshit. He can't take the throne from me. He wouldn't. What are his other options? Benedict would yield our sovereign power to the Roman Pope. Damien? My cousin Ingrid, who is still a child? Nightgardin would be licking its chops if that happened.

A hot copper taste fills my mouth. The inside of my cheek hurts from the involuntary bite.

Damien destroyed my world. His scandal nearly brought down our entire lineage. Now he is banished. Not even allowed to claim Edenvale citizenship. No, that bottom-feeder will never be permitted to call himself more than "King of Traitors."

Father has no other choice, if he wants to avoid passing the crown from his bloodline. He will have to relent, to compromise, come around and see things from my point of view. It is that or let the kingdom fall to ruin, and that—he knows—is not an option.

My shoulders relax. I'll indulge in Miss Winter's little game for the time being, but she doesn't know that I'm the one writing the rules, and that I only play to win.

"Ahem, Highness?" Her exaggerated throat clearing breaks my thoughts. "My eyes are up here."

I allow my gaze to slowly rake over the swell of her perfect breasts. "I know exactly where your eyes are, Miss Winter, and might I say that's a fetching color of shadow. Makes your eyes appear deeper than the Bottomless Lake."

Kate sucks in a ragged breath, one evidenced by the rapid rise and fall of her chest rather than heard.

"Can we get down to business?" Pleading fills her voice.

"That all depends. Would getting down to...*business* bring you pleasure?" I dribble innuendo over every sentence. My mask is perfect. I'm every inch the rakish rogue everyone has come to expect. Kate Winter has no idea that my heart accelerates in her vicinity, kicks into fifth faster than my Ferrari 250 Testa Rossa.

And she never will.

She balls her free hand into a fist while the other clutches a portfolio, her fingertips white from her grip. Bet Little Miss Ice Queen would love nothing better than landing a punch right in my arrogant smirk. She can take a number. There are many in the line before her.

Plus she's safer wanting nothing more to do with me than our business dealings.

"X," I call, not breaking my gaze. "The poles."

"Very good, Highness." He clicks his heels and strides to the trunk of the Rolls. Good old X. Familiar as my shadow.

"I'm not really a nature girl." She casts a baleful look at the long grass, swatting away a hovering insect. "But I am excited to get to work. Here is the dossier." She brandishes the portfolio. "I spent last night reviewing suitable prospects and have winnowed your choices to five viable candidates." She clears her throat. "Your parents offered some input as well, wishing the choice to be someone who would buoy your image and thereby the image of the throne. Your stepmother in particular took a keen interest. The queen is a woman of many opinions."

I arch a brow. My hag of a stepmother has many feelings about my existence, none of them good. "I thought we were to do some sort of personality profile."

She breaks eye contact. "Your stepmother didn't think it was necessary to invest too much in compatibility since—well—since you don't intend this to be much of an emotional connection. You've made that point crystal clear. So I've been instructed to provide you with *appropriate* choices."

"Fascinating." A cold front blows over my chest, transforming my tone to sheer ice. I spent last night milking my cock, dreaming of her sweet, soaked pussy, and all the while she'd been reviewing *appropriate* brides. Not once in five years have I given a single fuck what a woman thinks about after I've been with her.

Not once until today.

How much is Father paying her for this trouble? My stepmother would bankrupt the royal coffers if it meant having her revenge. She won't play me the fool the way her daughter did. Victoria made me believe that a kiss meant love, not a fast track to sink her claws into my wealth—or my future throne.

These days the only crown jewels I'm prepared to offer the opposite sex rest between my legs. It's likely she is conspiring with my stepmother. No doubt yesterday's unexpected encounter was part of her carefully constructed ruse designed to disarm me. Being heir to the Edenvale throne means living with an invisible target on my back. The thing is, though, that I already know there's a sniper in my midst, and she sleeps in my father's bed.

My smile is as cool as her name. If Kate Winter hopes to lie in wait to stab a proverbial blade between my shoulder blades, then I hope she has the patience of a saint, because I aim to give her no such satisfaction.

X returns, and her expression morphs from confused to horrified.

"Fishing poles?" She gasps. "Is this your idea of a joke?"

"Fishing is one of my many hobbies," I lie smoothly. "And it seems an apt metaphor given our current situation." I take a pole from X and hand it to her.

She grips it without complaint, understanding the gesture isn't a request, but an order from her prince.

I grab the dossier from her other hand, not bothering to look inside, and hand it to X. "We won't be needing that just yet," I say, then turn my attention to Kate. "After all, there are many fish in the sea, correct? Or should I say...river?" I pivot and stride toward the old Roman bridge. "And how can I be sure of your skills in catching one for me until I see you in action?"

Kate

It's a stone bridge, I remind myself. A sturdy, stone, won't-crumble-beneath-your-feet bridge. There's no need to tell him I can't swim.

Though the swelling in my ankle has gone down, the lingering ache still slows my gait. He walks a few paces ahead of me, not bothering to wait. Decidedly different behavior from yesterday when he carried me after my fall—saw to it that I made it home safe. Hell, he even sent me breakfast this morning. I knew I was stupid to think it meant anything more than feeding the help, that Nikolai Lorentz was anything other than what the media portrayed.

I catch up to him at the center of the bridge where nothing else waits for us other than two buckets, one of which must be bait, the other to hold what we catch. I swallow hard when I note the height—or lack thereof—of the stone wall separating us from the river below. Nikolai perches casually on the low barrier, reaches into the bucket and pulls from it what looks like a small slice of sausage.

"What is that?" I ask, wrinkling my nose.

He shrugs. "X prepared it. Says it's his best recipe for catching trout. You met Beatrice in the kitchen yesterday, yes? Our head cook? Tonight's royal meal depends on what you catch for us today."

His tone is more cold than playful, yet I decide to humor him.

"Well, then," I say. "I've got plenty of suggestions for takeout when this goes *royally* amiss."

He buries the hint of a smile, but I see it nonetheless and take it as a sign that I do have the power to break through whatever wall he's hiding behind today. I remind myself that my livelihood depends on it and let out a breath before reaching into the small bucket and pinching a slimy piece of bait between my thumb and forefinger.

I shudder at the feel of the foreign substance against my skin but do not dare complain. I watch as Nikolai fixes his bait to his hook and mimic his movements precisely. Maybe this won't be so difficult after all.

He raises a brow. "You've fished before?"

I shake my head. "I'm a quick learner," I say, realizing I've nowhere to wipe my hand and opt for the ledge of the wall I don't dare sit on myself.

He casts his line into the river, and again I follow suit.

Piece of disgusting, slimy cake.

He finally grins. "May the best fisherman win," he says. "Not that it's a competition."

I smile. "You're on, Your Highness."

We fish in silence, him still sitting on the wall while I stand a pace behind it. In less than three minutes his line tugs at the pole, and Nikolai whoops in response, standing to reel in his catch.

I can't help but marvel at the ease of his movements, the flex of his biceps as he rotates the crank on the pole. And it's this lapse in my attention, this gravitational pull he seems to have on me despite every bit of logic saying it shouldn't, that causes the tug on my own line to catch me off guard.

My body yanks forward, and I stumble. It all happens in the space of a few seconds. I don't even have time to scream before I knock into the wall and pitch right over it.

The water is cool, yet it burns my lungs and throat as I panic and breathe it in. I cough, but it only makes me take in more water. In this strange, suspended panic, I note the clarity of the river, that I can see through the surface and to the bridge to where it looks like something is falling toward me as I sink.

As quickly as I was yanked off the bridge, strong hands wrap around me and tug me toward the surface. When I break through, I cough up the water I couldn't release seconds ago and gasp for air. Instinct has me thrashing in his arms, but he doesn't let go.

"Kate!" he yells, his voice hoarse. "Christ, Kate! Stop fighting me and put your feet down. It's only five feet deep!"

His words register, and I cease movement, letting my legs straighten below me while I still cling to his arm with my own.

My shoes touch the riverbed, and I stand on my tiptoes, my five-foot-five height keeping my face well above water.

We reach the bank, and I collapse onto my ass, humiliation seeping in as I cough up another mouthful of water.

Nikolai falls onto his back, panting, his T-shirt and jeans plastered to his muscled frame.

"Christ almighty," he says, catching his breath. "Why didn't you tell me you couldn't swim?"

I try to convince myself that this job is worth it, that no matter what other disasters befall throughout the length of this contract, it will be worth it in the end. Because if I fail, it's Maddie and Gran who will pay the price.

"You're my prince," I say dully. "You said we were fishing, so I obeyed."

He bolts upright, brows pulled together. "Is that really—?" he sputters. "You think I would endanger—?" But he trails off again. He reaches for my face, resting a palm gingerly against my cheek, and it's almost as hard to breathe as being underwater. "Are you okay?"

Genuine concern laces his words. This is a Nikolai I've never seen in the pages of a magazine. This man did not exist in the maze yesterday.

"Yes," I whisper, the heat in his palm making me forget I'm soaking wet.

"I told you," he says, his gray eyes darkening to black, "I will not marry."

I nod slowly. "And your father will keep the throne from you if you do not. Nikolai, when you stormed out yesterday, he mentioned Damien…"

A soft, guttural sound emanates from his throat.

"If you want the throne," I continue, "then finding a bride is the only way." And the only way to keep my grandmother getting the best care that our country has to offer. But I don't tell him that. As much as I am drawn to him, I can't get close to another man. Especially not another bad boy who doesn't seem to care about anything other than his next thrill. My heart can only take so much.

He lets out a long breath. "So it is," he says, and my heart tightens at the sound of defeat in those words. "Then we find someone who will play by my rules, who knows she is queen in name only, and that I will govern Edenvale as I see fit when it's my time."

I nod again. "If that is your choice."

He lets out a bitter laugh. "Choice," he says through gritted teeth. "Wouldn't that be a luxury?"

I shiver, the cold setting in and seeping into my bones. He drops his hand to my neck, my collarbone and then to breast, my nipple hard against the cold, wet fabric of my blouse, a trail of heat in its wake.

"What if I choose to touch you like this?" he asks, his lips a fraction of an inch from mine. "Would you choose that, too?" He glances toward the river. Then his gaze burns into mine again. "Because you *have* a choice, Kate. You should have told me that you live along a river yet have never bathed in it."

I feel the prick of tears and try to will them away.

"Maddie and I—my sister—lost our parents when they drove off the road that winds along the mountain's edge. The river was deeper than five feet where their car plunged in." A single tear escapes, and he brushes it away, the gesture too sweet. Too intimate. "I was too young to remember them but not too young to develop a fear of the water. The funny thing is, Maddie says I was an excellent swimmer from a young age, but it's like my mind has blocked that part out. So…here we are."

He runs a hand through his soaked black hair. "You should have told me," he says again, and I startle to see the intensity in his eyes. "*You* have choice, Kate. With me. Nothing is an order. Do you understand that?"

"Yes," I whisper.

He places a hand behind my neck and lowers me to the ground, my body a willing accomplice.

"You will find me a royal bride," he says, hovering over me. A bead of water drips off his skin and splashes near the corner of my lips. It takes all my self-restraint not to lick it.

"Yes."

"I will not love her," he adds.

"I know," I whisper.

"I *cannot* love anyone." His voice is a low vibration, one I feel in his chest against mine.

"I know," I say again, cursing the beating of my heart that seems to speed up the nearer he gets. We might be from two different worlds, but we have that much in common. I *can* love, but I won't. Not when I've known so much loss.

"But I want you," he says, his breath warm against my lips.

"I want you, too," I admit.

He flicks out his tongue, running it along my bottom lip, and I grind my pelvis into his.

"Do you *choose* this, Kate? Do you choose what I'm offering?"

My body has already complied. All that's left is my voice.

"I do, Your Highness."

"Call me Nikolai."

I let out a trembling breath. "I do—Nikolai." His name tastes as delicious as his hungry mouth.

He kisses me, long and slow and deep until my toes curl and my core is on fire.

"Say my name again," he growls, his erection firm against my aching clit.

"Nikolai," I whisper, and his tongue plunges into my mouth again.

I may have the freedom of choice, but I also have the wisdom to know this is a foolish one to make. I'll have to add a note in my planner to regret this sometime tomorrow.

CHAPTER SIX

Nikolai

I BURY MY fingers into her thick coil of auburn hair and pull, not hard, but enough to deepen our kiss. Kate's tears place me on unfamiliar ground. The story of her loss threatens to undo my expertly built defenses. I don't know how to tell her this, but in some ways, I understand her pain. Once upon a time, many years ago, a car accident changed my own world. She and I share an unexpected connection, both forever marked by a tragedy that changed the course of our lives.

Damn it. My pulse thunders in my ears. I don't want to be curious about Kate, to be interested in her as a *person* and not another notch in my belt. I channel my frustration into tangling my tongue with hers, demanding more, demanding everything, and she moans into my open mouth, offering herself freely.

My chest tightens like a vise. I gasp a mumbled curse. This kiss is taking over, filling my veins, replacing the blood. *Slow the fuck down. Keep it physical.* Remember that's my MO—making women cry out my name and wanting nothing more in return than my own physical release. I reach down to circle my thumbs over her peaked nipples, hard nubs against her wet, silky top. She moans again. Louder.

I tear away, one foot in heaven and one in hell. It's time to get a grip, to calm myself and focus. After all, getting a woman off is what I do best. My uncertainty fades as I take charge, increasing the pressure. Not much, just enough to turn that moan into a gasp, followed by a soft squeak. I break our kiss and nip her plump lower lip, tasting the hint of cherry lip balm. Then I continue my leisurely torment down her jaw to the sensitive place on her neck, relishing her rapid pulse and trace of perfume that wasn't washed away in the river. Chanel No. 5.

She is killing me in the best of ways.

"God, you smell brilliant." I give her a soft bite. Not enough to leave a mark, but enough that I've got her full attention. She moans. All women enjoy a little domination in the bedroom. "Like that?"

"Mmmmm," she purrs.

I bite again, wiping away the sting with the flat of my tongue. "I asked you a question. I am your prince. I expect you to respond." My tone is authoritative, yet teasing. I want control, but I also want her to know she's safe—safe from the river, from the painful memories she buries. I'll erase it all with a swipe of my tongue. Another nip of teeth.

She presses her hips against me. "Feels so good," she murmurs. "If X wasn't close, I'd be on my knees filling my mouth with your cock."

So my prim-and-proper ice queen likes to talk dirty. Blood sings through my veins, a pounding chorus, as I thicken in an instant. "Good thing X took a drive."

She stills. "He's gone?"

"I heard him leave while we walked toward the bridge."

She frowns. "He knew you'd seduce me?"

I shrug. "Maybe he wanted a croissant?"

She slides away. My body aches at the gap, and for a moment, I falter. Who is really in control here?

"You seduce many women, don't you, Sire?"

No point lying. *"Nikolai,"* I remind her, my voice firm. I want my name dripping off her lips in a torrent of pleasure. "Call me by my name." Might as well admit there is more to wanting to hear her say it than a simple, sexual ego booster. Every cell in my being craves her closer, wanting to rub against her and smooth away my ragged edges, to see if she is the one who possesses whatever the fuck I need to be made whole.

Good God. I'm pussy drunk.

"You seduce many women, don't you, *Nikolai*?" She bites her bottom lip, and my cock strains against my jeans, but I force my voice to remain steady.

"Yes," I say simply. I'm Mr. Right Now. Not Mr. Right.

"A bad boy."

I crook my lips into an arrogant smile, the mask that she expects her future ruler to wear. I have a rake-hell reputation to uphold. "That seems to be the general opinion."

She shakes her head. "Why not give in?" she murmurs, more to herself than me. "Live dangerously for once in my life." She refocuses her gaze on me. "We can do whatever it is we are about to do and still remain professional."

My brows rise. "Your mouth sheathing my cock is

professional?" I swallow hard, and she notices, grinning, no doubt, at the effect she has on me.

She narrows her gaze as if to size me up. "Yes. Once
I know what you like, I'll be that much better posi-
tioned to find it for you."

"I can think of many positions I'd like to find you
in."

She purses her lips. Then a flicker of uncertainty
passes over her face. "Tell me how you like it."

"Pardon?" My own eyes widen. "How I like getting
sucked off?" She wants a lesson?

"Yes, tell me in thorough detail. If you teach me
well, perhaps you'll get a handsome reward." She palms
me over the wet denim of my jeans. "I'm a quick study
and also quite good at taking direction."

I decide right then and there that despite what she's
been hired to do—and how much I detest the thought
of finding a bride—I love being around this most surprising woman.

Wait...love? The word doesn't belong anywhere in
my vocabulary. This is no good. My heart better go
sit its ass in a corner. I clear my throat. "You want to
know how to suck a dick? Very well. First, the woman
in question needs to crave it. I want her to approach
my cock like it's a chocolate fucking fudge sundae and
she hasn't eaten in a week."

Her lids flutter. "Go on."

Shit. I can talk dirty in five languages, but I've never
given an explicit lesson in the art of performing a blow
job. And believe me—it is a goddamn art. "I need some
encouragement," I tell her, my voice growing hoarse
with need. "A little inspiration."

She arches a brow. "And how can I do that?"

I pretend to think it over. "Are you wearing a matching set?"

She nods with a shy smile. "I do own the bra to match my pink lace panties," she says, then licks her lips. "But I didn't wear it today."

My throat thickens. And if it's at all possible, my cock grows even harder, and I want nothing more than for her to rip my jeans from my legs. *Mission accomplished, Miss Winter.* The image of what lies beneath her drenched clothing will inspire me for days and nights to come.

What can I say? Kate Winter is my fucking muse. Literally.

"Shall we continue with the lesson?" I ask.

"Please," she says. "It's been a while since—well, I think I mentioned yesterday that it's been a while. Period."

I bury the surge of jealousy at the thought of her mouth on any other man and decide to give her exactly what she's asking for—so that she may give it to me.

"Outside of a sixty-nine, I prefer to stand," I tell her, already imagining her kneeling before me. "Gives me good control and a great view. Hands are important. Use them. I love a mouth on me, but touch is a must. Stroke my shaft. Massage my sac. Gradually increase the tempo. That's when I'll need some tongue on the tip, swirling and sucking like I'm your favorite flavor of Popsicle."

She rolls her eyes. "Cool it with the food references. You're making me hungry." Her tone is teasing, but I can tell from the way her pupils dilate that she is soaked.

"Never use your teeth. Simply lick and swirl until you're ready."

"For what?" She sounds drugged.

"To take me as deep as you can go. A gentleman never crams his cock into a lady's throat. He waits, patiently, but what he wants is for her to suck him down. And all the while, hold eye contact. Trust me on this. A guy loves it when you take it all and let him see how much you love every inch."

She runs a hand over her hair. "And for the end?"

"Swallow," I say bluntly and shrug. She asked, so I might as well give her the truth.

"I've never done that," she whispers. "I've always been too intimidated."

"Well, you don't have to," I tell her quickly. Again it comes, that inexplicable need to make her feel safe. "It's just…you asked what's the best. That is the best, Pet. Nothing like it."

She stays quiet for a long moment. Long enough that I start to wonder if I've pissed her off—or even worse, scared her from even wanting to try.

"Stand, Sire," she finally says, and I obey without question. She stands too, stepping forward to close the narrow distance between us, all the while keeping her gaze locked to my face.

Then she sinks to her goddamn knees.

"I've never mixed business and pleasure." She reaches to undo my fly. "But this is my most important job yet, so perhaps I should ensure you get the royal treatment."

My hands fist in her hair, and I know from the determined look in her eyes that I'm about to be destroyed.

Kate

His jeans are snug against his hard, muscled thighs, and despite them being soaked in the river, it only takes me seconds to pull them to his ankles.

My nipples peak against my cold, wet top, and I wonder if he knows how close to the edge I already am. Just from his words. It was never like this with Jean-Luc, and as soon as the thought enters my mind, I'm awash in a wave of guilt. How dare I compare what I'm about to do to a man I met yesterday to a man I'd planned to be with for the rest of my life?

And yet it's the truth.

I loved my fiancé, but I can't recall wanting him with this sort of hunger. I'd always felt performing oral sex to be more of an obligation than anything else. And he had always finished so quickly that I never knew what he really liked.

But I *want* to taste Nikolai so badly that my pulse throbs between my legs.

I start by placing a soft kiss on his inner thigh, then shift my heavy gaze to his.

"More," he says, and my core tightens at the command.

I kiss his other thigh, this time a little higher up, and I have to grab his backside to steady myself.

He lets out a groan.

"Hands," he says, his voice tight, and I do believe I've made it difficult for my prince to speak.

I look up at him and grin, releasing his ass with my right hand so I can cup his balls. Then, without warning, I swirl my tongue over his tip, the precum salty on my taste buds. We both moan.

His hands tug at my hair, and I move my own to join my mouth, taking him deeper as he slides slick through my palm.

"Fuck," he hisses. *"Yes*, Pet. More. Goddamn, I need more."

My clit swells at the sound of his need, a delicious, aching pulse between my thighs, and I can't hold back a whimper as he sinks deeper into my mouth, as I let the taste of him fill me.

Deeper and faster, my hand grips his throbbing shaft, and I feel his thighs begin to shake. I hold his gaze as I bury him to the hilt, and for the brief moment when he begins to teeter over the edge, I see past the facade to a brokenness that draws me further into his orbit.

He shudders and growls. I swallow his release, an intimate connection I never knew was possible. I back away, ready to force my trembling limbs to stand, but he collapses to his knees in front of me.

His hands cup my cheeks, and he stares into my eyes. Without a word he kisses me so hard and deep I can barely catch my breath. He lowers me to the ground, wordless still, his lips never leaving mine. His hand slides beneath my blouse, and I buck against him as he pinches my sensitive peak.

We are animals, communicating with nothing other than our shared savage need, and I *need* this. I *need* his hands on me, in me—I need Nikolai Lorentz everywhere. And because we speak the same language, he knows, and I find him wrenching my pants from my hips, down to my knees, all the while his tongue tangling with mine.

Finally, when two fingers plunge inside me, immediately hitting the right spot, I call out his name in an overwhelming torrent of sensation.

"Nikolai!"

And then I finally close my eyes and see nothing but stars.

I'm nothing short of a mess when we make our way to the road and find X waiting outside the Rolls. Nikolai, despite his dip in the river as well, looks nothing short of spectacular. Or maybe that's all I can see after what he's done to me.

What *has* he done? I feel satiated yet hungry. Re-made but ruined.

X opens the door as we approach, not once letting his impassive gaze give away that he knew Nikolai had planned to seduce me. But when I look inside the car and see my scones and fruit replaced by a small platter of croissants, I can't help but burst into a fit of laughter.

Nikolai's brows pull together, and it takes every ounce of control for me to simply motion toward the open door and say, *"Look."*

He does, and as soon as he sees the pastries, he's laughing too, and I am surprised the way my heart surges to hear such a sound—a genuine emotion from Prince Nikolai, and I get to bear witness.

X clears his throat and raises a brow.

"Your Highness. Miss Winter—I thought you might have worked up an appetite."

I decide not to deny it because damn—I *am* starving. So I reach inside the car and grab a chocolate croissant, tearing off a piece and shoving it into a surprised Nikolai's mouth before tearing into the rest of it with my teeth.

"You're right," I say, mouth full, hair tangled and probably full of sand, clothes still wet and plastered to my body. "I'm famished."

X nods. "Your Highness, I take it there are supplies to collect from the bridge?"

Nikolai swallows his bite of croissant. "Yes, thank you. One fishing pole, the bucket of bait and Miss Winter's dossier. You can throw the trout I caught back into the river."

"Yes, Your Highness," he says, not questioning why we are short one fishing pole.

Once X is out of earshot, I point at Nikolai with my half-eaten croissant.

"Hey, I thought you said tonight's royal meal depended on what I caught on our little fishing expedition."

He shrugs and gives me a sheepish grin, another expression I don't expect, and it disarms me completely.

"I despise seafood, actually," he says. "But I was hoping to enjoy putting you through the wringer."

I open my mouth at an attempt to unleash my fury on him, but he silences me with a kiss, and I'm caught so off guard that I simply melt into it.

"How about a truce?" he says against me, and I squeak out my answer, the momentary fury dissolving into dust.

"Okay," I whisper.

"Okay," he says.

"But this *cannot* happen again, Your Highness. We have— I mean *I* have a job to do."

He nods. "Of course. Never again, Miss Winter. You have my word."

I sigh. I know he's soon to be my king, that my job

is to find him a queen, but right now I don't believe his word for one tiny second. And that impish grin on his face tells me that neither does he.

CHAPTER SEVEN

Nikolai

"My, my, isn't His Highness in quite the chipper mood?" My wicked stepmother, Queen Adele, sizes me up from across the mahogany table. Even when it is just she, my father and I in residence at the palace, she insists on using the formal dining room that can accommodate up to fifty guests. Overhead hang three large crystal chandeliers, and lining the wood-paneled room are suits of armor interspersed with the images of frowning black-haired men, my ancestors, the kings of old.

From the looks of their faces, dark and brooding is a family tradition.

"As a matter of fact, *Majesty*, I *am* in good spirits." I wipe my lips with a linen napkin before crooking them into a smile as fake as her own. The queen's gaze narrows as she tries to see through my mocking mask.

Lots of luck, love.

My father cuts his roast, oblivious as always to the private war that I carry out with the hag. "I understand you met with the matchmaker this afternoon.

She seems a competent woman." He spears the beef with his fork. "Most enthusiastic."

"Quite." An image of Kate Winter flashes, one where she is on her knees, hair wet and wild, sucking my cock like some sort of mythic water goddess, and I suppress a satisfied grin.

"Rather common, if you ask me." My stepmother gives an audible sniff.

"Good thing no one did," I growl, my mouth flat-lining.

She ignores the warning in my voice. "I do admit to having second thoughts on Miss Winter. After all, how can a commoner have the proper breeding necessary to discern fine taste? Edenvale *is* the second-oldest throne in all of Europe. The realm expects certain standards."

White-hot fury builds behind my eyes. This snobby shrew isn't fit to lick the sole of one of Kate's heels, let alone dare to speak her name with such disdain. True, my favorite matchmaker isn't blue-blooded, but she has more natural grace and elegance in one of her little fingers than Adele has in her entire Botoxed body.

Who knows what prompted Father to marry her? I barely remember my real mother, but from all accounts, it was a love match. Queen Cordelia remains well-beloved by her people to this day, no thanks to Adele, who likes to pretend she never existed.

I study the fine lines that groove my stepmother's frown. She has always been a sourpuss, but since her only daughter Victoria's death she's turned downright wicked.

The last vestiges of my good mood vanish. When Adele married my lonely father the only bright spot to the arrangement came in the form of her beautiful and vivacious nineteen-year-old daughter, my stepsister and first love. I was a foolish twenty-three-year-old boy determined to make Victoria my queen. While Father disapproved of the relationship, Adele could not hide her ambition. She might not have liked the idea of me making love to her daughter but persuaded Father to allow the engagement to proceed because it would make Victoria a queen. She even argued that it would strengthen Edenvale's royal ties to have not one but two generations of our royal bloodlines matched. Their aristocratic family has always been one of the wealthiest and most influential in our kingdom. But they've always had a reputation for being ambitious.

Too ambitious for my liking.

Over the years, whenever I indulged in a whiskey too many and allowed my thoughts to wander, it had seemed conceivable that Adele might have masterminded the whole affair, put her only child in my path, advising her on how to best seduce her way into a lonely prince's heart. If Victoria had survived the accident, perhaps she'd have grown to be as calculating and bloodless as the woman sneering down her aristocratic nose at me. The question, though, will never be answered. My youngest brother, Damien, saw to that, ending her life with his usual recklessness, earning his banishment and my everlasting hatred.

"Well, do try to retain your good mood for Saturday evening," Adele says, dipping her spoon into the lobster bisque.

"What's Saturday?" I crook my finger, signaling the butler to bring me more wine. I am tempted to grab the whole damn bottle, get too drunk to dream. I don't want nightmares of Victoria disturbing my sleep tonight.

"Didn't Miss Winter tell you?" My stepmother's lifeless smile is stiff and doesn't reach her cruel eyes. "She has arranged your first date."

Kate

"No," I say, when I open my apartment door to find X standing there. "Absolutely not." Before I can close the door in the man's face—and I would feel horrid doing so, but this crosses the line—Maddie sidles up behind me.

"Who's your friend?" she asks, though I'm sure she can tell by his immaculate suit that he is not one who dwells on Market Street. I glance at my own attire, a freaking Fall Out Boy T-shirt and skinny jeans. I look like an American teenager.

"Maddie, this is X. He works for the royal family."

My sister pulls the door the rest of the way open. She, of course, is in a perfectly beautiful sundress, because *she* has a date. Which is fine because I was very much looking forward to Netflix, and ice cream, and not thinking about the strange events that have transpired this week. But no, the prince has to butt into my plans, my thoughts, my whatever—simply because he can.

X offers my sister a slight bow, and she backhands me on the shoulder.

"*This* is the prince's driver—the guy who picked you up the other morning? You didn't say he was a silver fox!" she whisper-shouts, but the man is standing right in front of us.

X's brows rise, the slightest hint of his amusement.

"Miss Kate," he says. "His Highness says it is part of your professional obligation."

I roll my eyes.

"What obligation?" Maddie asks.

"Tell him *no*," I say to X, ignoring my sister.

He pulls a phone from the inside pocket of his suit jacket and glances at the screen.

"Miss Kate declines your invitation," he says, and my stomach drops. The prince has been listening to our entire interaction.

When I hear his voice, my body tingles in response, and I silently curse Nikolai Lorentz.

"Kate," he says. X points the phone toward me and my sister. "I'm going to be late for the date that *you* set up if you don't get down here in the next three minutes."

I huff out a breath and try to ignore my sister's wide eyes and mouth open in a surprised O.

"Your Highness—" I start, but he clears his throat, interrupting me.

"Nikolai," he corrects me, and I repress an exasperated scream.

"*Nikolai.* I think you are confused. This is *your* date. I set it up, but believe me when I say that both you and the Countess of Wynberry will be most put out by me joining you for dinner."

Maddie backhands me again, this time harder, but she still says nothing.

Nikolai's raucous laugh rings out from the phone in X's hand.

"You won't actually *join* us," he says. "You'll be in the car with X. Beatrice has prepared a veritable feast for you to dine on while you wait for my cue."

My fists clench at my sides, and I don't bother stifling my groan.

"You have some nerve," I say.

"I need a wingman."

"No."

"I need to be called to an urgent meeting, an out if things go south. Because if the countess doesn't go for my proposed arrangement, I promise things will go— southerly," he adds, his words laced with amusement.

"No," I maintain.

There is silence for a few long beats, and I hold my breath until he speaks again.

"If I behave *badly*," he says, slowly drawing out each word, "which I've been known to do, I could scare off a potential prospect. But if someone is there to give me a more respectable exit should I need one, well, then, we all win. Don't we?" He pauses to let his words sink in before he puts the final nail in the coffin that is my fate for this evening. "You don't want to chance me *not* making it to the altar. Do you, Kate?"

White-hot fury pulses through me. Does he know the king and queen will refuse my fee—no matter how tireless I work—if he does not marry? How dare he use such leverage against me? But because I cannot let Maddie carry our grandmother's financial burden alone, I say what I need to say to shut him up before he reveals too much.

"Fine," I relent through gritted teeth. "I'll be right down."

X sighs and ends the call as I spin into my apartment. My sister follows.

"You're accompanying *the prince* on his date. Oh. My. God, Katie. Why didn't I get this freaking job?"

I grab my bag from the foot of my bed and sling it over my shoulder. "Right now, Maddie, I wish you had."

I don't even bother looking in the mirror. I storm toward the door where X waits patiently.

"You're not even going to change?" my sister asks from behind me, and I shake my head, answering her over my shoulder.

"You heard the man. He's going to be late, and I sure as hell don't want to keep the prince and the countess waiting."

"Have fun!" she calls, unable to mask her own giddy excitement.

Not likely.

"You too!" I offer, sincerely hoping her night goes better than mine is about to.

"If you succeed then we will have clients pouring in."

I fake a smile. "Yay!" My enthusiasm rings false, but my sister doesn't notice. She is too good to speak the language of sarcasm.

Maddie deserves all the happiness and success. She built our little company from nothing, and when my life fell apart two years ago, she gave me a place to stay and a job to dive into so I wouldn't waste away in my grief.

This is why, despite his behavior, I head downstairs and out to the Rolls-Royce parked at the curb. I'm doing this for *her*. For years I've depended on my sister, and now more than ever she's depending on me. I won't mess this up. She deserves for her business to succeed, and that means lessening the burden of paying for Gran's mounting medical bills. Every day it seems a new one arrives. She tries to hide her worry from me, but I see the dark shadows under her eyes.

X opens the door for me, and I slide into the seat opposite Nikolai. I cross my arms and try to level him with my glare.

"You look—" he starts, but I cut him off.

"Don't, Nikolai. Just don't."

He raises his brows. "I was only going to say *beautiful*. You look beautiful, Kate."

Don't, I tell myself in silence. *Don't let his words have any effect on you.*

"X," he says when the man appears behind the wheel. When did he even get there? I swear he just shut my door. "Do you know what a Fall Out Boy is?"

I snort. "Tell me you're joking." Then I see it again, the ghost of a smile on X's face. We're silently sharing a joke at Nikolai's expense.

Nikolai shrugs. "I'm assuming it is some sort of popular rock band. The music I listen to does not come with a T-shirt."

I laugh again and thrust my phone through the open partition to X.

"It's my top playlist," I say. "Can you put it on?"

The man nods, and seconds later my phone is hooked up to the car's speaker system.

The tightness in my throat loosens as "Immortals" wafts from the speakers, and I'm shocked once again when Nikolai's shoulders relax, and he cocks his head to the side and smiles.

"It's no Amadeus," he says, "but I quite like it. I suppose I'm learning I like a lot of new things these days, Miss Winter."

A chill runs along my spine, but I will it away.

Do not for one second think that he is charming.
You know full well that Prince Charming he is not.

But as the anger subsides I see him clearly, his jet-black hair slicked back from his face, charcoal gray suit to match his eyes, and a royal blue tie for a pop of color. He looks so—*princely*. And gorgeous. And when his smile reaches his eyes, I have to push away the surge of emotion that rises to the surface because I've suddenly lost my grip on the anger.

I shake my head and remind myself why I'm here—to make sure this date goes smoothly. To ensure that Prince Nikolai Lorentz is one step closer to marriage—and becoming my king.

"Thank you for coming," he says softly, and I force a smile.

"Of course," I say, regaining my composure. "Nikolai?"

"Kate?"

"Have you read the entire contract between Happy Endings and your family?"

He laughs. "What's to read? You were hired to find me a wife. You're finding me a wife. I'm not interested in the fine print."

I let out a breath. So he doesn't know the consequences for me—for my family—if I fail. My anger ebbs completely as I realize Nikolai's behavior this evening is simply him being Nikolai.

"Well, then," I say. "Tell me what I need to do to make this date a success."

At this, X pulls away from the curb, and we set off for Nikolai to meet his first potential match.

CHAPTER EIGHT

Nikolai

I MUST GIVE credit to Kate's skillful matchmaker profiling. The Countess of Wynberry fits my usual physical type to a T. Platinum blond hair, come-hither bedroom eyes and ripe breasts that she proudly displays in a low-cut black silk dress offset by a necklace of glittering rubies. Hell, I don't know a guy who wouldn't describe the countess as his type. She could be a sister to that American actress Scarlett Johansson.

We meet in my private room at La Coeur, a three-star Michelin restaurant set in an eighteenth-century manor. The view of the Alps through the wide windows is unparalleled, and the gorgeous woman lounging across the table looks like she'd rather take a bite out of me than the raspberry-and-chocolate confection on her gilded plate. Yet I feel nothing but faint boredom.

Dinner went well enough. The filet was perfectly cooked and the cabernet an excellent vintage. She chattered on and on about her family's approval of our union and then of all the filthy things she planned on doing to me once we left the restaurant. I should have been hard just from her depraved words. Instead all I want is to be in my Rolls beside an auburn-haired woman in jeans who makes me feel like something I haven't felt in years.

Myself.

"You don't talk much, do you?" the countess purrs, taking her time licking her spoon clean. Her bare foot caresses my shin under the table, and I curse my unresponsive cock. The countess could douse the fire inside, the embers burning for a woman who arranged this date, but she'd fail at snuffing out the blaze.

"I do if I have something to say," I answer blandly. Her dessert does look delightful. Too bad I ordered nothing to eat for our final course, just a scotch neat. She needs to stop playing seductive games and enjoy it. But then, I've made my decision, which means she won't have time to finish, so perhaps it is for the best.

She looks curious, missing the warning in my voice. "And do you have something to say?" she asks.

Enough time wasting. "I do." I crumple my napkin on my lap and get down to business.

I say what I must in short, clipped sentences. Her eyes grow slowly wider until the whites are perfectly visible around her nearly violet irises.

Within a minute she throws a glass of champagne in my face. She has more restraint than I credited her with. I expected her to last thirty seconds max.

"You are as they say." She gathers her fur stole and rises in a huff. "A twisted monster of a man."

I blow her a kiss, and she squeals with outrage before storming for the exit.

Kate arrives in less than a minute, exactly as I expected, disheveled from sprinting to my table.

"What happened?" She gasps for air. "I thought I was here to help you to *not* cause a scene!"

I wave my hand in the air. "Trust me when I tell you that what just transpired was *not* a scene. You have read the tabloids, yes? I'm capable of so much worse. Don't you think?"

She must have run the whole way and not bothered using the restaurant's elevator. Her cheeks are flushed to a rosy red, and her chest rises and falls, heaving her breasts against the thin cotton of her T-shirt. The sight captivates me more than all the silk in Spain.

"The countess left in a rage," Kate continues. "She threatened to kick X in the parking lot if he didn't get out of her way. I'm pretty sure that counts as a scene."

I chuckle at the thought of anyone accosting X. I've seen him pin a paparazzo against a wall with one hand while dismantling his camera with the other, the action as simple as flossing his teeth. I have no idea who the hell X was before he came to the palace, but one thing is for certain: he's survived worse than the Countess of Wynberry.

"We weren't a good fit," I say lazily, sitting back in my chair. "And because no photographers are allowed inside—"

Kate lets out a breathy laugh. "Oh, there were photographers outside. I can attest to that." She shakes her head. "I have to admit my surprise... On paper you and the countess were a *perfect* match." Her tone is disappointed even as the relief is plain on her face. Strange how I am in tune to the subtleties of her emotion when we've barely been acquainted for the span of a week.

"She had a hard time hearing key truths," I say.

"Truths?" She crosses her arms and lowers her chin.

A wayward auburn strand falls across her forehead. "Nikolai, what on earth did you tell that poor woman?"

Poor woman? Perhaps that was the perfect term for her. While the countess was rich in material wealth, she lacked human qualities like warmth, companionship and kindness, characteristics I can usually dismiss. But for some reason, tonight I cannot.

"Take a seat, Kate." I gesture to the chair opposite me. "I'll tell you exactly what I said *if* you allow me to feed you bite by bite."

Kate

I cross my arms. "I'm quite stuffed," I say, not daring to glance at the dessert on the table. Even out of the corner of my eye it looks heavenly. "Beatrice fed me well with yet another back-seat feast, and I will under no circumstances let you be seen in public feeding a palace employee." Never mind that we are in a private room.

He reaches over and takes a bite of the rich-looking confection, his tongue slowly stroking the spoon, and I swallow. Then I narrow my eyes at him.

"Oh, fine," he says. "Have it your way. I simply told her what we both already know, that whoever my bride will be, it will be nothing more than a business arrangement. There will be no physical obligation other than her providing me with my own heir—however long that may take. And I will be free to satisfy my needs with whomever suits my fancy. Oh, I may have also mentioned that she will under no circumstances have any say in how I rule this country."

I throw my hand over my mouth, but it doesn't stifle

my gasp. "Nikolai!" I shout, not caring that his private room is not exactly soundproof.

He shrugs. "Oh, come now," he says. "I explained she'd want for nothing—that she'd be free to dally with anyone she pleased, so long as she was discreet."

I clench my teeth. "I know you don't plan on taking your marriage seriously, but no woman deserves to be spoken to like that. You could have been more—more *delicate*, and you know it. But you care nothing for anyone other than yourself, so you did it the Nikolai way. I should have known this job would be impossible. That *you'd* be impossible. You didn't want me here to help. Did you? You wanted me here so I'd have a front-row seat to the Nikolai Lorentz show."

My cheeks burn as I bunch my fists at my sides. One minute I'm taken aback by how beautiful he is—how he can level me with his gaze. The next I am reminded all too clearly of who he is. He is my prince—and soon, my king. He has the power to behave as he does, and I am nothing more than a subject.

I push back my chair. "I'll call for a taxi," I say, trying to keep my voice even. Anger will get me nowhere. It won't get the countess the respect he should have paid her, and it certainly won't earn any for me. He owes me nothing.

He lets me get as far as the door before he speaks.

"Kate," he says, all pretense gone from his voice. "Wait." Then I hear him let out a breath. *"Please."*

I turn to face him, and he's standing, too. But I don't dare move any closer. Even across the table he feels too near now. Because if there's one word I never expected to hear directed at me from him, it is that last one. *Please.*

"What?" I ask, the fight draining from me as he holds me with his steely, intent stare.

He runs a hand through his perfectly styled hair, loosening it so he looks more as he did on the bridge— or after he'd dived into the river to save me.

"You're right," he says. "About most of it, but you're missing one important detail."

I cross my arms and raise my brows but say nothing.

"Of course I didn't need any help," he says, palms resting on his chair. "I care nothing for my reputation. I leave that to my father, my stepmother, to all those paid to give a fuck. I suppose I'll have to clean up my act a bit once I'm king, though."

He flashes that irresistible grin, but I don't let myself fall prey to it, not this time.

"I know you don't care what others think of you," I say. "But you put my reputation on the line tonight, too, Your Highness." He winces, and the sight is something so wholly unexpected, my heart tugs involuntarily. "You may have nothing to lose, but I do. My *sister* does. Her business supports our family. We have responsibilities. This whole marriage thing that you see as a joke is how we put a roof over our heads. It's how we—"

He steps around from the chair and nearer to where I stand, the movement stealing the words from my mouth. I suck in a breath as he takes a step closer and then hold it as he rests a palm on my cheek.

"I'm an ass," he says, and I nod. "One royal prick," he adds, and I don't disagree. "Perhaps I could have been more civil to the countess. But where I truly fucked up was that I wasn't thinking of how this would affect *you*."

I clear my throat. "Wh-what important detail?" I stammer. His brows pull together. "Before, you said I was missing one important detail." I can smell the sweet scotch in the warmth of his breath. I bite my lip to keep from reacting.

He rests his forehead against mine, the gesture far too intimate, and my breath hitches.

"I asked you to come tonight, Kate, because in the span of six days, I seem to have gone from wanting nothing to do with you and what you've been hired for to not wanting you out of my sight."

He braces a palm against the door behind me, and I take a step back so I'm flush against it.

"Nikolai," I whisper. "We can't." My insistence is different than the other day at the bridge. I could take his teasing—could even pretend that we might continue our encounters and leave it at just sex. But now? What he is suggesting now is beyond possibility.

"What if there was a way?" he asks, his lips dangerously close to my own. "What if I could make you truly mine?"

My throat tightens at the thought. "But I was hired to—"

"I know," he says. "And I will continue to see the women with whom you match me. I will even be civil. But I make you this promise. I'll marry none of them."

As much as the idea of him touching another woman, let alone marrying one, already hurts in a way it should not be able to, I need him to do it because my family depends on it. *Irony, you're a cruel bitch.*

"When do you need to be married by?" I'm playing with him because I already know. Maybe if I smile the pain will ebb. One can always hope.

"My twenty-ninth birthday."

"Which is…" As if the heir's birthday isn't a national holiday.

His lids narrow as he tries to figure out what game I'm playing. "Ninety days from now."

I close my eyes and take in a long breath. Then I press my palm to his chest. "I'll make you a wager."

He laughs softly. "Go on."

"I'll see you married by your birthday," I say, my fingers already itching to grab at his tie.

He surprises me with a soft kiss before he answers. "I look forward to disappointing you."

I grip his tie and pull him as close as he can get. "And what's more, I promise you will be happy with the woman." After all, I know exactly what His Highness likes. Who better to find him not just a queen but happiness as well?

I swallow the pang of regret, the one that has me wishing for what cannot be. I do not want for him a life of misery, but I cannot let my own family fall into ruin. I will succeed. For both of us.

"You'd have to be one hell of a matchmaker, sweetheart," he says.

"Trust me." I fight to keep the tremor from my voice. "I'm the best."

CHAPTER NINE

Nikolai

It isn't until nightfall that I realize that Kate never laid out the terms for our wager. I sit at my baby grand piano, my fingers flying over the keys, weaving a complex, sensual sound. Don't believe classical music can be sexy? Listen to Wagner's *Tristan and Isolde* before dismissing me. Harmony and dissonance. Brutal discord only to be thwarted by soaring passion. Music pours through me as I toy over the many ways I can extract payment from the lovely Miss Winter. Such an interesting paradox that her hair holds hints of flame even as her name promises coldness. She is both fire and ice.

I picture her lips sheathing my cock, taking me down to the root on the banks of the river. There had been a promise in her eyes, a promise that she'd be mine, if I reached out and made a claim. And so I will—at least physically, but the pleasure of the flesh is as much as I can offer. And pleasure I shall give her.

If only she had royal blood...then...perhaps she could make me overcome my vow.

"Who is the lucky lady?" a deep voice says behind me, and I strike a wrong key.

Damn it.

I turn around, ready to bite the head off whoever dares to venture into my inner sanctum, and find my brother Benedict regarding me with an arched brow.

We look so much alike save for the eye color and the goodness that emanates from him just as something wicked brews inside me. I am darkness and shadow. He is golden light. I hear the whispers. I know those that think him a bastard—Benedict himself included. I pay those words little heed. Full brother or half, he is my best and only true friend.

"Welcome home, Bastard," I say. It's a joke between us. We wear our vulnerabilities like armor. It's the way we survive as the lords of the land, all eyes on us.

"That was Wagner, no?" He cocks his head. "You only play that when a woman has you tied in knots."

His memory is keen.

"Dear brother, don't you know? If there is a woman and knots to consider, I am the one doing the tying. Apologies if I offend your holy sensibilities." I eye Benedict's simple clerical garb. My brother is a seminarian, a year away from taking his holy vows and entering the priesthood, much to the eternal pride of our father. When the idea of his virginity is not causing me nightmares, the idea is amusing in the extreme. Benedict is one of the most sought-after men in Europe, and he chooses to marry the church.

I hope God keeps his bed warm.

"What good is the spare to my heir if he is celibate?" Father likes to roar after a drink too many. While he speaks in jest, there is a glimmer of truth.

Benedict takes it all in stride. All he wants to do is please the king—to prove himself worthy of his lineage no matter what the rumors say. When Benedict declared his life belonged to the church, Father was the first to commend him.

How many times have I wondered if a woman could ever tempt him from his path? But he assures me that his destiny is fixed. That the pleasures of the flesh pale in comparison to the rhapsody of the soul.

I have to say, burying my face between Kate's thighs takes me to the gates of heaven. Imagine what burying my cock in her would do.

"I came to bid you good-night and let you know that I'll be taking up residence in the south tower for the foreseeable future."

Benedict long ago laid a claim to the ancient keep on the far northern border of the palace grounds. He prefers its austere environment for prayer and solitude.

"What happened to the Vatican?" I ask him. "Thought you were off to Italy for good."

He laughs softly. "The Vatican City is its own country," he reminds me. "As you should have learned when studying geography."

"Ah, didn't Mrs. Everdeen tutor us on that subject?"

He inclines his head.

"Well, I was too busy studying Mrs. Everdeen in other ways." I smirk. "She had this trick she could do with her tongue that—"

"You are incorrigible, brother," Benedict says. "And yet it is bloody good to see you."

I cross the room and enfold him in a warm bear hug, slapping him on the back. "You too."

"I hear you are to be wed. Is it your bride who has you playing Wagner?"

I shake my head. "The matchmaker." The words are out before I can stop them.

Damn Benedict. His kind eyes make a sinner like me yearn to confess.

He nods thoughtfully. "Sounds like a dilemma."

A flicker of hope lights in me. "You're the scholar in the family."

"Between you and Damien, it wasn't hard to do."

Benedict is also the only one not afraid to acknowledge our younger brother's existence in my presence.

I ignore it this once. "If there's a loophole to the Royal Marriage Decree, a way for me to make my own damned decisions without losing the kingdom, I need you to find it. I am determined not to wed. You know this."

He appears thoughtful. "Such an action will displease our father."

"Yes." And by extension, that will displease my too-good brother. "And Adele," I add. My lips curl into a grin as I know this point will make Benedict my ally.

He brightens at that thought. He and Adele have no love lost. That witch is the only person to ever make my saintly brother lose his temper.

"Very well," he says, a muscle twitching in his jaw at the mention of our stepmother. "I'll look into it."

"You are truly a glorious human. You'll be canonized yet."

He grins at that, but his normally clear green eyes remain dark.

"What's the reason you are back, brother?" My light

tone doesn't mask the hint of probing seriousness. "You haven't said."

His lips tilt in a smile that only I ever get to see, one that isn't all that angelic. "It appears the Lord's wish is to help prevent your sacrament of marriage." He clicks his heels and disappears out the door.

It takes me a moment to realize that he hasn't answered my question at all.

Kate

What the hell was I thinking, placing a wager against someone as strong-willed as Nikolai Lorentz? If there's anything a man like him thrives on, it's the game, and I've just upped the stakes of the one he'd been playing long before I came into the picture—thinking I will get him to play by his own kingdom's rules.

I pace the length of the conference room, the same one where I first met the prince two weeks ago, and the same one where, afterward, the king and queen called me to a private meeting without their son.

Shit.

The door opens, and I freeze midpace only to find Beatrice and another member of the kitchen staff with a silver cart laden with pastries, finger sandwiches and a sterling teapot. Each woman offers me a quick nod as they begin depositing the refreshments on the table.

"Will there be more than the king and queen joining me in here?" I ask nervously, and Beatrice shakes her head.

"No, Miss. These are Queen Adele's favorites. The king orders Her Majesty's most requested finger foods when she's in—" The other woman flashes Beatrice a look, but Beatrice waves her off and crosses over to where I stand. "It's really not my place, Miss, but I think you should know today is the anniversary of Miss Victoria's passing."

I swallow, and my eyes widen. I am to meet with the queen on the anniversary of her daughter's death—the daughter who was betrothed to Nikolai.

The date hadn't registered with me. Of course I knew of Nikolai and Victoria's relationship. The entire continent did. But it had been years since the car crash. It wasn't the type of thing that made news anymore. Nikolai saw to that—*sees* to that every moment he finds himself in the spotlight. Unless the king has any diplomatic dealings that call for broadcast coverage, Nikolai is the family's media darling.

Why, then? Why have my sovereign rulers called me here today, of all days, for a mere check-in on my list of possible brides for the prince?

A throat clears, and Beatrice and I both look up to see the other kitchen servant nodding toward the entrance of the room where Queen Adele stands in the double doorway, flanked by two guards.

She wears an exquisite black dress, long sleeved with a square neckline, the bodice hugging her womanly curves. I can see why King Nikolai was taken with her so soon after Queen Cordelia's death. The woman is a sight to behold, her golden hair in perfect pin curls framing her face, a ruby-studded tiara atop her head. She is elegance and grace, but there is ice in her emerald stare, and I can't help the shiver that makes my hair stand on end.

"That will be all, everyone," she says, and the two

guards, along with Beatrice and her assistant, leave the room, pulling the doors closed behind them.

I bow my head and curtsy as she walks toward the head of the table, and I wait for her to sit. I'm not sure where to seat myself, so like an idiot I ask, "May I pour you some tea, Your Highness?"

"Do sit, Miss Winter," she says, her voice laced with amusement when I expect to hear the remnants of grief. Surely she's come from visiting her daughter's grave. Or perhaps she will be on her way after our meeting.

Our meeting. It's only when I take a seat at the opposite end of the table that I realize the king is nowhere to be seen.

"Will His Highness, King Nikolai, be joining us soon?"

She laughs softly. "The king is away on matters of state business," she says. "It's just the two of us, I'm afraid." She places her palms flat atop the mahogany table. "Don't worry, Miss Winter. I shall be brief."

I nod as the breath catches in my throat. Something about the queen—being in her presence alone—has all my senses on high alert.

"I know how important this job is to you," she drawls, her tone like an animal toying with its prey.

"Yes, Your Highness. It is," I say.

She steeples her fingers before her and grins, the smile not quite reaching her deep green eyes.

"And that you and your sister stand to gain a great deal of fortune if all goes according to plan."

Double my fee *is* a generous offer. "Yes, Your Highness."

She leans forward, and though the length of the table separates us, I flinch at the movement.

"And if you do *not* succeed, your business will be in ruins."

I gasp. To lose the fee promised me would be a devastating blow, but Madeline and I would still be able to come back from it. We'd still—

"Stop trying to rationalize whatever it is you think you're going to say to me, Miss Winter. I'm not in the habit of ruining others—as long as we are on the same side. And I think we both want the same thing, don't we? To see my stepson walk down that aisle and the throne stay in the...immediate family?"

"Yes, of course," I say. I hold her gaze, determined not to flinch again.

Her posture relaxes, but only slightly. "Good. Then all you have to do is keep up business as usual. Seek out all the lovely, appropriate, *deserving* women. Build up Nikolai's image like his father hopes you will."

My teeth grind together in my mouth. Something is off here, but so far she's not asking anything other than what I'm already doing.

"May I ask you a question, Your Highness?"

Her brows rise. She is considering my boldness, no doubt, but then she nods her head.

"Forgive me if I'm being untoward. But are you trying to see to it that I fail or succeed? Because I can't for the life of me figure out why you called this meeting."

This time her eyes light up as her lips curl. "You *will* succeed, Miss Winter."

"How do you know?" I add, deciding to go for broke in my impropriety of speaking my uncensored thoughts in front of my leader.

"Because," she says, standing from her chair. I stand as well. "*I'm* going to find the woman most deserving of a life with my stepson, and we will present her to him when the time is right."

"But my list—"

She shakes her head, closing her eyes as she does. When she looks at me again, I see something so cold in that stare that I shudder. "My match won't be on any such list, but when I've found the one, you'll know. All you have to do is convince Nikolai she's the one, as well." She narrows her eyes at me. "That boy trusts you already. I've seen the way he looks at you. All you have to do is maintain that trust—keep him occupied while I set everything in place. You'll get your doubled fee and maybe even an additional bonus. I get what's rightfully mine and Nikolai gets what he deserves."

"Rightfully yours?" I ask, unable to stop the question even though I know I should not speak out of turn with her.

But the queen doesn't bother to respond.

She plucks a cucumber finger sandwich from the top of a tiered plate and pops it in her mouth, smirking as she devours it. Then she saunters out of the room, not waiting for me to say another word.

Double my fee. A bonus. Or a ruined business if we're not playing for the same side.

Maybe Nikolai does play his games, but he no longer makes the rules.

I wonder now if he ever did.

CHAPTER TEN

Nikolai

I WAKE TO harsh late-morning light striking my sleep-dry eyes. Crimson silk sheets tangle at the base of my four-poster ebony wood bed.

I'm buck naked.

No big surprise there. I never sleep with clothes. This rock-hard morning wood isn't unusual, either. The only strange part to this scenario is that I'm not reaching for my phone. No mad urge within me craves a speed dial to any of my usual female liaisons. There is no shortage of nubile women eager to serve as my royal lover for the morning. But I have made a great effort to ensure that my personal speed dial is discreet and only includes women interested in keeping things horizontal. Commitment types get deleted.

But today is different.

I close my fist around my shaft, circling the tip with my thumb. It's already slick with a bead of pre-cum. Must have been having one hell of a dream. A flash of it glimmers in the back of my mind, Kate's auburn waves spilling over her shoulders, her milk-white breasts rising and falling with her gasps as I bury myself inside her.

I bite on the inside of my cheek. Even the fleeting memory of the tantalizing dream is enough to make me moan out loud.

As if sensing my need, my phone buzzes. But it's no perfectly timed offer from a casual lover. I stare at the name on the screen as all the extra blood in my brain rushes off to pool in my cock.

Kate Winter: Morning, Sunshine. Ready when you are!

I give myself a few more hard pumps, remember how Kate's tangy sweet pussy tastes, and my hips buck off the mattress. "Oh, I'm ready, Pet."

The phone buzzes again. I'm with X.

X. The mention of my personal guard almost throws me off my game. He is like another brother. We even shared women in depraved threesomes, once upon a time when I was younger and even wilder than I am now. But that doesn't mean I want to share Kate. A muffled growl rises in my throat. I don't want to share her with anyone else in the world.

Strange. Normally I'm a love-the-one-you're-with kind of guy. After I'm with a woman, it's out of sight and out of mind. But with Kate it's different. There is an unfamiliar pull inside me to know more than her body, but I have no idea what to do with this—feeling.

The notion leaves me unsettled. I remove my hand from my dick and text her back.

Nikolai: Still in bed.

Kate: What!?!?!?!? Are you coming?

Nikolai: Not without you…

Kate: Excuse me?

Nikolai: A real man never comes first, Pet.

Kate: OMG

Nikolai: ;)

Kate: You did not just winky face me.

Nikolai: What are you going to do about it? ;)

Kate: I've just eaten my weight in Beatrice's white chocolate scones waiting for you or I'd march up there and drag you down myself.

Nikolai: I have a king-size bed. Perfect place to sleep off a food coma.

Kate: I have an heiress to a screw company waiting at the airfield.

Nikolai: ?

Kate: Your next date is Regina Bjorn. Her father is Vlad Bjorn, owner of Big Bjorn Screws, one of Edenvale's largest exports. We are meeting her at the royal hangar at noon. You're flying her in your personal helicopter.

Nikolai: I'm so screwed.

Kate: ;)

I swing my bare feet to the cold floorboards, my grin from our banter quickly morphing into a sneer. I know Vlad Bjorn. He is titled with a minor barony and is a large man with blotchy skin. He calls himself the Big Screw, but in my opinion he resembles a stick of bologna. I know he has twelve daughters but can't picture any of their faces at the moment. That fact alone leaves me numb. I don't want to fly this Regina anywhere, not when I could be flirting with my feisty matchmaker, who can't learn that my brother Benedict is looking for a loophole to break the Royal Marriage Decree. Until then I must play my hand well by making nice with the dates Kate sets up for me. Not to raise so much as an eyebrow of suspicion.

Lucky for me, I am a most excellent actor.

Kate

My eyes widen as I stare out the window toward the airfield. I knew the palace grounds were substantial, but each time I see something new, it still catches me off guard. My world is so small compared to his.

"Impressed?" Nikolai whispers in my ear, his warm breath sending tingles all the way to my toes.

I nod. "This *car* would barely fit in my apartment. The concept of an airfield is a lot to take in."

"You never listed your terms," he says softly, his voice like velvet, and I know exactly what he means.

I turn to face him, and he barely backs away. My heart races as my eyes meet his.

"Well," I say, keeping my voice steady. "I know money—or anything of material value—is of no consequence to you, which I guess bodes well for me since I have nothing of material value to offer."

"Kate—" he starts, but I shake my head. I don't want him to apologize for his wealth, nor will I apologize for my lack thereof.

"Nikolai. We come from different worlds, and that's okay." His eyes darken at this, and I wish I had the time to ask him what he's thinking, but the car slows, and I know we're approaching the hangar. "And because I'm going to win," I tease, trying to lighten whatever heaviness has taken over his features, "I'll keep it simple."

"Simple?" he asks, raising a brow, painting on that prince of a smile, one I know he is readying for the heiress.

"A favor," I say simply. "If I win—which I plan to do—you do me one favor. If *you* win—which is highly unlikely—then you get to ask a favor of me."

"Are there limits?" he asks. "To what we can ask?"

I shake my head. "No limits on my end. If you are not wed by your birthday, you can ask me for anything you want. Do *you* have any limits?"

"None," he says quickly, his voice suddenly rough. "Ask me anything right now, Kate. Tell me what you'd want from me."

But the car halts, effectively ending our conversation.

"Time for you to fly to Zurich," I say, forcing a smile.

"It's just lunch," he says. "You and X should—"

"I am *not* tagging along on any more dates. If you want to bring X, fine. I'm only here to make sure you aren't late and to remind you to be a gentleman."

He winks at me. "Darling, have you forgotten who I am? I'll do nothing of the sort."

"Nikolai..."

He kisses me on the cheek, effectively shutting me up.

"No worries, Pet. I'll be on my best behavior."

I groan. "That's what I'm afraid of."

Nikolai's door opens, and X stands ready to usher him out of the vehicle and to the hangar.

"I'll be back by dusk," he says on his way out. "And I'd like you here when I arrive."

He doesn't wait for me to protest but assumes I'll obey his every whim.

What if I had plans tonight? I want to ask—even though I don't. As much as it warms me from within that he wants to see me this evening, I can't help but feel like the afterthought that I am and can only ever be.

X joins me in the car, and I watch as Nikolai strides toward Regina Bjorn, a regal, platinum-haired beauty who stands in front of a BMW with windows tinted so black I'm not even sure you can see through them at all.

Zurich was my idea, to have him take her to her mother's homeland, a place I learned she hadn't visited since childhood but had always missed. He'd score points in the thoughtfulness department before they'd even left the helipad, which I glance at in front of the hangar. Nikolai holds her hand as she climbs into the helicopter. Her azure scarf billows in the breeze, floating against Nikolai's crisp white oxford—a picture-perfect couple.

My breath hitches.

I knock on the window in front of me, and X lowers the glass.

"Shall I take you home, Miss?"

The confines of the apartment that doubles as the home office for Happy Endings do not comfort me, especially if it means the third degree from Maddie. If I don't want to think about Nikolai on his date, I certainly don't want to *talk* about Nikolai on his date. So I decide to do something I rarely do—something for *me*.

"X," I say, my mood brightening. "We're going to the cinema."

"Miss, there is a private theater in the palace—"

"Absolutely not. No palace. No royal treatment. Just you and me and that car-chase-with-tons-of-explosions action film that premiered last weekend."

"But, Miss—the palace theater has that film or any other—"

I lean through the open partition. "No. Royal. Treatment."

He clears his throat and starts the engine. "As you wish, Miss Kate."

He backs away from the hangar as the propeller blades begin to spin. And when the helicopter lifts off the ground, I allow myself a few seconds to marvel that the strong hands controlling that beast of a machine have touched me in ways no other man has.

Then I sink into my seat.

"Thank you, X." I hand him my phone. "And maybe my Fall Out Boy playlist while we drive. Crank up the volume so I can't hear myself think." Drowning out my

thoughts seems preferable to drowning *in* them. I reach
for a bottle and glass from the minibar across from my
seat. "And—and I'm going to have some of the prince's
cognac even though it's before noon."

"As you wish, Miss."

Seconds later the music blares.

X's eyes remain on the road as we approach the palace gates, but I swear I see a devilish grin take over
his stoic countenance. Yet as quickly as it appears, it
is gone.

I pour myself a drink and then take a long sip. After
a few seconds I tip my head back and laugh.

"No royal treatment," I say with a snort. "I'm in a
Rolls-Royce with a private driver and a bottle of cognac.
And I have to return at dusk to meet up with the prince."
I snort again, but damn it, the laughter feels good.

No royal treatment indeed.

CHAPTER ELEVEN

Nikolai

THE MOUNTAINS EN ROUTE to Zurich are as sculpted as Regina Bjorn's high cheekbones, and yet the experience feels empty. Emotionally at least. Regina has done a damn good job of filling the airspace, making it clear that she knows a thing or two about screwing.

"It is, after all, the family business," she chatters into the microphone with a giggle. We both wear helmets with headsets.

"Nothing about that innuendo is remotely appealing," I mutter and grip the cyclical stick that gives me control of the aircraft.

My surly comment flies straight over her head. As does anything else I say for the rest of our time together—unless it's an attempt to feign interest in her father's company.

Screws.

By the time we return to the Royal Airfield, landing with the setting sun, I'm convinced that I've endured paper cuts more enjoyable than Regina Bjorn.

Kate paired me with this woman through her matchmaking service? What does this say about me and the persona that I have cultivated with such care? Has the shallow, arrogant, vain Prince Nikolai finally become Mr. Hyde, overriding the respectable Dr. Jekyll? Is the facade I've so long shown the world really the man I want to be? I've nearly convinced myself the mask is real. But when Kate looks at me, it's as if she can see someone else. The person that I might have been if life hadn't kicked me in the teeth with a stiletto then had my youngest brother drive it off a cliff.

The thought unsettles me, and I push it from my mind as we exit the helicopter. I escort Regina back to her driver. She still talks of—what else?—screws. In the last hours I've endured lectures about cap screws, machine screws, tag screws, setscrews and—I shit you not—self-tapping screws.

A few weeks ago I would have been able to turn the day's conversation into an activity that required no words at all—unless it was Regina purring my bloody name. Now I hope those self-tapping wonders are Regina's favorite because I don't know anyone who could stay awake through one of her conversations long enough to get it up.

When I wish her good-night, I am not entirely convinced she notices.

The Rolls is parked in my usual spot. As I stride closer, eager to put distance between myself and the Heiress of Screws, I am surprised to hear music playing. It's an American classic, "Sweet Caroline." More to the point, the two people in the car are belting out the words—and X can apparently more than hold a tune. This man… I shake my head. He's full of surprises. Not only is he an expert tattoo artist responsible for all the tribal ink on my body, he's also a ninth-degree Grand

Master black belt in Tae Kwon Do, and my on-again, off-again threesome wingman. Now he can harmonize better than Neil Diamond?

Sneaky fuck.

Who the hell *is* X? So often I've asked myself this, but it is to no avail. X has been my bodyguard since I reached maturity. I barely remember life without him. And yet I know nothing of him when he's not in my immediate presence, while he knows all there is of me.

I guess he can add charismatic crooner to his résumé.

I open the door, and he and Kate both clam up, staring at me.

"I didn't know you were back yet," she says, clutching what appears to be a giant bucket of popcorn.

"You didn't hear the chopper blades?" I inquire, lifting an eyebrow. I fly a Eurocopter Mercedes-Benz, the most pimped-out helicopter in the world, able to get high and fly fast. For one not to notice such an aircraft, well—what the hell could pry her interest from awaiting my arrival?

I scowl to myself. Perhaps I *am* the pompous persona I've cultivated.

"Sorry. It's the Golden Oldies Hour on Royal Radio. Our favorite," she said.

"Our?" My eyebrow goes higher.

"Sir." X is matter-of-fact and unapologetic as he starts the engine. "Would you like to take a seat?"

"I'd like to know who you are and what you've done with my bodyguard," I shoot back as an unexpected wave of possessive jealousy rolls between my clenched shoulder blades.

"Was your outing with Miss Bjorn satisfactory?"

Kate asks, popping a piece of popcorn into her mouth with wide eyes.

"No. And where the hell did you get that?"

She pops another kernel into her mouth. "We went to the movies. They were showing the live action *Beauty and the Beast* at the discount theater and X had never seen it."

"An oversight he must be happy to have rectified," I snap.

Kate shrugs. "I was prepared to share with him my love of all things fast and furious, but the Disney classic won out. Apparently X is impressed by royalty. Me, not so much." She bites back a grin, and all I can do is bite back my own rage.

X's eyes shoot to mine in the rearview, and I glare out the window. Stupid to be jealous of my bodyguard. But the entire day I suffered with Regina *Bore*, he was with Kate. Enjoying himself. Enjoying *her*. I've shared women with X in the past, but this is one time that I don't want to. I don't want to share her with *anyone*. The idea of her with another man, even if I'm there as well, makes my stomach turn over as my fingers curl into themselves.

I stare back at her as white-hot possession shoots through me.

Mine.

The word is powerful and pure. My blood pounds with the echo. *Mine. Mine. Mine.*

This is the truth. And it's time she knows it.

"X, to the palace."

"I need to get back to the office," Kate protests. "If your second date was another bust, then I need to review lucky number three and figure out a game plan."

"I want to use the back entrance," I continue as if she hasn't spoken. A vague headache pounds in my temples. I want to drop the pretense for two seconds. I will never marry. I'm not made for the institution, and Kate is wasting her time.

That shouldn't be my problem, but I don't want her to leave. At least not yet. I want to enjoy the pleasure of her company a little while longer.

"Sir?" X asks, and I know what he really means. "Are you sure about this?"

No woman has ever accompanied me back to the palace, to my private quarters. Not until now.

I nod my head. "And make it fast."

Kate

"Where are the king and queen this fine evening?" Nikolai asks X as we pull to a side of the palace I haven't seen before.

"In Paris until tomorrow for the queen's—" he coughs "—rejuvenation treatments."

Nikolai grins at me. "Do you need to let your sister know you won't be coming home this evening?"

I cross my arms and narrow my eyes. "I don't have a curfew, *Your Highness*. But I do have work to do if we are going to make the perfect match, so I really should—"

"Stay," he says, the grin fading, those gray eyes dark with something too intense to deny. Because I feel it too—have felt it since he left for Zurich despite the comfort of X's presence and our day of distraction.

I won't ask him why. Or what this means. I won't let logic override the ache in my belly. I can do this and not endanger the business. I force myself to believe it because the word is already forming on my lips.

"Okay," I answer.

Nikolai's door opens, and X stands at the ready. The man is the epitome of stealth. I didn't even realize he'd exited the vehicle.

Nikolai turns toward the opened door. "Miss Winter will be staying this evening, X."

X nods. "A moment alone with your guest, please, Your Highness. I shall then escort her to your quarters."

Nikolai laughs quietly. "A bit bold today, aren't we, X?"

X nods but doesn't crack a smile. "When it's called for, Your Highness."

Nikolai faces me again, gently grabbing my palm and bringing it to his lips. "See you soon," he whispers, and then he's gone.

Moments later my door opens, and X offers a hand to help me out of the vehicle.

"Let me guess," I say, as he leads me through a small door and into a dimly lit stairwell. "You want to finish our Neil Diamond duet."

No smile or any indication that only several minutes ago the two of us could have turned every chair on *The Voice*. Instead he simply holds out an arm for me to grab as we begin to ascend the steep stairs.

"The prince," he says, "is very private."

I snort.

"What the world sees in the media is what he wants them to see, Miss. And while I am not at liberty to divulge his past, I can say as much as this. Save for Victoria, the queen's late daughter, no woman has ascended these stairs. Not before—and not since."

There is no time for me to respond as we reach a small landing at the top, a tall oak door—partially ajar— before us. He nods for me to enter, and I do. I hear the door click shut behind me and turn to see X standing with his back to it, the faintest hint of a smile on his face. Then, as quick as a blink, he steps to his left, where soft curtains billow beside an open window—and he leaps through it like we aren't on the third story of a palace.

I yelp.

Nikolai rounds the corner, a bottle of Moët in one hand, two crystal flutes in the other.

"Let me guess," he says. "X took the window."

My hand covers my mouth as I nod, imagining my silver-fox companion splattered against the brick pavers below.

Nikolai laughs and shakes his head. "He often prefers scaling the brick to the stairs. Sometimes I wonder who X was before he came here, but I've learned to not question the man's abilities and thank the stars we're on the same team." He moves closer, his feet bare beneath the dark denim of his jeans and his now-wrinkled oxford unbuttoned. "He's fine. I promise."

"I'm not looking out that window," I say, goose bumps raising the hairs on my bare arms. The sundress was perfect for the day, but now that the sun has set, I shiver in the open-air breeze. "I'll take your word for it."

Nikolai nods toward the direction from which he came.

"You're cold," he says. "Come. Let me warm you up."

I follow him around a corner and note a small galley kitchen with dark marble counters, a sturdy wooden table—round—with four high-backed chairs beyond the breakfast bar. I don't have time to take in the modest living space other than a baby grand piano against a floor-to-ceiling window beyond a leather couch. The next thing I know, I'm walking through another door and into my prince's bedroom.

He sets the bottle and flutes on a night table and turns back to me. His strong hands run the length of my arms, warming me from the outside in. I let out a breath.

"Why am I here, Nikolai?" I can't hold out any longer, my curiosity getting the best of me. My chest tightens at the thought of his answer.

He kisses my neck, and my head falls back. A small sigh escapes my lips.

"I don't want to share you," he says against my skin, his lips making their way up to my jaw, then my cheek.

"But I haven't been—" I stop myself before telling him that I have not been with any other man since he first laid his hands on me—that for two years before that there hadn't been anyone, either.

His mouth finds mine, and my lips part, inviting him in—craving the taste of him like I didn't know I could.

"I don't like that X got to see a side of you today that I've never seen."

The sentence comes out almost as a growl, and my breath hitches.

"It was a movie," I whisper. "Not a helicopter ride to another country for an intimate lunch." I don't regret the words—or laying my jealousy out before him, not when he is blatantly doing the same. I want him, more than I've been able to admit, and right now I'm ready to give him all of me in return.

He backs toward the four-poster ebony bed, red silk sheets pulled back to reveal the space where his body last lay. I grin against his lips.

"What?" he asks, feeling the change in my expression.

"No one comes in to clean? To make your bed, Your Highness?"

He sits on the edge of the mattress, pulling me close so I straddle his lap.

"No one enters other than those closest to me," he says, his eyes dark with need. "And I want you closest, Kate. Tonight I want you more than anyone else."

I answer him by unbuttoning his shirt the rest of the way and sliding it down his arms. He closes his eyes and breathes in deep as my fingers trace the lines of ink on his shoulder, as they circle the tattoo of a compass that rests above his heart.

"It's beautiful," I say, a slight tremor in my voice. "*You're* beautiful, Nikolai."

He opens his eyes and wordlessly lifts my dress over my head so I'm left in nothing but my white lace panties.

"You're exquisite," he says. Then he takes one of my breasts into his mouth. I arch against him. "Finer than any woman who bears a title." His tongue swirls around the peaked nipple of my other breast, and I gasp. "Open your eyes and look at me," he says, and I obey. "No matter what I do, you *see* me."

I cradle his beautiful face in my palms. "I do."

"And you *want* me," he says.

I nod.

"*Only* me."

I nod again, taking each of his palms in mine and pressing them to my breasts. "Only you."

"I'll win our wager," he says with a grin. "I will not walk down the aisle."

"You *will* marry," I remind him and swallow back the reality of what that means.

"Not tonight, though." He falls onto the bed, pulling me over him.

"No," I say. "Not tonight."

CHAPTER TWELVE

Nikolai

FOR HOW LONG has my soul been trapped in a vise of loneliness? For years I have passed through countless nights as restless and insatiable as a vampire. Instead of feeding on mortal blood, I devoured what distraction and comfort was available in the form of sexual release—the more depraved, the better.

I take and take and take with a relentlessness matched only by my many lovers who are eager to use me in turn for the proximity to limitless power and wealth.

But tonight? All I want is to give. Kate Winter shall experience nothing less than absolute, exquisite pleasure.

She is stretched above me. My hands roam the soft swells of her body, the dip of her small hourglass waist. Her loose curls tumble over my face, forming a curtain of fire. Again I am stricken by the paradox—Miss Winter, whose hair burns brighter than the sun, whose undeniable beauty burns my heart.

"Are you sure this is a good idea?" she whispers, and as her lips part, I catch a glimpse of her teeth, her tongue. Oh yes, that pink clever tongue, which swirled around my cock until I nearly forgot my birthright. And that was in a hurried riverside tryst. Tonight the hours spread before us, and I intend to put each one to good use.

"A good idea?" I give my head a single shake. "No, Pet. It is *the best* idea."

A hitched breath escapes her perfect lips as I cradle her face in my hands. My mouth finds hers, and our groans collide. I place my palms over her breasts again, and her heart careens against my hand. My thumbs circle her nipples before teasing them with a flick. She gasps in appreciation, sinking her nails deep into my biceps. I coax her forward.

Her breasts tumble into my face. I suck one gorgeous nipple into my mouth, then the other, feasting as if she is languorously feeding me champagne grapes. One small press of my teeth against her sensitive flesh, a teasing nip, and she arches, her pelvis rocking over mine.

I snarl from need mixed with acute frustration. Tonight I had planned to take it slow, savor every last inch of her body, worship her skin with my tongue. But animal that I am, lust consumes me, and a deeper feeling, an urgency comes over me to be *home*, as if her body is the safe harbor in the violent black storms that have rocked my world for so long. Turbulence has since become my new normal.

"My turn," she whispers, moving over me, traveling the ridges of my flexed abdomen with her pouty lips. Then lower, until she reaches my belt buckle, unhooks it, and with a pop of a button and the grind of a zipper, my entire proud length is revealed.

She takes me by the root and swirls her tongue around the end. "Mmm," she murmurs. "So good."

I prop myself up on my elbows, letting her take me for a few wet strokes. "Fuck," I groan.

"You like that?" she asks in a flirtatious tone, before adding, "Your *Majesty*."

Naughty minx.

"Hell yes, I do, Pet. And you know what I'll like even more?"

She arches a brow in question.

"Tasting you at the same time." I reach down and with one deft motion flip her around so her pert ass is in my face. "Spread those thighs for me," I growl, slapping one cheek, and she moans loudly, parting her legs wide enough to let me see the sheen on her intimate flesh.

"You are so goddamn gorgeous," I groan and slam her against me. With both hands I give her hips a firm rock, encouraging her to fuck my face, seizing her pleasure as she works over my cock, taking every inch that I have to give.

I flex my tongue over her swollen folds, making sure her clit is well-attended, and when her breath grows ragged, I press harder, giving her hearty licks, writing my name on the soaked, silky skin, marking my territory with flourishing circles and swirls, an intimate calligraphy.

As she falls apart, I plunge my tongue deep inside her tight hole, ravage her with smooth strokes, hinting at the delirious euphoria that is about to be hers.

"Nikolai, oh, God, Nikolai," she gasps, rising up to sit on the back of her heels, spastically jerking then grinding over me in a slow, rhythmic, figure-eight fashion. "Oh God! Your Highness!" She gasps. "Fuck me harder!"

I could come this very second. Sweet, sweet Kate has one filthy mouth. And I obediently comply. The bed shakes. Someday I'll control this entire land, but right now this firecracker is begging to be ruled. Before I take what is mine, I plunge my full face against her pretty pink pussy.

Tonight is about the journey, not the destination. I lick and fuck her until she is dripping and on all fours, hot, tangy juices running down my chin. Two orgasms. Three. Fuck. I lose count of how many I give her. But now my cock is so thick, the need so intense, that I need to join her in this mad passion. Ours won't be a mindless rutting. A fleeting pleasure.

I freeze as the realization takes hold.

There is a chance that entering her will tear asunder the very fiber of my soul.

Kate

I don't know what's come over me. I've never spoken like that. Not to Jean-Luc. Not to anyone. But this man—this man turns me into my basest self. A woman in need who will do or say whatever it takes to satisfy the hunger. And I hunger for Nikolai Lorentz, with everything that I am.

He lifts his head from between my legs, his dark hair a beautiful mess of ravaged waves.

"I need you," he says, his voice strained. "Fuck, Kate. I *need* you."

There is something akin to pain in his words, an

ache I'm not expecting, and the animal in me gives way to something else entirely so that all I can do is nod.

He stands from the bed, and despite how hard I already came, I need him inside me. I need *him*, too.

How can any good come of feeling like this?

He disappears into the bathroom, and I hear the faucet run. When I can't stand not knowing how long it will be until he returns, I follow him in there, not caring that he knows how desperate I am to keep him close.

His head dips toward the sink as he splashes water over his face again and again. I rest my palm on his back, and he shudders.

"Nikolai," I say softly.

He straightens enough for me to see his beautiful face in the mirror.

"I thought I could clear my thoughts. I thought I could cleanse away this feeling." He shakes his head. "But I *need* you," he says again to our mirrored selves. "I'm not supposed to *need* anyone."

I see the foil packet on the counter, grab it and tear it open.

"Look at me," I say. "No hiding behind a reflection."

The muscles in his shoulders and back flex as he moves, and when our eyes meet, I don't hesitate as I roll the condom down his thick, pulsing length. He sucks in a breath.

"Remember," I say. "No matter what sort of mask you give to the rest of the world, I *see* you."

As much as this man turns me to animal, I shift to caring lover just as quickly. Because who truly takes care of a prince?

He dips his head toward mine but stops before our lips barely touch.

"You're the only one who can."

And then he kisses me with such tenderness I have to fight back tears. I rise to the tips of my toes, and he nudges my entrance. I grab the base of his shaft and urge him inside. His palms clamp against my thighs, and he lifts me. I wrap my legs around his waist as he sinks into my warmth, and a growl tears from his lips.

Nikolai walks with me like this until we're back at the bed. He lays me on the elegant silk sheet and climbs over me, burying himself as deep as he can go.

I cry out. Not from pleasure or pain but from the undeniable ache of both. The walls around my heart crumble to dust, letting my prince inside.

My prince.

"My prince." This time I say it aloud as he slides out and back in again—slow, controlled, deliberate. He claims me with each thrust. Heart and soul.

My prince.

My prince.

My prince.

His lips are strong and fierce against mine. Each sweep of his tongue is a taste sweeter than any confection and richer than the royal coffers.

The pressure builds, and his momentum picks up. My muscles throb around him as I feel him pulse inside me. So close. He's so close. But I know he's waiting for me.

And because he knows me like no man ever has, he knows what is necessary to send me over the edge.

He slips a hand between us, at the place where two

bodies become one, and presses his thumb to my swollen clit. I cry out again and again and again.

He roars as he tumbles off the cliff with me, shuddering above me until we both shatter into a million pieces.

He opens his eyes and traps me in his steel gaze.

"My *queen*," he says before collapsing beside me.

I stroke his sweat-dampened hair as he peppers my shoulder with kisses so achingly tender. I try not to take his words to heart. What we have is only temporary, until I find him a proper bride.

He combs my hair out of my face, his fingers grazing my chin. "My beautiful, fiery winter queen," he says, and I start to wish those words to be truth, though I know full well they never could be. Even if he would marry, a commoner like me could never be in the running.

"Your *what*?" I hear, and gasp when I see a figure looming over us where we lie.

Nikolai turns his head lazily toward our intruder.

"Fucking hell, Christian," he says with nothing more than mild annoyance in his words. "How in God's name did you get in here? And do you ever bloody knock?"

The man steps closer, a muscle ticking in his chiseled jaw. "Give me one good reason why I shouldn't lay you out like the bloody prick you are. Royal law or not, you know I can fucking do it, and it looks like your shadow isn't here to stop me."

I suck in a breath. Am I about to witness a royal brawl? Or worse—get caught in the middle of it? Regardless of my ability to do so or not, a fierce urge to protect my prince takes hold.

"Who are you?" I ask, but the man ignores me, his gaze still fixed on His Royal Highness.

Nikolai sits up, not at all concerned that he's conducting this conversation completely naked. In fact, he uses his other hand to free his princely cock from its condom.

"Come now, Christian. Answer the lady's question as you know I'm too bored to keep answering yours."

The man clenches his teeth. "Lady?" he says. "I'll do no such thing. But you can bloody tell me why you called this commoner *queen*."

Nikolai glances back at me and winks, and with that tiny gesture the intimacy of our connection falls away.

He laughs. "If you'd been given the royal treatment like I had, you'd bow to the woman who performed such a deed and call her your sovereign, as well."

I know this act. Something about this man—this Christian—instills a quiet fear in the prince, one that causes him to protect our connection. To protect *me*.

"I'm hungry, Your Highness. Can I fix you a snack?"

I slide off the edge of the bed, taking the sheet with me as a robe as I brush past our visitor.

"That would be lovely, Pet."

I grin at the term of endearment as I make my way to the kitchen. Only when I'm out of the room do the pieces start to click in place.

I know that man. Christian. Christian *Wurtzer*.

He is the Baron of Rosegate, the disputed land between Edenvale and our ancient enemies to the north, the Kingdom of Nightgardin. For now Rosegate is under King Nikolai's protection and rule. I squeeze my eyes shut, remembering that the baron also has a supermodel sister. Her face has been splashed across the tabloids almost as much as Nikolai's. Sometimes *together*. Whatever his visit entails, it cannot be good.

And despite what just occurred in Nikolai's room before our interruption, it's only now that I feel royally screwed.

CHAPTER THIRTEEN

Nikolai

"JESUS." CHRISTIAN PACES my room, disgust marring his features. I find a pair of trousers and yank them on. "I'm a fucking idiot. How much time have I wasted worrying that I'd been an overhasty judge, that maybe my little sister, as shallow and conniving as she is, and as depraved and arrogant as you are, had made an unexpected love match?"

He tears a hand through his clipped blond hair. "Instead you're up to your usual tricks, except now you're bedding women in the prince's wing. So much for all your high-minded talk about keeping your chamber as a sanctuary. Now any gold-digging sex kitten can—"

He ceases speaking. Mostly because my hand closes on his throat and squeezes. X once told me he could break a man's neck with a simple flick of the wrist. Good thing he refused to share the trick because, so help me, I would use it against my old friend for besmirching what happened between Kate and me in this room tonight. Our lovemaking was by turns savage and sensual, raw and romantic, two sides of a single emotion, one that hums through me like liquid gold.

I don't dare give it an official name. I don't even think too hard on the word's existence because it feels so fragile, like a soap bubble that could pop in a brisk wind.

Christian's feet kick at the empty air because even as my feelings toward Kate beckon from a place of light, darkness still owns my soul. And my friend dares to condescend an amazing woman such as she.

"Please," he wheezes, hands clawing uselessly at my strength. "Nikolai." He may be skilled in a boxing ring, but I have undiluted fury on my side.

"I don't need a goddamn bodyguard to deal with you, *Baron*. I could break your neck as easily as I could break the alliance with Rosegate," I grind out. "How many hours would it take for Nightgardin to invade if I call off our military protection?"

There is the sound of wood sliding along a groove. Then a warning hand on my shoulder. "Put him down," X's quietly authoritative voice insists.

"Thought I told you to quit using secret passages," I say, releasing Christian and letting him tumble to the floor, gasping for oxygen.

X shakes with noiseless laughter. He doesn't so much as smile, but I know he is amused.

"Don't you get claustrophobic in there?" I ask. The palace is riddled with secret chambers, a veritable rabbit warren within the walls. X seems to liken them to his own personal sanctum.

"After the month I spent as a prisoner in the Russian nuclear sub in the Arctic Sea, the passages here are as roomy as a Versailles ballroom, Your Highness."

"Jesus. Who are you?" I ask him, and not for the first time. I'm never entirely sure if the guy is joking.

"What are you going to do with him?" Per usual, X

evades my question to gesture at Christian, who now pushes himself to standing.

"He disrespected Kate," I snap.

Christian stares at me, eyes wide. "Your face, when you say her name. You *feel* something for this woman. Don't you? I never thought it possible."

"I don't owe you—or anyone, for that matter—any explanations," I remind him. I might sound arrogant as hell, but I never denied that I am a royal prick.

"Your Highness," he says, bowing his head. "I apologize for barging in on you. And for assuming the worst. I actually came to warn you about Catriona, in the vain hope that you and she had forged a connection. After you didn't call, it appears she has gone sour. She had delusions of herself on the Edenvale throne. And I thought that if there was any chance you *did* feel something for her... But I know the truth, that Catriona is only capable of loving herself. Still, she is my sister. When I saw you with—"

"Kate," I say, before he calls her a commoner again and I *do* rip his throat out.

"Of course," he says. "Kate. I just wasn't expecting you felt something for another."

"Thank you," I say curtly. I am not yet ready to forgive, but I appreciate the warning.

I don't have time for Catriona's petty scheming. What I said to Kate tonight was the truth.

She is my addiction; I can't stay away. Every kiss, every caress, every damn moment in her presence hits my body like a drug. I can't seem to get enough and crave fix after fix. It's not that I want her so much as I *need* her. There must be a way to make her my queen and keep my royal inheritance.

Kate

I open the stainless-steel refrigerator in Nikolai's kitchen to find nothing but a bowl of strawberries that look freshly cut.

"They go perfectly with the champagne."

I yelp and almost lose my sheet—the only thing covering my naked body—to find X using a pocket square to clean what looks like berry juice—or possibly blood—from a small knife. I opt to believe it is the former. When he's done, he slips the knife into a sheath inside his suit jacket.

"How did you…? I mean, where did you…?" I glance toward an open window near the grand piano across the great room, but X shakes his head.

"Not tonight, Miss. My travels are *within* the walls this evening rather than without."

I shake my own head and decide not to press the issue. Instead I tuck my sheet tight around me and remove the bowl of berries from the fridge, cradling them against my body. I inhale and sigh.

"How do these smell so good?" I ask, my mouth watering. "I can already taste them."

X reaches into another coat pocket and hands me my cell phone.

"The reason I left the prince alone with the baron. You seem to have missed a call. Also, my apologies for him interrupting you and His Highness. Save for his brother Benedict, Christian Wurtzer is the only one with unrestricted security clearance to the annex, an oversight that will soon be remedied." The corner of his mouth twitches into the ghost of a smile. "The strawberries are a gift. I thought you and the prince might need a bit of—sustenance."

X dips his head in a mild bow and disappears around a corner. I hear the sound of what must be a sliding door on a track and then what I swear is a chuckle coming from within the very walls.

Who is that guy?

The caller identification on my phone steals my attention from the mystery of X. My sister. It's not even eight o'clock. I know I told Nikolai I don't have a curfew, but maybe Maddie is worried after all. I ignore her voice mail and move straight to calling her back.

"Oh, Katie, thank God," she says when she answers.

"I'm okay," I tell her. "I guess I should have called. I'm with Nikolai and—"

"It's Grandmother," she says, and all the air rushes out of my lungs with her utterance of those two words.

"Is she—?"

"She's still with us," Maddie says quickly. "But do you remember the cough she had last time I visited? It turns out it was the onset of pneumonia. They started her on medication, but she wasn't responding. We're at the Royal Hospital. She's on a respirator and IV meds. They say she can recover, but, Katie—the money it will cost for all of this. We're barely making our rent at the moment. Can they not pay you a small advance?"

I swallow back the lump in my throat. "Can we get by for two more months?" I ask.

"If we're very careful," she says. "Maybe." Her voice sounds ready to crack. Poor Maddie. She's shouldered so much responsibility since our parents died. Too much.

I take a deep breath and back myself into a corner of the kitchen, a feeble attempt at privacy.

"As long as I get Nikolai down the aisle, we get double our fee."

I hear her gasp. "But what if you don't?" she asks.

I shake my head. "That won't matter. He will marry. I'm sure of it."

Nikolai won't let the kingdom slip away from his family. As much as he embraces the part of the careless playboy, I know deep down he is a man of duty, which means he *will* have to choose a bride—one who is fit to rule beside him. There is no one better than me to find his perfect match, even if it's only perfect on paper.

As much as the thought kills me, I can't let down my own family. My grandmother was there for me and my sister in our darkest hour. She deserves nothing less from us in kind. To see out her final days in peace and comfort.

"I trust you," Maddie says.

"I won't let you down." I step out of the kitchen and glance toward Nikolai's room and see our uninvited guest on his way toward me. "I have to go," I say.

"Okay. I'll be with Gran all day tomorrow. Only one visitor is allowed at a time. Relieve me in the evening?"

"Of course," I tell her. "I'll be there by five. But I won't be home tonight," I add. "Love you, Maddie." And then I end the call before she can question where I am—before the guilt for not being with Gran now can set in. Because I know what happened between Nikolai and me wasn't just sex.

He called me his queen.

Christian offers me a slight nod as he walks by but

says nothing before letting himself out the apartment's front door.

I pad into Nikolai's room, strawberries in hand. He sits on the edge of his bed, hair rumpled and jeans on but unbuttoned. He pops the bottle of champagne and fills the two flutes.

"Sorry about that, Pet." He offers me a glass.

I set the strawberries on the night table and take it willingly. He pulls me onto his lap and then lifts his own glass, tapping the crystal against mine.

"Stay the night," he says.

I nod, and when I lift my glass to drink, the sheet loosens and falls below my breasts.

"My God, you are beautiful," he says, and I don't bother covering myself again.

He sets down his flute and plucks a strawberry from the bowl, bringing it to my lips. I bite, and juice dribbles onto my lips and my chin. Nikolai kisses me, licking my skin clean. I swallow the rest of my champagne in one sip, the bubbles tickling my tongue, and I'm swept away in a giddiness I've never felt before.

He lays me out on the bed, unwrapping me from the sheet as if I am a gift.

"I'm yours," I say. And we make love again, this time achingly yet wonderfully slow, and I know when he buries himself in me again and again that I'm in trouble. *Big* trouble.

I must help him marry another.

Both of our futures depend on it.

In the morning I slide out from the crook of his arm. I kiss the inked compass above his heart and silently wish for it to point us both in the right direction.

X is surprisingly absent this morning, so I exit the prince's quarters as discreetly as possible, leaving him a note that I've gone for a walk.

I need to clear my head.

Soon after I leave the secluded wing, I find a chapel on the outskirts of the grounds. Perhaps someone inside can offer guidance when I have no direction of my own.

I enter to find the place empty but for the rows of pews. A few moments of silence will do me good, as well.

When I take a seat in the rear, I bow my head and close my eyes.

So... I've never actually done this, I think, rationalizing that if there is some higher power, he or she can hear my thoughts. No need to speak them aloud. *But I have loved. It was a good love, but not a great one. I know that now. Because my chest—my body—doesn't feel like it can contain what I have for Nikolai. But whatever this is will fade. It must. We've only known each other for a few short weeks. And he must marry another.*

"I'm frightened of what I feel," I say aloud.

"That which scares us is the most important to face."

The deep voice comes from behind, and I suck in a breath.

"God?" I ask, afraid to face whoever is chuckling. But I'm being a fool, so I turn.

"Not exactly the risen Lord, but I like to think we're close." A dark-haired man, dressed head to toe in black, stares at me with the loveliest green eyes. He wears the white collar of the seminary.

"Oh! Father!" I stand quickly, bumping my knee

on the pew in front of me, and hiss out a curse before covering my mouth. "I'm so sorry," I say.

The man smiles, and his kind eyes put me at ease. "You should hear some of the phrases that come out of my brother's mouth when he's here. I assure you none of them are accidental."

My eyes widen. It has been quite some time since any photographs of him have shown up in newspapers or magazines, but I recognize him now.

"You're Prince Benedict," I say, but he shakes his head.

"I prefer Father Benedict, if that's okay with you, Miss—"

"Kate," I say, extending a hand. Though I'm not sure that's the appropriate gesture. He obliges me nonetheless.

"The matchmaker, I presume?"

I swallow. "How did you know?"

"Come," he says, nodding toward the exit. "It's such a beautiful morning. Let us sit in the sun."

I follow him to a small garden where we settle on a stone bench. He tilts his head toward the sky and closes his eyes, breathing in the morning air.

"Has Nikolai spoken of me?" I ask, ashamed at my boldness, but I don't have time to beat around the bush.

Benedict folds his hands in his lap and simply nods.

"Do you truly care for my brother, Kate?"

My cheeks grow hot, and tears prick the backs of my eyes. I have not even told Nikolai of my feelings. Caring for him is not allowed. He is destined for another woman.

Benedict smiles again. "Your reaction is answer enough," he says. "So I will tell you two things. The first is that I love Nikolai, and I will do anything I can to protect him—and anything I can to help him find happiness, something I don't believe he's been capable of feeling for quite some time."

I swipe a finger under my eye, clearing away an escaping tear.

"The second is that if his happiness lies with someone who does not fit the parameters of the Royal Marriage Decree, I will do all that I can to find a way around it if Nikolai is ready to stop playing his games and fight for something real. Do you understand this, Miss Kate?"

I nod and fight the urge to hug him.

Nikolai and I have an ally. It is not a solution, but it is hope.

"Thank you," I whisper instead, but I grab his hand, pressing it between my own. "Thank you so much."

I decide not to overstay my welcome. I don't want to worry Nikolai if I'm gone too long. But as I'm walking away, Benedict calls after me.

"You may very well secure his heart," he says, and I pause midstep. "Just remember that if you do, it is not only yours to cherish, it is yours to protect."

I don't turn around or respond but instead continue on my way.

He knows I heard.

He knows I understand.

He knows Nikolai might just secure my heart, as well.

CHAPTER FOURTEEN

Nikolai

KATE RETURNS FROM her walk in a pensive mood.

"Everything okay, Pet?" I ask with no small concern. Her cheeks are white as marble.

She presses her lips into a grin, but it doesn't quite reach her eyes. So I make that my singular purpose for the hours ahead, to wash away whatever plagues her and get her beautiful blue eyes to smile again.

Today is the sole day in the month when tourists flood the palace and our extensive grounds. Social media shall soon be filled with #royalday #palacelife #princenikolaiwhereareyou #princenikolaihereicome posts.

And the women who flock inside aren't lying.

Invariably, a few overenthusiastic subjects attempt to break into my royal suite. Once, a coed from the University of Edenvale evaded the guards and made it all the way to my door wearing nothing but a yellow rain slicker and a pair of Wellingtons. Luckily, X was brushing up on his Japanese ninja star throwing skills in the antechamber off my residence, and the sight of him clutching a deadly iron *shuriken* halted her explorations and sent her fleeing for friendlier environments.

But today, I don't want to mix among my subjects. Nor do I want the public world to have a peek at the intimacy developing between me and Kate. All I want is to whisk her somewhere far away from prying eyes, and thanks to my helicopter, this is an entirely plausible option.

"I have a surprise," I tell her, picking up a woven brown picnic basket. X would normally be happy to carry such items, but I want this date to be all from me. For the next few hours there won't be any sign of bad boy Prince Nikolai putting his signature moves on a woman. Instead, she will be with a man who is taking a wonderful woman to a place that couldn't match her vibrant beauty, but comes close.

"We're having a picnic?"

"I made the sandwiches myself…and got lost trying to find the palace kitchen," I admit with a rueful grin.

She giggles, half in horror and half in amusement. "Please tell me you are joking."

I shrug. "In my world, you ring a silver bell, and whatever you need appears."

She stares at me with her signature intense gaze for long enough that my heart pounds. Does she see me as nothing more than a spoiled, overgrown brat?

"So if you tinkle your little bell, your wishes all come true."

I nod. "The palace staff pride themselves on this point."

She glances around the room. "Would this magic bell work for me?"

A thought scuttles through my brain like a menacing cockroach. *Does she value your worth more than you?* I stomp the passing notion into a million unrecognizable pieces. This is Kate. She isn't a gold digger. She could never be. "But of course. It's there on the table, beside the chaise lounge."

She eyes it and gives her chin a musing rub. "What if I ring for Hugh Jackman? The Wolverine version."

I choke on my breath, coughing into my fist.

"What can I say?" She stares with wide-eyed innocence. "I like my men with a sharp edge."

I cross the room, settle my hands on her hips to pull her as close as possible to me and my rapidly thickening needs. "You want me to snarl?"

"Maybe," she says, her voice lilting, teasing, driving me mad.

"You are playing with fire, Pet."

She nods. "Are you saying that I make you burn?" She rocks herself against me with a wink.

I nearly groan aloud. "Come, before I ravish you here and waste all these Nutella sandwiches."

She claps her hands. "You made *Nutella* sandwiches?"

I grin. "With bananas from Hawaii sliced over sourdough imported from San Francisco."

Her eyes brighten, finally, and the sight of her unencumbered joy makes my heart race.

"Nutella sandwiches with banana are my favorite. How did you know?"

"I may or may not have perused your Facebook account. You don't post often. I was hoping for a few more selfies."

Her mouth makes a perfect O, utterly adorable and unassumingly sexy as hell.

"The profile *About Me* section says…" I clear my throat. "'The quickest way to my heart is through a Nutella sandwich.'"

"Guilty as charged," she says with a giggle. "If you read the rest, you'd see it says you'd capture my heart forever if you added bananas." She raises a brow.

"Does it now?" I ask, and she merely shrugs.

We start to walk before I hold up a hand. "Wait, I need to get you something." I open the hallway closet door and pull out two hangers, one with a brand-new sundress and another with one of my jackets. "X procured you fresh garments for our journey, and I want to make sure you don't get cold on the way."

She smiles at the floral printed dress, but her brows knit together when I hand her the jacket. "You're planning on blasting the air-conditioning in the Rolls?"

I click my tongue. "No, we'll be flying at ten thousand feet." I smile into her uncomprehending face. "We're taking my helicopter to a little place I know." I lean over to kiss her forehead. "Me, you and the most beautiful place on Earth. What can go wrong?"

Kate

Nikolai fastens my seat belt and affixes the helmet strap.

"Are you shaking, Pet?" he asks, planting the sweetest of kisses on my nose.

I inhale a trembling breath. "I guess now wouldn't be the *best* time to tell you I've never flown before?"

He grins. "In a helicopter, you mean."

I shake my head. "I've never gone farther than a train could take me, and even then I never left the outskirts of Edenvale," I tell him, almost ashamed of my words. My fiancé was the adventurer, but he always took that to the extreme. It was never my desire to join him. Plus, Gran's health has been declining for years. "I don't know," I say, not wanting to burst Nikolai's bubble of excitement. Then I shrug. "I guess I'm the kind of girl who plays it safe."

Until I let my country's future king pleasure me in the royal gardens.

My head spins. My world is so small compared to his, and each revelation of my upbringing must remind him of this.

He rests his hands on my hips, so strong and reassuring. And as ridiculous as I must look in this helmet, he kisses me, his lips a promise that he will keep me safe.

"I want to show you so much," he whispers against me. "I want to give you the world."

I suck in a sharp breath. "I want that, too," I tell him. And with one more kiss, he hops from my side of the helicopter and makes his way to his own.

His helmet on and seat belt fastened, he flips a few switches and grips what looks like a very complicated gearshift. And then my stomach plummets from my body and probably through the cockpit floor as the ground drops out from under us.

I yelp.

"Shit. Are you okay?"

Concern laces Nikolai's voice as it pipes through the small speakers close to my ears. It's then that I start giggling.

"This…is…amazing!" I squeal as the palace shrinks beneath us—as all of Edenvale, the only home I've ever known, begins to disappear. I turn to him, eyes wide in amazement. *"Nikolai."*

He nods. "I know, Pet. I know."

We rise above mountains and valleys. The outskirts of our country's rolling green hills spread out before us like an emerald blanket.

"Grab the cyclic," he says, nodding toward the joystick next to my leg.

I shake my head violently.

"Don't worry. I won't let us fall."

I swallow and do as he says. He flips another couple of switches and then grins at me.

"Now—tilt it ever so slightly to the right."

I do it, my hands shaking yet gentle on what will either fly us in the direction he wants or be the instrument of our doom. To my surprise, the helicopter veers right, and I squeal with delight.

"I'm flying it!" I cry.

"You're flying it, Kate."

My heart surges at his utterance of my name. Though I enjoy his term of endearment, something about him calling me *Kate* makes whatever today is all the more real.

Nearly two hours later we land in an open field that is lusher and greener than any I've seen. Nikolai leads me several yards away to a country road, a motorbike parked on the gravel beside it.

"How did you—?" I start, and Nikolai answers me with a kiss so deep and full of need that my knees buckle.

"Careful there, Pet. The day's only just begun."

My grandmother, I think, the real world intruding

on the fantasy about to begin. "Nikolai, I need to get back—"

He kisses my nose. "Let go of home, if only for today. I promise to get you back to your life...and me back to mine." There is regret in his tone. "Just give me this day."

I nod and swallow back the threat of tears.

He fastens the picnic basket to the back of the bike and once again fastens a helmet to my head. He helps me onto the seat and then hops on in front of me.

"Don't let go," he says as I wrap my arms around his waist, and I squeeze him tight, my silent promise to obey.

The hills we ride are bumpy, on the verge of treacherous at times as we wind through the mountains. Nikolai has not told me where we are, but when we arrive at our destination, I know without the day having really begun that it will be the best one of my life.

"Nikolai," I say again as he helps me off the motorbike. I open my mouth to say more, but tears prick at my eyes, and I am left speechless, staring out over white rocks and turquoise water, a small bathing pool with a cascading waterfall at its end.

He removes his helmet and then my own as I continue to gape at the site before me.

"I wanted to bring you somewhere as beautiful as you," he says. "Such a place doesn't exist, but I do believe this is the closest I'll get."

This time I'm powerless against the few tears that fall. I don't recall knowing happiness like this.

He pulls the basket from the bike and then lifts a small hatch beneath the basket's perch, pulling out a pair of socks and hiking boots.

I laugh as I look at my ballet flats. Sensible shoes, yet not sensible enough for the terrain we are about to traipse.

"Your glass slippers, Cinderella," he says, and I lean against the vehicle, allowing him to lace me into the boots. On the second one, his hands travel up the length of my leg, and his lips trail sweet kisses in their wake.

I give his head a playful tap. "Not until I get my Nutella sandwich," I say, though if he truly wanted to, he could have me right here on the side of the road.

We make our way to the pool, and Nikolai spreads a blanket upon an embankment.

"Are we the only ones here?" I ask. "And by the way, *where* is here?"

He retrieves a sandwich from the basket, removes it from its parchment wrapper and tears off a small piece.

"We are in the secluded hills of western Rosegate." He pops the sandwich bite into my mouth, and I hum my approval as chocolate, hazelnut and banana converge upon my tongue. "And I can assure you that *no one* will be visiting this pool today."

I swallow. "How—how deep is it?" I ask, and Nikolai's eyes soften.

"Not more than four feet, even at the deepest end. We don't have to go in. I knew you might not want to, but I also knew I couldn't *not* show you this place."

I shake my head, wanting to be brave for him—to be brave for *me*. I've been in water before—willingly. I just don't remember knowing how to swim.

"You'll keep me safe?" I ask.

His hands cradle my cheeks. "God, yes, Kate. Of course. *Always*."

His gray eyes bore into mine, and I know he's telling the truth. It's that last word, *always*, that seals the deal.

I back away from him and kick off my boots. Then I pull my dress over my head, revealing my one surprise for him today.

"Where—where are your undergarments?" he stammers, and I beckon for him with my index finger.

"You've already given me the world today. I wanted to give something to you." As he steps closer, I begin to unbutton his shirt. "I want to tell you something. I—I hadn't been with anyone else for a couple of years before you." I squeeze my eyes shut and wait for the embarrassment to subside. When I feel his fingertips caress my cheeks, I open them again to see nothing but pure adoration in his gaze. "I was engaged and—he died. I didn't say anything before because—"

"It's okay," he says, surprising me with his reassurance as his hand still cradles my face. "I guess we are more alike than we thought."

He means Victoria. And maybe he's right. Maybe our worlds aren't so far apart after all.

I nod. "What I'm trying to say is… I've been on birth control the whole time. Because it was easier… because I hoped that maybe someday…"

He grins. "I'm clean," he says, knowing what I'm trying to ask. "I may be a wicked rake much of the time, but I'm always careful. If you want to know how many times a year I get tested…"

I shake my head, deciding to trust him rather than wonder how the frequency of doctor's visits factors into the ratio of women he's been with.

"I want to *be* with you, Nikolai. Like this. If you want to be with me."

"There's only been one other I've been with—like this." He growls softly in my ear. "And there is *nothing* I want more right now."

So I free him of his clothes, marveling at his naked body—each ridge of his muscles, the black ink of his tattoos.

"Tell me what it means," I say, tracing the compass with my finger as I've done before.

He brings my hand to his lips, pressing a kiss into my palm.

"It means I was lost," he says. "But I'm not anymore."

I nod, unable to speak. So we step carefully from our perch, down the rocks and into the warm crystal waters below.

"Make love to me," I say, wrapping my arms around his neck, his hard cock already nudging me open. I am slick and ready—just from his words—to take him in.

He pushes inside, and I cry out as my legs wrap around his hips. I am weightless in the water. Weightless in his arms. Gravity no longer exists.

And I never, ever want to come back down.

CHAPTER FIFTEEN

Nikolai

MY COCK SHEATHES itself inside Kate, her intimate muscles clenching my length, and a single word hits like a punch to the soul. *Home.* I have traveled the world, set foot on every continent, skied sky-kissing alpine slopes, explored tiger-filled jungles and indulged in exclusive VIP sex clubs in most major cities, yet I've always felt adrift, empty, as if I live my life surrounded by an invisible moat.

Kate might never have set a single stiletto beyond our small kingdom's borders, but when we lock gazes, it is as if the whole fucking universe is in her eyes.

She is my home.

I withdraw, take my hard cock in one hand and press the tip to her clit, stroking her hot wet center in a slow, hip-grinding circle. This realization makes me dizzy. I knew she'd attracted me, then entranced me. But this feeling requires me to get out a thesaurus, search for superlatives. And yet it might be simple. So goddamn simple.

Her lips part as her pupils dilate.

"Good, Pet?" My voice is husky with emotion. I

want to make her come so hard that the memory of the pleasure imprints on her skin, engraves in her bones.

"Amazing, but…" She trails off, lowering her lids.

I smooth a strand of fiery hair from her cheek. "No secrets between us. No barriers. I am here, raw, skin to skin. I demand no less from you."

"I need you back inside me."

The urgency lacing her plea is almost my undoing. "Your wish is my command, m'lady."

I hike her off her feet and position her slender thighs around my hips. She tries to wiggle lower, but I hold her firmly as I begin my trek toward the waterfall.

"Please. Nikolai. In me. Now."

I intend to bury myself in her so deep that I no longer know where she ends and I begin. But first she needs her surprise.

We pass under the fall, and the intense pounding rush is nothing to the thundering pulse of my blood in my ears.

Inside the cave there is a small crack in the ceiling, and a shaft of perfect buttery sunlight sparkles over the crystal walls.

Kate gasps. "What is this magical place?"

I bury my face in her porcelain neck and breathe in her essence, the faint hint of Chanel No. 5. "The Grotto of Diamonds," I rumble. "Stunning, isn't it?"

Her chest heaves against me.

"Absolutely breathtaking," she says.

I cup her chin, refuse to let her grow demure, to be shy. "Wasn't talking about the grotto."

With a pump, I am back inside. Fucking Christ. My ass muscles clench. She feels softer than spun silk, tight, wet and perfect. As much as I want to lose myself in a series of punishing, dominating thrusts, this is for her. This day. This trip. This moment. So I take the time to ensure every stroke glides over her clit in the slow, steady rhythm that she craves. When I settle her ass against a smooth rock, she hisses with pleasure.

"There's a hot spring running down the wall here," I rasp.

She hums. "This feels amazing." The warm water seeps between her legs, splashing my own thighs.

She arches with pleasure like a naughty kitten and I slide the final inch. Fuck. Her pussy milks me in micropulses. Savage pleasure claws my chest. She is so close already. My darling Kate is responsive as hell. But I won't find my release until she gets hers.

I dip over her sensitive nipple and trace the rosy bud with the flat of my tongue while I enter her over and over, deeper and deeper. Her nails claw my back helplessly. Those micropulses become quakes.

"Watch me, Pet. Watch *us*. Watch your sweet pussy take all that I have to give."

We stare through the crystalline water, hypnotized at the erotic sight of my thick root working through her pink entrance. It's the most goddamn beautiful sight that has ever existed.

"This is where I belong," I say. "In you. Giving you everything you deserve."

"I love watching you take me," she gasps.

"Love watching you get it."

Then her dizzy gasp turns to a small cry. "It's so good. It's too much. I'm coming."

"And who is giving it to you?"

"Nikolai."

As she breathes my name I shoot inside her, my own

groan losing itself in her mouth as I taste the ecstasy on her tongue.

We spend the day like this. Lovemaking in the Grotto of Diamonds. Nibbling Nutella sandwiches. Sharing funny stories about our childhoods. Each moment is the best one of my life.

When at last I fly us home, she falls asleep in her seat, too satiated to fear the helicopter, and among the night sky, I tell the stars my secrets, the truth that's burning a hole in my heart. The one that I am not yet ready to confess to her face.

For now, the truth lies in the sky above—and buried deep within my long-darkened soul.

Kate

I feel his fingertips softly caress my face, and I stir in my seat. I'm vaguely aware of my surroundings—a helicopter, I think—but I don't want to leave the dream, one where Nikolai tells me he loves me.

"We're home, Pet. Time to wake."

His voice is soft in my ear, and my body betrays me as my eyes flutter open, exiting the fairy tale I so long to stay in. Because of course he never spoke those words, and I'm not the princess who gets her happily ever after. Yet after this day, I can't help but hope for the possibility that one day I will be.

The propeller blades are still, and Nikolai no longer wears his helmet. I reach a hand to my own head and find that neither do I.

"Wow," I say. "I was really out. What time is it?" It's only then that I realize the setting sun—that I remember Maddie spending the day at the hospital with Gran.

"It's nearly six," he says. "Is everything okay?"

I fling off my seat belt and fidget with the door. "I'm sorry. Today was—it was everything, but I'm late. It's a family thing. I—I have to go."

I must sound as frantic as I feel because he rushes from the helicopter and around to my side, helping me out.

"Whatever you need. Where do you have to go? I'll take you there myself."

We race from the helipad where I expect to see X waiting with the Rolls-Royce, but instead I find two guards along with Queen Adele. Christian Wurtzer. And a young woman I recognize from the covers of various magazines—Catriona Wurtzer. She stands with a self-satisfied grin plastered on her face and one hand distinctively rubbing her flat belly.

"What is all this?" Nikolai asks, more annoyed than concerned.

Christian's jaw is tight, and I can tell he is using monumental restraint. Whatever is going on, this man looks at Nikolai like he wants to tear his throat out.

The queen purses her lips and narrows her eyes at me. "Come now, Nikolai. Really. Dallying with the hired *help*. I'd like to know how she plans to earn double her fee for getting you down the aisle if she can't keep her legs crossed in your presence." She sets her cold gaze on me. "And *you*." The queen raises her brows. "I know I told you to earn his trust, but I had no idea you'd seduce him, as well. I guess that *is* one way to go about it."

Her lips part into a satisfied, victorious grin.

"Double fee? What the fuck is this about a double fee?" Nikolai asks.

The world seems to spin around me. I might be sick.

Christian's jaw ticks. Catriona stifles a laugh. And when I look at Nikolai, the light in his eyes snuffs out as I watch his gaze cool and then turn completely to ice.

"Double your fee?" he repeats, his tone achingly bitter.

"The contract," I say, but it comes out as a strangled sob. "You have the copy. The money wasn't a secret." But he told me he hadn't read it, which means I let the lie of omission stand. I let myself believe that what he didn't know wouldn't hurt him. I let myself believe that we could beat the queen at her own game, but I never really stood a chance. Did I?

"I trusted you," he says. "But I guess that was just part of your job too. I didn't think I needed a contract to prove to me that you weren't like every other woman who's schemed to get in my bed. If it wasn't meant to be kept from me, then why not say something?" he asks, his words biting and bitter. "Is this why you challenged me? Why you were so confident you'd succeed? Because you were allied with the person who despises me most?"

He steps toward me, his face inches from mine, but I don't for one second think he will kiss me, not with his teeth clenched. Or that vein in his neck throbbing with the hot anger rising from his body.

"Was. Any. Of. It. Real?"

Each word stabs me like a poisoned dagger.

"Nikolai, you *know* it was real," I say, but how can he trust me now when the queen speaks the truth? She didn't request my help. She demanded it, under veiled threats. I *was* her ally. I had no choice but to comply. And even though I gained his trust, I never really gave him mine. Or I'd have been brave enough to tell him everything.

I knew I was falling for him today, and the possibility of us made me think I wasn't afraid of her anymore—that I could tell Nikolai about Gran. About why I needed to succeed even if it meant breaking my own heart.

She played me. She played him. And now she is going to win.

"Money," he says, his voice so distant I almost don't believe it's the same man who woke me moments ago. "That's what you really hoped to gain. Wasn't it?"

I shake my head, refusing to believe things can change with one utterance from the queen. "You know that's not true. She *made* me agree. I had no choice. I should have told you everything, but that doesn't mean—"

"Stop," he says. "Just stop. Why would you say anything if *seducing* me could earn you double your fee?" His eyes flash to the queen and back to me. "Do you want to know why I refuse to marry?" he asks, but he doesn't wait for an answer. "Because the last woman I asked to be my queen was willing to accept my hand even though she loved another. All because she thought the title more important than all else. Now she is gone, my brother banished, and I right back where I started, fooling myself that any woman could see past the facade."

He takes another step closer to me, and I flinch. I do not know this Nikolai. *This* is not my prince.

"I told you. I will. Not. Marry."

Laughter bubbles from the queen's lips, and she claps her hands slowly.

"Lovely speech. Really. Lovely. But here is the thing. It was only a matter of time before your—dalliances— got you into trouble. Thankfully, the countless times you've *dallied* with the baroness seem to have worked in your favor." Her lips curled into a malicious grin. "Catriona is pregnant with your heir. You *will* marry and secure an alliance with Rosegate...or lose the throne."

Nikolai's eyes widen as his gaze meets that of his former lover, and then falls to where her hand rests on her belly.

My tears fall hot and fast because I know now we never had a chance—Nikolai and I. The queen had said she would find his match and that I would support it. Benedict searching for a loophole was nothing more than a distraction. This was always going to end.

"Take her away until I decide what to do with her," the queen says.

And before I can comprehend that she means me, both of her guards appear at my sides, my arms firm in their grip.

"What are you doing?" I cry.

"Your Highness," Christian starts. "You never said anything about locking her up!"

But the queen waves him off.

"Take. Her. Away," she says again, and the guards start dragging me toward a car at the edge of the grounds.

"Nikolai!" I call. "Listen to me. You know it was never about the money. I know you do."

But he doesn't respond as the guards pull me farther and farther from him.

I want to cry out again, but for whom? Nikolai stands there, dumbfounded and shattered. I have no ally.

As I collapse into the back of the car, my eyes blur

with tears—so much so that it takes me several seconds to get my bearings.

A minibar. A bottle of cognac. And when I look up, the window between me and the driver lowers.

"To the dungeon, then, Miss?" the driver asks, and I dare to let myself hope.

"X?"

CHAPTER SIXTEEN

Nikolai

"Tsk, tsk." Adele clicks her tongue. Her mouth's sympathetic purse only serves to make the triumph in her eyes more grotesque. Not for the first time I wonder just how she managed to capture my father's heart. She hails from an old Edenvale family, aristocratic to the core, but besmirched by a long line of traitors who over time have betrayed our throne's integrity to cut lucrative deals with Nightgardin, hoping to profit in the destabilization. A few of her ancestors' heads decorated the palace bridge as a warning to other transgressors.

I flex my fist, wishing for an ancient ax and a chopping block.

"Naughty, naughty, Nikolai, leading that pathetic matchmaker on. I hope you had fun with your little game. I'm sure she'll get over it in, oh, ten or twenty years." She glances to Catriona, and they share the same tinkling, malevolent laugh.

I don't know what the fuck to think. Two hours ago I was making love to a woman who I'd have sworn looked into my pitch-black soul and saw a man worthy of her heart. Now I'm being told it was a lie? That she was in it for a double fee. It's not even the money that gets me this time. It's that she kept her alliance with the queen rather than me. I've been enough of a royal idiot to be duped into thinking Kate had grown to care for me for my own sake.

Idiot.

Self-disgust roils through me. But I don't allow a trace of feeling to reveal itself on my face.

Instead, I twist my own lips into a sneer. "Pity." I ensure my words are ice, that they drip with scorn. "For a commoner, she was uncommon good fun." I allow my gaze to fall on Catriona. Her white-blond hair. Her porcelain perfect skin and pale blue eyes nearly the same shade of water. Nothing warm or welcoming. No. Twin pools of an Arctic lake. I take my time scanning every inch of her perfect body. "Darling," I drawl. "You didn't need to fake a pregnancy to keep my interest. The way I recall, we have unfinished business. You promised me a backstage pass and never delivered." I arch a brow.

"You bastard," Christian says, lunging for me. The two guards, already returned, restrain him.

"I think you meant to say Your Highness." I dust off my shirtfront. "I do believe the proper terminology in addressing your liege lord is Sire, Prince, Majesty. You could go for Your Most Exalted Worshipfulness for extra credit. You always were an ass kisser back in school."

And he was. Perfect grades. Awards for chivalry. While my extracurricular activities consisted of fucking Miss Teatree, the student French teacher, in the back of my Rolls-Royce during lunch breaks.

"I am going to cut out your disgusting tongue," he hisses.

"Your loyalty to your sister is commendable," I answer easily. "But problematic. Because either she is lying, in which case you are a fool, or she is telling the truth, and you are threatening violence not only on your future king but also the father of your nephew. A child who will be the only one to carry on your noble line given your...dilemma."

Christian stares at me with fire in his eyes. He contracted mumps during our school days, and the nurse told him he was probably sterile. A pity as it puts his small but highly coveted territory in jeopardy. Rosegate needs an heir. Edenvale needs to solidify the alliance. Despite the circumstances, it would be an advantageous match.

"My money is that you are a fool," I say, turning back to Catriona. "How do you know that you are pregnant? Will you have me believe you are some sort of modern-day Princess and the Pea? That you can magically sense if my child is growing within you?"

"Don't be ridiculous," Adele snaps, beckoning to a butler who stands off to the side, holding a silver platter covered by a swan-shaped lid.

He hurries over and removes the lid with a flourishing bow. On the tray lies a pregnancy stick with two lines.

"I do not read hieroglyphics," I mumble.

"Idiocy doesn't become you. It's obvious that's a positive sign." Victory is stamped on my stepmother's every smug feature. "You coated her womb with your depraved seed. Time to do your duty."

"A little baby," Catriona says, her mouth curving into an uncertain smile. "A future king or queen. Plus, Rosegate will unite with Edenvale at last, and Nightgardin won't ever have a chance of taking it over."

My stepmother inclines her head as if truer words had never been spoken. What is her poisonous endgame? I have to think, but my brain is flatlining, my neurons only able to process one thing. That I let another woman pretend to care for me. That I let down my defenses and gave Kate entry into my inner keep.

My stepmother hates me, blames me for her daughter's death, but why the fuck is she so intent on marrying me off to Catriona, or marrying me off period? I am not buying her giving a flying fuck over solidifying ties to Rosegate.

The cogs in my dulled brain begin to creak back to life. Doubt slides up my spine like a serpent. I used condoms with Catriona. She said she was also on birth control. If Kate was working with Adele, why not Catriona, too?

If it looks like a duck and quacks like a duck…

"The wedding will be in three days' time," Adele says. "A very private, very legally binding ceremony."

The queen might be crafty, but she isn't exactly a rocket scientist. And about as subtle as a doorpost.

"I don't think so." It takes all my strength not to gnash my teeth. "I know I've been nothing but a crushing disappointment to your selfish motives, so just add this latest mistake to my tab."

I turn away, thoughts reeling. If Catriona is carrying my child, I can't abandon her or the innocent baby, but I can't marry her. I'll order a blood test and then figure things out. Even if the ache of betrayal floods my body as I think of the woman who just disappeared into the night, I know it was real for me, so much so that I can barely breathe thinking it was all a game for her. I want to fall to my knees and scream. I want to find a wall and punch it until my fists run with blood.

Love is my curse, never my salvation. When Father dies, I will sit on the Stone Throne, but my heart will be as impenetrable as a block of uncut granite. Perhaps Catriona will bear my bastard, but she will never be my queen.

X. I need X. He'll know what to do. Even if it is to get me mind-numbingly drunk until today is blacked out of memory—he'll know.

"I will make you happy," Catriona says, putting the perfect quaver in her voice. She's such a drama queen that I'm half tempted to give her access to the throne, just to watch the spectacle.

"Sweetheart, there is only one reason why I stuck my dick in you. Fine, two. But the primary reason was this... I was trying to find out if your brother was selling me out to the tabloids again."

"What are you bloody talking about?" Christian yells.

"Every time I went out in the past year, images would appear of me online and in the print media. Despite my reputation, I do value discretion when it suits me. I knew someone in my entourage was spilling the proverbial beans. Squeaking to the press. But it was you all along. You were the little mouse." I'm unleashing the asshole attitude that's made me infamous, going full scale royal prick.

There is no one that I can trust. I am as I have always been—alone.

Catriona presses a hand to her heart. "How could you accuse me of such base behavior?"

My shoulders shake with my cold laugh. "The minute Christian found me with you, I knew it wasn't him. He was so upset. Then nothing leaked afterward. Except there was an attempt to sell something to a national magazine, wasn't there?"

She blanches. If she was pale before, now Catriona is a living ghost.

"X intercepted the messages. You were going to sell a tell-all exposé to the highest bidder. Did you think that texting your brother to come find you in my bed was going to force him to badger me to marry you? Or that you'd achieve notoriety as my lover?"

Catriona draws her hand back and slaps me hard on the cheek. "You are a monster. No wonder Victoria ran off with Damien. You can't love. Your heart is complete and utter stone."

"Enough!" Adele commands in her usual imperious tone. "Someone escort my sniveling future daughter-in-law back inside the palace. And her brother, before he murders the heir to the throne."

The crowd clears, and within minutes it's just my stepmother and me.

"Why are you doing this?" I ask at last, breaking the silence. No more pretense. I just want answers.

"I've waited for this moment a long time," she purrs. "Ever since I buried my daughter in the cold, hard ground."

And I believe her. I just don't believe that is the

whole truth. But do I trust this inner voice, the same intuition that whispered that I should take a chance on Kate? The one that has led me back here, to this black place of pain and bone-crushing loneliness? Victoria hurt my heart. Kate detonated it with the precision of a lobbed grenade. It will never be whole.

As I begin to search for answers, one truth is certain. Not only will I never marry, I will never love again.

Kate

A heavy gated door scrapes across stone as it slams shut behind me. I stumble into the cold, dank cell and stare with wide eyes back at the man who just threw me in here.

"X," I say, my voice shaking. "Why?"

He stares at me without expression, and my fear starts to morph into something fierce. I throw myself at the bars separating me from him, shaking them to no avail.

"I care about him—so much! You know I do."

My heart beats wildly in my chest. I can't even say it to X, that I *love* Nikolai. But he watched me get carted away thinking I betrayed him because I was too afraid to tell him the truth.

Because I'm a fool to have ever thought I could bridge the divide between his world and mine.

"This—this is all the queen," I continue. "She told me she would choose his bride, that if I didn't comply my sister's business would be ruined. You know she has the power to do that. You know she set this whole thing up!"

Still he stands, arms crossed, impassive as ever.

I pace, shivering in the damp air, tears pouring along my cheeks. When X says nothing, I collapse onto a stone bench at the rear of the cell and let out a bitter laugh.

"I didn't think places like this were real, you know. Castles? Sure. But dungeons? This is the stuff of fairy tales," I tell my emotionless captor. "But I never expected to be the princess. I only ever wanted to take care of my family."

I meet X's stare. There is no sign that he's even heard a word I've said, yet I swear I see a twinkle in his eyes that wasn't there before.

"The money?" I say, my voice steady now because even if Nikolai won't hear me out, he will know the truth. "My sister and I live and work out of our small apartment. Every cent that doesn't go toward our monthly payments, toward food or keeping the business afloat—it goes to the elderly care center where our grandmother lives. And now it will go to the hospital that's keeping her alive. That's where I'm supposed to be now, X. *Please.* Let me go to her."

X's jaw tightens, the only sign that any of this is getting through to him.

I open my mouth to say something more but am interrupted by what sounds like a sack of potatoes hitting the stone floor.

X looks to his left, and his features finally relax.

"You have three minutes to decide if you trust me,

Miss Kate. Three minutes to decide if you are willing to put your life in my hands."

I rise from the stone bench and make my way to the iron gate that separates me from him, pressing my face against the bars so I can see what X sees—a burly palace guard slumped on the floor next to a stool, an empty beer stein tipped over next to him.

"Yes, I drugged his ale." X waves a hand. "It won't be the first time he's fallen asleep on watch, but it is the first time it's of my doing. He'll be lucky not to piss himself with relief when he wakes to find he hasn't been caught."

The corner of his mouth quirks ever so slightly into the hint of a grin, and my heart surges with hope.

"You don't need to prove your love, Kate. Not to me," he says, his voice a firm whisper. And just like Nikolai calling me Kate somehow made me know that what we had was real, X doing the same—dropping that ridiculous *Miss*—tells me I can trust him, too.

"I've known of your family's situation since the king and queen hired you," he goes on. "But the prince—he has been in the dark, and you are one of those responsible for keeping him there."

My breath hitches, and I swallow back a sob. He is right. Nikolai hid nothing from me, but I hid my life from him. Even if it was for my own protection, I betrayed his trust in doing so.

I nod. "This isn't my world," I tell him. "I'm out of my depth. And as much as he means to me—as much as my silly secret wish has been for him to choose *me*—I knew it was a fool's errand to think he could ever truly be mine. I must think about my family right now. And Nikolai—" I stutter on the next thought, but it is the only way. "Nikolai must marry Catriona. If she's carrying his baby, he must." I swallow hard against the ache in my chest, against the cavern that will replace my heart after my next words. "Tell the queen I forfeit my fee. Tell *Nikolai*. I will not cause trouble for the prince. I just need to get to my family."

X nods somberly at me. "Queen Adele plans to leave you here until after the wedding." My whole body begins to shake as his words sink in.

Another tear slides down my cheek. "When will that be?" I ask.

X clears his throat. "Three days' time," he says. "I hope you understand I *had* to bring you here. The prince's safety depends on it."

I glance around my cell and shudder not just at the thought of being locked here for three days or of losing Nikolai—but that such cruelty exists in the queen's heart.

"Father Benedict is working tirelessly to find a loophole," X continues. "If this baby is not Nikolai's—and if there is a way out of the decree—he will find it within these three days. If I let you go, though," he says, "the queen will expedite the wedding, and Nikolai will have no chance at true happiness. But if you trust me—if you trust that my one and only mission is to protect my prince—then you can leave here tonight."

I wipe the tears from my face, my hands now covered in dirt from the filthy cell bars. I'm sure I look as frightened as I feel, but I don't care. I don't care about anything but protecting my family and the man that I love, even if he will never know my true feelings.

Everything inside me trembles so hard I fear my bones will shatter. But I hold my head high and look straight into X's unwavering stare.

"I trust you," I say. "For Maddie. For my grandmother. For Nikolai, all whom I love. I trust you, X."

He pulls a small vial from his coat pocket and hands it to me through the bars.

"Then drink."

CHAPTER SEVENTEEN

Nikolai

"WALK WITH ME." Adele gathers her crimson skirts and strides toward the gloomy entrance to the maze.

I follow as if in a trance. My head pounds, and my brain is reeling. Too many questions. Too many years living with lies and pain and never knowing who to trust. Who, if anyone has, ever loved me for me?

Maybe no one.

A feeling of utter loneliness swallows me.

Do I want to be king? It's never been a question that I've consciously asked myself before. It's as inevitable as drawing a breath. The next beat of my heart. Someday I will sit on the Stone Throne in the Reception Hall and lead my people into what I have always hoped in my deepest heart would be a prosperous and bright future.

But I don't want to be king at this price. My birthright isn't worth letting Adele win at her twisted game. But I don't know the rules. I don't know how to beat her when she holds all the cards. But the worst thing that can happen is to let her sense my uncertainty. That would be like slicing my wrists in a shark tank. Better to square my shoulders, set my jaw and figure this the fuck out. She will make a mistake. I just need to stay sharp, be ready to pounce at the first misstep.

"So quiet, no? As if the world holds its collective breath." Adele runs her fingers over the hedgerow. "Why the long face? I'd think you would enjoy taking a stroll down memory lane." Her voice is steeped in innuendo.

I ball my hands into tight fists. "I don't know what you are talking about."

"Now, now. Coy's not a good look on you, Nikolai," she croons. "We might *dislike* each other, but do let's be frank. I know how you ravished the lovely Kate Winter here on the ground of the maze. You feasted and rutted on her with your face like the wild beast that you are, depraved by lust. Disgusting and yet fascinating."

I stare at her, blinking slowly.

"How do I know your...*activities*?" She leers. "Please. You think your father runs this place? Why do you think I encourage all of his travels for diplomacy? This is *my* kingdom, and I have eyes *everywhere*." She enunciates each syllable of that last word. "A mouse doesn't so much as shit in this palace without me getting an update." She shakes her head in mock sorrow. "Now don't get all pouty. No one likes a sore loser." Her eyes gleam. "And you've lost, my sweet prince. You have lost so much that I'd be tempted to pity you if I wasn't so absolutely delighted."

Her laugh cuts my skin like glass shards before it morphs into a hysterical sob. "My daughter should have been queen!" she snaps. "It was *her* destiny to save Rosegate, not that dimwit Catriona."

My jaw clenches. "I *loved* Victoria." I choke out the

bitter truth. "But she was sleeping with my traitor of a brother."

She scoffs, sneering as she looks me up and down. "You are unfit to be king. A real man worries about affairs of the state, not of the heart. You are nothing but a weak fool. So what if Victoria didn't love you? She would have bedded you, born you an heir. She knew her duty. And your duty was to keep her safe! There were greater plans at work."

Every cell in my body recoils. "Wouldn't you want more for your daughter than to serve as a broodmare to a man she didn't love?"

"I wanted her to be queen," she hisses. "And to... and to... It doesn't matter! There is no more worthy goal than the pursuit of power. *You* took that away from her. And now I get to take your happiness from you."

Bile rises in my throat. "She loved my brother! *He* took her life, Adele. And he's been paying the price for years." An unexpected twinge of sympathy pierces me. I loved Victoria and lost her. Damien loved her and lost everything. I will not forgive my youngest brother, but only now when I have lost Kate—when I stand to lose everything if Adele has her way—do I have the slightest idea what life might be like to be banished.

"Damien was third in line to the throne." She speaks so forcefully spittle flies from her mouth. "You ran her off so she could be what? An insignificant nobody? Do you know who my family is, that we are a bloodline even more ancient than yours?"

I swipe my cheek, not having the slightest interest in getting into a snobby pissing match over who is the most royal. "I ran them both off after discovering them fucking like dogs in the Royal Library. And do you know what I think? I think she wanted me to catch her. I think she wanted me to *free* her from a future she never wanted as much as you did."

My chest heaves. I have to squeeze my eyes shut as the memory takes hold. It's not as if I don't hold some of the guilt. For years I've wondered if it could have gone differently. If there was something I could have done that would have set in motion a different course of events that did not end with Victoria dead. But the fact remains that she loved another, that she betrayed me and was all too happy to leave once she was caught.

"She'd still be alive if it wasn't for you." Adele flies at me, claws outstretched, grief taking her to the point of insanity.

This is my moment.

I've been waiting for a misstep. If she was playing a political game, her feelings for Victoria, the grief at losing not only a daughter but also a future meal ticket, muddles her thinking. She isn't calculating now. She is ready to tear me apart limb from limb, unleash her long-simmering resentment, the fact that she has had to kowtow to the Lorentz family to wear the crown, and now the best she will ever get is a puppet in Catriona, a weak-minded, selfish woman easily manipulated to do her bidding.

As for me, I'm ready to go to hell and bring Adele along for the ride. I am at the brink of endurance, and below me lies the bleak roiling blackness, the void that is there, always there. I'm done resisting. I'm ready to give myself over to the void.

She is right.

I've lost.

I've lost everything that matters.

The world goes crimson before a strong steady hand clamps my shoulder.

"Sire," X says in a grave voice, pulling me back. "Come quick. There is no time."

Kate

You will be able to hear all too clearly but see nothing. You'll feel the touch of others all too keenly but will be paralyzed from any movement yourself. You will be alive, but to anyone without sharp medical training, you will appear dead. Heartbeat too slow to detect, breathing too shallow to recognize.

This is what X tells me before I drink. There isn't time to ask him how he knows of such a drug or if he's seen it work before. I have mere seconds to decide that I trust him before everything goes black and I lose myself completely.

I feel the cold stone beneath my cheek but see nothing at all. I hear the frantic scuffle of shoes in the distance. The sound grows louder, and then there is nothing but silence for several long moments before the unmistakable click-clack of high heels approach.

"She was delirious. Screaming nonsense about how the queen threatened her livelihood if she did not get you down the aisle. Of course it was all rubbish," X says. "After her tirade she complained of shortness of breath. I knew she was just looking for a way out, so I ignored her pleas. And then she just—collapsed."

Metal clangs, and I swear the ground beneath me shakes.

"You *ignored* her?" His voice is hoarse, frantic, and I can feel his pain. It is as tangible as the stone against my cheek.

Nikolai! I want to cry out his name, but I'm stuck in this blackness, forced to do nothing but listen and to trust that I will be out of here soon.

"You bastard!" he growls, his voice wild. "I will kill you, X. I will fucking kill you!"

Laughter trills through Nikolai's madness. The queen. They are all here, staring at my prone body. And Nikolai thinks— Oh God. X. What have we done to him?

"Oh, this is too good," Adele says. "Not even in the plan, but it certainly makes things much easier for me. Tell me, X. Is she dead?"

"Unlock the fucking cell!" Nikolai bellows, interrupting her question.

"Oh, very well," the queen concedes. "Have your last look if you must."

Metal grates over stone, and I feel the faint warmth of skin against my own.

"There is no pulse," X says gravely. "Sire, my deepest condolences."

I hear a sickening crack and then Nikolai's broken voice. "I *will* kill you for this," he says again, and I'm not sure if he's speaking to the queen, or X, or both.

The scraping of heels comes nearer, and icy fingers touch my neck. If I wasn't already paralyzed, the queen's cold touch would do it.

"You didn't actually think I'd trust your word, X.

Did you? But it looks as if you're being truthful. The girl is dead."

Her skin leaves mine, and I fight to claw my way out of my body, out of this cell and away from her even though I know there's nothing more she can do to me—so long as she thinks I'm gone.

Seconds later I am weightless. No, I'm in someone's arms. I feel warm liquid splash on my cheek and know that it is my prince who cradles me.

"I'm so sorry," he whispers, and I feel his trembling lips press against my forehead. "I believe you," he whispers. "I trusted you, and I know in my gut it was the right thing to do, but I let the goddamn past get the better of me. I will never forgive myself for doubting you. I don't deserve your love, but I know you gave it to me today. I let my fear blind me to the truth, but know this, Kate. I love you. And I promise you this—I will *not* love another." And then in a voice so soft I almost miss it, I hear, "I win our wager," he says, his whisper cracking on that last word. "I will not marry—not if it means the woman beside me is not you. You owe me a favor, Kate. Those were our terms." I hear him take a shuddering breath. "Please. Come back."

My body rocks in his arms. Again and again warm drops of liquid splatter my cheek, and my heart cracks wide-open for the broken man who holds me. "Come back, Kate," he pleads, louder this time, and then his lips are on mine.

I taste the salt of his tears, and if I wasn't sure that I was, in fact, paralyzed, I would swear that my eyes leaked tears of their own. Kiss after soft kiss, he doesn't let go of me, not even when the queen groans.

"Enough already," she hisses. "You'll never know

loss like I do, Nikolai. But now you will live with yours for a lifetime. Now, X. Wipe the blood from your lip and do something with Miss Winter's body. I'm sure you can conjure a reasonable explanation for the Royal Guard, and I trust it will be kept from the papers."

"Yes, Your Highness," I hear X say.

I feel Nikolai lift my palm to his cheek, and my fingers twitch against his tear-soaked skin.

A throat clears. "Your Highness," X says, "is the king not arriving back at the palace shortly? Surely you want to be the first to break the news about the prince and Catriona. I will—take care of things here."

"Yes. Fine," she says. "Nikolai, clean yourself up and join us in the grand dining hall for dinner. You can announce your impending nuptials yourself."

Nikolai says nothing, only holds my palm flat against his cheek as I listen to the piercing blows of her heels against the stone until the sound grows farther and farther away. Finally, I hear the far-off clank of the heavy cellar door closing.

Nikolai lets go of my hand, but it doesn't fall. My fingers twitch against his skin again, and I hear a sharp intake of breath.

"X?" He draws out his servant's name.

"Really, Sire," X says, the slightest admonishment in his voice, "I thought you had more faith in me than that."

My eyes flutter open, and Nikolai's head is turned toward the man who hopefully saved us both. I gasp as my sluggish lungs gulp at the air while my heartbeat feels like it's increasing at an exponential rate.

Both of their heads snap toward mine. X stares at me with a satisfied grin on his face despite a split lower lip. It's the first genuine smile I've seen from him, and I can't help but feel the slightest bit victorious. I vowed to make the man smile, and I did, even if I had to nearly die to do it.

Nikolai still holds me, his eyes wide and red rimmed.

I regain movement in my other arm and cradle his face in my palms.

"I *love* you, Nikolai," I say, my thumb swiping at a remaining tear on his cheek. "The money was never—"

But his lips are on mine before I get a chance to explain, and that's when I realize that I don't have to. He trusts that my love is real, and it is. God, it is. He pulls me closer, deepening the kiss as my lips part for him. My limbs are still weak, but he holds me so tight I know I won't fall.

"Sire," X interrupts. "We don't have much time. The drug was supposed to last longer. Perhaps I measured incorrectly in my haste. We must get Miss Kate to the hospital."

Nikolai pulls away. "But I thought—" he stammers. "I thought she was okay," he says to X and then turns back to me. "You cannot leave me again," he says.

I shake my head. "This is all X's doing," I say. "I trust I will be okay soon. But my sister. My grandmother." A tear escapes. "I need to get to them."

In the distance the cellar door grinds open again.

"I will explain everything in the car, Sire," X says, an edge in his voice I do not like. "But we are out of time!"

"I can't walk," I whisper, fear lacing my words. If Adele was happy to find me dead, what will she do if she finds me still alive?

Nikolai stands with me still in his arms, and I wrap mine tight around his neck.

"We cannot exit the cell without being seen," he says.

X raises a brow. "Of course we can, Your Highness. Just not through the door."

CHAPTER EIGHTEEN

Nikolai

X PRESSES A moss-covered stone on the dungeon wall, and it sinks back like a button on a keyboard.

"This palace is full of surprises." He turns with a wink. "Designed that one myself."

Of course I've wondered about X's background story. He is so tight-lipped that it is possible to believe he is anything or anyone. When I came of age he was assigned as my personal bodyguard and soon became my most trusted friend and adviser. I have given him free rein to indulge in any number of curious hobbies from Kenjutsu Japanese swordsmanship to breeding poison dart frogs. But it appears secret passages have also been a keen interest, for I thought I knew them all, and I have just been proved wrong.

"It's a tight squeeze, but it will bring us out at the Gates of Victory," X says.

"And from there we can proceed to the back entrance," I say, unable to believe Kate is still alive in my arms. That this nightmare has turned into a dream.

"The guards in the back keep were sent a flagon of ale from you tonight, as thanks for their service."

"I ordered no such thing," I tell him.

X arches a brow. "I did. And saw it dosed with six seeds of the Evernight Poppy before delivery. The men should be dreaming of busty Edenvale milkmaids this very moment." He glances back at us. "Miss Kate here, however, consumed one entire blossom. She *should* have been out for at least twenty-four hours. I do wonder about that kiss, though..." He trails off.

"What about the kiss?" I ask.

X shakes his head. "Even I don't believe in such tales," he says. "True love's kiss being more powerful than poison? There just is no logical explanation for her early rousing."

I open my mouth to respond, but Kate interrupts me.

"I've never heard of an Evernight Poppy," she murmurs, rubbing my bicep and attempting to shift her body in my arms.

"Of course not," X snaps. "No one outside of a nomadic tribe of Kazakhstani master poison makers knows of the flower's existence." His mouth quirks. "Except me."

Kate attempts to lower herself and take a step but immediately crumples. I sweep her off her feet once more.

"What's happening to me?" Her eyes cloud over with fright. "Why won't my legs work?"

"You were mostly dead. Intermittent paralysis is an unfortunate side effect from the poison."

Kate moans.

"Damn it, X, for how long?" I snarl, hating Kate's fear. She moans again, this time more breathless. "For how fucking long?"

The voices in the corridor grow louder. Whoever is coming for Kate's supposed dead body is almost here.

X beckons me forward and we slip into the secret passage. He pulls a crank and the door slides effortlessly closed. "Not long," he says at last.

"Then why do you look unsettled?" I rumble. The idea of Kate suffering another second more has me in agony.

We wind through the complex twisting labyrinth that X has built through the ancient walls. The corridor is pitch-black except for the powerful flashlight beam that X shines from his wristwatch.

"There is another side effect," he says in a tight voice.

Kate writhes in my arms. "Oh, God," she breathes in a husky whisper unlike any I've ever heard. "Oh, my Jesus God."

I freeze, unwilling to take another step until X fills me in on every last fucking detail.

X sucks in an audible breath. "Unbridled sexual desire is the other effect."

"I need you inside me or I'll die." Kate licks the side of my neck while sliding her hand to cup my bulge. "Feed me that gorgeous royal prick, Your Highness. Inch by majestic inch."

"This side effect, Sire... It won't abate on its own," X says grimly. "It's the poison attacking the part of her brain that controls pleasure."

"I need it so bad," Kate moans. "It hurts. It hurts to want this badly."

My eyes widen. "What do I do?" My cock is granite hard the instant Kate's palm caresses it through my pants. We need to escape, but Kate's sensual moans are making me mad with roaring lust, and soon others will hear her pleas on the other side of the wall.

X turns to regard me in full. His normally inscrutable expression is even harder to read than ever before. "The only cure for this side effect is for someone to bring her to orgasm."

Kate

"X," I growl. "You said I would feel things more keenly in my sleep state." I writhe in Nikolai's arms as we slide through the narrow corridor. "I'm not asleep anymore, and I can't turn it off!" I cry. "The pain is going to kill me!"

I thrash and grind against my prince's hands. "Touch me, Nikolai. God, please, touch me!"

"My apologies, Miss," X says as he leads the way. "The sharp awareness of your senses—of your needs—it is more intense when you wake. And you woke early. You still have much of the drug in your system. Sire, you must pleasure her at once."

"Kate," he says. "I need to know it's not just the drug. I need to be sure that after everything that's happened, you still truly want me like this."

His tortured eyes bore into me, and for one short moment, everything is clear.

"I love you, Nikolai. Of *course* I still want you like this."

"Very well," he says.

My prince repositions me in his arms so that one of his hands is now underneath my dress where I'm wearing nothing at all. A finger grazes my clit and I nearly black out as I scream from the sensation.

"Silence is of the utmost importance," X says, reminding me of our predicament...and that Nikolai and I have an audience.

"Fuck you, X," Nikolai hisses. "You saved her only to torture her?"

We come to a screeching halt, and Nikolai's finger slips inside me. I buck and moan. Nikolai kisses me, no doubt to quiet me, and I'm ravenous for him, teeth gnashing and tongues swirling. I nip at his bottom lip and draw blood, the copper tang filling my taste buds.

A stone door slides open, and we burst into a stair-well and then up and out into the night air.

"Hang in there, Pet. I'm going to take care of you."

But I can't even answer him. I am an animal, biting and scratching in his arms as X flings open the door to the Rolls and Nikolai practically throws me inside. I lie sprawled on my back when he climbs in and kneels beside me. He glances up to the open window where X climbs into the driver's seat.

"Drive!" Nikolai yells, and I feel the car lurch forward.

Tears stream. "Now, Nikolai! Fuck. I need you *now*!"

"As you wish, my lady," he says with a wicked grin.

He shoves my dress up past my hips, spreads my legs wide and plunges two fingers inside me. I cry out in such exquisite agony I think I may burst at the seams. His face disappears between my legs as his tongue assists his fingers, lapping the length of my folds and swirling around my aching clit.

I tear at my hair and writhe along the seat of the Rolls.

"Don't stop! Oh, my God, Nikolai. Don't you fuck-ing stop!" I growl and moan and buck into his face.

And he doesn't stop. He is relentless in his savage

feast—lips, tongue, *teeth* working me to the brink of insanity while his fingers pump inside me.

One of his fingers hits the spot, and his tongue sends me straight over the edge.

I cry out my prince's name as fresh tears stain my cheeks. The relief is overwhelming.

His head collapses between my knees, and for several long moments, no one says a thing.

The car rolls to a stop and X announces our arrival through the still-open divider. "The Royal Hospital of Edenvale," he says. "Shall I give you two a minute?" he asks, not even trying to hide his amusement.

Neither Nikolai nor I say a word. I'm not even sure I've retained the ability to speak.

"And, Miss," X adds. "Congratulations. You're cured."

I wiggle my toes and note that I am no longer paralyzed *or* in sex-starved agony. It would appear that X is correct on all accounts.

"Nikolai?" I say softly when I find my voice again.

He finally lifts his head. His hair is wild and his eyes glazed over.

"Are you truly okay?" he asks.

I push myself to a sitting position and slide my dress back down.

"I'm okay," I assure him. "Thank you."

He runs a hand through his black hair, and I note the weariness in his gray eyes. It finally hits me that I'm not the only one who's endured today.

"I want to make sure *you're* okay," I say. "But—I have to get inside. My sister must be worried sick, and my grandmother…" My voice catches on the word. "She's the reason we needed the money. This was never about deceiving you, Nikolai. Only about saving my family. I should have told you." Tears prick at the backs of my eyes once again.

"Don't worry about me," Nikolai says. "I understand. And I never should have doubted you." His eyes are so tender and full of love. "Whatever you need, Pet. And I'm coming with you."

He reaches for my hand, and I see that the knuckle is split on his own.

"Did you really punch X?" I ask.

His gaze grows dark and all too somber for a moment. "I thought you were dead."

The door opens to my right, and X stands there extending a hand.

"I've a salve for the wound when we get back to the palace, Your Highness." X grins at us, patting his bloodied lip with a silk handkerchief. He closes the door after Nikolai and I exit the vehicle. I marvel at my ability to stand after being paralyzed minutes ago. Then I catch sight of myself in the tinted window of the Rolls and gasp.

Dirt streaks my face, and my hair? I look as if I've been living in the forest like a wild animal.

"You're the most beautiful woman I've ever seen," Nikolai whispers in my ear.

I decide not to chide him for lying because time is everything.

"I have to get in there," I say.

Nikolai laces his fingers through mine. "Let's go."

X leads us inside the main entrance, and it only takes seconds for the gawks and whispers to begin. Before we even make it to the information desk, a camera flashes violently in my face.

"Look!" the paparazzo cries. "It's Prince Nikolai and his latest conquest! How about a quote, Your Highness? Who's the flavor du jour?"

In a flurry of movement, Nikolai has the man by the throat and shoved up against a wall.

"Be careful with your words," he hisses through gritted teeth as the man drops his camera to the floor, his face turning blue.

My eyes widen, and X leans in close, whispering in my ear. "I taught him that."

Before I have time to react, Nikolai lets the man go and is by my side again. In seconds, we've obtained my grandmother's room number. We bypass the elevator and race up the stairs to the fourth floor and stop short just outside her room.

Standing in front of the door are the queen and three guards, Christian and Catriona Wurtzer, and Brother Benedict.

"I almost trusted your little charade," the queen says with a self-satisfied grin. "But imagine my confusion when the prince failed to show up to dinner and I tracked the Rolls to the hospital. Surely X wasn't going to *dispose* of Miss Winter here." She raises a brow. "I suppose I'll have to take care of the disposal myself."

"What the *hell* is this, Adele?" Nikolai growls.

The queen simply nods in our direction. "Arrest them all for treason."

CHAPTER NINETEEN

Nikolai

ONE OF ADELE'S thuggish goons lunges at Kate. But before the oversize gorilla with the neck tattoos can set a single finger on my love's skin, I lay him out with a swift uppercut to the underside of his mean jaw.

"Oof." He hits the floor like a sack of rotten potatoes and doesn't move again.

"That's going to be one hell of a migraine when he comes around," X says with approval, rolling the henchman over with his toe. "Well-played, Sire."

"Who's next?" I roar at the remaining guards. They forget what blood pulses through my veins, that of generations of fierce warriors and plunderers. I am descended from a long and noble line of men and women who got and secured what they wanted by any means necessary. I call on them now to aid me in this hour of dire need. My gut tells me that Nightgardin is using her as their puppet, but I don't have the proof to make an accusation now. Better to wait and watch. For now, the threat is neutralized. She is going down, and Kate will be protected.

Adele snaps her fingers. Sven and Sval, giant twins

who reportedly did time in a Siberian prison as hit men for the Russian mafia, swagger forward, cracking their scarred knuckles.

"Want to tag team, X?" I call out. "A little fun for old times' sake?"

"Only if we challenge ourselves to taking these amateurs in under ten seconds." My bodyguard's wager enrages the twins.

"We *amateurs* eat little worms like you for breakfast." Sven opens his mouth to reveal a row of gold-plated teeth.

"Scared, pretty boy?" Sval jeers.

"I am, actually." I yawn. "Scared that by the time X and I finish with you, there will be nothing left to interrogate."

Sven slowly blinks. "But the queen—"

"Is not heir to the throne." I draw myself to my full height. "And is acting without a signed decree from the royal liege and is therefore in breach of the law. She doesn't have a leg to stand on legally with this attempt at a coup. Treason is being committed here, but it's not by me. With whom do you want to align loyalties, gentlemen?"

"Catriona is not with heir, either!" Christian says, stepping forward, his sister's upper arm in his grasp. "I mean, she's not carrying *your* heir. She made the mistake of confiding her and the queen's little scheme to me. My sister actually thought I'd be party to her own treason to further Rosegate's interests alongside Adele's bigger and more diabolical ambitions. But it's not your child she carries, Nikolai. She has said so herself."

Catriona wrenches from her brother's grasp and

slaps him across the face. "You spoiled everything for me. Everything! The queen will make you pay. *All* of you!"

"I will ruin you," Adele says to my friend, her voice as threatening as the hiss of an adder.

"So be it," Christian says. "But you will *not* ruin the prince." He turns to me. "I'm so sorry, Your Highness. I will never doubt you again." Then he grabs Catriona's arm again and hauls her away.

"Well," I say, eyeing the queen. "That solves the problem of my upcoming nuptials, X. Wouldn't you agree?"

X steps beside me, removing a deadly-looking blade with a jewel-encrusted handle from his black boot. He uses it to casually clean his nails. We are in a hospital, after all, and do wish to remain civil.

"Don't be fools, my good men," I order Adele's remaining brutes. "I am prepared to be reasonable based on the fact you have a combined IQ that is smaller than today's date, but if you come one step closer to Kate, you will be dead." I'll resurrect Edenvale's old beheading customs and do the deed myself.

"Blood doesn't need to be spilled," Benedict breaks in with his deep, commanding voice, as if sensing my murderous urges. A crucifix dangles from his wrist beneath his black clerical habit.

But I am not to be reasoned with. "Anyone here who makes the mistake of touching a single square inch of Kate's body will be chewing on my boot." My voice echoes through the hospital corridor.

The door behind us creaks open.

"Kate?" A fiery-haired woman with creamy skin

and a smattering of freckles peers out. "What's going on? You brought company?"

"Maddie!" Kate sounds on the verge of tears. "Is Gran—?"

"Still touch and go," Maddie says, hugging herself. "She has moments of consciousness, but they are few and far between. Where have you been? You were supposed to relieve me hours ago. I need to step outside for five minutes. Feel fresh air on my face."

"I said arrest them!" the queen shouts to Sven and Sval, but they remain motionless. "Or I shall make sure you are both the first volunteers in my new all-eunuch squadron."

"I must insist that everyone listen to me," Benedict says in a calm voice that silences the chaos. He has always been good at that. "Nikolai has been ordered to marry according to the proclamation, but I have recently learned of the Wagmire Defense."

"The what?" Adele waves her hand. "Never mind— I don't care. Arrest them all."

"If true love can be proven…" Benedict catches and holds my gaze as if the queen hasn't opened her mouth. "Then the marriage may proceed."

Kate gasps behind me.

"Is this true?" I ask, unable to grasp the fact that I might be able to somehow get everything I want.

"I read all eight hundred pages of *The Lesser Known Edenvale Royal Bylaws and Subcommands*." Benedict raises a finger. "There is one catch. To prove true love the couple must swim unassisted across the Bottomless Lake to the Island of Atonement, in accordance with our ancient customs, thereby passing a test of the heart."

I flex my jaw. A mighty challenge awaits us, but I

am determined we shall prove our love's worth. After so many years in the darkness, I am ready to fight for this shot at the light.

"Did you just say swim?" Kate asks in a tiny voice shot through with fear.

An ominous medical device alarm sounds from the room Maddie has just emerged from. Two nurses run up the hall. Kate steps forward, the panic on her face from her fear of water twisting to an expression of pure anguish.

"Gran, no!"

Kate

The nurses rush past me and nearly knock Maddie out of the way. The queen and her two guards are forced to move as well. Nikolai doesn't waste a breath, grabbing my hand and spiriting me inside the room.

I can't see anything other than the nurses, a flurry of movement around my grandmother's bed. My breathing hitches as I prepare myself for the worst.

"Sophia," one of them chides, calling Gran by her first name. "You gave us quite a fright. Next time press the call button, and we'll be in as soon as you need us."

One of the nurses turns to face my sister and me, and her eyes widen when she recognizes Nikolai.

"Your—Your Highness. I didn't realize—"

"Ignore me," he commands. "Let the two Miss Winters know what has happened with their grandmother at once. That should be all that matters here."

Her cheeks redden with embarrassment. "Of course, Your Highness." She turns to Maddie, the one who's been here all day. I swallow back the guilt. I should have come last night when she called. I should have thought about something other than my own fleeting chance at happiness. Then half the ruling body of Edenvale wouldn't be waiting in the hall to take me from my family for good.

"Miss Winter, it seems as if your grandmother is ready to breathe on her own, and she took to telling us by turning off her heart monitor."

Maddie gasps and covers her mouth. I let out a strangled sob.

"She's—she's okay?" I ask, tears of happiness overpowering whatever awaits me when I walk out this door.

The nurse nods, her warm brown eyes immediately setting me at ease. "Please, if you all step out for a few minutes, we can get the doctor in here so we can remove the tube and check her vitals. We'll call you as soon as she's ready."

I nod eagerly, grabbing Maddie's hand. Nikolai holds my other one, and I squeeze them both, two people I love dearly standing beside me.

We step out into the hall, where I find the Royal Police leading away the queen's brutish guards.

"I've spoken with Father," Benedict says to Nikolai. Both men shoot a glance toward Adele, who is also being detained by two officers. "It sounds as if much has gone on tonight that he was unaware of. He'd like to see you for a full statement when you're through here."

Adele growls at us and spits at Nikolai's feet. "You don't deserve happiness," she says. "Not after any chance of it was taken from me because of you and your miserable family. I know people. Powerful people. This is *not* the last you'll hear from me, Prince Nikolai," she vows, her words dripping with both anguish and disdain.

"I'm sure it's not," he says. "But for now I want you out of my sight." He eyes the officers. "Detain her somewhere safe—where she cannot harm others or herself. My father will be in contact with further instructions."

The men nod and take hold of her under the arms, leading her away with heels dragging.

I understand her sadness. I've known great loss, too, as has Nikolai. I'd even shut myself away from the prospect of happiness again after Jean-Luc. For two years I played it safe, afraid to move on. But the queen—she is stuck in a cycle of hate and blame so big that it's blinded her to the world around her.

I shudder.

"No, Pet," I hear Nikolai say. Then my eyes meet his. "I know what you're thinking, and no. I would not have ended up like that."

A tear rolls down my cheek, not only because he's read my thoughts but that he knows what I was thinking about him.

He cups my face in his palms. "It could have been me. I admit that wholly and completely. But it only could have happened had you not walked into my life—or had Adele truly sent you to your death."

He kisses me, his lips fierce and insistent against mine. I can taste the salt of my own tears.

"No," I say. "Your heart may have been dark, but hers is black and cruel. Yours was always salvageable."

"Only by you, Kate."

I smile. "Only by me."

Benedict clears his throat, and I'm reminded that we are not alone.

"The Wagmire Defense," he says.

My grandmother's door opens, and the nurse ushers us in.

"Did someone just say the Wagmire Defense?"

Her voice is like the sweetest music. I keep from throwing myself on her frail body, but I grab Gran's hand and press it to my cheek.

"Yes." I laugh through falling tears. "The Wagmire Defense. Do you—do you know something of it?"

She huffs out a breath as if whatever she's about to say she's told me a million times.

"I knew your mother," she says, and I frown as I realize she's not lucid after all.

"Yes, Grandmother. I know. My mother was your daughter-in-law, remember?"

She waves me off, and the focus of her gaze fixes not on me, not Maddie, but—Nikolai and Benedict.

"I knew *your* mother," she says to the two men. "Knew her when she was a commoner and even after she'd met the terms of the Defense. A great woman, she was—your mother. Pity her history couldn't be shared, sworn to secrecy as we all were."

Nikolai's normally golden skin blanches while Benedict's expression remains impassive.

"She did what she had to do to protect her sons," Gran says, and her gaze returns to me. "And you, my Katie. Love will carry you across the Bottomless Lake. I am sure of it as I'm sure their mother isn't—"

She pauses, and a far-off look takes over her features.

"Nurse," she says, eyeing the woman who's wheeling the ventilator to the other side of the room. The woman turns to face us. "Nurse, would you introduce me to my visitors?"

"We're just volunteers," Maddie says, understanding that Gran's memories have left her. We are once again strangers to her. "Happy to see you're feeling well."

Maddie puts an arm around my shoulders and backs me away from the bed.

"She's gone for now," she whispers. "But it looks like the worst is over."

I nod and swallow back any more tears, for Gran's sake.

"She knew Mother," Benedict says, and I don't miss the hint of bitterness in his voice.

"If your grandmother is telling the truth..." Nikolai starts, but I cut him off.

"She's ill," I tell him. "She could be confusing your mother for someone else."

He shakes his head. "Confusion or not, she knew the Wagmire Defense. Our very own mother found the loophole," Nikolai says softly. "And now Kate—"

I shake my head. "I can't swim," I remind him.

"You can," he says and kisses me. "We can together. And then you'll be my bride."

"I'm terrified," I admit. "And also, that was a terrible proposal. If we survive this Bottomless Lake, I want a real one," I tell him.

He laughs. "And then you'll say yes?"

I shrug but can't fight the giddy smile taking over my face. "I guess we'll see."

He whisks me into the hall, where we hardly have any more privacy, but then, Nikolai loves to put on a show when he has a proper audience. He surprises me, though, with nothing more than a sweet, tender kiss that makes me positively melt.

"I love you," he whispers. "Just so we're clear on that."

I swallow as the words sink in, the words I never thought I'd hear, words he now cannot stop saying. "I love you, too."

"Then that settles it. You *will* be my queen."

I can't help but laugh.

"Still not a proposal," I say.

But yes, I think quietly to myself. *My answer is most certainly yes.*

CHAPTER TWENTY

Nikolai

MY STEPMOTHER IS sent to recuperate on a private therapeutic island in the Indian Ocean. Father is still blinded by his love for her, trusting that her betrayal comes only from a place of grief. But I know better, as does X. He promises to continue a private investigation into Adele's past. Something will turn up.

X briefs me on all the particulars as we race home at top speed. The Rolls-Royce screeches through the palace gates. It is time to face Father.

"Pet." I take Kate's hand between mine and kiss each fingertip. We step out of the car and into the palace's grand entrance. "X can escort you to my chambers. Ensure you get a proper shower and that the cooks prepare a batch of fresh scones."

Kate spent some time with her grandmother before we left the hospital. But now that she is off the ventilator, she and her sister no longer have to remain vigilant at her bedside.

"I don't want to leave you alone to confront your father," she says, setting her jaw in the stubborn manner that I love.

"I don't need anyone to fight my battles for me," I snap, harder than I intend to.

She is unmoved. "Of course you don't. But you deserve to have the woman who loves you by your side no matter what. In good times and bad."

"My father's temper is worse than mine," I warn.

"I don't scare easily," she says with a small smile. Given that she is still beside me despite everything that has happened, I can only choose to believe her. Love for this amazing woman ignites my veins. She is a spark of everlasting fire. When I am beside her the darkness doesn't stand a chance.

X clicks his heels. "I'll inform air traffic control that we intend to depart for the Bottomless Lake within the hour?"

I nod. "Yes. The sooner the better." I squeeze Kate's hand. "I want you to be mine."

She squeezes back, but then I feel her go rigid.

"Something is wrong," I say.

She worries her bottom lip between her teeth. "Won't it—won't it be dark when we arrive?"

The sun already dips beyond the horizon.

I nod. "Yes. But X will see to it that torches are lit so we can find our way. We can wait until morning, though." I kiss her. "Patience is not one of my finer traits, but I can do it—for you."

She shakes her head. "You're right. The sooner the better. I don't want to chance anything else getting in the way of you being mine, as well." She offers me a nervous smile, and my whole being is set ablaze. What this woman has already risked for me—what she's willing to still chance on my behalf—knocks the air straight out of my lungs. I've never known love like this, and I'm still not sure what I've done to deserve it. She needs to know I'd do the same for her.

I turn her toward me and settle my hands on her shoulders. She seems so delicate. Yet behind that fragility is a strength that threatens to bring me to my knees. "The lake, it is deep beyond measure."

She mashes her lips. "Hence the name."

"I will not force you to swim for me. This kingdom isn't worth making you feel like you're in danger for even a moment."

She swallows. "You'd walk away from all this for me?" Her face is pale even as her blue eyes shine bright.

"Without a second thought," I rumble. "Outside of telling you that I love you, these are the truest words that I have ever spoken."

She dips her head. "You think I'm strong enough for this?"

I tilt her chin up and fix my gaze on her. "I think you are strong enough for *anything*. Never doubt that, Kate. Not for one second, my beautiful, courageous *queen*."

Her eyes glisten, but she holds her head high and smiles. "Then I won't back down. Not an inch. You and I shall rule this kingdom, and I will start demonstrating my future courage as a queen by not letting the Bottomless Lake stand between me and my dreams."

She wraps her arms around my neck and presses her lips to mine. There is the sound of slow clapping.

I glance over, and Father stands in a nearby doorway, studying us with a sardonic expression. "Touching," he says in his deep voice. "The best performance I've seen in years."

Kate

I freeze. Yes, I've spoken to the king before, but it was for business purposes only. His voice hadn't sent ice flowing through my veins then. It does now.

"Don't, Father," Nikolai says, his voice firm, but I'm so attuned to him now that I can hear the strain. The worry.

The prince has his father's eyes, but King Nikolai's irises grow dark as he takes a step toward his son. His salt-and-pepper hair is perfectly in place, his suit tailored to an older yet still ruggedly fit body. If he's any indication of what I have to look forward to as Nikolai ages... I shake my head, banishing the thought. Because other than his distinguished good looks, the king stares at me with utter condescension and disapproval, his own gray eyes mired in distaste.

"How dare you speak to me as such," the man says, standing inches from his son. "How dare you bring your whore into our home when you've broken it beyond repair. The queen is *ruined*, you selfish, ungrateful child."

I gasp. The king opens his mouth to speak again, but Nikolai cuts him off.

"Enough, Father!" he roars, enough so that the man takes a step back. Nikolai's hand still grips mine fiercely, enough so that I feel pain, but I stand my ground along with him. "The true *queen* was my mother. And I know everything. I know about the Bottomless Lake, about the Wagmire Defense, and that my own mother was not of royal blood." He holds up his arm. "Look, Father. Take a good look at where common blood flows through my veins all because you wanted to marry for love. And you dare to deny me the same?"

Nikolai's chest heaves with every breath. All of his words, his passion—it's for *me*.

The king's eyes widen. His skin grows pale, and he stumbles back another step. Yet he says nothing.

"If you ever, *ever* refer to Kate as my whore again, I won't be so kind with you as I was with Adele. She is not fit to be queen, Father. And I think, deep down, you know it. But also know this. If you loved my mother enough to risk the kingdom for her, then you might understand a fraction of what I feel for Kate. We will swim the lake. We will make it to the Island of Atonement. And I will prove that I am worthy of her love."

I take in a sharp breath. "No," I finally interrupt. "Nikolai—I must prove myself to *you*."

He lessens his grip on my hand and brings my palm to his lips, pressing a soft kiss against my skin.

"You never had anything to prove," he said. "You and your sister have given everything of yourselves to take care of the only family you have left. I know this was never about money for you but about unconditional and unwavering love. I've spent too long surrounded by people who are with me for their own gain that I forgot what love was. Perhaps this test of will is meant to prove something to the rest of the royal court, but know that whether we make it to the end of this quest or not, we've already won."

I let out a hiccuping sob, yet my smile is as broad as my love for this amazing man.

I cup his hands in my palms. "We've already won," I echo.

X appears in the doorway behind the king, which is odd considering he should have had to walk past us to arrive there. Then again—as I'm beginning to learn—X is capable of far more than we know.

"Sire. My Lady," he says. "The jet is fueled and ready to go. Are you ready?"

We both nod without hesitation, but the king approaches his son again, this time planting his hands on Nikolai's shoulders. Nikolai stiffens.

"You really love her," he says, and then he begins to laugh. "You *love* her!"

"Father, have you gone mad?"

The king laughs again, his head tilted toward the ceiling. "How," he says, "after all these years, could you expect me to believe your feelings were true? You've never so much as brought a woman to dine with us, yet you are willing to swim the lake for a commoner."

Nikolai's jaw tightens, and his father's laughing ceases.

"Commoner or not, your mother had more royal blood than any queen before her. No one—and I mean *no one*—shall ever be her equal."

Nikolai swallows hard, understanding what I know to be true, as well.

Theirs was a great love—Nikolai's mother and father's. Perhaps that is why someone like Adele was able to manipulate her way to the throne. No one could ever replace the love the king lost, but the kingdom needed a queen. Adele must have been the perfect aristocratic fit—on paper.

But there is so much more to finding the perfect

match, as I've found mine in the most unlikely of places.

"I know the feeling," Nikolai says, the slightest tremor in his otherwise determined voice.

"How did you know?" the king asks, scrubbing a hand across his jaw. "How did you know about your mother?"

I clear my throat. "My grandmother, Your Highness," I say, taking a steady breath. "She's not well, mentally speaking, but she has moments of clarity. I believe she might have known the late queen many years ago."

The king pulls both Nikolai and I into an unexpected embrace, and I respond on instinct, wrapping one arm around each of the men at my sides.

"Go," King Nikolai whispers to us both. "Go prove your love to the rest of the world. You've already proven it to me."

He releases us, and both Nikolai and I bow our heads to our respected ruler.

"Why, though?" Nikolai asks. "Why did you never tell us?"

The king shudders his expression, and I wait for him to repeat what Gran said, something about protecting her sons.

"My father wasn't so understanding," he simply says. "So we were forced to live a lie, to tell all that she came from an ancient royal line only recently uncovered. And because I loved your mother, I didn't fight him on it. She was my queen. That was all that mattered."

It's a nice enough story, but for reasons I cannot explain, I think he's lying. Maybe it's that Nikolai is so much like his father, that being able to read one allows me to read the other.

But Nikolai's beautiful smile is his acceptance, so I let it go. Because Nikolai is my prince. And that's all that matters to me.

"Thank you, My Liege," Nikolai says, and it's in this moment I know he will be the king this country needs…and the man I cannot live without.

As X leads us toward the doors from where we came, Nikolai stops and turns toward his father once more.

"I'd like to move Kate's grandmother—and sister, if she chooses—to the palace after the wedding. Her grandmother will need constant care, so I'll be hiring nursing staff, as well."

His father nods. "Tell me her name, and I'll see to it the preparations are made."

"Sophia Winter," Nikolai says before spinning back toward X so that only I see the look of complete and utter astonishment take over the king's countenance. But it lasts no longer than a second before he is a mask of calm again, so much so that I believe it must have been my imagination playing tricks on me.

"Consider it done," the king says, and before I know it, I'm spirited out the palace gates and to the airfield once again.

"It's time to claim our future," Nikolai says as we stand before the steps leading up to the aircraft.

And then he kisses me until I forget that I almost died tonight, until I forget the king's strange reaction to my grandmother's name, until I forget that I have anything to fear.

I will claim my future, I think, as his tongue sweeps past my lips and I taste victory already.

And then I whisper against him. "My future—is *you*."

CHAPTER TWENTY-ONE

Nikolai

THE BOTTOMLESS LAKE is located in the most remote region on the eastern borders of my kingdom. We fly over fifteen-thousand-foot mountain peaks until we reach a high-altitude meadow with a runway. Long golden grass waves in the wind while white flowers bob as if in greeting. After we disembark the jet, I take Kate's hand in mine, leading the way along the narrow trail. No words pass between us. At least nothing that can be spoken aloud. The trail swings out onto a cliff, and I hear her gasp. Not because of the sheer granite wall and vertigo drop-off. But because of what lies so far down below.

It is the deepest lake in the world. There are rumors of ancient creatures trolling these mysterious waters—sea monsters, mermaids and other such nonsense. But I don't take much stock in the old storytelling.

Still, it's disconcerting to peer into water that blue, visible even in the luminescence of the moon, that pitiless color that seems to attract all available light, to suck it down into its icy heart.

I lace my fingers with Kate's, let our palms slide in

a gentle caress, a delicious promise of later. Heat ignites my veins. Soon, so soon, this beautiful woman will be mine.

X guides us down the stone steps to the lakeshore, and as he sets to work lighting floating torches to blaze our trail, I strip from my clothing in easy, unconcerned movements. As I remove my pants I smile as she stares at my cock.

"See something you like, Pet?" I ask her with a wry smile. I love that my body gives her such wicked, carnal pleasure.

She opens her mouth, and I expect a witty insult. Instead, she sucks in a breath and falls to her knees, bracing her hands on the gravelly beach.

My flirtatious instincts evaporate as I slip into pure protection mode. "What is it?" I drop into a low crouch.

"It's a stupid thing to be this afraid of water, isn't it?" She lifts her gaze, and the pain stamped there almost levels me. "But try rationalizing that with my body."

"Kate, my love, I have told you before, I don't require you to do this. My kingdom pales in comparison to your safety and happiness."

"I want to be brave for you, for me, for us, for love. But it's not the memory of what I've lost at the depths of a river shallower than this. It's what I could lose. I don't just mean us losing our freedom to marry, Nikolai. What if something happened? What if I lost *you*?" Kate shakes her head, and then her jaw takes on that determined set that makes me want her all the more. "Promise me you can do this, and I won't let fear win." She removes her dress and is bare before me, all creamy skin and soft angles. Her perfect breasts make my mouth water.

I step forward. "I can do this, Kate. *We* can do this. Though I can't help feeling that I don't deserve you."

She presses a cool hand to the side of my cheek, skimming my stubble. "We could stand here debating that claim, or we could swim to the Island of Atonement and get on with the rest of our lives."

We stare out to the middle of the lake, now dotted with small licks of flame, to where a modest, heart-shaped island is covered by a thick blanket of trees. In the middle is a tall stone tower, glittering in the brilliant moonlight, that looks as ancient as the mountains.

"What is waiting for us out there?" she whispers.

"I can't say for certain." I cover her hand with mine. "But whatever dangers or mysteries we are about to face, we'll face them together."

"Just as we will anything else in life."

She nods and wades into the water, and I've never seen anything more stunning. This woman is willing to sacrifice anything for me, for us.

I feel the same way.

And so I follow after.

Kate

The water is surprisingly warm, yet I inhale a shuddering breath. Nikolai's hand is still in mine as we wade deeper, following the line of X's torchlights, though X himself is nowhere to be seen.

Because we must do this alone.

Nikolai suddenly halts.

"What is it?" I ask.

He squeezes my hand. "The bottom will drop out soon," he warns, and I can tell he fights to keep his voice even. "You said once that your sister said you could swim, that you'd just blocked it out. I can't let you go any farther, Kate. Not if you are putting your life at risk."

I nod, knowing what he is asking of me—what I am asking of him. The water is halfway up my torso, my breasts nearly covered, and despite the balmy air, I tremble. Then I squeeze my eyes shut and drop beneath the surface, letting go of Nikolai's hand. The last thing I hear is him frantically calling my name.

I force my eyes open. The water is clear but dark, and in the places below a floating torch, I catch the movement of a fish or whatever else dwells beneath the surface. My heart races as panic threatens to take hold of my senses, but I remind myself that there is clean air above me, that I am not alone, and that I am not trapped as my parents were.

I am not trapped. But Nikolai is. And he is depending on me to set him free.

I kick my legs out behind me and push my palms and my outstretched arms through the water. And then I burst through the surface. My feet no longer reach the ground, yet I am still here. I am in control.

I am triumphant.

"Kate!" Nikolai cries, his voice hoarse as he swims out to meet me. "Fucking hell, Kate. What are you doing?"

I grin as my arms and legs make circles through the inky blue. "I'm pretty sure I'm swimming," I say, and my heart thunders in my chest. "Oh, my God, Nikolai. I'm swimming!"

His eyes gleam silver in the moonlight, and the terror I know I caused washes from his face.

"You did it," he says. "Jesus, fuck, you did it!"

I narrow my eyes. "Don't let Benedict hear you speaking like that."

He lets out a broad, bellowing laugh and kisses me as he keeps himself afloat.

"Let's go get our future," I say. He nods, and we set out for the island.

We swim from torch to torch, each one a beacon. As my adrenaline wanes and the long minutes set in, my limbs grow weary.

"Just make it to the next torch," Nikolai says, when he senses my exhaustion.

And so I vow to make it to the next torch. And then the next one. And the one after that until I stumble as my toes unexpectedly dig into sand.

I straighten and stand as tears spring from my eyes. Nikolai doesn't waste a second as he scoops me into his arms and kisses me hard, unrelenting, and I realize my only fear now is that I will never be able to get enough of this man.

He doesn't let go, doesn't release me from the kiss as he strides onto shore, his strong arms holding me close. It is a mirror image of the day we met, when he carried me to safety in the maze. Then I was determined to marry him off to another. But today I risk everything to make him mine.

I cling to his solid, naked form as he marches straight for the stone monument, and he only releases me when we stand before a carved-out doorway that beckons us to enter.

We do.

I gasp as Nikolai whispers, *"Look."* His head tilts toward the ceiling—or at least where there should be one. But instead the stone opens to the star-speckled sky, to the full moon in all her brilliance, lighting us from above. I spin, my eyes taking in the walls that surround us, and see that they are covered with rich, painted murals, all different versions of two lovers discovering this land.

"Oh, Nikolai." Those are my only words, though. I am not sure I have breath to give life to what I wish to say.

"I know," he says, relieving me from the burden as we simply marvel and stare.

I run my hands along the painted stone walls until I come to a spot of empty canvas, a section of a wall waiting for the next painting. It's then that my fingers nick a loose stone, sending it crashing to the floor.

I gasp. "I'm sorry! Oh, my God. I broke the monument. I survived that swim to come here and ruin this sacred place, and I—" But I gasp again as Nikolai, without hesitation, reaches his arm inside the shadowy opening. This is the thing horror stories are made of, and I brace myself for him to cry out as some deadly creature takes his hand, but instead he pulls out a blue wooden box no bigger than a schoolchild's pencil case. A piece of parchment is wrapped around it, fastened with a waxen seal.

Now it is Nikolai who gasps.

"What is it?" I ask, and he stares up at me, his gray eyes glistening.

He smiles as a tear escapes down his beautiful, chiseled cheek.

"This is the royal seal," he says. "I think—I think this is from my parents."

I step into his grasp, wrapping my arms around his torso. Then he breaks open the seal and unfolds the parchment, holding it up for both of us to see.

"Read it to me," he says. "I'm too fucking nervous."

I swallow and do as he asks, reading the letter aloud as my own eyes well with tears again.

To Our Dearest Nikolai,

Generations have gone before us, those that have abided by the ancient decree. And should you go that route as well, we pray that you are happy. That if and when it is necessary, this finds your heir; that generations do not pass before Edenvale is rewarded once again with a king and queen who are pure of heart. For we have found the way to true happiness.

Our only hope is that you are able to do the same. Should you find the one who fills your heart, then she shall also be the one to fill your soul. There is no room for blackness, for hate, for anything to cloud the mind of a king who shall rule with a just hand if he has true love in his heart. If you've found this gift, do not take such treasure for granted. Populate the palace with heirs, with products of a love immeasurable, and the kingdom will prosper as does your devotion.

To love and be loved in return—there is no greater reward we can bestow upon you. But take what is in this box and use it as a token of that love. Then, when the time is right, come back to this place and paint your story upon these walls. Leave a token for those who come after you.

With all the love in our hearts, King Nikolai and Queen Cordelia

I wipe away tears as I finish, my arms still around my prince. He says nothing as he opens the box and removes a glorious sapphire-and-diamond ring—a ring fit only for a queen.

He pulls away and stares down at me with shining eyes, his beautiful naked body bathed in radiant moonlight. He lets the box and parchment clatter to the stone floor as he drops to his knee.

"You said you wanted a real proposal," he says, no hint of the rogue I met barely a month ago in his gaze or in his tone.

I cover my mouth and nod, unable to speak without the possibility of sobbing.

"Then here it is, Kate. There is nothing more real than my love for you. Words cannot capture it. The entire kingdom cannot contain it. It is as deep as a lake with no bottom and as vast as the infinite universe. I would have given up my birthright for you, but instead you gave up your fear for me. I can think of no greater act of love than the one you have performed. I beg you to give me a lifetime to repay you. Be my life. Be my love. Be my queen."

I sink to my knees in front of him, pressing my lips together to keep from falling apart. Then I stand and take his face in my hands.

"Yes," I whisper, and I kiss him again and again and again. "Yes, Nikolai." He kisses me back, pulling my left hand free so he can slide the ring onto my finger. It is a perfect fit. "Infinite times—*yes*. But wait. First we have to take care of one pesky detail."

His face blanches. "What. What more do you need? Kate, I'll do anything to win your hand."

I take a step toward him, splaying my palms against his chest. "We had a wager."

And there it is, that feline grin of his that tells me he wants to devour me whole. I might let him.

"Why, yes, my love. We did have a wager. And I do believe you won. Didn't you?"

I nod. "Do you remember the terms?"

His brows furrow, and he scrubs a hand across his beautifully stubbled jaw. "I owe you nothing more than a favor. Would you like me to make payment? What is your price?"

I nod again then stand on my toes and whisper in his ear. Nikolai's eyes widen, and he lets out a guttural sound.

"As you wish, Beloved," he says.

My skin is pebbles of gooseflesh. I'm wearing nothing but the glittering jewels on my finger. I marvel at his stiff length, ready for me as the heat coils in my belly, so very ready for him. I let him guide me back into the water. He speaks no words at all as he pulls me over his beautiful body.

The lake water is cool against my skin, but his tip is warm and wet at my opening where he nudges until slick heat envelops his perfect, thick erection. I sink over it, burying him to the hilt.

He bites my shoulder and growls.

I slide up slowly and let him swirl around my swollen center before plummeting over him again.

He cradles my face in his hands and stares intently into my eyes—eyes I know are reddened from tears of disbelief, of love, of complete and utter joy.

"We may rule this kingdom for a lifetime, but you—my future wife and my future queen—shall rule my heart for eternity. Just as those paintings on the island's tower wall, my love for you lives beyond this life and beyond this world."

"Nikolai," I gasp as he moves inside me. "I love you, too."

"But," he says, flicking his tongue against my lips, the devil in his stare, "just because you rule me doesn't mean you'll ever tame me."

He pinches my pebbled nipple, and I shriek at the exquisite pleasure and pain.

"After all—I'm still one royal prick."

And he is my royal temptation. I will never, ever get enough.

EPILOGUE

X

I WIPE REMNANTS of drywall from my shoulder as the sound of drilling whines through the ceiling.

"You're getting sloppy, X," she scolds from the shadows. "You've been followed."

I step to the left and watch the drywall dust on the carpet to my right.

I raise my brows, knowing that she can see me even though I cannot see her.

"Really?" I ask. "Because if that were true, why are they a floor above?" I nod toward the flashing blue light on the desk in front of her. "Perhaps they have no idea *I'm* here. Perhaps they weren't even looking until a server signal popped up on their screen." I imagine her dark eyes boring holes through me.

She lets out a sigh. "You are still as arrogant as ever."

I grin and take a step forward. She doesn't stop me because she knows I'm still not close enough to see.

"And you're still as easy to ruffle as ever. And, my Lady, I do enjoy ruffling you."

There is a long silence but for the drilling overhead.

They will break through soon. We're on borrowed time, but then again, we always are.

"Tell me," she says, her voice firm, though I detect the slightest tremor. Our parrying is over. "Is he safe?"

I open my mouth to say her name—or maybe her call sign, *D*. But I stop myself as I always do. If I don't speak it aloud, no one else can hear. If I don't see her in the flesh, they cannot torture her existence from me.

I bite back a self-satisfied grin. I've survived the worst any captor has had to offer—whips, brands, knives sharp enough to draw blood yet small enough that bleeding out would be a long, slow death.

Much to the disappointment of all who've tried, I'm not dead. Unfortunately for them—they are.

"X," she pleads, as if I'd ever falter on a mission.

"He is safe," I say. "He and the princess are enjoying an extended honeymoon on a private island off the coast. They will return soon, but plans for the celebration have been postponed until the king decides what to do with the traitorous queen. The prince, though, will rule at his father's side, and the princess will serve as ambassador to our neighbors."

"And Rosegate?" she asks.

A chunk of ceiling falls to the floor.

"We don't have much time," I say. "They *will* break through. And Rosegate is secure for the time being, but we're still trying to figure out if the queen's motive was merely to take the throne or to aid Nightgardin in Edenvale's fall."

She pulls the thumb drive, the source of the flashing light, from the laptop's USB port.

"We won't be here when they break through," she says, and I hold up my palm, my hand curling into a fist to catch the small projectile. "I want the oldest prince to remain under surveillance, but you are relieved of immediate duty when it comes to him."

I nod. More drywall falls. I clip the carabiners to the belt loops on my trousers and wonder for the first time if the material will hold. I guess we're about to find out.

"What is the next mission?" I ask, knowing there is one.

I hear the wheels of her chair roll and can tell from the cadence of her breathing that she's now standing.

"It's all on the drive," she says.

I look down at the blue light in my palm. "The heir spare," I say, knowing without a computer monitor in front of me to corroborate. This is exactly what Nikolai wanted anyway. He will be none the wiser when my attentions shift.

"He is lost," she says, "the second son." Her voice grows distant as she does what she does best and disappears into a world that used to recognize her in seconds— one that now knows nothing of her existence.

Lost, I think. *What if he doesn't want to be found?*

The ceiling caves in, and because being found is not on *my* agenda for the day, I unhook one of the carabiners and leap from the fifteenth-floor window.

I throw the bungee cable over the line and let gravity and the southerly wind do their job.

I skim over taxis, buses, locals and tourists, none of them aware of my existence overhead.

When I land on the hotel balcony, I make a mental note to thank the tailor of this suit. The strength of the belt loops is exquisite.

I brush away any further signs of ceiling dust and pick up my tumbler from the balcony ledge, draining the rest of my scotch. Then I thrust open the balcony doors to find a delicious brunette naked on the bed, a blindfold over her eyes and her wrists still bound to the bedpost. She purses her luscious, red-painted lips into a pout.

"You said you were running out to grab your drink. You've been gone for at least five minutes, X."

I check my watch. "Seven, darling."

She writhes against the satin sheet and bites her lip. "Well, I'm counting the minutes until you fuck me."

I tap my breast pocket and make sure the flash drive is stored securely. Then I tear off the jacket.

"Spread your legs and count down from three," I command, and she writhes again.

I unbutton my shirt.

"Three," she moans.

I lose the pants.

"Two."

I press my knees into the edge of the bed and run a hand up her thigh, my thumb teasing her folds where I left her drenched with anticipation.

"One," she whimpers.

Time's up.

* * * * *

THE MAVERICK PRINCE

CATHERINE MANN

To my favourite little princesses and princes – Megan, Frances, James and Zach. Thank you for inviting Aunt Cathy to your prince and princess tea parties. The snack cakes and Sprite were absolutely magical!

Prologue

GlobalIntruder.com
Exclusive: For Immediate Release

Royalty Revealed!

Do you have a prince living next door? Quite possibly!

Courtesy of a positive identification made by one of the GlobalIntruder.com's very own photojournalists, we've successfully landed the scoop of the year. The deposed Medina monarchy has not, as was rumored, set up shop in a highly secured fortress in Argentina. The three Medina heirs—with their billions—have been living under assumed names and rubbing elbows with everyday Americans for decades.

We hear the sexy baby of the family, Antonio, is already taken in Texas by his waitress girlfriend

Shannon Crawford. She'd better watch her back now that word is out about her secret shipping magnate!

Meanwhile, never fear, ladies. There are still two single and studly Medina men left. Our sources reveal that Duarte dwells in his plush resort in Martha's Vineyard. Carlos—a surgeon, no less—resides in Tacoma. Wonder if he makes house calls?

No word yet on their father, King Enrique Medina, former ruler of San Rinaldo, an island off the coast of Spain. But our best reporters are hot on the trail.

For the latest update on how to nab a prince, check back in with the GlobalIntruder.com. And remember, you heard it here first!

One

"**K**ing takes the queen." Antonio Medina declared his victory and raked in the chips, having bluffed with a simple high-card hand in Texas Hold'Em.

Ignoring an incoming call on his iPhone, he stacked his winnings. He didn't often have time for poker since his fishing charter company went global, but joining backroom games at his pal Vernon's Galveston Bay Grille had become a more frequent occurrence of late. Since Shannon. His gaze snapped to the long skinny windows on either side of the door leading out to the main dining area where she worked.

No sign of Shannon's slim body, winding her way through the brass, crystal and white linen of the five-star restaurant. Disappointment chewed at him in spite of his win.

A cell phone chime cut the air, then a second right

afterward. Not his either time, although the noise still forced his focus back to the private table while two of Vernon Wolfe's cronies pressed the ignore button, cutting the ringing short. Vernon's poker pals were all about forty years senior to Antonio. But the old shrimp-boat captain turned restaurateur had saved Antonio's bacon back when he'd been a teen. So if Vernon beckoned, Antonio did his damnedest to show. The fact that Shannon also worked here provided extra oomph to the request.

Vernon creaked back in the leather chair, also disregarding his cell phone currently crooning "Son of a Sailor" from his belt. "Ballsy move holding with just a king, Tony," he said, his voice perpetually raspy from years of shouting on deck. His face still sported a year-round tan, eyes raccoon ringed from sunglasses. "I thought Glenn had a royal flush with his queen and jack showing."

"I was taught to bluff by the best." Antonio—or Tony Castillo as he was known these days—grinned.

A smile was more disarming than a scowl. He always smiled so nobody knew what he was thinking. Not that even his best grin had gained him forgiveness from Shannon after their fight last weekend.

Resisting the urge to frown, Tony stacked his chips on the scarred wooden table Vernon had pried from his boat before docking himself permanently at the restaurant. "Your pal Glenn needs to bluff better."

Glenn—a coffee addict—chugged his java faster when bluffing. For some reason no one else seemed to notice as the high-priced attorney banged back his third brew laced with Irish whiskey. He then simply shrugged, loosened his silk tie and hooked it on the back of the chair, settling in for the next round.

Vernon swept up the played cards, flipping the king of hearts between his fingers until the cell stopped singing vintage Jimmy Buffett. "Keep winning and they're not going to let me deal you in anymore."

Tony went through the motions of laughing along, but he knew he wasn't going anywhere. This was his world now. He'd built a life of his own and wanted nothing to do with the Medina name. He was Tony Castillo now. His father had honored that. Until recently.

For the past six months, his deposed king of a dad had sent message after message demanding his presence at the secluded island compound off the coast of Florida. Tony had left that gilded prison the second he'd turned eighteen and never looked back. If Enrique was as sick as he claimed, then their problems would have to be sorted out in heaven...or more likely in somewhere hotter even than Texas.

While October meant autumn chills for folks like his two brothers, he preferred the lengthened summers in Galveston Bay. The air conditioner still cranked in the redbrick waterside restaurant in the historic district.

Muffled live music from a flamenco guitarist drifted through the wall along with the drone of dining clientele. Business was booming for Vernon. Tony made sure of that. Vernon had given Antonio a job at eighteen when no one else would trust a kid with sketchy ID. Fourteen years and many millions of dollars later, Tony figured it was only fair some of the proceeds from the shipping business he'd built should buy the aging shrimp-boat captain a retirement plan.

Vernon nudged the deck toward Glenn to cut, then dealt the next hand. Glenn shoved his buzzing BlackBerry beside his spiked coffee and thumbed his cards up for a peek.

Tony reached for his...and stopped...tipping his ear toward the sound from outside the door. A light laugh cut through the clanging dishes and fluttering strum of the

Spanish guitar. *Her* laugh. Finally. The simple sound made him ache after a week without her.

His gaze shot straight to the door again, bracketed by two windows showcasing the dining area. Shannon stepped in view of the left lengthy pane, pausing to punch in an order at the servers' station. She squinted behind her cat-eye glasses, the retros giving her a naughty schoolmarm look that never failed to send his libido surging.

Light from the globed sconces glinted on her pale blond hair. She wore her long locks in a messy updo, as much a part of her work uniform as the knee-length black skirt and form-fitting tuxedo vest. She looked sexy as hell—and exhausted.

Damn it all, he would help her without hesitation. Just last weekend he'd suggested as much when she'd pulled on her clothes after they'd made love at his Bay Shore mansion. She'd shut him down faster than the next heartbeat. In fact, she hadn't spoken to him or returned his calls since.

Stubborn, sexy woman. It wasn't like he'd offered to set her up as his mistress, for crying out loud. He was only trying to help her and her three-year-old son. She always vowed she would do anything for Kolby.

Mentioning that part hadn't gone well for him, either.

Her lips had pursed tight, but her eyes behind those sexy black glasses had told him she wanted to throw his offer back in his face. His ears still rang from the slamming door when she'd walked out. Most women he knew would have jumped at the prospect of money or expensive gifts. Not Shannon. If anything, she seemed put off by his wealth. It had taken him two months to persuade her just to have coffee with him. Then two more months to work his way into bed with her. And after nearly four weeks of mind-bending sex, he was still no closer to understanding her.

Okay, so he'd built a fortune from Galveston Bay being

one of the largest importers of seafood. Luck had played a part by landing him here in the first place. He'd simply been looking for a coastal community that reminded him of home.

His real home, off the coast of Spain. Not the island fortress his father had built off the U.S. The one he'd escaped the day he'd turned eighteen and swapped his last name from Medina to Castillo. The new surname had been plucked from one of the many branches twigging off his regal family tree. Tony *Castillo* had vowed never to return, a vow he'd kept.

And he didn't even want to think about how spooked Shannon would be if she knew the well-kept secret of his royal heritage. Not that the secret was his to share.

Vernon tapped the scarred wooden table in front of him. "Your phone's buzzing again. We can hold off on this hand while you take the call."

Tony thumbed the ignore button on his iPhone without looking. He only disregarded the outside world for two people, Shannon and Vernon. "It's about the Salinas Shrimp deal. They need to sweat for another hour before we settle on the bottom line."

Glenn rolled his coffee mug between his palms. "So when we don't hear back from you, we'll all know you hit the ignore button."

"Never," Tony responded absently, tucking the device back inside his suit coat. More and more he looked forward to Shannon's steady calm at the end of a hectic day.

Vernon's phone chimed again—Good God, what was up with all the interruptions?—this time rumbling with Marvin Gaye's "Let's Get It On."

The grizzled captain slapped down his cards. "That's my wife. Gotta take this one." Bluetooth glowing in his ear, he shot to his feet and tucked into a corner for semiprivacy. "Yeah, sugar?"

Since Vernon had just tied the knot for the first time seven months ago, the guy acted like a twenty-year-old newlywed. Tony walled off flickering thoughts of his own parents' marriage, not too hard since there weren't that many to remember. His mother had died when he was five.

Vernon inhaled sharply. Tony looked up. His old mentor's face paled under a tan so deep it almost seemed tattooed. What the hell?

"Tony." Vernon's voice went beyond raspy, like the guy had swallowed ground glass. "I think you'd better check those missed messages."

"Is something wrong?" he asked, already reaching for his iPhone.

"You'll have to tell us that," Vernon answered without once taking his raccoonlike eyes off Tony. "Actually, you can skip the messages and just head straight for the internet."

"Where?" He tapped through the menu.

"Anywhere." Vernon sank back into his chair like an anchor thudding to the bottom of the ocean floor. "It's headlining everywhere. You won't miss it."

His iPhone connected to the internet and displayed the top stories—

> Royalty Revealed!
> Medina Monarchy Exposed!

Blinking fast, he stared in shock at the last thing he expected, but the outcome his father had always feared most. One heading at a time, his family's cover was peeled away until he settled on the last in the list.

Meet the Medina Mistress!

The insane speed of viral news… His gaze shot straight to the windows separating him from the waiters' station, where seconds ago he'd seen Shannon.

Sure enough, she still stood with her back to him. He wouldn't have much time. He had to talk to her before she finished tapping in her order or tabulating a bill.

Tony shot to his feet, his chair scraping loudly in the silence as Vernon's friends all checked their messages. Reaching for the brass handle, he kept his eyes locked on the woman who turned him inside out with one touch of her hand on his bare flesh, the simple brush of her hair across his chest until he forgot about staying on guard. Foreboding crept up his spine. His instincts had served him well over the years—steering him through multimillion-dollar business decisions, even warning him of a frayed shrimp net inching closer to snag his feet.

And before all that? The extra sense had powered his stride as he'd raced through the woods, running from rebels overthrowing San Rinaldo's government. Rebels who hadn't thought twice about shooting at kids, even a five-year-old.

Or murdering their mother.

The Medina cover was about more than privacy. It was about safety. While his family had relocated to a U.S. island after the coup, they could never let down their guard. And damn it all, he'd selfishly put Shannon in the crosshairs simply because he had to have her in his bed.

Tony clasped her shoulders and turned her around. Only to stop short.

Her beautiful blue eyes wide with horror said it all. And if he'd been in doubt? The cell phone clutched in Shannon's hand told him the rest.

She already knew.

* * *

She didn't want to know.

The internet rumor her son's babysitter had read over the phone had to be a media mistake. As did the five follow-up articles she'd found in her own ten-second search with her cell's internet service.

The blogosphere could bloom toxic fiction in minutes, right? People could say whatever they wanted, make a fortune off click-throughs and then retract the erroneous story the next day. Tony's touch on her shoulders was so familiar and stirring he simply couldn't be a stranger. Even now her body warmed at the feel of his hands until she swayed.

But then hadn't she made the very same mistake with her dead husband, buying into his facade because she *wanted* it to be true?

Damn it, Tony wasn't Nolan. All of this would be explained away and she could go back to her toe-curling affair with Tony. Except they were already in the middle of a fight over trying to give her money—an offer that made her skin crawl. And if he was actually a prince?

She swallowed hysterical laughter. Well, he'd told her that he had money to burn and it could very well be he'd meant that on a scale far grander than she could have ever imagined.

"Breathe," her ex-lover commanded.

"Okay, okay, okay," she chanted on each gasp of air, tapping her glasses more firmly in place in hopes the dots in front of her eyes would fade. "I'm okay."

Now that her vision cleared she had a better view of her place at the center of the restaurant's attention. And when had Tony started edging her toward the door? Impending doom welled inside her as she realized the local media would soon descend.

"Good, steady now, in and out." His voice didn't sound any different.

But it also didn't sound Texan. Or southern. Or even northern for that matter, as if he'd worked to stamp out any sense of regionality from himself. She tried to focus on the timbre that so thoroughly strummed her senses when they made love.

"Tony, please say we're going to laugh over this misunderstanding later."

He didn't answer. His square jaw was set and serious as he looked over her shoulder, scanning. She found no signs of her carefree lover, even though her fingers carried the memory of how his dark hair curled around her fingers. His wealth and power had been undeniable from the start in his clothes and lifestyle, but most of all in his proud carriage. Now she took new note of his aristocratic jaw and cheekbones. Such a damn handsome and charming man. She'd allowed herself to be wowed. Seduced by his smile.

She'd barely come to grips with dating a rich guy, given all the bad baggage that brought up of her dead husband. A crooked sleaze. She'd been dazzled by Nolan's glitzy world, learning too late it was financed by a Ponzi scheme.

The guilt of those destroyed lives squeezed the breath from her lungs all over again. If not for her son, she might very well have curled inside herself and given up after Nolan took his own life. But she would hold strong for Kolby.

"Answer me," she demanded, hoping.

"This isn't the place to talk."

Not reassuring and, oh God, why did Tony still have the power to hurt her? Anger punched through the pain. "How long does it take to say *damned rumor?*"

He slid an arm around her shoulders, tucking her to his side. "Let's find somewhere more private."

"Tell me now." She pulled back from the lure of his familiar scent, minty patchouli and sandalwood, the smell of exotic pleasures.

Tony—Antonio—Prince Medina—whoever the hell he was—ducked his head closer to hers. "Shannon, do you really want to talk here where anyone can listen? The world's going to intrude on our town soon enough."

Tears burned behind her eyes, the room going blurry even with her glasses on. "Okay, we'll find a quiet place to discuss this."

He backed her toward the kitchen. Her legs and his synched up in step, her hips following his instinctively, as if they'd danced together often...and more. Eyes and whispers followed them the entire way. Did everyone already know? Cell phones sang from pockets and vibrated on tabletops as if Galveston quivered on the verge of an earthquake.

No one approached them outright, but fragments drifted from their huddled discussions.

"Could Tony Castillo be—"

"—Medina—"

"—With that waitress—"

The buzz increased like a swarm of locusts closing in on the Texas landscape. On her life.

Tony growled lowly, "There's nowhere here we can speak privately. I need to get you out of Vernon's."

His muscled arm locked her tighter, guiding her through a swishing door, past a string of chefs all immobile and gawking. He shouldered out a side door and she had no choice but to follow.

Outside, the late-day sun kissed his bronzed face, bringing his deeply tanned features into sharper focus. She'd always known there was something strikingly foreign about him. But she'd believed his story of dead parents, bookkeepers who'd emigrated from South America. Her own parents had died in a car accident before she'd graduated from college. She'd thought they'd at least shared similar childhoods.

Now? She was sure of nothing except how her body still betrayed her with the urge to lean into his hard-muscled strength, to escape into the pleasure she knew he could bring.

"I need to let management know I'm leaving. I can't lose this job." Tips were best in the evening and she needed every penny. She couldn't afford the time it would take to get her teaching credentials current again—if she could even find a music-teaching position with cutbacks in the arts.

And there weren't too many people out there in search of private oboe lessons.

"I know the owner, remember?" He unlocked his car, the remote chirp-chirping.

"Of course. What was I thinking? You have connections." She stifled a fresh bout of hysterical laughter.

Would she even be able to work again if the Medina rumor was true? It had been tough enough finding a job when others associated her with her dead husband. Sure, she'd been cleared of any wrongdoing, but many still believed she must have known about Nolan's illegal schemes.

There hadn't even been a trial for her to state her side. Once her husband had made bail, he'd been dead within twenty-four hours.

Tony cursed low and harsh, sailor-style swearing he usually curbed around her and Kolby. She looked around, saw nothing... Then she heard the thundering footsteps a second before the small cluster of people rounded the corner with cameras and microphones.

Swearing again, Tony yanked open the passenger door to his Escalade. He lifted her inside easily, as if she weighed nothing more than the tray of fried gator appetizers she'd carried earlier.

Seconds later he slid behind the wheel and slammed the door a hair's breadth ahead of the reporters. Fists pounded on the tinted windows. Locks auto-clicked. Shannon sagged in the leather seat with relief.

The hefty SUV rocked from the force of the mob. Her heart rate ramped again. If this was the life of the rich and famous, she wanted no part.

Shifting into Reverse then forward, Tony drove, slow but steady. People peeled away. At least one reporter fell on his butt but everyone appeared unharmed.

So much for playing chicken with Tony. She would be wise to remember that.

He guided the Escalade through the historic district a hint over the speed limit, fast enough to put space between them and the media hounds. Panting in the aftermath, she still braced a hand on the dash, her other gripping the leather seat. Yet Tony hadn't even broken a sweat.

His hands stayed steady on the wheel, his expensive watch glinting from the French cuffs of his shirt. Restored brick buildings zipped by her window. A young couple dressed for an evening out stepped off the curb, then back sharply. While the whole idea of being hunted by the paparazzi scared her to her roots, right here in the SUV with Tony, she felt safe.

Safe enough for the anger and betrayal to come bubbling to the surface. She'd been mad at him since their fight last weekend over his continued insistence on giving her money.

But those feelings were nothing compared to the rage that coursed through her now. "We're alone. Talk to me."

"It's complicated." He glanced in the rearview mirror. Normal traffic tooled along the narrow street. "What do you want to know?"

She forced herself to say the words that would drive a permanent wedge between her and the one man she'd dared let into her life again.

"Are you a part of that lost royal family, the one everybody thought was hiding in Argentina?"

The Cadillac's finely tuned engine hummed in the silence. Lights clicked on automatically with the setting sun, the dash glowing.

His knuckles went white on the steering wheel, his jaw flexing before he nodded tightly. "The rumors on the internet are correct."

And she'd thought her heart couldn't break again.

Her pride had been stung over Tony's offer to give her money, but she would have gotten over it. She would have stuck to her guns about paying her own way, of course. But *this?* It was still too huge to wrap her brain around. She'd slept with a prince, let him into her home, her body, and considered letting him into her heart. His deception burned deep.

How could she have missed the truth so completely, buying into his stories about working on a shrimp boat as a teen? She'd assumed his tattoo and the closed over pierced earlobe were parts of an everyman past that seduced her as fully as his caresses.

"Your name isn't even Tony Castillo." Oh God. She pressed the back of her hand against her mouth, suddenly nauseated because she didn't even know the name of the guy she'd been sleeping with.

"Technically, it could be."

Shannon slammed her fists against the leather seat instead of reaching for him as she ached to do. "I'm not interested in technically. Actually, I'm not interested in people who lie to me. Can I even trust that you're really thirty-two years old?"

"It isn't just my decision to share specific details. I have other family members to consider. But if it's any consolation, I really am thirty-two. Are you really twenty-nine?"

"I'm not in a joking mood." Shivering, she thumbed her bare ring finger where once a three-carat diamond had rested. After Nolan's funeral, she'd taken it off and sold it along with everything else to pay off the mountain of debt. "I should have known you were too good to be true."

"Why do you say that?"

"Who makes millions by thirty-two?"

He cocked an arrogant eyebrow. "Did you just call me a moocher?"

"Well, excuse me if that was rude, but I'm not exactly at my best tonight."

His arms bulged beneath his Italian suit—she'd had to look up the exclusive Garaceni label after she'd seen the coat hanging on his bedpost.

Tony looked even more amazing out of the clothes, his tanned and muscled body eclipsing any high-end wardrobe. And the smiles he brought to her life, his uninhibited laughter were just what she needed most.

How quiet her world had been without him this week. "Sorry to have hurt your feelings, pal. Or should I say, Your Majesty? Since according to some of those stories I'm 'His Majesty's mistress.'"

"Actually, it would be 'Your Highness.'" His signature smile tipped his mouth, but with a bitter edge. "Majesty is for the king."

How could he be so flippant? "Actually, you can take your title and stuff it where the sun—"

"I get the picture." He guided the Escalade over the Galveston Island Causeway, waves moving darkly below. "You'll need time to calm down so we can discuss how to handle this."

"You don't understand. There's no calming down. You lied to me on a fundamental level. Once we made l—" she stumbled over the next word, images of him moving over her, inside her, stealing her words and breath until her stomach churned as fast as the waters below "—after we went to bed together, you should have told me. Unless the sex didn't mean anything special to you. I guess if you had to tell every woman you slept with, there would be no secret."

"Stop!" He sliced the air with his hand. His gleaming Patek Philippe watch contrasted with scarred knuckles, from his sailing days he'd once told her. "That's not true and not the point here. You were safer not knowing."

"Oh, it's for my own good." She wrapped her arms around herself, a shield from the hurt.

"How much do you know about my family's history?"

She bit back the urge to snap at him. Curiosity reined in her temper. "Not much. Just that there was a king of some small country near Spain, I think, before he was overthrown in a coup. His family has been hiding out to avoid the paparazzi hoopla."

"Hoopla? This might suck, but that's the least of my worries. There are people out there who tried to kill my family and succeeded in murdering my mother. There are people who stand to gain a lot in the way of money and power if the Medinas are wiped off the planet."

Her heart ached for all he had lost. Even now, she wanted to press her mouth to his and forget this whole insane mess.

To grasp that shimmering connection she'd discovered with him the first time they'd made love in a frenzied tangle at his Galveston Bay mansion.

"Well, believe it, Shannon. There's a big bad world outside your corner of Texas. Right now, some of the worst will start focusing on me, my family and anyone who's close to us. Whether you like it or not, I'll do whatever it takes to keep you and Kolby protected."

Her son's safety? Perspiration froze on her forehead, chilling her deeper. Why hadn't she thought of that? Of course she'd barely wrapped her brain around Tony... Antonio. "Drive faster. Get me home now."

"I completely agree. I've already sent bodyguards ahead of us."

Bodyguards?

"When?" She'd barely been able to think, much less act. What kind of mother was she not to have considered the impact on Kolby? And what kind of man kept bodyguards on speed dial?

"I texted my people while we were leaving through the kitchen."

Of course he had people. The man was not merely the billionaire shipping magnate she'd assumed, he was also the bearer of a surname generations old and a background of privilege she couldn't begin to fathom.

"I was so distracted I didn't even notice," Shannon whispered, sinking into her seat. She wasn't even safe in her own neighborhood anymore.

She couldn't wish this away any longer. "You really are this Medina guy. You're really from some deposed royal family."

His chin tipped with unmistakable regality. "My name is Antonio Medina. I was born in San Rinaldo, third son of King Enrique and Queen Beatriz."

Her heart drumming in her ears, panic squeezed harder at her rib cage. How could she have foreseen this when she met him five months ago at the restaurant, bringing his supper back to the owner's poker game? Tony had ordered a shrimp po'boy sandwich and a glass of sweet tea.

Poor Boy? How ironic was that?

"This is too weird." And scary.

The whole surreal mess left her too numb to hurt anymore. That would return later, for sure. Her hands shook as she tapped her glasses straight.

She had to stay focused now. "Stuff like this happens in movies or a hundred years ago."

"Or in my life. Now in yours, too."

"Nuh-uh. You and I?" She waggled her hand back and forth between them. "We're history."

He paused at a stop sign, turning to face her fully for the first time since he'd gripped her shoulders at the restaurant. His coal black eyes heated over her, a bold man of uninhibited emotions. "That fast, you're ready to call an end to what we've shared?"

Her heart picked up speed from just the caress of his eyes, the memory of his hands stroking her. She tried to answer but her mouth had gone dry. He skimmed those scarred knuckles down her arm until his hand rested on hers. Such a simple gesture, nothing overtly erotic, but her whole body hummed with awareness and want.

Right here in the middle of the street, in the middle of an upside down situation, her body betrayed her as surely as he had.

Wrong. Wrong. Wrong. She had to be tough. "I already ended things between us last weekend."

"That was a fight, not a breakup." His big hand splayed over hers, eclipsing her with heat.

"Semantics. Not that it matters." She pulled herself

away from him until her spine met the door, not nearly far enough. "I can't be with you anymore."

"That's too damn bad, because we're going to be spending a lot of time together after we pick up your son. There's no way you can stay in your apartment tonight."

"There's no way I can stay with *you*."

"You can't hide from what's been unleashed. Today should tell you that more than anything. It'll find you and your son. I'm sorry for not seeing this coming, but it's here and we have to deal with it."

Fear for her son warred with her anger at Tony. "You had no right," she hissed between clenched teeth, "no right at all to play with our lives this way."

"I agree." He surprised her with that. However, the reprieve was short. "But I'm the only one who can stand between you both and whatever fallout comes from this revelation."

Two

A bodyguard stood outside the front door of her first-floor apartment. A bodyguard, for heaven's sake, a burly guy in a dark suit who could have passed for a Secret Service employee. She stifled the urge to scream in frustration.

Shannon flung herself out of the Escalade before it came to a complete stop, desperate to see her child, to get inside her tiny apartment in hopes that life would somehow return to normal. Tony couldn't be serious about her packing up to go away with him. He was just using this to try to get back together again.

Although what did a *prince* want with her?

At least there weren't any reporters in the parking lot. The neighbors all seemed to be inside for the evening or out enjoying their own party plans. She'd chosen the large complex for the anonymity it offered. Multiple three-story buildings filled the corner block, making it difficult to tell one apartment from another in the stretches of yellow units with tiny white balconies. At the center of it all, there was a pool and tiny playground, the only luxuries she'd allowed herself. She might not be able to give Kolby a huge yard, but he would have an outdoor place to play.

Now she had to start the search for a haven all over again.

"Here," she said as she thrust her purse toward him, her keys in her hand, "please carry this so I can unlock the door."

He extended his arm, her hobo bag dangling from his big fist. "Uh, sure."

"This is not the time to freak out over holding a woman's purse." She fumbled for the correct key.

"Shannon, I'm here for you. For you and your handbag."

She glanced back sharply. "Don't mock me."

"I thought you enjoyed my sense of humor."

Hadn't she thought just the same thing earlier? How could she say good-bye to Tony—he would never be Antonio to her—forever? Her feet slowed on the walkway between the simple hedges, nowhere near as elaborate as the gardens of her old home with Nolan, but well maintained. The place was clean.

And safe.

Having Tony at her back provided an extra layer of protection, she had to admit. After he'd made his shocking demand that she pack, he'd pulled out his phone and began checking in with his lawyer. From what she could tell hearing one side of the conversation, the news was spreading fast, with no indication of how the Global Intruder's people had cracked his cover. Tony didn't lose his temper or even curse.

But her normally lighthearted lover definitely wasn't smiling.

She ignored the soft note of regret spreading through her for all she would leave behind—this place. *Tony.* He strode alongside her silently, the outside lights casting his shadow over hers intimately, moving, tangling the two together as they walked.

Stopping at her unit three doors down from the corner, Tony exchanged low words with the guard while she slid the key into the lock with shaking hands. She pushed her way inside and ran smack into the babysitter already trying to open up for her. The college senior was majoring in elementary education and lived in the same complex. There might only be seven years between her and the girl in a concert T-shirt, but Shannon couldn't help but feel her own university days spent studying to be a teacher happened eons ago.

Shannon forced herself to stay calm. "Courtney, thanks for calling me. Where's Kolby?"

The sitter studied her with undisguised curiosity—who could blame her?—and pointed down the narrow hall toward the living room. "He's asleep on the couch. I thought it might be better to keep him with me in case any reporters started showing up outside or something." She hitched her bulging backpack onto one shoulder. "I don't think they would stake out his window, but ya never know. Right?"

"Thank you, Courtney. You did exactly the right thing." She angled down the hall to peek in on Kolby.

Her three-year-old son slept curled on the imported leather sofa, one of the few pieces that hadn't been sold to pay off debts. Kolby had poked a hole in the armrest with a fountain pen just before the estate sale. Shannon had strapped duct tape over the tear, grateful for one less piece of furniture to buy to start her new life.

Every penny she earned needed to be tucked away for

emergencies. Kolby counted on her, her sweet baby boy in his favorite Thomas the Tank Engine pj's, matching blanket held up to his nose. His blond hair was tousled and spiking, still damp from his bath. She could almost smell the baby-powder sweetness from across the room.

Sagging against the archway with relief, she turned back to Courtney. "I need to pay you."

Shannon took back her hobo bag from Tony and tunneled through frantically, dropping her wallet. Change clanked on the tile floor.

What would a three-year-old think if he saw his mother's face in some news report? Or Tony's, for that matter? The two had only met briefly a few times, but Kolby knew he was Mama's friend. She scooped the coins into a pile, picking at quarters and dimes.

Tony cupped her shoulder. "I've got it. Go ahead and be with your son."

She glanced up sharply, her nerves too raw to take the reminder of how he'd offered her financial help mere moments after sex last weekend. "I can pay my own way."

Holding up his hands, he backed away.

"Fine, Shannon. I'll sit with Kolby." He cautioned her with a look not to mention their plans to pack and leave.

Duh. Not that she planned to follow all *his* dictates, but the fewer who knew their next move the better for avoiding the press and anyone else who might profit from tracking their moves. Even the best of friends could be bought off.

Speaking of payoffs… "Thank you for calling me so quickly." She peeled off an extra twenty and tried not to wince as she said goodbye to ice cream for the month. She usually traded babysitting with another flat-broke single mom in the building when needed for work and dates.

Courtney was only her backup, which she couldn't—and didn't—use often. "I appreciate your help."

Shaking her head, Courtney took the money and passed back the extra twenty. "You don't need to give me all that, Mrs. Crawford. I was only doing my job. And I'm not gonna talk to the reporters. I'm not the kind of person who would sell your story or something."

"Really," Shannon urged as she folded the cash back into her hand, "I want you to have it."

Tony filled the archway. "The guard outside will walk you home, just to make sure no one bothers you."

"Thanks, Mr. Castillo. Um, I mean…" Courtney stuffed the folded bills into her back pocket, the college coed eyeing him up and down with a new awareness. "Mr. Medina… Sir? I don't what to call you."

"Castillo is fine."

"Right, uh, bye." Her face flushed, she spun on her glitter flip-flops and took off.

Shannon pushed the door closed, sliding the bolt and chain. Locking her inside with Tony in a totally quiet apartment. She slumped back and stared down the hallway, the ten feet shrinking even more with the bulk of his shoulders spanning the arch. Light from the cheap brown lamp glinted off the curl in his black hair.

No wonder Courtney had been flustered. He wasn't just a prince, but a fine-looking, one-hundred-percent *man*. The kind with strong hands that could finesse their way over a woman's body with a sweet tenderness that threatened to buckle her knees from just remembering. Had it only been a week since they'd made love in his mammoth jetted tub? God knows she ached as if she'd been without him for months.

Even acknowledging it was wrong with her mind, her body still wanted him.

* * *

Tony wanted her.

In his arms.

In his bed.

And most of all, he wanted her back in his SUV, heading away from here. He needed to use any methods of persuasion possible and convince her to come to his house. Even if the press located his home address, they wouldn't get past the gates and security. So how to convince Shannon? He stared down the short tiled hallway at her.

Awareness flared in her eyes. The same slam of attraction he felt now and the first time he'd seen her five months ago when he'd stopped by after a call to play cards. Vernon had mentioned hiring a new waitress but Tony hadn't thought much of it—until he met her.

When Tony asked about her, the old guy said he didn't know much about Shannon other than her crook of a husband had committed suicide rather than face a jury. Shannon and her boy had been left behind, flat broke. She'd worked at a small diner for a year and a half before that and Vernon had hired her on a hunch. Vernon and his softie heart.

Tony stared at her now every bit as intently as he had that first time she'd brought him his order. Something about her blue-gray eyes reminded him of the ocean sky just before a storm. Tumultuous. Interesting.

A challenge. He'd been without a challenge for too long. Building a business from nothing had kept him charged up for years. What next?

Then he'd seen her.

He'd spent his life smiling his way through problems and deals, and for the first time he'd found someone who saw past his bull. Was it the puzzle that tugged him? If so, he wasn't any closer to solving the mystery of Shannon.

Every day she confused him more, which made him want her more.

Pushing away from the door, she strode toward him, efficiently, no hip swish, just even, efficient steps. Then she walked out of her shoes, swiping one foot behind her to kick them to rest against the wall. No shoes in the house. She'd told him that the two times he'd been allowed over her threshold for no more than fifteen minutes. Any liaisons between them had been at his bayside mansion or a suite near the restaurant. He didn't really expect anything to happen here with her son around, even asleep.

And given the look on her face, she was more likely to pitch him out. Better to circumvent the boot.

"I'll stay with your son while you pack." He removed his shoes and stepped deeper into her place, not fancy, the sparse generic sort of a furnished space in browns and tan—except for the expensive burgundy leather sofa with a duct-taped *X* on the armrest.

Her lips thinned. "About packing, we need to discuss that further."

"What's to talk about?" He accepted their relationship was still on hold, but the current problems with his identity needed to be addressed. "Your porch will be full by morning."

"I'll check into a hotel."

With the twenty dollars and fifty-two cents she had left in her wallet? He prayed she wasn't foolish enough to use a credit card. Might as well phone in her location to the news stations.

"We can talk about where you'll stay *after* you pack."

"You sound like a broken record, Tony."

"*You*'re calling *me* stubborn?"

Their standoff continued, neither of them touching, but he was all too aware of her scrubbed fresh scent.

Shannon, the whole place, carried an air of some kind of floral cleaner. The aroma somehow calmed and stirred at the same time, calling to mind holding her after a mind-bending night of sex. She never stayed over until morning, but for an hour or so after, she would doze against his chest. He would breathe in the scent of her and him and *them* blended together.

His nose flared.

Her pupils widened.

She stumbled back, her chest rising faster. "I do need to change my clothes. Are you sure you'll be all right with Kolby?"

It was no secret the couple of times he'd met the boy, Kolby hadn't warmed up to him. Nothing seemed to work, not ice cream or magic coin tricks. Tony figured maybe the boy was still missing his father.

That jerk had left Shannon bankrupt and vulnerable. "I can handle it. Take all the time you need."

"Thank you. I'm only going to change clothes though. No packing yet. We'll have to talk more first, Tony—um, Antonio."

"I prefer to be called *Tony*." He liked the sound of it on her tongue.

"Okay...Tony." She spun on her heel and headed toward her bedroom.

Her steps still efficient, albeit faster, were just speedy enough to bring a slight swing to her slim hips in the pencil-straight skirt. Thoughts of peeling it down and off her beautiful body would have to wait until she had the whole Antonio/Tony issue sorted out.

If only she could accept that he'd called himself Tony Castillo almost longer than he'd remembered being Antonio Medina.

He even had the paperwork to back up the Castillo

name. Creating another persona hadn't been that difficult, especially once he'd saved enough to start his first business. From then on, all transactions were shuttled through the company. Umbrella corporations. Living in plain sight. His plan had worked fine until someone, somehow had pierced the new identities he and his brothers had built. In fact, he needed to call his brothers, who he spoke to at most a couple of times a year. But they might have insights.

They needed a plan.

He reached inside his jacket for his iPhone and ducked into the dining area where he could see the child but wouldn't wake him. He thumbed the seven key on his speed dial…and Carlos's voice mail picked up. Tony disconnected without leaving a message and pressed the eight key.

"Speak to me, my brother." Duarte Medina's voice came through the phone. They didn't talk often, but these weren't normal circumstances.

"I assume you know." He toyed with one of Shannon's hair bands on the table.

"Impossible to miss."

"Where's Carlos? He's not picking up." Tony fell back into their clipped shorthand. They'd only had each other growing up and now circumstances insisted they stay apart. Did his brothers have that same feeling, like they'd lost a limb?

"His secretary said he got paged for an emergency surgery. He'll be at least another couple of hours. Apparently Carlos found out as he was scrubbing in, but you know our brother." Duarte, the middle son, tended to play messenger with their father. The three brothers spoke and met when they could, but there were so many crap memories from their childhood, those reunions became further apart.

Tony scooped up the brown band, a lone long strand

of her blond hair catching the light. "When a patient calls…"

"Right."

It could well be hours before they heard from Carlos, given the sort of painstaking reconstructive surgeries he performed on children. "Any idea how this exploded?"

His brother hissed a long angry curse. "The Global Intruder got a side-view picture of me while I was visiting our sister."

Their half sister Eloisa, their father's daughter from an affair shortly after they had escaped to the States. Enrique had still been torn up with grief from losing his wife… not to mention the guilt. But apparently not so torn up and remorseful he couldn't hop into bed with someone else. The woman had gone on to marry another man who'd raised her daughter as his own.

Tony had only met his half sister once as a teen, a few years before he'd left the island compound. She'd only been seven at the time. Now she'd married into a high-profile family jam-packed with political influence and a fat portfolio. Could she be at fault for bringing the media down on their heads for some free PR for her new in-laws? Duarte seemed to think she wanted anonymity as much as the rest of them. But could he have misjudged her?

"Why were you visiting Eloisa?" Tony tucked the band into his pocket.

"Family business. It doesn't matter now. Her in-laws were there. Eloisa's sister-in-law—a senator's wife—slipped on the dock. I kept her from falling into the water. Some damn female reporter in a tree with a telephoto lens caught the mishap. Which shouldn't have mattered, since Senator Landis and his wife were the focus of the picture. I still don't know how the photographer pegged me from a side view, but there it is. And I'm sorry for bringing this crap down on you."

Duarte hadn't done anything wrong. They couldn't live in a bubble. In the back of Tony's mind, he'd always known it was just a matter of time until the cover story blew up in their faces. He'd managed to live away from the island anonymously for fourteen years, his two older brothers even longer.

But there was always the hope that maybe he could stay a step ahead. Be his own man. Succeed on his own merits. "We've all been caught in a picture on occasion. We're not vampires. It's just insane that she was able to make the connection. Perfect storm of bad luck."

"What are your plans for dealing with this perfect storm?"

"Lock down tight while I regroup. Let me know when you hear from Carlos."

Ending the call, Tony strode back into the living room, checked on Kolby—still snoozing hard—and dropped to the end of the sofa to read messages, his in-box already full again. By the time Tony scrolled through emails that told him nothing new, he logged on to the internet for a deeper peek. And winced. Rumors were rampant.

That his father had died of malaria years ago—false.

Supposition that Carlos had plastic surgery—again, false.

Speculation that Duarte had joined a Tibetan monastery—definitely false.

And then there were the stories about him and Shannon, which actually happened to be true. The whole "Monarch's Mistress" was really growing roots out there in cyberspace. Guilt kicked him in the gut that Shannon would suffer this kind of garbage because of him. The media feeding frenzy would only grow, and before long they would stir up all the crap about her thief of a dead husband. He tucked away his phone in disgust.

"That bad?" Shannon asked from the archway.

She'd changed into jeans and a simple blue tank top. Her silky blond hair glided loosely down her shoulders, straight except for a slight crimped ring where she'd bound it up on her head for work. She didn't look much older than the babysitter, except in her weary—wary—eyes.

Leaning back, he extended his legs, leather creaking as he stayed on the sofa so as not to spook her. "The internet is exploding. My lawyers and my brothers' lawyers are all looking into it. Hopefully we'll have the leak plugged soon and start some damage control. But we can't stuff the genie back into the bottle."

"I'm not going away with you." She perched a fist on one shapely hip.

"This isn't going to die down." He kept his voice even and low, reasonable. The stakes were too important for all of them. "The reporters will swarm you by morning, if not sooner. Your babysitter will almost inevitably cave in to one of those gossip rag offers. Your friends will sell photos of the two of us together. There's a chance people could use Kolby to get to me."

"Then we're through, you and I." She reached for her sleeping son on the sofa, smoothing his hair before sliding a hand under his shoulders as if to scoop him up.

Tony touched her arm lightly, stopping her. "Hold on before you settle him into his room." As far as Tony was concerned, they would be back in his Escalade in less than ten minutes. "Do you honestly think anyone's going to believe the breakup is for real? The timing will seem too convenient."

She sagged onto the arm of the sofa, right over the silver X. "We ended things last weekend."

Like hell. "Tell that to the papers and see if they believe you. The truth doesn't matter to these people. They probably printed photos of an alien baby last week. Pleading a breakup isn't going to buy you any kind of freedom from their interest."

"I know I need to move away from Galveston." She glanced around her sparsely decorated apartment, two pictures of Kolby the only personal items. "I've accepted that."

There wouldn't be much packing to do.

"They'll find you."

She studied him through narrowed eyes. "How do I know you're not just using this as an excuse to get back together?"

Was he? An hour ago, he would have done anything to get into her bed again. While the attraction hadn't diminished, since his cover was blown, he had other concerns that overshadowed everything else. He needed to determine the best way to inoculate her from the toxic fallout that came from associating with Medinas. One thing for certain, he couldn't risk her striking out on her own.

"You made it clear where we stand last weekend. I get that. You want nothing to do with me or my money." He didn't move closer, wasn't going to crowd her. The draw between them filled the space separating them just fine on its own. "We had sex together. Damn good sex. But that's over now. Neither one of us ever asked for or expected more."

Her gaze locked with his, the room silent but for their breathing and the light snore of the sleeping child. Kolby. Another reminder of why they needed to stay in control.

In fact, holding back made the edge sharper. He skimmed his knuckles along her collarbone, barely touching. A week ago, that pale skin had worn the rasp of his beard. She didn't move closer, but she didn't back away, either.

Shannon blinked first, her long lashes sweeping closed while she swallowed hard. "What am I supposed to do?"

More than anything he wanted to gather her up and tell her everything would be okay. He wouldn't allow anything less. But he also wouldn't make shallow promises.

Twenty-seven years ago, when they'd been leaving San Rinaldo on a moonless night, his father had assured them everything would be fine. They would be reunited soon.

His father had been so very wrong.

Tony focused on what he could assure. "A lot has happened in a few hours. We need to take a step back for damage assessment tonight at my home, where there are security gates, alarms, guards watching and surveillance cameras."

"And after tonight?"

"We'll let the press think we are a couple, still deep in that affair." He indulged himself in one lengthy, heated eye-stroke of her slim, supple body. "Then we'll stage a more public breakup later, on our terms, when we've prepared a backup plan."

She exhaled a shaky breath. "That makes sense."

"Meanwhile, my number one priority is shielding you and Kolby." He sifted through options, eliminating one idea after another until he was left with only a single alternative.

Her hand fell to rest on her sleeping son's head. "How do you intend to do that?"

"By taking you to the safest place I know." A place he'd vowed never to return. "Tomorrow, we're going to visit my father."

Three

"Visit your father?" Shannon asked in total shock. Had Tony lost his mind? "The King of San Rinaldo? You've got to be kidding."

"I'm completely serious." He stared back at her from the far end of the leather sofa, her sleeping son between them.

Resisting Tony had been tough enough this past week just knowing he was in the same town. How much more difficult would it be with him in the same house for one night much less days on end? God, she wanted to run. She bit the inside of her lip to keep from blurting out something she would regret later. Sorting through her options could take more time than they appeared to have.

Kolby wriggled restlessly, hugging his comfort blanket tighter. Needing a moment to collect her thoughts and her resolve, she scooped up her son.

"Tony, we'll have to put this discussion on hold." She

cradled her child closer and angled down the hall, ever aware of a certain looming prince at her back. "Keep the lights off, please."

Shadows playing tag on the ceiling, she lowered Kolby into the red caboose bed they'd picked out together when she moved into the apartment. She'd been trying so hard to make up for all her son had lost. As if there was some way to compensate for the loss of his father, the loss of security. Shannon pressed a kiss to his forehead, inhaling his precious baby-shampoo smell.

When she turned back, she found Tony waiting in the doorway, determination stamped on his square jaw. Well, she could be mighty resolute too, especially when it came to her son. Shannon closed the curtains before she left the room and stepped into the narrow hall.

She shut the door quietly behind her. "You have to know your suggestion is outrageous."

"The whole situation is outrageous, which calls for extraordinary measures."

"Hiding out with a king? That's definitely what I would call extraordinary." She pulled off her glasses and pinched the bridge of her nose.

Before Nolan's death she'd worn contacts, but couldn't afford the extra expense now. How much longer until she would grow accustomed to glasses again?

She stared at Tony, his face clear up close, everything in the distance blurred. "Do you honestly think I would want to expose myself, not to mention Kolby, to more scrutiny by going to your father's? Why not just hide out at your place as we originally discussed?"

God, had she just agreed to stay with him indefinitely?

"My house is secure, up to a point. People will figure out where I live and they'll deduce that you're with me.

There's only one place I can think of where no one can get to us."

Frustration buzzed in her brain. "Seems like their telephoto lenses reach everywhere."

"The press still hasn't located my father's home after years of trying."

But she thought… "Doesn't he live in Argentina?"

He studied her silently, the wheels almost visibly turning in his broad forehead. Finally, he shook his head quickly.

"No. We only stopped off there to reorganize after escaping San Rinaldo." He adjusted his watch, the only nervous habit she'd ever observed in him. "My father did set up a compound there and paid a small, trusted group of individuals to make it look inhabited. Most of them also escaped San Rinaldo with us. People assumed we were there with them."

What extreme lengths and expense their father had gone to. But then wasn't she willing to do anything to protect Kolby? She felt a surprise connection to the old king she'd never met. "Why are you telling me this much if it's such a closely guarded secret?"

He cupped her shoulder, his touch heavy and familiar, *stirring*. "Because it's that important I persuade you."

Resisting the urge to lean into him was tougher with each stroke of his thumb against the sensitive curve of her neck. "Where *does* he live then?"

"I can't tell you that much," he said, still touching and God, it made her mad that she didn't pull away.

"Yet you expect me to just pack up my child and follow you there." She gripped his wrist and moved away his seductive touch.

"I detect a note of skepticism in your voice." He shoved his hands in his pockets.

"A note? Try a whole freaking symphony, Tony." The sense of betrayal swelled inside her again, larger and larger until it pushed bitter words out. "Why should I trust you? Especially now?"

"Because you don't have anyone else or they would have already been helping you."

The reality deflated her. She only had a set of in-laws who didn't want anything to do with her or Kolby since they blamed her for their son's downfall. She was truly alone.

"How long would we be there?"

"Just until my attorneys can arrange for a restraining order against certain media personnel. I realize that restraining orders don't always work, but having one will give us a stronger legal case if we need it. It's one thing to stalk, but it's another to stalk and violate a restraining order. And I'll want to make sure you have top-of-the-line security installed at your new home. That should take about a week, two at the most."

Shannon fidgeted with her glasses. "How would we get there?"

"By plane." He thumbed the face of his watch clean again.

That meant it must be far away. "Forget it. You are not going to isolate me that way, cut me off from the world. It's the equivalent of kidnapping me and my son."

"Not if you agree to go along." He edged closer, the stretch of his hard muscled shoulders blocking out the light filtering from the living area. "People in the military get on planes all the time without knowing their destination."

She tipped her chin upward, their faces inches apart. Close enough to feel his heat. Close enough to kiss.

Too close for her own good. "Last time I checked, I wasn't wearing a uniform." Her voice cracked ever so slightly. "I didn't sign on for this."

"I know, Shanny...." He stroked a lock of her hair intimately. "I *am* sorry for all this is putting you through, and I will do my best to make the next week as easy for you as possible."

The sincerity of his apology soothed the ragged edges of her nerves. It had been a long week without him. She'd been surprised by how much she had missed his spontaneous dates and late-night calls. His bold kisses and intimate caresses. She couldn't lie to herself about how much he affected her on both an emotional and physical level. Otherwise this mess with his revealed past wouldn't hurt her so deeply.

Her hand clenched around her glasses. He gently slid them from her hand and hooked them on the front of her shirt. The familiarity of the gesture kicked her heart rate up a notch.

Swaying toward him, she flattened her hands to his chest, not sure if she wanted to push him away or pull him nearer. Thick longing filled the sliver of space between them. An answering awareness widened his pupils, pushing and thinning the dark brown of his eyes.

He lowered his head closer, closer still until his mouth hovered over hers. Heated breaths washed over her, stirring even hotter memories and warm languid longing. She'd thought the pain of Nolan's deceit had left her numb for life...until she saw Tony.

"Mama?"

The sound of her son calling out from his room jolted her back to reality. And not only her. Tony's face went from seductive to intent in a heartbeat. He pulled the door open just as Kolby ran through and into his mother's arms.

"Mama, Mama, Mama..." He buried his face in her neck. "Monster in my window!"

* * *

Tony shot through the door and toward the window in the child's room, focused, driven and mentally kicking himself for letting himself be distracted.

He barked over his shoulder, "Stay in the hall while I take a look."

It could be nothing, but he'd been taught at a young age the importance of never letting down his guard. Adrenaline firing, he jerked the window open and scanned the tiny patch of yard.

Nothing. Just a Big Wheel lying on its side and a swing dangling lazily from a lone tree.

Maybe it was only a nightmare. This whole blast from the past had him seeing bogeymen from his own childhood, too. Tony pushed the window down again and pulled the curtains together.

Shannon stood in the door, her son tucked against her. "I could have sworn I closed the curtains."

Kolby peeked up. "I opened 'em when I heard-ed the noise."

And maybe this kid's nightmare was every bit as real as his own had been. On the off chance the boy was right, he had to check. "I'm going outside. The guard will stay here with you."

She cupped the back of her child's head. "I already warned the guard. I wasn't leaving you to take care of the 'monster' by yourself."

Dread kinked cold and tight in his gut. What if something had happened to her when she had stepped outside to speak to the guard? He held in the angry words, not wanting to upset her son.

But he became more determined by the second to persuade her and the child to leave Galveston with him.

"Let's hope it was nothing but a tree branch. Right, kiddo?"

Tony started toward the door just as his iPhone rang. He glanced at the ID and saw the guard's number. He thumbed the speaker phone button. "Yes?"

"Got him," the guard said. "A teenager from the next complex over was trying to snap some pictures on his cell phone. I've already called the police."

A sigh shuddered through Shannon, and she hugged her son closer, and God, how Tony wanted to comfort her.

However, the business of taking care of her safety came first. "Keep me posted if there are any red flags when they interview the trespasser. Good work. Thanks."

He tucked his phone back into his jacket, his heart almost hammering out of his chest at the close call. This could have been worse. He knew too well from past experience how bad it could have been.

And apparently so did Shannon. Her wide blue eyes blinked erratically as she looked from corner to corner, searching shadows.

To hell with giving her distance. He wrapped an arm around her shoulders until she leaned on him ever so slightly. The soft press of her against him felt damn right in a day gone wrong.

Then she squeezed her eyes closed and straightened. "Okay, you win."

"Win what?"

"We'll go to your home tonight."

A hollow victory, since fear rather than desire motivated her, but he wasn't going to argue. "And tomorrow?"

"We'll discuss that in morning. Right now, just take us to your house."

* * *

Tony's Galveston house could only be called a mansion.

The imposing size of the three-story structure washed over Shannon every time they drove through the scrolled iron gates. How Kolby could sleep through all of this boggled her mind, but when they'd convinced him the "monster" was gone—thanks to the guard—Kolby had been all yawns again. Once strapped into the car seat in the back of Tony's Escalade, her son had been out like a light in five minutes.

If only her own worries could be as easily shaken off. She had to think logically, but fears for Kolby nagged her. Nolan had stolen so much more than money. He'd robbed her of the ability to feel safe, just before he took the coward's way out.

Two acres of manicured lawn stretched ahead of her in the moonlight. The estate was intimidating during the day, and all the more ominously gothic at night with shadowy edges encroaching. It was one thing to visit the place for a date.

It was another to take shelter here, to pack suitcases and accept his help.

She'd lived in a large house with Nolan, four thousand square feet, but she could have fit two of those homes inside Tony's place. In the courtyard, a concrete horse fountain was illuminated, glowing in front of the burgundy stucco house with brown trim so dark it was almost black. His home showcased the Spanish architecture prevalent in Texas. Knowing his true heritage now, she could see why he would have been drawn to this area.

Silently he guided the SUV into the garage, finally safe and secure from the outside world. For how long?

He unstrapped Kolby from the seat and she didn't argue. Her son was still sleeping anyway. The way Tony's big hands managed the small buckles and shuffled the sleeping child onto his shoulder with such competence touched her heart as firmly as any hothouse full of roses.

Trailing him with a backpack of toy trains and trucks, she dimly registered the house that had grown familiar after their dates to restaurants, movies and the most amazing concerts. Her soul, so starved for music, gobbled up every note.

Her first dinner at his home had been a five-course catered meal with a violinist. She could almost hear the echoing strains bouncing lightly off the high-beamed ceiling, down to the marble floor, swirling along the inlay pattern to twine around her.

Binding her closer to him. They hadn't had sex that night, but she'd known then it was inevitable.

That first time, Tony had been thoughtful enough to send out to a different restaurant than his favored Vernon's, guessing accurately that when a person worked eight hours a day in one eating establishment, the food there lost its allure.

He'd opted for Italian cuisine. The meal and music and elegance had been so far removed from paper plate dinners of nuggets and fries. While she adored her son and treasured every second with him, she couldn't help but be wooed by grown-up time to herself.

Limited time as she'd never spent the night here. Until now.

She followed Tony up the circular staircase, hand on the crafted iron banister. The sight of her son sleeping so limp and relaxed against Tony brought a lump to her throat again.

The tenderness she felt seeing him hold her child reminded her how special this new man in her life was. She'd chosen him so carefully after Nolan had died, seeing

Tony's innate strength and honor. Was she really ready to throw that away?

He stopped at the first bedroom, a suite decorated in hunter green with vintage maps framed on the walls. Striding through the sitting area to the next door, he flipped back the brocade spread and set her son in the middle of the high bed.

Quietly, she put a chair on either side as a makeshift bed rail, then tucked the covers over his shoulders. She kissed his little forehead and inhaled his baby-fresh scent. Her child.

The enormity of how their lives had changed tonight swelled inside her, pushing stinging tears to the surface. Tony's hand fell to rest on her shoulder and she leaned back....

Holy crap.

She jolted away. How easily she fell into old habits around him. "I didn't mean..."

"I know." His hand fell away and tucked into his pocket. "I'll carry up your bags in a minute. I gave the house staff the night off."

She followed him, just to keep their conversation soft, not because she wasn't ready to say good-night. "I thought you trusted them."

"I do. To a point. It's also easier for security to protect the house with fewer people inside." He gestured into the sitting area. "I heard what you said about feeling cut off from the world going to my father's and I understand."

His empathy slipped past her defenses when they were already on shaky ground being here in his house again. Remembering all the times they'd made love under this very roof, she could almost smell the bath salts from last weekend. And with him being so understanding on top of everything else...

He'd lied. She needed to remember that.

"I realize I have to do what's right for Kolby." She sagged onto the striped sofa, her legs folding from an emotional and exhausting night. "It scares the hell out of me how close a random teenager already got to my child, and we're only a couple of hours into this mess. It makes me ill to think about what someone with resources could do."

"My brothers and I have attorneys. They'll look into pressing charges against the teen." He sat beside her with a casual familiarity of lovers.

Remember the fight. Not the bath salts. She inched toward the armrest. "Let me know what the attorneys' fees are, please."

"They're on retainer. Those lawyers also help us communicate with each other. My attorney will know we're going to see my father if you're worried about making sure someone is aware of your plans."

Someone under his employ, all of this bought with Tony's money that she'd rejected a few short days ago. And she couldn't think of any other way. "You trust this man, your lawyer?"

"I have to." The surety in his voice left little room for doubt. "There are some transactions that can't be avoided no matter how much we want to sever ties with the past."

A darker note in his voice niggled at her. "Are you talking about yourself now?"

He shrugged, broad shoulders rippling the fabric of his fine suit.

Nuh-uh. She wasn't giving up that easily. She'd trusted so much of her life to this man, only to find he'd misled her.

Now she needed something tangible, something honest from him to hold on to. Something to let her know if that honor and strength she'd perceived in him was real. "You said you didn't want to break off our relationship. If that's true, this would be a really good time to open up a little."

Angling toward her, Tony's knee pressed against hers, his eyes heating to molten dark. "Are you saying we're good again?"

"I'm saying..." She cleared her throat that had suddenly gone cottony dry. "Maybe I could see my way clear to forgiving you if I knew more about you."

He straightened, his eyes sharp. "What do you want to know?"

"Why Galveston?"

"Do you surf?"

What the hell? She watched the walls come up in his eyes. She could almost feel him distancing himself from her. "Tony, I'm not sure how sharing a *Surf's Up* moment is going to make things all better here."

"But have you ever been surfing?" He gestured, his hands riding imaginary waves. "The Atlantic doesn't offer as wild a ride as the Pacific, but it gets the job done, especially in Spain. Something to do with the atmospheric pressure coming down from the U.K. I still remember the swells tubing." He curled his fingers around into the cresting circle of a wave.

"You're a *surfer?*" She tried to merge the image of the sleek business shark with the vision of him carefree on a board. And instead an image emerged of his abandon when making love. Her breasts tingled and tightened, awash in the sensation of sea spray and Tony all over her skin.

"I've always been fascinated with waves."

"Even when you were in San Rinaldo." The picture of him began to make more sense. "It's an island country, right?"

She'd always thought the nautical art on his walls was tied into his shipping empire. Now she realized the affinity for such pieces came from living on an island. So much about him made sense.

His surfing hand soared to rest on the gold flecked globe beside the sofa. Was it her imagination or was the gloss dimmer over the coast of Spain? As if he'd rubbed his finger along that area more often, taking away the sheen over time.

He spun the globe. "I thought you didn't know much about the Medinas."

"I researched you on Google on my phone while we were driving over." Concrete info had been sparse compared to all the crazy gossip floating about, but there were some basics. Three sons. A monarch father. A mother who'd been killed as they were escaping. Her heart squeezed thinking of him losing a parent so young, not much older than Kolby.

She pulled a faltering smile. "There weren't any surfer pictures among the few images that popped up."

Only a couple of grainy formal family portraits of three young boys with their parents, everyone happy. Some earlier photos of King Enrique looking infinitely regal.

"We scrubbed most pictures after we escaped and regrouped." His lighthearted smile contrasted with the darker hue deepening his eyes. "The internet wasn't active in those days."

The extent of his rebuilding shook her to her shoes. She'd thought she had it rough leaving Louisiana after her husband's arrest and death. How tragic to have your past wiped away. The enormity of what had happened to his family, of how he'd lived since then, threatened to overwhelm her.

How could she not ache over all he'd been through? "I saw that your mother died when I read up on your past. I'm so sorry."

He waved away her sympathy. "When we got to…where my father lives now, things were isolated. But at least we still had the ocean. Out on the waves, I could forget about everything else."

Plowing a hand through his hair, he stared just past her, obviously locked in some deep memories. She sensed she was close, so close to the something she needed to reassure her that placing herself and her son in his care would be wise, even if there weren't gossip seekers sifting through her trash.

She rested her hand on his arm. "What are you thinking?"

"I thought you might like to learn next spring. Unless you're already a pro."

"Not hardly." Spring was a long way off, a huge commitment she wasn't anywhere near ready to make to anyone. The thought of climbing on a wave made her stomach knot almost as much as being together that long. "Thanks for the offer, but I'll pass."

"Scared?" He skimmed his knuckles over her collarbone, and just that fast the sea-spray feel tingled through her again.

"Hell, yes. Scared of getting hurt."

His hand stilled just above her thumping heart. Want crackled in the air. Hers? Or his? She wasn't sure. Probably equal measures from both of them. That had never been in question. And too easily he could draw her in again. Learning more about him wasn't wise after all, not tonight.

She pulled away, her arms jerky, her whole body out of whack. She needed Tony's lightness now. Forget about serious peeks into each other's vulnerable pasts. "No surfing for me. Ever try taking care of a toddler with a broken leg?"

"When did you break your leg?" His eyes narrowed. "Did he hurt you? Your husband?"

How had Tony made that leap so quickly?

"Nolan was a crook and a jerk, but he never raised a hand to me." She shivered, not liking the new direction their conversation had taken at all. This was supposed to teach her more about him. Not the other way around. "Do we have to drag more baggage into this?"

"If it's true."

"I told you. He didn't abuse me." Not physically. "Having a criminal for a husband is no picnic. Knowing I missed the signs... Wondering if I let myself be blind to it because I enjoyed the lifestyle... I don't even know where to start in answering those questions for myself."

She slumped, suddenly exhausted, any residual adrenaline fizzling out. Her head fell back.

"Knowing you as I do, I find it difficult to believe you would ever choose the easy path." Tony thumbed just below her eyes where undoubtedly dark circles were all but tattooed on her face. "It's been a long day. You should get some rest. If you want, I'll tuck you in," he said with a playful wink.

She found the old Tony much easier to deal with than the new. "You're teasing, of course."

"Maybe..." And just that fast the light in his eyes flamed hotter, intense. "Shanny, I would hold you all night if you would let me. I would make sure no one dared threaten you or your son again."

And she wanted to let him do just that. But she'd allowed herself to depend on a man before... "If you hold me, we both know I won't get any rest, and while I'll have pleasure tonight, I'll be sorry tomorrow. Don't you think we have enough wrong between us right now without adding another regret to the mix?"

"Okay...." Tony gave her shoulder a final squeeze and stood. "I'll back off."

Shannon pushed to her feet alongside him, her hands fisted at her sides to keep from reaching for him. "I'm still mad over being kept in the dark, but I appreciate all the damage control."

"I owe you that much and more." He kissed her lightly on the lips without touching her anywhere else, lingering long enough to remind her of the reasons they clicked. Her breath hitched and it was all she could do not to haul him in closer for a firmer, deeper connection.

Pulling back, he started toward the door.

"Tony?" Was that husky voice really hers?

He glanced over his shoulder. So easily she could take the physical comfort waiting only a few feet away in his arms. But she had to keep her head clear. She had to hold strong to carve out an independent life for her and her son and that meant drawing clear boundaries.

"Just because I might be able to forgive you doesn't mean you're welcome in my bed again."

Four

She wasn't in her own bed.

Shannon wrestled with the tenacious grip of her shadowy nightmare, tough as hell to do when she couldn't figure out where she was. The ticking grandfather clock, the feel of the silky blanket around her, none of it was familiar. And then a hint of sandalwood scent teased her nose a second before...

"Hey." Tony's voice rumbled through the dark. "It's okay. I'm here."

Her heart jumped. She bolted upright, the cashmere afghan twisting around her legs and waist. Blinking fast, she struggled to orient herself to the surroundings so different from her apartment, but the world blurred in front of her from the dark and her own crummy eyesight. Shannon pressed her hands to the cushiony softness of a sofa and everything came rushing back. She was at Tony's, in the sitting room outside where Kolby slept.

"It's okay," Tony continued to chant, squeezing her shoulder in his broad hand as he crouched beside the couch.

Swinging her feet to the ground, she gathered the haunting remnants of her nightmare. Shadows smoked through her mind, blending into a darker mass of memories from the night Nolan died, except Tony's face superimposed itself over that of her dead husband.

Nausea burned her throat. She swallowed back the bite of bile and the horror of her dream. "Sorry, if I woke you." Oh, God, her son. "Is Kolby all right?"

"Sleeping soundly."

"Thank goodness. I wouldn't want to frighten him." She took in Tony's mussed hair and hastily hauled on jeans. The top button was open and his chest was bare. Gulp. "I'm sorry for disturbing you."

"I wasn't asleep." He passed her glasses to her.

As she slid them on, his tattoo came into focus, a nautical compass on his arm. Looking closer she realized his hair was wet. She didn't want to think about him in the shower, a tiled spa cubicle they'd shared more than once. "It's been a tough night all around."

"Want to talk about what woke you up?"

"Not really." Not ever. To anyone. "I think my fear for Kolby ran wild in my sleep. Dreams are supposed to help work out problems, but sometimes, it seems they only make everything scarier."

"Ah, damn, Shanny, I'm sorry for this whole mess." He sat on the sofa and slid an arm around her shoulders.

She stiffened, then decided to hell with it all and leaned back against the hard wall of chest. With the nightmare so fresh in her mind, she couldn't scavenge the will to pull away. His arms banded around her in an instant and her head tucked under his chin. Somehow it was easier to accept this comfort when she didn't have to look in his eyes. She'd been alone with her bad dreams for so long. Was it wrong to take just a second's comfort from his arms roped so thick with muscles nothing could break through to her? She would be strong again in a minute.

The grandfather clock ticked away minutes as she stared at his hands linked over her stomach—at the lighter band of skin where his watch usually rested. "Thanks for coming in to check on us, especially so late."

"It can be disconcerting waking in an unfamiliar place alone." His voice vibrated against her back, only her thin nightshirt between them and his bare chest.

Another whiff of his freshly showered scent teased her nose with memories of steam-slicked bodies.

"I've been here at least a dozen times, but never in this room. It's a big house." They'd met five months ago, started dating two months later…had starting sleeping together four weeks ago. "Strange to think we've shared the shower, but I still haven't seen all of your home."

"We tended to get distracted once our feet hit the steps," he said drily.

True enough. They'd stayed downstairs on early dinner dates here, but once they'd ventured upstairs…they'd always headed straight for his suite.

"That first time together—" Shannon remembered was after an opera when her senses had been on overload and her hormones on hyperdrive from holding back "—I was scared to death."

The admission tumbled out before she could think, but somehow it seemed easier to share such vulnerabilities in the dark.

His muscles flexed against her, the bristle of hair on his arms teasing goose bumps along her skin. "The last thing I ever want to do is frighten you."

"It wasn't your fault. That night was a big leap of faith for me." The need to make him understand pushed past walls she'd built around herself. "Being with you then, it was my first time since Nolan."

He went completely still, not even breathing for four ticks of the clock before she felt his neck move with a swallow against her temple. "No one?"

"No one." Not only had Tony been her sole lover since Nolan, he'd been her second lover ever.

Her track record for picking men with secrets sucked.

His gusty sigh ruffled her hair. "I wish you would have told me."

"What would that have changed?"

"I would have been more...careful."

The frenzy of their first time stormed her mind with a barrage of images...their clothes fluttering to carpet the stairs on their way up. By the top of the steps they were naked, moonlight bathing his olive skin and casting shadows along the cut of muscles. Kissing against the wall soon had her legs wrapped around his waist and he was inside her. That one thrust had unfurled the tension into shimmering sensations and before the orgasm finished tingling all the way to the roots of her hair, he'd carried her to his room, her legs still around him. Again, she'd found release in bed with him, then a languid, leisurely completion while showering together.

Just remembering, an ache started low, throbbing between her legs. "You were great that night, and you know it." She swatted his hand lightly. "Now wipe the arrogant grin off your face."

"You can't see me." His voice sounded somber enough.

"Am I right, though?"

"Look at me and see."

She turned around and dared to peer up at him for the first time since he'd settled on the couch behind her. Her intense memories of that evening found an echo in his serious eyes far more moving than any smile.

Right now, it was hard to remember they weren't a couple anymore. "Telling you then would have made the event too serious."

Too important.

His offer to "help" her financially still loomed unresolved between them, stinging her even more than last weekend after the enormous secret he'd kept from her. Why couldn't they be two ordinary people who met at the park outside her apartment complex? What would it have been like to get to know Tony on neutral, normal ground? Would she have been able to see past the pain of her marriage?

She would never know.

"Shannon." His voice came out hoarse and hungry. "Are you okay to go back to sleep now? Because I need to leave."

His words splashed a chill over her heated thoughts. "Of course, you must have a lot to take care of with your family."

"You misunderstand. I *need* to leave, because you're killing me here with how much I've hurt you. And as if that wasn't enough to bring me to my knees, every time you move your head, the feel of your hair against my chest just about sends me over the edge." His eyes burned with a coal-hot determination. "I'll be damned before I do anything to break your trust again."

Before she could unscramble her thoughts, he slid his arms from her and ducked out the door as silently as he'd arrived. Colder than ever without the heat of Tony all around her, she hugged the blanket closer.

No worries about any more nightmares, because she was more than certain she wouldn't be able to go back to sleep.

By morning, Tony hadn't bothered turning down the covers on his bed. After leaving Shannon's room, he'd spent most of the night conferring with his lawyer and a security firm. Working himself into the ground to distract himself from how much he hurt from wanting her.

With a little luck and maneuvering, he could extend his week with her into two weeks. But bottom line, he *would* ensure her safety.

At five, he'd caught a catnap on the library sofa, jolting awake when Vernon called him from the front gate. He'd buzzed the retired sea captain through and rounded up breakfast.

His old friend deserved some answers.

Choosing a less formal dining area outside, he sat at the oval table on the veranda shaded by a lemon tree, Vernon beside him with a plate full of churros. Tony thumbed the edge of the hand-painted stoneware plate—a set he'd picked up from a local craftsman to support the dying art of the region.

Today of all days, he didn't want to think overlong on why he still ate his same childhood breakfast—deep fried strips of potato dough. His mother had always poured a thick rich espresso for herself and mugs of hot chocolate for her three sons, an informal ritual in their centuries-old castle that he now knew was anything but ordinary.

Vernon eyed him over the rim of his coffee cup. "So it's all true, what they're saying in the papers and on the internet?"

Absurd headlines scrolled through his memory, along-side reports that had been right on the money. "My brother's not a Tibetan monk, but the general gist of that first report from the Global Intruder is correct."

"You're a prince." He scrubbed a hand over his dropped jaw. "Well, hot damn. Always knew there was something special about you, boy."

He preferred to think anything "special" about him came from hard work rather than a genetic lottery win. "I hope you understand it wasn't my place to share the details with you."

"You have brothers and a father." He stirred a hefty dollop of milk into his coffee, clinking the spoon against the edges of the stoneware mug. "I get that you need to consider their privacy, as well."

"Thanks, I appreciate that."

He wished Shannon could see as much. He'd hoped bringing her here would remind her of all that had been good between them. Instead those memories had only come back to bite him on the ass when she'd told him that he was her first since her husband died. The revelation still sucker punched the air from his gut.

Where did they go from there? Hell if he knew, but at least he had more time to find out. Soon enough he would have her in his private jet that waited fueled and ready a mile away.

The older man set down his mug. "I respect that you gotta be your own man."

"Thank you again." He'd expected Vernon to be angry over the secrecy, had even been concerned over losing his friendship.

Vernon's respect meant a lot to him, as well as his advice. From day one when Tony had turned in his sparse job application, Vernon had treated him like a son, showing him the ropes. They had a lot of history. And just like fourteen years ago, he offered unconditional acceptance now.

His mentor leaned forward on one elbow. "What does your family have to say about all of this?"

"I've only spoken with my middle brother." He pinched off a piece of a churro drizzled with warm honey. Popping it into his mouth, he chewed and tried not think of how much of his past stayed imprinted on him.

"According to the papers, that would be Duarte. Right?" When Tony nodded, Vernon continued, "Any idea how the story broke after so many years?"

And wasn't that the million-dollar question? He, his brothers and their lawyers were no closer to the answer on that one today than they'd been last night. "Duarte doesn't have any answers yet, other than some photojournalist caught him in a snapshot and managed to track down details. Which is damn strange. None of us look the same since we left San Rinaldo as kids."

"And there are no other pictures of you in the interim?"

"Only a few stray shots after I became Tony. Carlos's face has shown up in a couple of professional magazines." But the image was so posed and sterile, Tony wasn't sure he would recognize his own sibling on the street. For the best.

His father always insisted photos would provide dangerous links, as if he'd been preparing them from the beginning to split up. Or preparing them for his death.

Not the normal way for a kid to live, but they weren't a regular family. He'd grown accustomed to it eventually... until it almost seemed normal. Until he was faced with a regular person's life, like Shannon's treasured photos of her son.

He broke off another inch of a churro. His hand slowed halfway to his mouth as he got that feeling of "being watched." He checked right fast—

Kolby stood in the open doorway, blanket trailing from his fist.

Uh, okay. So now what? He'd only met the child a few times before last night and none had gone particularly well. Tony had chalked it up to Kolby being shy around strangers or clingy. Judging by the thrust of his little jaw and frown now, there was no mistaking it. The boy didn't like him.

That needed to change. "Hey, kiddo. Where's your mom?"

Kolby didn't budge. "Still sleepin'."

Breaking the ice, Vernon tugged out a chair. "Wanna have a seat and join us?"

Never taking his eyes off Tony, Kolby padded across the tile patio and scrambled up to sit on his knees. Silently, he simply blinked and stared with wide blue-gray eyes just like Shannon's, his blond hair spiking every which way.

Vernon wiped his mouth, tossed his linen napkin on the plate and stood. "Thanks for the chow. I need to check on business. No need to see me out."

As his old friend deserted ship, unease crawled around inside Tony's gut. His experience with children was nonexistent, even when he'd been a kid himself. He and his brothers had been tutored on the island. They'd been each other's only playmates.

The island fortress had been staffed with security guards, not the mall cop sort, but more like a small deployed military unit. Cleaning staff, tutors, the chef and groundskeepers were all from San Rinaldo, older supporters of his father who'd lost their families in the coup. They shared a firm bond of loyalty, and a deep-seated need for a safe haven.

Working on the shrimp boat had felt like a vacation, with the wide open spaces and no boundaries. Most of all he enjoyed the people who didn't wear the imprint of painful loss in their eyes.

But still, there weren't any three-year-olds on the shrimp boat.

What did kids need? "Are you hungry?"

"Some of that." Kolby pointed to Tony's plate of churros. "With peanut bubber."

Grateful for action instead of awkward silence, he shoved to his feet. "Peanut butter it is then. Follow me."

Once he figured out where to look. He'd quit cooking for himself about ten years ago and the few years he had, he wasn't whipping up kiddie cuisine.

About seven minutes later he unearthed a jar from the cavernous pantry and smeared a messy trail down a churro before chunking the spoon in the sink.

Kolby pointed to the lid on the granite countertop. "We don't waste."

"Right." Tony twisted the lid on tight. Thinking of Shannon pinching pennies on peanut butter, for crying out loud, he wanted to buy them a lifetime supply.

As he started to pass the plate to Kolby, a stray thought broadsided him. Hell. Was the kid allergic to peanuts? He hadn't even thought to ask. Kolby reached. Tony swallowed another curse.

"Let's wait for your mom."

"Wait for me why?" Her softly melodic voice drifted over his shoulder from across the kitchen.

He glanced back and his heart kicked against his ribs. They'd slept together over the past month but never actually *slept*. And never through the night.

Damn, she made jeans look good, the washed pale fabric clinging to her long legs. Her hair flowed over her shoulders and down her back, still damp from a shower. He remembered well the silky glide of it through his fingers... and so not something he should be thinking about with her son watching.

Tony held up the plate of churros. "Can he eat peanut butter?"

"He's never tried it that way before, but I'm sure he'll like it." She slipped the dish from his grip. "Although, I'm not so certain that breakable stoneware is the best choice for a three-year-old."

"Hey, kiddo, is the plate all right with you?"

"'S okay." Kolby inched toward his mother and wrapped an arm around her leg. "Like trains better. And milk."

"The milk I can handle." He yanked open the door on the stainless steel refrigerator and reached for the jug. "I'll make sure you have the best train plates next time."

"Wait!" Shannon stopped him, digging into an oversized bag on her shoulder and pulling out a cup with a vented lid. "Here's his sippy cup. It's not Waterford, but it works better."

Smoothly, she filled it halfway and scooped up the plate. Kolby held on to his mother all the way back to the patio.

For the first time he wondered why he hadn't spent more time with the boy. Shannon hadn't offered and he hadn't pushed. She sat and pulled Kolby in her lap, plate in front just out of his reach. The whole family breakfast scenario wrapped around him, threatening his focus. He skimmed a finger along his shirt collar— Hell. He stopped short, realizing he wasn't wearing a tie.

She pinched off a bite and passed it to her son. "I had a lot of time to think last night."

So she hadn't slept any better than he had. "What did you think about after I left?"

Her eyes shot up to his, pink flushing her face. "Going to see your father, of course."

"Of course." He nodded, smiling.

"Of course," Kolby echoed.

As the boy licked the peanut butter off the churro, she traced the intricate pattern painted along the edge of the plate, frowning. "I would like to tell Vernon and your lawyer about our plans for the week and then I'll come with you."

He'd won. She would be safe, and he would have more time to sway her. Except it really chapped his hide that she trusted him so little she felt the need to log her travel itinerary. "Not meaning to shoot myself in the foot here, but why Vernon instead of my lawyer? Vernon is my friend. I financed his business."

"You own the restaurant?" Her slim fingers gravitated back to the china. "*You* are responsible for my paychecks? I thought the Grille belonged to Vernon."

"You didn't know?" Probably a good thing or he might well have never talked her into that first date. "Vernon was a friend when I needed one. I'm glad I could return the favor. He's more than delivered on the investment."

"He gave you a job when your past must have seemed spotty," she said intuitively.

"How did you figure that out?"

"He did the same for me when I needed a chance." A bittersweet smile flickered across her face much like how the sunlight filtered through the lemon tree to play in her hair. "That's the reason I trust him."

"You've worked hard for every penny you make there."

"I know, but I appreciate that he was fair. No handouts, and yet he never took advantage of how much I needed that job. He's a good man. Now back to our travel plans." She rested her chin on her son's head. "Just to be sure, I'll also be informing my in-laws—Kolby's grandparents."

His brows slammed upward. She rarely mentioned them, only that they'd cut her out of their lives after their son died. The fact that she would keep such cold fish informed about their grandson spoke of an innate sense of fair play he wasn't sure he would have given in her position.

"Apparently you trust just about everyone more than me."

She dabbed at the corners of her mouth, drawing his attention to the plump curve of her bottom lip. "Apparently so."

Not a ringing endorsement of her faith in him, but he would take the victory and focus forward. Because before sundown, he would return to his father's island home off the coast of Florida.

She was actually in a private plane over...
Somewhere.

Since the window shades were closed, she had no idea whether they were close to land or water. So where were they? Once airborne, she'd felt the plane turn, but quickly lost any sense of whether they were going north or south, east or west. Although north was unlikely given he'd told her to pack for warm weather.

How far had they traveled? Tough to tell since she'd napped and she had no idea how fast this aircraft could travel. She'd been swept away into a world beyond anything she'd experienced, from the discreet impeccable service to the sleeping quarters already made up for her and Kolby on arrival. Questions about her food preferences had resulted in a five-star meal.

Shannon pressed a hand to her jittery stomach. God,

she hoped she'd made the right decision. At least her son seemed oblivious to all the turmoil around them.

The cabin steward guided Kolby toward the galley kitchen with the promise of a snack and a video. As they walked toward the back, he dragged his tiny fingers along the white leather seats. At least his hands were clean.

But she would have to make a point of keeping sharp objects out of Kolby's reach. She shuddered at the image of a silver taped X on the luxury upholstery.

Her eyes shifted to the man filling the deep seat across from her couch. Wearing gray pants and a white shirt with the sleeves rolled up, he focused intently on the laptop screen in front of him, seemingly oblivious to anyone around him.

She hated the claustrophobic feeling of needing his help, not to mention all the money hiding out entailed. Dependence made her vulnerable, something she'd sworn would never happen again. Yet here she was, entrusting her whole life to a man, a man who'd lied to her.

However, with her child's well-being at stake, she couldn't afford to say no.

More information would help settle the apprehension plucking at her nerves like heart strings. Any information, since apparently everything she knew about him outside of the bedroom was false. She hadn't even known he owned the restaurant where she worked.

Ugh.

Of course it seemed silly to worry about being branded as the type who sleeps with the boss. Having an affair with a drop-dead sexy prince trumped any other gossip. "How long has it been since you saw your father?"

Tony looked up from his laptop slowly. "I left the island when I was eighteen."

"Island?" Her hand grazed the covered window as she

envisioned water below. "I thought you left San Rinaldo as a young boy."

"We did." He closed the computer and pivoted the chair toward her, stretching his legs until his feet stopped intimately close to hers. "I was five at the time. We relocated to another island about a month after we escaped."

She scrunched her toes in her gym shoes. Her scuffed canvas was worlds away from his polished loafers and a private plane. And regardless of how hot he looked, she wouldn't be seduced by the trappings of his wealth.

Forcing her mind back on his words rather than his body, she drew her legs away from him. Was the island on the east coast or west coast? Provided Enrique Medina's compound was even near the U.S. "Your father chose an island so you and your brothers would feel at home in your new place?"

He looked at her over the white tulips centered on the cherry coffee table. "My father chose an island because it was easier to secure."

Gulp. "Oh. Right."

That took the temperature down more than a few degrees. She picked at the piping on the sofa.

Music drifted from the back of the plane, the sound of a new cartoon starting. She glanced down the walkway. Kolby was buckled into a seat, munching on some kind of crackers while watching the movie, mesmerized. Most likely by the whopping big flat screen.

Back to her questions. "How much of you is real and what's a part of the new identity?"

"My age and birthday are real." He tucked the laptop into an oversized briefcase monogrammed with the Castillo Shipping Corporation logo. "Even my name is technically correct, as I told you before. Castillo comes from my mother's family tree. I took it as my own when I turned eighteen."

Resting her elbow on the back of the sofa, she propped her head in her palm, trying her darnedest to act as casual as he appeared. "What does your father think of all you've accomplished since leaving?"

"I wouldn't know." He reclined, folding his hands over his stomach, drawing her eyes and memories to his rock-hard abs.

Her toes curled again until they cracked inside her canvas sneakers. "What does he think of us coming now?"

"You'll have to ask him." His jaw flexed.

"Did you even tell him about the extra guests?" She resisted the urge to smooth the strain away from the bunched tendons in his neck. How odd to think of comforting him when she still had so many reservations about the trip herself.

"I told his lawyer to inform him. His staff will make preparations. Kolby will have whatever he needs."

Who was this coolly factual man a hand stretch away? She almost wondered if she'd imagined carefree Tony... except he'd told her that he liked to surf. She clung to that everyday image and dug deeper.

"Sounds like you and your father aren't close. Or is that just the way royalty communicates?" If so, how sad was that?

He didn't answer, the drone of the engines mingling with the cartoon and the rush of recycled air through the vents. While she wanted her son to grow up independent with a life of his own, she also planned to forge a bond closer than cold communications exchanged between lawyers and assistants.

"Tony?"

His eyes shifted to the shuttered window beside her

head. "I didn't want to live on a secluded island any longer. So I left. He disagreed. We haven't resolved the issue."

Such simple words for so deep a breach where attorneys handled *all* communiqués between them. The lack of communication went beyond distant to estrangement. This wasn't a family just fractured by location. Something far deeper was wrong.

Tucking back into his line of sight, she pressed ahead. This man had already left such a deep imprint on her life, she knew she wouldn't forget him. "What have your lawyers told your father about Kolby and me? What did they tell your dad about our relationship?"

"Relationship?" He pinned her with his dark eyes, the intensity of his look—of him—reaching past the tulips as tangibly as if he'd taken that broad hand and caressed her. He was such a big man with the gentlest of touches.

And he was thorough. God, how he was thorough.

Her heart pounded in her ear like a tympani solo, hollow and so loud it drowned out the engines.

"Tony?" she asked. She *wanted.*

"I let him know that we're a couple. And that you're a widow with a son."

It was one thing to carry on a secret affair with him. Another to openly acknowledge to people—to family—that they were a couple.

She pressed hard against her collarbone, her pulse pushing a syncopated beat against her fingertips. "Why not tell your father the truth? That we broke up but the press won't believe it."

"Who says it's not the truth? We slept together just a week ago. Seems like less than that to me, because I swear I can still catch a whiff of your scent on my skin." He leaned closer and thumbed her wrist.

Her fingers curled as the heat of his touch spread farther. "But about last weekend—"

"Shanny." He tapped her lips once, then traced her rounded sigh. "We may have argued, but when I'm in the room with you, my hand still gravitates to your back by instinct."

Her heart drummed faster until she couldn't have responded even if she tried. But she wasn't trying, too caught up in the sound of him, the desire in his every word.

"The pull between us is that strong, Shannon, whether I'm deep inside you or just listening to you across a room." A half smile kicked a dimple into one cheek. "Why do you think I call you late at night?"

She glanced quickly at the video area checking to make sure her son and the steward where still engrossed in Disney, then she whispered, "Because you'd finished work?"

"You know better. Just the sound of you on the other end of the line sends me rock—"

"Stop, please." She pressed her fingers to his mouth. "You're only hurting us both."

Nipping her fingers lightly first, he linked his hand with hers. "We have problems, without a doubt, and you have reason to be mad. But the drive to be together hasn't eased one bit. Can you deny it? Because if you can, then that is it. I'll keep my distance."

Opening her mouth, she formed the words that would slice that last tie to the relationship they'd forged over the past few months. She fully intended to tell him they were through…. But nothing came out. Not one word.

Slowly, he pulled back. "We're almost there."

Almost where? Back together? Her mind scrambled to keep up with him, damn tough when he kept jumbling her brain. She was a flipping magna cum laude graduate. She resented feeling like a bimbo at the mercy of her libido. But how her libido sang arias around this man...

He shoved to his feet and walked away. Just like that, he cut their conversation short as if they both hadn't been sinking deep into a sensual awareness that had brought them both such intense pleasure in the past. She tracked the lines of his broad shoulders, down to his trim waist and taut butt showcased so perfectly in tailored pants.

Her fingers dug deep into the sofa with restraint. He stopped by Kolby and slid up the window covering.

"Take a look, kiddo, we're almost there." Tony pointed at the clear glass toward the pristine sky.

Ah. *There*. As in they'd arrived there, at his father's island. She'd been so caught up in the sensual draw of undiluted Tony that she'd temporarily forgotten about flying away to a mystery location.

Scrambling down the sofa, she straightened her glasses and stared out the window, hungry for a peek at their future—temporary—home. And yes, curious as hell about the place where Tony had grown up. Sure enough, an island stretched in the distance, nestled in miles and miles of sparkling ocean. Palm trees spiked from the lush landscape. A dozen or so small outbuildings dotted a semicircle around a larger structure.

The white mansion faced the ocean in a *U* shape, constructed around a large courtyard with a pool. She barely registered Kolby's "oohs" and "aahs" since she was pretty much overwhelmed by the sight herself.

Details were spotty but she would get an up-close view soon enough of the place Tony had called home for most of his youth. Even from a distance she couldn't miss the grand scale of the sprawling estate, the unmistakable sort that housed royalty.

The plane banked, lining up with a thin islet alongside the larger island. A single strip of concrete marked the private runway. As they neared, a ferryboat came into focus. To ride from the airport to the main island? They sure were serious about security.

The intercom system crackled a second before the steward announced, "We're about to begin our descent to our destination. Please return to your seats and secure your lap belts. Thank you, and we hope you had a pleasant flight."

Tony pulled away from the window and smiled at her again. Except now, the grin didn't reach his eyes. Her stomach fluttered, but this time with apprehension rather than arousal.

Would the island hold the answers she needed to put Tony in her past? Or would it only break her heart all over again?

Five

Daylight was fading fast and a silence fourteen years old between him and his father was about to be broken.

Feet braced on the ferry deck, Tony stared out over the rail at the island where he'd spent the bulk of his childhood and teenage years. He hated not being in command of the boat almost as much as he hated returning to this place. Only concern for Shannon and her son could have drawn him back where the memories grew and spread as tenaciously as algae webbing around coral.

Just ahead, a black skimmer glided across the water, dipping its bill into the surface. With each lap of the waves against the hull, Tony closed off insidious emotions before they could take root inside him and focused on the shore.

An osprey circled over its nest. Palm trees lined the beach with only a small white stucco building and a two-lane road. Until you looked closer and saw the guard tower.

When he'd come to this island off the coast of St. Augustine at five, there were times he'd believed they were home…that his father had moved them to another part of San Rinaldo. In the darkest nights, he'd woken in a cold sweat, certain the soldiers in camouflage were going to cut through the bars on his windows and take him. Other nights he imagined they'd already taken him and the bars locked him in prison.

On the worst of nights, he'd thought his mother was still alive, only to see her die all over again.

Shannon's hand slid over his elbow, her touch tentative, her eyes wary. "How long did I sleep on the plane?"

"A while." He smiled to reassure her, but the feeling didn't come from his gut. Damn, but he wished the past week had never happened. He would pull her soft body against him and forget about everything else.

Wind streaked her hair across her face. "Oh, right. If you tell me, I might get a sense of how far away we are from Galveston. I might guess where we are. Being cut off from the world is still freaking me out just a little."

"I understand, and I'll to do my best to set things right as soon as possible." He wanted nothing more than to get off this island and return to the life he'd built, the life he chose. The only thing that made coming back here palatable was having Shannon by his side. And that rocked the deck under his feet, realizing she held so much influence over his life.

"Although, I have to admit," she conceded as she tucked her son closer, "this place is so much more than I expected."

Her gaze seemed to track the herons picking their way along the shore, sea oats bowing at every gust. Her grayish-blue eyes glinted with the first hints of excitement. She must not have noticed the security cameras tucked in trees and the guard on the dock, a gun strapped within easy reach.

Tony gripped the rail tighter. "There's no way to prepare a person."

Kolby squealed, pitching forward in his mother's arms.

"Whoa..." Tony snagged the kid by the back of his striped overalls. "Steady there."

A hand pressed to her chest, Shannon struggled for breath. "Thank God you moved so fast. I can't believe I looked away. There's just so much to see, so many distractions."

The little guy scowled at Tony. "Down."

"Buddy," Tony stated as he shook his head, "sometime you're going to have to like me."

"Name's not buddy," Kolby insisted, bottom lip out.

"You're right. I'm just trying to make friends here." Because he intended to use this time to persuade Shannon breaking up had been a crappy idea. He wondered how much the child understood. Since he didn't know how else to approach him, he opted for straight up honesty. "I like your mom, so it's important that you like me."

Shannon's gasp teased his ear like a fresh trickle of wind off the water. As much as he wanted to turn toward her, he kept his attention on the boy.

Kolby clenched Tony's shirt. "Does you like *me?*"

"Uh, sure." The question caught him off guard. He hadn't thought about it other than knowing it was important to win the son over for Shannon's sake. "What do you like?"

"Not you." He popped his bottom lip back in. "Down, pwease."

Shannon caught her son as he leaned toward her. Confusion puckering her brow, her eyes held Tony's for a second before she pointed over the side. "Is that what you wanted to see, sweetie?"

A dolphin zipped alongside the ferry. The fin sliced through the water, then submerged again.

Clapping his tiny hands, Kolby chanted, "Yes, yes, yes."

Again, Shannon saw beauty. He saw something entirely different. The dolphins provided port security. His father had gotten the idea from his own military service, cutting-edge stuff back then. The island was a minikingdom and money wasn't an object. Except this kingdom had substantially fewer subjects.

Tony wondered again if the secluded surroundings growing up could have played into his lousy track record with relationships as an adult. There hadn't been any teenage dating rituals for practice. And after he left, he'd been careful with relationships, never letting anything get too complicated. Work and a full social life kept him happy.

But the child in front of him made things problematic in a way he hadn't foreseen.

For years he'd been pissed off at his father for the way they'd had to live. And here he was doing the same to Kolby. The kid was entertained for the moment, but that would end fast for sure.

Protectiveness for both the mother and son seared his veins. He wouldn't let anything from the Medina past mark their future. Even if that meant he had to reclaim the very identity he'd worked his entire adulthood to shed.

The ferry slid against the dock. They'd arrived at the island.

And Prince Antonio Medina was back.

What was it like for Tony to come back after so long away? And it wasn't some happy homecoming, given the estrangement and distance in this family that communicated through lawyers.

Shannon wanted to reach across the limousine to him, but Tony had emotionally checked out the moment the ferry docked. Of course he'd been Mr. Manners while leaving the ferry and stepping into the Mercedes limo.

Watch your step… Need help? However, the smiles grew darker by the minute.

Maybe it was her own gloomy thoughts tainting her perceptions. At least Kolby seemed unaffected by their moods, keeping his nose pressed to the window the whole winding way to the pristine mansion.

Who wouldn't stare at the trees and the wildlife and finally, the palatial residence? White stucco with a clay tiled roof, arches and opulence ten times over, the place was the size of some hotels or convention centers. Except no hotel she'd stayed in sported guards armed with machine guns.

What should have made her feel safer only served to remind her money and power didn't come without burdens. To think, Tony had grown up with little or no exposure to the real world. It was a miracle he'd turned out normal.

If you could call a billionaire prince with a penchant for surfing "normal."

The limousine slowed, easing past a towering marble fountain with a "welcome" pineapple on top—and wasn't that ironic in light of all those guards? Once the vehicle stopped, more uniformed security appeared from out of nowhere to open the limo. Some kind of servant—a butler perhaps—stood at the top of the stairs. While Tony had insisted he wanted nothing to do with his birthplace, he seemed completely at ease in this surreal world. For the first time, the truth really sunk in.

The stunningly handsome—stoically silent—man walking beside her had royal blood singing through his veins.

"Tony?" She touched his elbow.

"After you," he said, simply gesturing ahead to the double doors sweeping open.

Scooping Kolby onto her hip, she took comfort in his sturdy little body and forged ahead. Inside. *Whoa.*

The cavernous circular hall sported gold gilded archways leading to open rooms. Two staircases stretched up either side, meeting in the middle. And, uh, stop the world, was that a Picasso on the wall?

Her canvas sneakers squeaked against marble floors as more arches ushered her deeper into the mansion. And while she vowed money didn't matter, she still wished she'd packed different shoes. Shannon straightened the straps on Kolby's favorite striped overalls, the ones he swore choo-choo drivers wore. She'd been so frazzled when she'd tossed clothes into a couple of overnight bags, picking things that would make him happy.

Just ahead, French doors opened on to a veranda that overlooked the ocean. Tony turned at the last minute, guiding her toward what appeared to be a library. Books filled three walls, interspersed with windows and a sliding brass ladder. Mosaic tiles swirled outward on the floor, the ceiling filled with frescos of globes and conquistadors. The smell of fresh citrus hung in the air, and not just because of the open windows. A tall potted orange tree nestled in one corner beneath a wide skylight.

An older man slept in a wingback by the dormant fireplace. Two large brown dogs—some kind of Ridgeback breed, perhaps?—lounged to his left and right.

Tony's father. A no-kidding king.

Either age or illness had taken a toll, dimming the family resemblance. But in spite of his nap, he wasn't going gently into that good night. No slippers and robe for this meeting. He wore a simple black suit with an ascot rather than a tie, his silver hair slicked back. Frailty and his pasty pallor made her want to comfort him.

Then his eyes snapped open. The sharp gleam in his coal dark eyes stopped her short.

Holy Sean Connery, the guy might be old but he hadn't lost his edge.

"Welcome home, *hijo prodigo.*" *Prodigal son.*

Enrique Medina spoke in English but his accent was still unmistakably Spanish. And perhaps a bit thick with emotion? Or was that just wishful thinking on her part for Tony's sake?

"Hello, Papa." Tony palmed her back between her shoulder blades. "This is Shannon and her son Kolby."

The aging monarch nodded in her direction. "Welcome, to you and to your son."

"Thank you for your hospitality and your help, sir." She didn't dare wade into the whole *Your Highness* versus *Your Majesty* waters. Simplicity seemed safest.

Toying with a pocket watch in his hand, Enrique continued, "If not for my family, you would not need my assistance."

Tony's fingers twitched against her back. "Hopefully we won't have to impose upon you for long. Shannon and her son only need a place to lay low until this blows over."

"It won't blow over," Enrique said simply.

Ouch. She winced.

Tony didn't. "Poor choice of words. Until things calm down."

"Of course." He nodded regally before shifting his attention her way. "I am glad to have you here, my dear. You brought Tony home, so you have already won favor with me." He smiled and for the first time, she saw the family resemblance clearly.

Kolby wriggled, peeking up from her neck. "Whatsa matter with you?"

"Shhh…Kolby." She pressed a quick silencing kiss to his forehead. "That's a rude question."

"It's an honest question. I do not mind the boy." The king shifted his attention to her son. "I have been ill. My legs are not strong enough to walk."

"I'm sorry." Kolby eyed the wheelchair folded up and tucked discreetly alongside the fireplace. "You musta been bery sick."

"Thank you. I have good doctors."

"You got germs?"

A smile tugged at the stern face. "No, child. You and your mother cannot catch my germs."

"That's good." He stuffed his tiny fists into his pockets. "Don't like washin' my hands."

Enrique laughed low before his hand fell to rest on one dog's head. "Do you like animals?"

"Yep." Kolby squirmed downward until Shannon had no choice but to release him before he pitched out of her arms. "Want a dog."

Such a simple, painfully normal wish and she couldn't afford to supply it. From the pet deposit required at her apartment complex to the vet bills… It was out of her budget. Guilt tweaked again over all she couldn't give her child.

Yet hadn't Tony been denied so much even with such wealth? He'd lost his home, his mother and gained a gilded prison. Whispers of sympathy for a motherless boy growing up isolated from the world softened her heart when she most needed to hold strong.

Enrique motioned Kolby closer. "You may pet my dog.

Come closer and I will introduce you to Benito and Diablo. They are very well trained and will not hurt you."

Kolby didn't even hesitate. Any reservations her son felt about Tony certainly didn't extend to King Enrique—or his dogs. Diablo sniffed the tiny, extended hand.

A cleared throat startled Shannon from her thoughts. She glanced over her shoulder and found a young woman waiting in the archway. In her late twenties, wearing a Chanel suit, she obviously wasn't the housekeeper.

But she was stunning with her black hair sleeked back in a simple clasp. She wore strappy heels instead of sneakers. God, it felt silly to be envious of someone she didn't know, and honestly, she only coveted the pretty red shoes.

"Alys," the older man commanded, "enter. Come meet my son and his guests. This is my assistant, Alys Reyes de la Cortez. She will show you to your quarters."

Shannon resisted the urge to jump to conclusions. It wasn't any of her business who Enrique Medina chose for his staff and she shouldn't judge a person by their appearance. The woman was probably a rocket scientist, and Shannon wouldn't trade one single sticky hug from her son for all the high-end clothes on the planet.

Not that she was jealous of the gorgeous female with immaculate clothes, who fit perfectly into Tony's world. After all, he hadn't spared more than a passing glance at the woman.

Still, she wished she'd packed a pair of pumps.

An hour later, Shannon closed her empty suitcases and rocked back on her bare heels in the doorway of her new quarters.

A suite?

More like a luxury condominium within the mansion. She sunk her toes into the Persian rug until her chipped pink polish disappeared in the apricot and gray pattern. She and Kolby had separate bedrooms off a sitting area with an eating space stocked more fully than most kitchens. The balcony was as large as some yards.

Had the fresh-cut flowers been placed in here just for her? She dipped her face into the crystal vase of lisianthus with blooms that resembled blue roses and softened the gray tones in the decor.

After Alys had walked them up the lengthy stairs to their suite, Kolby had run from room to room for fifteen minutes before winding down and falling asleep in an exhausted heap under the covers. He hadn't even noticed the toy box at the end of his sleigh bed yet, he'd been so curious about their new digs. Tony had given them space while she unpacked, leaving for his quarters with a simple goodbye and another of those smiles that didn't reach his eyes.

The quiet echoed around her, leaving her hyperaware of other sounds…a ticking grandfather clock in the hall… the crashing ocean outside… Trailing her fingers along the camelback sofa, she looked through the double doors, moonlight casting shadows along her balcony. Her feet drew her closer until the shadows took shape into the broad shoulders of a man leaning on the railing.

Tony? He felt like a safe haven in an upside down day. But how had he gotten there without her noticing his arrival?

Their balconies must connect, which meant someone had planned for them to have access to each other's rooms. Had he been waiting for her? Anticipation hummed through her at the notion of having him all to herself.

Shannon unlocked and pushed open the doors to the patio filled with topiaries, ferns and flowering cacti. A swift ocean breeze rolled over her, lifting her hair and fluttering her shirt along her skin in whispery caresses. God, she was tired and emotional and so not in the right frame of mind to be anywhere near Tony. She should go to bed instead of staring at his sinfully sexy body just calling to her to rest her cheek on his back and wrap her arms around his waist. Her fingers fanned against her legs as she remembered the feel of him, so much more intense with his sandalwood scent riding the wind.

Need pooled warm and languid and low, diluting her already fading resistance.

His shoulders bunched under his starched white shirt a second before he glanced over his shoulder, his eyes haunted. Then they cleared. "Is Kolby asleep?"

"Yes, and thank you for all the preparations. The toys, the food...the flowers."

"All a part of the Medina welcome package."

"Perhaps." But she'd noticed a few too many of their favorites for the choices to have been coincidental. She moved forward hesitantly, the tiles cool against the bottoms of her feet. "This is all...something else."

"Leaving San Rinaldo, we had to downsize." He gave her another of those dry smiles.

More sympathy slid over her frustration at his secrets. "Thank you for bringing us here. I know it wasn't easy for you."

"I'm the reason you have to hide out in the first place until we line up protection for you. Seems only fair I should do everything in my power to make this right."

Her husband had never tried to fix any of his mistakes, hadn't even apologized after his arrest in the face of irrefutable evidence. She couldn't help but appreciate the way Tony took responsibility. And he cared enough to smooth the way for her.

"What about you?" She joined him at the swirled iron

railing. "You wouldn't have come here if it weren't for me. What do you hope to accomplish for yourself?"

"Don't worry about me." He leaned back on his elbows, white shirt stretching open at the collar to reveal the strong column of his neck. "I always look out for myself."

"Then what are you gaining?"

"More time with you, at least until the restraining order is in place." The heat of his eyes broadcast his intent just before he reached for her. "I've always been clear about how much I want to be with you, even on that first date when you wouldn't kiss me good-night."

"Is that why you chased me? Because I said no?"

"But you didn't keep saying no and still, here I am turned on as hell by the sound of your voice." He plucked her glasses off, set them aside and cradled her face in his palms. "The feel of your skin."

While he owned an empire with corporate offices that took up a bayside block, his skin still carried the calluses of the dockworker and sailor he'd been during his early adulthood. He was a man who certainly knew how to work with his hands. The rasp as he lightly caressed her cheekbones reminded her of the sweet abrasion when he explored farther.

He combed through along her scalp, strands slithering across his fingers. "The feel of your hair."

A moan slipped past her lips along with his name, "Tony..."

"Antonio," he reminded her. "I want to hear you say my name, know who's here with you."

And in this moment, in his eyes, he was that foreign prince, less accessible than her Tony, but no less exciting and infinitely as irresistible, so she whispered, "Antonio."

His touch was gentle, his mouth firm against hers. She parted her lips under his and invited in the familiar sweep, taste and pure sensation. Clutching his elbows, she swayed, her breasts tingling, pulling tight. Before she could think or stop herself, she brushed slightly from side to side, increasing the sweet pleasure of his hard chest teasing her. His hard thigh between her legs.

She stepped backward.

And tugged him with her.

Toward the open French doors leading into her bedroom, her body overriding her brain as it always seemed to do around Tony. She squeezed her legs together tighter against the firm pressure of his muscled thigh, so close, too close. She wanted, *needed* to feel him move inside her first.

Sinking her fingernails deeper, she ached to ask him to stay with her, to help her forget the worries waiting at home. "Antonio—"

"I know." He eased his mouth from hers, his chin scraping along her jaw as he nuzzled her hair and inhaled. "We need to stop."

Stop? She almost shrieked in frustration. "But I thought... I mean, you're here and usually when we let things go this far, we finish."

"You're ready to resume our affair?"

Affair. Not just one night, one satisfaction, but a relationship with implications and complications. Her brain raced to catch up after being put on idle while her body took over. God, what had she almost done? A few kisses along with a well-placed thigh, and she was ready to throw herself back in his bed.

Planting her hands on his chest, she stepped away. "I can't deny that I miss you and I want you, but I have no desire to be labeled a Medina mistress."

His eyebrows shot up toward his hairline. "Are you saying you want to get married?"

Six

"Married?" Shannon choked on the word, her eyes so wide with shock Tony was almost insulted. "No! No, definitely not."

Her instant and emphatic denial left zero room for doubt. She wasn't expecting a proposal. Good thing, since that hadn't crossed his mind. Until now.

Was he willing to go that far to protect her?

She turned away fast, her hands raised as she raced back into the sitting area. "Tony—Antonio—I can't talk to you, look at you, risk kissing you again. I need to go to bed. To sleep. Alone."

"Then what do you want from me?"

"To end this craziness. To stop thinking about you all the time."

All the time?

He homed in on her words, an obvious slip on her part because while she'd been receptive and enthusiastic in bed, she'd given him precious little encouragement once they had their clothes back on again. Their fight over his simple offer of money still stung. Why did she have to reject his attempt to help?

She paced, restlessly lining up her shoes beside the sofa, scooping Kolby's tiny train from a table, lingering to rearrange the blue flowers. "You've said you feel the same. Who the hell wants to be consumed by this kind of ache all the time? It's damned inconvenient, especially when it can't lead anywhere. It's not like you were looking for marriage."

"That wasn't my intention when we started seeing each other." Yet somehow the thought had popped into his head out there on the patio. Sure, it had shocked the crap out of him at first. Still left him reeling. Although not so much that he was willing to reject the idea outright. "But since you've brought it up—"

Her hands shot up in front of her, between them. "Uh-uh, no sirree. You were the one to mention the *M* word."

"Fine, then. The marriage issue is out there, on the table for discussion. Let's talk it through."

She stopped cold. "This isn't some kind of business merger. We're talking about our lives here, and not just ours. I don't have the luxury of making another mistake. I already screwed up once before, big time. My son's well-being depends on my decisions."

"And I'm a bad choice because?"

"Do not play with my feelings. Damn it, Tony." She jabbed him in the chest with one finger. "You know I'm attracted to you. If you keep this up, I'll probably cave and we'll have sex. We probably would have on the plane if the steward and my son hadn't been around. But I would have been sorry the minute the orgasm chilled and is that really how you want it to be between us? To have me waking up regretting it every time?"

With images of the two of them joining the mile-high club fast-tracking from his brain to his groin, he seriously considered saying to hell with regrets. Let this insanity between them play out, wherever it took them.

Her bed was only a few steps away, offering a clear and tempting place to sink inside her. He would sweep away her clothes and the covers— His gaze hooked on the afghan draped along the end corner of the mattress.

Damn. Who had put that there? Could his father be deliberately jabbing him with reminders of their life as a family in hopes of drawing him back into the fold? Of course Enrique would, manipulative old cuss that he was.

That familiar silver blanket sucker punched him back to reality. He would recognize the one-of-a-kind afghan anywhere. His mother had knitted it for him just before she'd been killed, and he'd kept it with him like a shield during the whole hellish escape from San Rinaldo. Good God, he shouldn't have had to ask her why he was a bad choice. He knew the reason well.

Tony stumbled back, away from the memories and away from this woman who saw too much with her perceptive gray-blue eyes.

"You're right, Shannon. We're both too exhausted to make any more decisions today. Sleep well." His voice as raw as his memory-riddled gut, he left.

Dazed, Shannon stood in the middle of the sitting room wondering what the hell had just happened.

One second she'd been ready to climb back into Tony's arms and bed, the next they'd been talking about marriage.

And didn't that still stun her numb with thoughts of how horribly things had ended with Nolan?

But only seconds after bringing up the marriage issue, Tony had emotionally checked out on her again. At least he'd prevented them from making a mistake. It was a mistake, right?

Eyeing her big—empty—four-poster bed, she suddenly wasn't one bit sleepy. Tony overwhelmed her as much as the wealth. She walked into her bedroom, studying the Picasso over her headboard, this one from the artist's rose period, a harlequin clown in oranges and pinks. She'd counted three works already by this artist alone, including some leggy elephant painting in Kolby's room.

She'd hidden the crayons and markers.

Laughing at the absurdity of it all, she fingered a folded cashmere afghan draped over the corner of the mattress. So whispery soft and strangely worn in the middle of this immaculately opulent decor. The pewter-colored yarn complemented the apricot and gray tones well enough, but she wondered where it had come from. She tugged it from the bed and shook it out.

The blanket rippled in front of her, a little larger than a lap quilt, not quite long enough for a single bed. Turning in a circle she wrapped the filmy cover around her and padded back out to the balcony. She hugged the cashmere wrap tighter and curled up in a padded lounger, letting the ocean wind soothe her face still warm from Tony's touch.

Was it her imagination or could she smell hints of him even on the blanket? Or was he that firmly in her senses as well as her thoughts? What was it about Tony that reached to her in ways Nolan never had? She'd responded to her husband's touch, found completion, content with her life right up to the point of betrayal.

But Tony... Shannon hugged the blanket tighter. She

hadn't been hinting at marriage, damn it. Just the thought of giving over her life so completely again scared her to her toes.

So where did that leave her? Seriously considering becoming exactly what the media labeled her—a monarch's mistress.

Tony heard…the silence.

Finally, Shannon had settled for the night. Thank God. Much longer and his willpower would have given out. He would have gone back into her room and picked up where they'd left off before he'd caught sight of the damn blanket.

This place screwed with his head, so much so he'd actually brought up marriage, for crying out loud. It was like there were rogue waves from his past curling up everywhere and knocking him off balance. The sooner he could take care of business with his father the sooner he could return to Galveston with Shannon, back to familiar ground where he stood a better chance at reconciling with her.

Staying out of her bed for now was definitely the wiser choice. He walked down the corridor, away from her and that blanket full of memories. He needed his focus sharp for the upcoming meeting with his father. This time, he would face the old man alone.

Charging down the hall, he barely registered the familiar antique wooden benches tucked here, a strategic table and guard posted there. Odd how quickly he slid right back into the surroundings even after so long away. And even stranger that his father hadn't changed a thing.

The day had been one helluva ride, and it wasn't over yet. Enrique had been with his nurse for the past hour, but should be ready to receive him now.

Tony rounded the corner and nodded to the sentinel outside the open door to Enrique's personal quarters. The space was made for a man, no feminine touches to soften the room full of browns and tans, leather and wood. Enrique saved his Salvador Dali collection for himself, a trio of the surrealist's "soft watches" melting over landscapes.

The old guy had become more obsessed with history after his had been stolen from him.

Enrique waited in his wheelchair, wearing a heavy blue robe and years of worries.

"Sit," his father ordered, pointing to his old favored chair.

When Tony didn't jump at his command, Enrique sighed heavily and muttered under his breath in Spanish. "Have a seat," he continued in his native tongue. "We need to talk, *mi hijo*."

They did, and Tony had to admit he was curious—concerned—about his father's health. Knowing might not have brought him home sooner, but now that he was here, he couldn't ignore the gaunt angles and sallow pallor. "How sick are you really?" Tony continued in Spanish, having spoken both languages equally once they'd left San Rinaldo. "No sugar coating it. I deserve the truth."

"And you would have heard it earlier if you had returned when I first requested."

His father had never *requested* anything in his life. The stubborn old cuss had been willing to die alone rather than actually admit how ill he was.

Of course Antonio had been just as stubborn about ignoring the demands to show his face on the island. "I am here now."

"You and your brothers have stirred up trouble." A great big *I told you so* was packed into that statement.

"Do you have insights as to how this leaked? How did

that reporter identify Duarte?" His middle brother wasn't exactly a social guy.

"Nobody knows, but my people are still looking into it. I thought you would be the one to expose us," his father said wryly. "You always were the impetuous one. Yet you've behaved decisively and wisely. You have protected those close to you. Well done."

"I am past needing your approval, but I thank you for your help."

"Fair enough, and I'm well aware that you would not have accepted that help if Shannon Crawford was not involved. I would be glad to see one of my sons settled and married before I die."

His gut pitched much like a boat tossed by a wave. "Your illness is that bad?" An uneasy silence settled, his father's rattling breaths growing louder and louder. "Should I call a nurse?"

Or his assistant? He wasn't sure what Alys Reyes de la Cortez was doing here, but she was definitely different from the older staff of San Rinaldo natives Enrique normally hired.

"I may be old and sick, but I don't need to be tucked into bed like a child." His chin tipped.

"I'm not here to fight with you."

"Of course not. You're here for my help."

And he had the feeling his father wasn't going to let him forget it. They'd never gotten along well and apparently that hadn't changed. He started to rise. "If that's all then, I will turn in."

"Wait." His father polished his eighteen-karat gold pocket watch with his thumb. "My assistance comes at a price."

Shocked at the calculating tone, Tony sank back into his chair. "You can't be serious."

"I am. Completely."

He should have suspected and prepared himself. "What do you want?"

"I want you to stay for the month while you wait for the new safety measures to be implemented."

"Here? That's all?" He made it sound offhand but already he could feel the claustrophobia wrap around his throat and tighten. The Dali art mocked him with just how slippery time could be, a life that ended in a flash or a moment that extended forever.

"Is it so strange I want to see what kind of man you have matured into?"

Given Enrique had expected Tony to break their cover, he must not have had high expectations for his youngest son. And that pissed him off. "If I don't agree? You'll do what? Feed Shannon and her son to the lions?"

"Her son can stay. I would never sacrifice a child's safety. The mother will have to go."

He couldn't be serious. Tony studied his father for some sign Enrique was bluffing...but the old guy didn't have a "tell." And his father hadn't hesitated to trust his own wife's safety to others. What would stop him from sending Shannon off with a guard and a good-luck wish?

"She would never leave without her child." Like his mother. Tony restrained a wince.

"That is not my problem. Are you truly that unwilling to spend a month here?"

"What if the restraining order comes through sooner?"

"I would ask you to stay as a thanks for my assistance. I have risked a lot for you in granting her access to the island."

True enough, or so it would feel to Enrique with his near agoraphobic need to stay isolated from the world.

"And there are no other conditions?"

A salt and pepper eyebrow arched. "Do you want a contract?"

"Do you? If Shannon decides to leave by the weekend, I could simply go, too. What's the worst you can do? Cut me out of the will?" He hadn't taken a penny of his father's money.

"You always were the most amusing of my sons. I have missed that."

"I'm not laughing."

His father's smile faded and he tucked the watch into a pocket, chain jingling to a rest. "Your word is sufficient. You may not want any part of me and my little world here, but you are a Medina. You are my son. Your honor is not in question."

"Fair enough. If you're willing to accept my word, then a month it is." Now that the decision was made, he wondered why his father had chosen that length of time. "What's your prognosis?"

"My liver is failing," Enrique said simply without any hint of self-pity. "Because of the living conditions when I was on the run, I caught hepatitis. It has taken a toll over the years."

Thinking back, Tony tried to remember if his father had been sick when they'd reunited in South America before relocating to the island...but he only recalled his father being coolly determined. "I didn't know. I'm sorry."

"You were a child. You did not need to be informed of everything."

He hadn't been told much of *anything* in those days, but even if he had, he wasn't sure he would have heard. His grief for his mother had been deep and dark. That, he remembered well. "How much longer do you have?"

"I am not going to kick off in the next thirty days."

"That isn't what I meant."

"I know." His father smiled, creases digging deep. "I have a sense of humor, too."

What had his father been like before this place? Before the coup? Tony would never know because time was melting away like images in the Dali paintings on the wall.

While he had some memories of his mother from that time, he had almost none of his father until Enrique had met up with them in South America. The strongest memory he had of Enrique in San Rinaldo? When his father gathered his family to discuss the evacuation plan. Enrique had pressed his pocket watch into Tony's hands and promised to reclaim it. But even at five, Tony had known his father was saying goodbye for what could have been the last time. Now, Enrique wanted him back to say goodbye for the last time again.

How damned ironic. He'd brought Shannon to this place because she needed him. And now he could only think of how much he needed to be with her.

Seven

Where was Tony?

The next day after lunch, Shannon stood alone on her balcony overlooking the ocean. Seagulls swooped on the horizon while long legged blue herons stalked prey on the rocks. Kolby was napping. A pot of steeped herbal tea waited on a tiny table along with dried fruits and nuts.

How strange to have such complete panoramic peace during such a tumultuous time. The balcony offered an unending view of the sea, unlike the other side with barrier islands. The temperature felt much the same as in Galveston, humid and in the seventies.

She should make the most of the quiet to regain her footing. Instead, she kept looking at the door leading into Tony's suite and wondering why she hadn't seen him yet.

Her morning had been hectic and more than a little overwhelming learning her way around the mansion with Alys. As much as she needed to resist Tony, she'd missed having his big comforting presence at her side while she explored the never-ending rooms packed nonchalantly with priceless art and antiques.

And they'd only toured half of the home and grounds.

Afterward, Alys had introduced two women on hand for sitter and nanny duties. Shannon had been taken aback by the notion of turning her son over to total strangers, although she had to confess, the guard assigned to shadow Kolby reassured her. She'd been shown letters of recommendation and résumés for each individual. Still, Shannon had spent the rest of the morning getting to know each person in case she needed to call on their help.

Interestingly, none of the king's employees gave away the island's location despite subtle questions about traveling back to their homes. Everyone on Enrique's payroll seemed to understand the importance of discretion, as well as seeing to her every need. Including delivering a closet full of clothes that just happened to fit. Not that she'd caved to temptation yet and tried any of it on. A gust rolling off the ocean teased the well-washed cotton of her sundress around her legs as she stood on the balcony.

The click of double doors opening one suite down snapped her from her reverie. She didn't even need to look over her shoulder to verify who'd stepped outside. She knew the sound of his footsteps, recognized the scent of him on the breeze.

"Hello, Tony."

His Italian loafers stopped alongside her feet in simple pink and brown striped flip-flops. *Hers.* Not ones from the new stash.

Leaning into her line of sight, he rested his elbows on the iron rail. "Sorry not to have checked in on you sooner. My father and I spent the morning troubleshooting on a conference call with my brothers and our attorneys."

Of course. That made sense. "Any news?"

"More of the same. Hopefully we can start damage control with some valid info leaked to the press to turn the tide. There's just so much out there." He shook his head sharply then forced a smile. "Enough of that. I missed you at lunch."

"Kolby and I ate in our suite." The scent of Tony's sandalwood aftershave had her curling her toes. "His table manners aren't up to royal standards."

"You don't have to hide in your rooms. There's no court or ceremony here." Still, he wore khakis and a monogrammed blue button-down rolled up at the sleeves rather than the jeans and shorts most everyday folks would wear on a beach vacation.

And he looked mighty fine in every starched inch of fabric.

"Formality or not, there are priceless antiques and art all easily within a child's reach." She trailed her fingers along the iron balustrade. "This place is a lot to absorb. We need time. Although I hope life returns to normal sooner rather than later."

Could she simply pick up where she'd left off? Things hadn't been so great then, given her nearly bankrupt account and her fight with Tony over more than money, over her very independence. Yet hadn't she been considering resuming the affair just last night?

Sometimes it was tough to tell if her hormones or her heart had control these days.

He extended his hand. "You're right. Let's slow things down. Would you like to go for a walk?"

"But Kolby might wake up and ask for m—"

"One of the nannies can watch over him and call us the second his eyes open. Come on. I'll update you on the wackiest of the internet buzz." A half grin tipped one side of his tanned face. "Apparently one source thinks the Medinas have a space station and I've taken you to the mother ship."

Laughter bubbled, surprising her, and she just let it roll free with the wind tearing in from the shore. God, how she needed it after the stressful past couple of days—a stressful week for that matter, since she had broken off her relationship with Tony. "Lead the way, my alien lover."

His smile widened, reaching his eyes for the first time since their ferry had pulled up to the island. The power outshone the world around her until she barely noticed the opulent surroundings on their way through the mansion to the beach.

The October sun high in the sky was blinding and warm, hotter than when she'd been on the balcony, inching up toward eighty degrees perhaps. Her mind started churning with possible locations. Could they be in Mexico or South America? Or were they still in the States? California or—

"We're off the coast of Florida."

Glancing up sharply, she swallowed hard, not realizing until that moment how deeply the secrecy had weighed on her. "Thank you."

He waved aside her gratitude. "You would have figured it out on your own in a couple of days."

Maybe, but given the secrecy of Enrique's employees, she wasn't as certain. "So, what about more of those wacky internet rumors?"

"Do you really want to discuss that?"

"I guess not." She slid off her flip-flops and curled her toes in the warm sand. "Thank you for all the clothes for me and for Kolby, the toys, too. We'll enjoy them while we're here. But you know we can't keep them."

"Don't be a buzz kill." He tapped her nose just below the

bridge of her glasses. "My father's staff ordered everything. I had nothing to do with it. If it'll make you happy, we'll donate the lot to Goodwill after you leave."

"How did he get everything here so fast?" She strode into the tide, her shoes dangling from her fingers.

"Does it matter?" He slid off his shoes and socks and joined her, just into the water's reach.

With the more casual and familiar Tony returning, some of the tension left her shoulders. "I guess not. The toys are awesome, of course, but Kolby enjoys the dogs most. They seem incredibly well trained."

"They are. My father will have his trainers working with the dogs to bond with your son so they will protect him as well if need be while you are here."

She shivered in spite of the bold beams of sunshine overhead. "Can't a dog just be a pet?"

"Things aren't that simple for us." He looked away, down the coast at an osprey spreading its wings and diving downward.

How many times had he watched the birds as a child and wanted to fly away, too? She understood well the need to escape a golden cage. "I'm sorry."

"Don't be." He rejected her sympathy outright.

Pride iced his clipped words, and she searched for a safer subject.

Her eyes settled on the rippling crests of foam frosting the gray-blue shore. "Is this where you used to surf?"

"Actually, the cove is pretty calm." He pointed ahead to an outcropping packed with palm trees. "The best spot is about a mile and a half down. Or at least it was. Who knows after so many years?"

"You really had free rein to run around the island." She stepped onto a sandbar that fingered out into the water. As a mother, she had a tough time picturing her child exploring this junglelike beach at will.

"Once I was a teenager, pretty much. After I was through with schooling for the day, of course." A green turtle popped his head from the water, legs poking from the shell as he swam out and slapped up the beach. "Although sometimes we even had class out here."

"A field trip to the beach? What fun teachers you had."

"Tutors."

"Of course." The stark difference in their upbringings wrapped around her like seaweed lapping at her ankles. She tried to shake free of the clammy negativity. "Surfing was your P.E.?"

"Technically, we had what you would call phys ed, but it was more of a health class with martial arts training."

During her couple of years teaching high school band and chorus before she'd met Nolan, some of her students went to karate lessons. But they'd gone to a gym full of other students, rather than attending in seclusion with only two brothers for company. "It's so surreal to think you never went to prom, or had an after-school job or played on a basketball team."

"We had games here...but you're right in that there was no stadium of classmates and parents. No cheerleaders." He winked and smiled, but she sensed he was using levity as a diversion.

How often had he done that in the past and she'd missed out hearing his real thoughts or feelings because she wanted things to be uncomplicated?

Shannon squeezed his bulging forearm. "You would have been a good football player with your size."

"Soccer." His bicep twitched under her touch. "I'm from Europe, remember?"

"Of course." Unlikely she would ever forget his roots now that she knew. And she wanted to learn more about this strong-jawed man who thought to order a miniature motorized Jeep for her son—and then give credit to his father.

She tucked her hand into the crook of his arm as she swished through the ebbs and flow of the tidewaters. "So you still think of yourself as being from Europe? Even though you were only five when you came to the U.S.?"

His eyebrows pinched together. "I never really thought of this as the U.S. even though I know how close we are."

"I can understand that. Everything here is such a mix of cultures." While the staff spoke English to her, she'd heard Spanish spoken by some. Books and magazines and even instructions on labels were a mix of English, Spanish and some French. "You mentioned thinking this was still San Rinaldo when you got here."

"Only at first. My father told us otherwise."

What difficult conversations those must have been between father and sons. So much to learn and adjust to so young. "We've both lost a lot, you and I. I wonder if I sensed that on some level, if that's what drew us to each other."

He slid an arm around her shoulders and pulled her closer while they kicked through the surf. "Don't kid yourself. I was attracted to how hot you looked walking away in that slim black skirt. And then when you glanced over your shoulder with those prim glasses and do-me eyes." He whistled long and low. "I was toast from the get-go."

Trying not to smile, her skin heating all the same, she elbowed him lightly. "Cro-Magnon."

"Hey, I'm a red-blooded male and you're sexy." He traced the cat-eye edge of her glasses. "You're also entirely too serious at the moment. Life will kick us in the ass all on its own soon enough. We're going to just enjoy the moment, remember? No more buzz kills."

"You're right." Who knew how much longer she would have with Tony before this mess blew up in her face? "Let's go back to talking about surfing and high school dances. You so would have been the bad boy."

"And I'll bet you were a good girl. Did you wear those studious glasses even then?"

"Since I was in the eighth grade." She'd hated how her nose would sweat in the heat when she'd marched during football games. "I was a dedicated musician with no time for boys."

"And now?"

"I want to enjoy this beautiful ocean and a day with absolutely nothing to do." She bolted ahead, kicking through the tide, not sure how to balance her impulsive need for Tony with her practical side that demanded she stay on guard.

Footsteps splashed behind her a second before Tony scooped her up. And she let him.

The warm heat of his shoulder under her cheek, the steady pump of his heart against her side had her curling her arms around his neck. "You're getting us all wet."

His eyes fell to her shirt. His heart thumped faster. "Are you having fun?"

"Yes, I am." She toyed with the springy curls at the nape of his neck. "You always make sure of that, whether it's an opera or a walk by the beach."

"You deserve to have more fun in your life." He held her against his chest with a familiarity she couldn't deny. "I would make things easier for you. You know that."

"And you know where I stand on that subject." She cupped his face, his stubble so dark and thick that he wore a perpetual five o'clock shadow. "This—your protection, the trip, the clothes and toys—it's already much more than I'm comfortable taking."

She needed to be clear on that before she even considered letting him closer again.

He eased her to her feet with a lingering glide of her body down his. "We should go back."

The desire in his eyes glinted unmistakably in the afternoon sun. Yet, he pulled away.

Her lips hungered and her breasts ached—and *he* was walking away again, in spite of all he'd said about how much he wanted her. This man confused the hell out of her.

Five days later, Shannon lounged on the downstairs lanai and watched her son drive along the beach in his miniature Jeep, dogs romping alongside. This was the first time she'd been left to her own devices in days. She'd never been romanced so thoroughly in her life. True to his word, over the past week Tony had been at his most charming.

Could her time here already be almost over?

Sipping freshly squeezed lemonade—although the drink tasted far too amazing for such a simple name—she savored the tart taste. Of course everything seemed sharper, crisper as tension seeped from her bones. The concerns of the world felt forever away while the sun warmed her skin and the waves provided a soothing sound track to her days.

And she had Tony to thank for it all. She'd never known there were so many entertainment options on an island. Of course Enrique Medina had spared no expense in building his compound.

A movie screening room with all the latest films piped in for private viewing.

Three different dining rooms for everything from family style to white-tie.

Rec room, gym, indoor and outdoor swimming pools. She could still hear Kolby's squeal of delight over the stable of horses and ponies.

Throughout it all, Tony had been at her side with tantalizing brushes of his strong body against hers. All the while his rich chocolate brown eyes reminded Shannon that the next move was up to her. Not that they stood a chance at finding privacy today. The grounds buzzed with activity, and today, no sign of Tony.

Behind her, the doors snicked open. Tony? Her heart stuttered a quick syncopation as she glanced back.

Alys walked toward her, high heels clicking on the tiled veranda as she angled past two guards comparing notes on their twin BlackBerry phones. Shannon forced herself to keep the smile in place. It would be rude to frown in disappointment, especially after how helpful the woman had been.

Too bad the disappointment wasn't as easy to hide from herself. No doubt about it, Tony was working his way back into her life.

The king's assistant stopped at the fully stocked outdoor bar and poured a glass of lemonade from the crystal pitcher.

Shannon thumbed the condensation on the cold glass. "Is there something you need?"

"Antonio wanted me to find you, and I have." She tapped her silver BlackBerry attached to the waistband of her linen skirt. Ever crisp with her power suit and French manicure. As usual the elegant woman didn't have a wrinkle in sight, much less wince over working in heels all day. "He'll be out shortly. He's finishing up a meeting with his father."

"I should get Kolby." She swung her feet to the side.

How silly to be glad she'd caved and used some of the new clothes. She had worn everything she brought with her twice and while the laundry service easily kept up with her limited wardrobe, she'd begun to feel a little ungrateful not to wear at least a few of the things that someone had gone to a lot of trouble to provide. Shannon smoothed the de la Renta scoop-necked dress, the fabric so decadently soft it caressed her skin with every move.

"No need to stop the boy's fun just yet. Antonio is on his way." Alys perched on the edge of the lounger, glass on her knee.

Shannon rubbed the hem of her dress between two fingers much like Kolby with his blanket when he needed soothing. "I hear you're the one who ordered all the new clothes. Thank you."

Alys saw to everything else in this smoothly run place. "No need for thanks. It's my job."

"You have excellent taste." She tugged the hem back over her knees.

"I saw your photo online and chose things that would flatter your frame and coloring. It's fun to shop on someone else's dime."

More than a dime had gone into this wardrobe. Her closet sported new additions each morning. Everything from casual jeans and designer blouses to silky dresses and heels to wear for dinner. An assortment of bathing suits to choose from....

And the lingerie. A decadent shiver slid down her spine at the feel of the fine silks and satins against her skin. Although it made her uncomfortable to think of this woman choosing everything.

Alys turned her glass around and around on her knee. "The expense you worry about is nothing to them. They can afford the finest. It would bother them to see you struggling. Now you fit in and that gives the king less to worry about."

God forbid her tennis shoes should make the king uncomfortable. But saying as much would make her sound ungrateful, so she toyed with her glasses, pulling them off and cleaning them with her napkin even though they were already crystal clear. The dynamics of this place went beyond any household she'd ever seen. Alys seemed more comfortable here than Tony.

Shannon slid her glasses back on. "If you don't mind my asking, how long have you been working for the king?"

"Only three months."

How long did she intend to stay? The island was luxurious, but in more of a vacation kind of way. It was so cut off from the world, time seemed to stand still. What kind of life could the woman build in this place?

Abruptly, Alys leaped to her feet. "Here is Antonio now."

He charged confidently through the door, eyes locked on Shannon. "Thank you for finding her, Alys."

The assistant backed away. "Of course." Alys stepped out of hearing range, giving them some privacy.

Forking a hand through his hair—messing up the precise combing from his conference with his father—Tony wore a suit without a tie. The jacket perhaps a nod toward meeting with his father? His smile was carefree, but his shoulders bore the extra tension she'd come to realize accompanied time he had spent with the king.

"How did your meeting go?"

"Don't want to talk about that." Tony plucked a lily from the vase on the bar, snapped the stem off and tucked the bloom behind her ear. "Would much rather enjoy the view. The flower is almost as gorgeous as you are."

The lush perfume filled each breath. "All the fresh flowers are positively decadent."

"I wish I could take credit, but there's a hothouse with a supply that's virtually unlimited."

Yet another amenity she wouldn't have guessed, although it certainly explained all the fresh-cut flowers. "Still," she repeated as she touched the lily tucked in her hair, "I appreciate the gesture."

"I would make love to you on a bed of flowers if you let me." He thumbed her earlobe lightly before skimming his knuckles along her collarbone.

How easy it would be to give over to the delicious seduction of his words and his world. Except she'd allowed herself to fall into that trap before.

And of course there was that little technicality that *he* had been the one holding back all week. "What about thorns?"

He laughed, his hand falling away from her skin and palming her back. "Come on, my practical love. We're going out."

Love? She swallowed to dampen her suddenly cottony mouth. "To lunch?"

"To the airstrip."

Her stomach lurched. This slice of time away was over already? "We're leaving?"

"Not that lucky, I'm afraid. Your apartment is still staked out with the press and curious royalty groupie types. You may want to consider a gated community on top of the added security measures. I know the cost freaks you out, but give my lawyer another couple of days to work on those restraining orders and we can take it from there. As for where we're going today, we're greeting guests and I'd like you to come along."

They weren't leaving. Relief sang through her so intensely it gave her pause.

Tony cocked his head to the side. "Would you like to come with me?"

"Uh, yes, I think so." She struggled to gather her scrambled thoughts and composure. "I just need to settle Kolby."

Alys cleared her throat a few feet away. "I've already notified Miss Delgado, the younger nanny. She's ordering a picnic lunch and bringing sand toys. Then of course she will watch over him during his naptime if needed. I assume that's acceptable to you?"

Her son would enjoy that more than a car ride and waiting around for the flight. She was growing quite spoiled having afternoons completely free while Kolby napped safely under a nanny's watchful care. "Of course. That sounds perfect."

Shannon smiled her thanks and reached out to touch the woman's arm. Except Alys wasn't looking at her. The king's assistant had her eyes firmly planted elsewhere.

On Tony.

Shock nailed her feet to the tiles. Then a fierce jealousy vibrated through her, a feeling that was most definitely ugly and not her style. She'd thought herself above such a primitive emotion, not to mention Tony hadn't given the woman any encouragement.

Still, Shannon fought the urge to link her arm with his in a great big "mine" statement. In that unguarded moment, Alys revealed clearly what she hoped to gain from living here.

Alys wanted a Medina man.

Eight

Tony guided the Porsche Cayenne four-wheel drive along the island road toward the airstrip, glad Shannon was with him to ease the edge on the upcoming meeting. Although having her with him brought a special torment all its own.

The past week working his way back into her good graces had been a painful pleasure, sharpening the razor edge on his need to have her in his bed again. Spending time with her had only shown him more reasons to want her. She mesmerized him with the simplest things.

When she sat on the pool edge and kicked her feet through the water, he thought of those long legs wrapped around him.

Seeing her sip a glass of lemonade made him ache to taste the tart fruit on her lips.

The way she cleaned her glasses with a gust of breath

fogging the frames made him think of her panting in his ear as he brought her to completion.

Romancing his way back into her good graces was easier said than done. And the goal of it all made each day on this island easier to bear.

And after they returned to Galveston? He would face that then. Right now, he had more of his father's past to deal with.

"Tony?" Bracing her hand against the dash as the rutted road challenged even the quality shock absorbers, she looked so right sitting in the seat next to him. "You still haven't told me who we're picking up. Your brothers, perhaps?"

Steering the SUV under the arch of palm trees lining both sides of the road, he searched for the right words to prepare Shannon for something he'd never shared with a soul. "You're on the right track." His hands gripped the steering wheel tighter. "My sister. Half sister, actually. Eloisa."

"A sister? I didn't know...."

"Neither does the press." His half sister had stayed under the radar, growing up with her mother and stepfather in Pensacola, Florida. Only recently had Eloisa reestablished contact with their father. "She's coming here to regroup, troubleshoot. Prepare. Now that the Medina secret is out, her story will also be revealed soon enough."

"May I ask what that story might be?"

"Of course." He focused on the two-lane road, a convenient excuse to make sure she didn't see any anger pushing past his boundaries. "My father had a relationship with her mother after arriving in the U.S., which resulted in Eloisa. She's in her mid-twenties now."

Shannon's eyes went wide behind her glasses.

"Yeah, I know." Turning, he drove from the jungle road

onto a waterside route leading to the ferry station. "That's a tight timeline between when we left San Rinaldo and the hookup." Tight timeline in regard to his mother's death.

"That must have been confusing for you. Kolby barely remembers his father and it's been tough for him to accept you. And we haven't had to deal with adding another child to the mix."

A child? With Shannon? An image of a dark-haired baby—his baby—in her arms blindsided him, derailing his thoughts away from his father in a flash. His foot slid off the accelerator. Shaking free of the image was easier said than done as it grew roots in his mind—Kolby stepping into the picture until a family portrait took shape.

God, just last week he'd been thinking how he knew nothing about kids. She was the one hinting at marriage, not him. Although she said the opposite until he didn't know what was up.

Things with Shannon weren't as simple as he'd planned at the outset. "My father's affair was his own business."

"Okay, then." She pulled her glasses off and fogged them with her breath. She dried them with the hem of her dress. "Do you and your sister get along?"

He hauled his eyes from Shannon's glasses before he swerved off onto the beach. Or pulled onto the nearest side road and to hell with making it to the airstrip on time.

"I've only met her once before." When Tony was a teenager. His father had gone all out on that lone visit with his seven-year-old daughter. Tony didn't resent Eloisa. It wasn't her fault, after all. In fact, he grew even more pissed off at his father. Enrique had responsibilities to his daughter. If he wanted to stay out of her life, then fine. Do so. But half measures were bull.

Yet wasn't that what he'd been offering Shannon? Half measures?

Self-realization sucked. "She's come here on her own since then. She and Duarte have even met up a few times, which in a roundabout way brought on the media mess."

"How so?" She slid her glasses back in place.

"Our sister married into a high-profile family. Eloisa's husband is the son of an ambassador and brother to a senator. He's a Landis."

She sat up straighter at the mention of America's political royalty. Talk about irony.

Tony slowed for a fuel truck to pass. "The Landis name naturally comes with media attention." He accelerated into the parking lot alongside the ferry station, the boat already close to shore. An airplane was parked on the distant airstrip. "Her husband—Jonah—likes to keep a low profile, but that's just not possible."

"What happened?"

"Duarte was delivering one of our father's messages, which put him on a collision course with a press camera. We're still trying to figure out how the Global Intruder made the connection. Although, it's a moot point now. Every stray photo of all of us has been unearthed, every detail of our pasts."

"Of my past?" Her face drained of color.

"I'm afraid so."

All the more reason for her to stay on the island. Her husband's illegal dealings, even his suicide, had hit the headlines again this morning, thanks to muckrakers looking for more scandal connected to the Medina story. He would only be able to shield Shannon from that for so long. She had a right to know.

"I've grown complacent this week." She pressed a hand to her stomach. "My poor in-laws."

The SUV idled in the parking spot, the ferry already

preparing to dock. He didn't have much time left alone with her.

Tony skimmed back her silky blond hair. "I'm sorry all this has come up again. And I hate it that I can't do more to fix things for you."

Turning toward his touch, she rested her face in his hand. "You've helped this week."

He wanted to kiss her, burned to recline the seats and explore the hint of cleavage in her scoop-necked dress. And damned if that wasn't exactly what he planned to do.

Slanting his mouth over her, he caught her gasp and took full advantage of her parted lips with a determined sweep of his tongue. Need for her pumped through his veins, fast-tracked blood from his head to his groin until he could only feel, smell, taste undiluted *Shannon*. Her gasp quickly turned to a sigh as she melted against him, the curves of her breasts pressed to his chest, her fingernails digging deeply into his forearms as she urged him closer.

He was more than happy to accommodate.

It had been so long, too long since they'd had sex before their argument over his damned money. Nearly fourteen days that seemed like fourteen years since he'd had his hands on her this way, fully and unrestrained, tunneling under her clothes, reacquainting himself with the perfection of her soft skin and perfect curves. She fit against him with a rightness he knew extended even further with their clothes off. A hitch in her throat, the flush rising on the exposed curve of her breasts keyed him in to her rising need, as if he couldn't already tell by the way she nearly crawled across the seat to get closer.

Shannon wanted sex with him every bit as much as he wanted her. But that required privacy, not a parking lot in clear view of the approaching ferry.

Holding back now was the right move, even if it was killing him.

"Come on. Time to meet my sister." He slid out of her arms and the SUV and around to her door before she could shuffle her purse from her lap to her shoulder.

He opened the door and she smiled her thanks without speaking, yet another thing he appreciated about her. She sensed when he didn't want to talk anymore. He'd shared things with women over the years, but until her, he'd never found one with whom he could share silence.

The lapping waves, the squawk of gulls, the endless stretch of water centered him, steadying his steps and reminding him how to keep his balance in a rocky world.

Resting his head on Shannon's back, he waited while the ferry finished docking. His sister and her husband stood at the railing. Eloisa's husband hooked an arm around her shoulders, the couple talking intently.

Eloisa might not be a carbon copy of their father, but she carried an air of something unmistakably Medina about her. His father had once said she looked like their grandmother. Tony wouldn't know, since he couldn't remember his grandparents who'd all died before he was born.

The loudspeaker blared with the boat captain announcing their arrival. Disembarking, the couple stayed close together, his brother-in-law broadcasting a protective air. Jonah was the unconventional Landis, according to the papers. If so, they should get along just fine.

The couple stepped from the boat to the dock, and up close Eloisa didn't appear nearly as calm as from a distance. Lines of strain showed in her eyes.

"Welcome," Tony said. "Eloisa, Jonah, this is Shannon Crawford, and I'm—"

"Antonio, I know." His sister spoke softly, reserved. "I recognize you both from the papers."

He'd met Eloisa once as a child when she'd visited the island. She'd come back recently, but he'd been long gone by then.

They were strangers and relatives. Awkward, to say the least.

Jonah Landis stepped up. "Glad you could accommodate our request for a visit so quickly."

"Damage control is important."

Eloisa simply took his hand, searching his face. "How's our father?"

"Not well." Had Shannon just stepped closer to him? Tony kept his eyes forward, knowing in his gut he would see sympathy in her eyes. "He says his doctors are doing all they can."

Blinking back tears, Eloisa stood straighter with a willowy strength. "I barely know him, but I can't envision a world without him in it. Sounds crazy, I'm sure."

He understood too well. Making peace was hard as hell, yet somehow she seemed to have managed.

Jonah clapped him on the back. "Well, my new bro, I need to grab Eloisa's bags and meet you at the car."

A Landis who carried his own luggage? Tony liked the unpretentious guy already.

And wasn't that one of the things he liked most about Shannon? Her down-to-earth ways in spite of her wealthy lifestyle with her husband. She seemed completely unimpressed with the Medina money, much less his defunct title.

For the first time he considered she might be right. She may be better off without the strain of his messed-up family.

Which made him a selfish bastard for pursuing her. But

he couldn't seem to pull back now when his world had been rocked on its foundation. The sailor in him recognized the only port in the storm, and right now, only a de la Renta dress separated him from what he wanted—needed—more than anything.

However, he needed to choose his time and place carefully with the private island growing more crowded by the minute.

The next afternoon, Shannon sat beside Tony in the Porsche four-wheel drive on the way to the beach. He'd left her a note to put on her bathing suit and meet him during Kolby's naptime. She'd been taken aback at the leap of excitement in her stomach over spending time alone with him.

The beach road took them all the way to the edge of the shoreline. He shifted the car in Park, his legs flexing in black board shorts as he left the car silently. He'd been quiet for the whole drive, and she didn't feel the need to fill the moment with aimless babbling. Being together and quiet had an appeal all its own.

Tugging on the edge of the white cover-up, she eyed the secluded stretch of beach. Could this be the end of the "romancing" and the shift back to intimacy? Her stomach fluttered faster.

She stepped from the car before he could open her door. Wind ruffled his hair and whipped his shorts, low slung on his hips. She knew his body well but still the muscled hardness hitched her breath in her throat. Bronzed and toned—smart, rich and royal to boot. Life had handed him an amazing hand, and yet he still chose to work insane hours. In fact, she'd spent more time with him this past week than during the months they'd dated in Galveston.

And everything she learned confused her more than solving questions.

She jammed her hands in the pockets of her cover-up. "Are you going to tell me why we're here?"

"Over there." He pointed to a cluster of palm trees with surfboards propped and waiting.

"You're kidding, right? Tony, I don't surf, and the water must be cold."

"You'll warm up. The waves aren't high enough today for surfing. But there're still some things even a beginner can do." He peeled off his T-shirt and she realized she was staring, damn it. "You won't break anything. Trust me."

He extended a hand.

Trust? Easier said than done. She eyed the boards and looked back at him. They were on the island, she reminded herself, removed from real life. And bottom line, while she wasn't sure she trusted him with her heart, she totally trusted him with her body. He wouldn't let anything happen to her.

Decision made, she whipped her cover-up over her head, revealing her crocheted swimsuit. His eyes flamed over her before he took her cover-up and tossed it in the SUV along with his T-shirt. He closed his hands around hers in a warm steady grip and started toward the boards.

She eyed the pair propped against trees—obviously set up in advance for their outing. One shiny and new, bright white with tropical flowers around the edges. The other was simpler, just yellow, faded from time and use. She looked at the water again, starting to have second—

"Hey." He squeezed her hand. "We're just going to paddle out. Nothing too adventurous today, but I think you're going to find even slow and steady has some unexpected thrills."

And didn't that send her heart double timing?

Thank goodness he moved quickly. Mere minutes later she was on her stomach, on the board, paddling away from shore to…nowhere. Nothing but aqua blue waters blending into a paler sky. Mild waves rolled beneath her but somehow never lifted her high enough to be scary, more of a gentle rocking. The chilly water turned to a neutral sluice over her body, soothing her into becoming one with the ocean.

One stroke at a time she let go of goals and racing to the finish line. Her life had been on fast-paced frenetic since Nolan died. Now, for the first time in longer than she could remember, she was able to unwind, almost hypnotized by the dip, dip, dip of her hands and Tony's into the water.

Tension she hadn't even realized kinked her muscles began to ease. Somehow, Tony must have known. She turned her head to thank him and found him staring back at her.

She threaded her fingers through the water, sun baking her back. "It's so quiet out here."

"I thought you would appreciate the time away."

"You were right." She slowed her paddling and just floated. "You've given over a lot of your time to make sure Kolby and I stayed entertained. Don't you need to get back to work?"

"I work from the island using my computer and telecoms." His hair, even darker when wet, was slicked back from his face, his damp skin glinting in the sun. "More and more of business is being conducted that way."

"Do you ever sleep?"

"Not so much lately, but that has nothing to do with work." He held her with his eyes locked on her face, no suggestive body sweep, just intense, undiluted Tony.

And she couldn't help but wonder why he went to so much trouble when they weren't sleeping together anymore.

If his conscience bothered him, he could have assigned guards to watch over her and she wouldn't have argued for Kolby's sake. Yet here he was. With her.

"What do you see in me?" She rested her cheek on her folded hands. "I'm not fishing for compliments, honest to God, it's just we seem so wrong for each other on so many levels. Is it just the challenge, like building your business?"

"Shanny, you take *challenge* to a whole 'nother level."

She flicked water in his face. "I'm being serious here. No joking around, please."

"Seriously?" He stared out at the horizon for a second as if gathering his thoughts. "Since you brought up the business analogy, let's run with that. At work you would be someone I want on my team. Your tenacity, your refusal to give up—even your frustrating rejection of my help— impress the hell out of me. You're an amazing woman, so much so that sometimes I can't even look away."

He made her feel strong and special with a few words. After feeling guilty for so long, of wondering if she could hold it all together for Kolby, she welcomed the reassurance coursing through her veins as surely as the current underneath her.

Tony slid from his board and ducked under. She watched through the clear surface as he freed the ankle leash attaching him to his board.

Resurfacing beside her, he stroked the line of her back. "Sit up for a minute."

"What?" She'd barely heard him, too focused on the feel of his hand low on her waist.

"Sit up on the board and swing your legs over the side." He held the edge. "I won't let you fall."

"But your board's drifting." She watched the faded yellow inch away.

"I'll get it later. Come on." He palmed her back, helping her balance as finally, she wriggled her way upright.

She bobbled. Stifled a squeal. Then realized what was the worst that could happen? She would be in the water. Big deal. And suddenly the surfboard steadied a little, still rocking but not out of control. The waters lapped around her legs, cool, exciting.

"I did it." She laughed, sending her voice out into that endlessness.

"Perfect. Now hold still," he said and somehow slid effortlessly behind her.

Her balance went haywire again for a second, the horizon tilting until she was sure they would both topple over.

"Relax," he said against her ear. "Out here, it's not about fighting, it's the one place you can totally let go."

The one place *he* could let go? And suddenly she realized this was about more than getting her to relax. He was sharing something about himself with her. Even a man as driven and successful as himself needed a break from the demands of everyday life. Perhaps because of moments like these he kept it all together rather than letting the tension tighten until it snapped.

She fit herself against him, his legs behind hers as they drifted. Her muscles slowly melted until she leaned into him. The waves curled underneath, his chest wet and bristly against her skin. A new tension coiled inside her, deep in her belly. Her swimsuit suddenly felt too tight against her breasts that swelled and yearned for the brush of the air and Tony's mouth.

His palms rested on her thighs. His thumbs circled a light massage, close, so close. Water ebbed and flowed over her heated core, waves sweeping tantalizing caresses on her aching flesh. Her head sagged onto his shoulder.

With each undulation of the board, he rocked against her, stirring, growing harder until he pressed fully erect along her spine. Every roll of the board rubbing their bodies against each other had to be as torturous for him as it was for her. His hands moved higher on her legs, nearer to what she needed. Silently. Just as in tune with each other as when they'd been paddling out.

She worried at first that someone might see, but with their backs to the shore and water…she could lose herself in the moment. Already his breaths grew heavier against her ear, nearly as fast as her own.

They could both let go and find completion right here without ever moving. Simply feeling his arousal against her stirred Shannon to a bittersweet edge. And good God, that scared the hell out of her.

The wind chilled, and she recognized the sting of fear all too well. She'd thought she could ride the wave, so to speak, and just have an affair with Tony.

But this utter abandon, the loss of control, the way they were together, it was anything but simple, something she wasn't sure she was ready to risk.

Scavenging every bit of her quickly dwindling willpower, she grabbed his wrists, moved his hands away…

And dived off the side of the board.

Nine

Tony propped his surfboard against a tree and turned to take Shannon's. The wariness in her eyes frustrated the hell out of him. He could have sworn she was just as into the moment out there as he was—an amazing moment that had been seconds away from getting even better.

And then she'd vaulted off the board and into the water.

Staying well clear of him, she'd said she was ready to return to shore. She hadn't spoken another word since. Had he blown a whole week's worth of working past her boundaries only to wreck it in one afternoon? Problem was, he still didn't know what had set her off.

She stroked a smudge of sand from his faded yellow board. "Is it all right to leave them here so far from where we started?"

They'd drifted at least a mile from the SUV. "I'll buy new ones. I'm a filthy rich prince, remember?"

Yeah, sexual frustration was making him a little cranky, and he suspected no amount of walking would take the edge off. Worse yet, she didn't even rise to the bait of his crabby words full of reminders of why they'd broken up in the first place.

Fine. Who the hell knew what she needed?

He started west and she glided alongside him. The wind picked up, rustling the trees and sweeping a layer of sand around his ankles.

Shannon gasped.

"What?" Tony looked fast. "Did you step on something? Are you getting chilly?"

Shaking her head, she pointed toward the trees, branches and leaves sweeping apart to reveal the small stone chapel. "Why didn't I notice that when we drove here?"

"We approached the beach from a different angle."

"It's gorgeous." Her eyes were wide and curious.

"No need to look so surprised. I told you that we lived here 24/7. My father outfitted the island with everything we would need, from a small medical clinic to that church." He took in the white stone church, mission bell over the front doors. It wasn't large, but big enough to accommodate everyone here. His older brother had told him once it was the only thing on the island built to resemble a part of their old life.

"Were you an altar server?"

Her voice pulled him back to the present.

"With a short-lived tenure." He glanced down at her, so damn glad she was talking to him again. "I couldn't sit still and the priest frowned on an altar server bringing a bag of books and Legos to keep himself entertained during the service."

"Legos?" She started walking again. "Really?"

"Every Sunday as I sat out in the congregation. I would

have brought more, but the nanny confiscated my squirt gun."

"Don't be giving Kolby any ideas." She elbowed him lightly, then as if realizing what she'd done, picked up her pace.

Hell no, he wasn't losing ground that fast. "The nanny didn't find my knife though."

Her mouth dropped open. "You brought a knife to church?"

"I carved my initials under the pew. Wanna go see if they're still there?"

She eyed the church, then shook her head. "What's all this about today? The surfing and then stories about Legos?"

Why? He hadn't stopped to consider the reasons, just acting on instinct to keep up with the crazy, out-of-control relationship with Shannon. But he didn't do things without a reason.

His gut had pointed him in this direction because... "So that you remember there's a man in here." He thumped his chest. "As well as a filthy rich prince."

But no matter what he said or how far he got from this place, the Medina heritage coursed through his veins. Regardless of how many times he changed his name or started over, he was still Antonio Medina. And Shannon had made it clear time and time again, she didn't want that kind of life. Finally, he heard her.

Several hours later, Shannon shoved her head deeper into the industrial sized refrigerator in search of a midnight snack. A glass of warm milk just wasn't going to cut it.

Eyeing the plate of *trufas con cognac* and small cups of *crema catalana,* she debated whether to go for the brandy truffles or cold custard with caramel on top.... She picked one of each and dropped into a seat at the steel table.

Silence bounced and echoed in the cavernous kitchen. She was sleepy and cranky and edgy. And it was all Tony's fault for tormenting her with charming stories and sexy encounters on the water—then shutting her out. She nipped an edge of the liqueur-flavored chocolate. Amazing. Sighing, she sagged back in the chair.

Since returning from their surfing outing, he'd kept his distance. She'd thought they were getting closer on a deeper level when he'd shared about his sister and even the Lego, then, wham. He'd turned into the perfect—distant—host at the stilted family dinner.

Not that she'd been able to eat a bite.

Now, she was hungry, in spite of the fact she'd finished off the truffle. She spooned a scoop of custard into her mouth, although she suspected no amount of gourmet pastries would satisfy the craving gnawing her inside.

When she'd started dating Tony, she'd taken a careful, calculated risk because her hormones had been hollering for him and she'd been a long, long time without sex. Okay, so her hormones hadn't been shouting for just any man. Only Tony. A problem that didn't seem to have abated in the least.

"Ah, hell." Tony's low curse startled her upright in her seat.

Filling the archway, he studied her cautiously. He wore jeans and an open button-down that appeared hastily tossed on. He fastened two buttons in the middle, slowly shielding the cut of his six-pack abs.

Cool custard melted in her mouth, her senses singing. But her heart was aching and confused. She toyed with the neck of her robe nervously. The blue peignoir set covered her from neck to toes, but the loose-fitting chiffon and lace brushed sensual decadence against her skin. The froufrou little kitten heels to match had seemed over-the-top in her room, but now felt sexy and fun.

Her hands shook. She pressed them against the steel topped table. "Don't mind me. I'm just indulging in a midnight feeding frenzy. I highly recommend the custard cups in the back right corner of the refrigerator."

He hesitated in the archway as if making up his mind, then walked deeper into the kitchen, passing her without touching. "I was thinking in terms of something more substantial, like a sandwich."

"Are princes allowed to make their own snacks?"

"Who's going to tell me no?" He kicked the fridge closed, his hands full of deli meat, cheese and lettuce, a jar of spread tucked under his elbow.

"Good point." She swirled another spoonful. "I hope the cook doesn't mind I've been foraging around. I actually used the stove, too, when I cooked a late night snack for Kolby. He woke up hungry."

Tony glanced over from his sandwich prep. "Is he okay?"

"Just a little homesick." Her eyes took in the sight of the Tony she remembered, a man who wore jeans low-slung on his hips. And rumpled hair...she enjoyed the disobedient swirls in his hair most.

"I'm sorry for that." His shoulders tensed under the loose chambray.

"Don't get me wrong, I appreciate how everyone has gone out of their way for him. The gourmet kid cuisine makes meals an adventure. I wish I had thought to tell him rolled tortillas are snakes and caterpillars." Pasta was called worms or a nest. "I'm even becoming addicted to Nutella crepes. But sometimes, a kid just needs the familiar feel of home."

"I understand." His sandwich piled high on a plate, he took a seat—across from her rather than beside as he would have in the past.

"Of course you do." She clenched her hands together to keep from reaching out to him. "Well, I'll have to make sure the cook knows I tried to put everything back where I found it."

"He's more likely to be upset that you called him a cook rather than a chef."

"Ah, a chef. Right. All those nuances between your world and mine." How surreal to be having a conversation with a prince over a totally plebian hoagie.

Tony swiped at his mouth with a linen napkin and draped it over his knee again. "You ran in a pretty high-finance world with your husband."

Her husband's dirty money.

She shoved away the custard bowl. Thoughts of the media regurgitating that mess for public consumption made her nauseated. She wasn't close to her in-laws, but they would suffer hearing their precious son's reputation smeared again.

And God help them all if her own secrets were somehow discovered.

Best to lie low and keep to herself. Although she was finding it increasingly difficult to imagine how she would restart her life. Even if she was able to renew her teaching credentials, who was going to want to hire the infamous Medina Mistress who'd once been married to a crook? When this mess was over, she would have to dig deep to figure out how to recreate a life for herself and Kolby.

Could Tony be having second thoughts about their relationship? His strict code of honor would dictate he take care of her until the media storm passed, but she didn't want to be his duty.

They'd dated. They'd had sex. But she only just realized how much of their relationship had been superficial as they both dodged discussing deeper, darker parts of their past.

Still, she wasn't ready to plunge into the murkiest of waters that made up her life with Nolan. She wasn't even sure right now if Tony would want to hear.

But regardless of how things turned out between them, she needed him to understand the real her. "I didn't grow up with all those trappings of Nolan's world. My dad was a high school science teacher and a coach. My mom was the elementary school secretary. We had enough money, but we were by no means wealthy." She hesitated, realizing... "You probably already know all of that."

"Why would you think so?" he asked, although he hadn't denied what she said.

"If you've had to be so worried about security and your identity, it makes sense you or your lawyer or some security team you've hired would vet people in your life."

"That would be the wise thing to do."

"And you're a smart man."

"I haven't always acted wisely around you."

"You've been a perfect gentleman this week and you know it," she said, as close as she could come to hinting that she ached for his touch, his mouth on her body, the familiar rise of pleasure and release he could bring.

Tony shrugged and tore into his sandwich again, a grandfather clock tolling once in the background.

"Kolby thinks we're on vacation."

"Good." He finished chewing, tendons in his strong neck flexing. "That's how he should remember this time in his life."

"It's unreal how you and your father have shielded him from the tension in your relationship."

"Obviously not well enough to fool you." His boldly handsome face gave nothing away.

"I know some about your history, and it's tough to miss how little the two of you talk. Your father's an interesting man." She'd enjoyed after-dinner discussions with Enrique and Eloisa about current events and the latest book they'd read.

The old king may have isolated himself from the world, but he'd certainly stayed abreast with the latest news. The discussions had been enlightening on a number of levels, such as how the old king wasn't as clipped and curt with his daughter as he was with Tony.

Tony stared at the last half of his snack, tucking a straggly piece of lettuce back inside. "What did you make for Kolby?"

His question surprised her, but if it kept him talking…

"French toast. It's one of his favorite comfort foods. He likes for me to cut the toast into slices so he can dip it into the syrup. Independence means a lot, even to a three-year-old." It meant a lot to adults. She reached for her bowl to scrape the final taste of custard and licked the spoon clean. The caramel taste exploded into her starving senses like music in her mouth.

Pupils widening with awareness until they nearly pushed away his brown irises, Tony stared back at her across the table, intense, aroused. Her body recognized the signs in him well even if he didn't move so much as an inch closer.

She set the spoon down, the tiny clink echoing in the empty kitchen. "Tony, why are you still awake?"

"I'm a night owl. Some might call me an insomniac."

"An insomniac? I didn't know that." She laughed darkly. "Although how could I since we've never spent an entire night together? Have you had the problem long?"

"I've always been this way." He turned the plate around on the table. "My mother tried everything from warm milk to a 'magic' blanket before just letting me stay up. She used to cook for me too, late at night."

"Your mother, the queen, cooked?" She inched to the edge of her chair, leaning on her elbows, hoping to hold his attention and keep him talking.

"She may have been royalty even before she married my father, but there are plenty in Europe with blue blood and little money." Shadows chased each other across his eyes. "My mother grew up learning the basics of managing her own house. She insisted we boys have run of the kitchen. There were so many everyday places that were off-limits to us for safety reasons, she wanted us to have the normalcy of popping in and out of the kitchen for snacks."

Like any other child. A child who happened to live in a sixteenth-century castle. She liked his mother, a woman she would never meet but felt so very close to at the moment. "What did she cook for you?"

"A Cyclops."

"Excuse me?"

"It's a fried egg with a buttered piece of bread on top." He swirled his hand over his plate as if he could spin an image into reality. "The bread has a hole pinched out of the middle so the egg yolk peeks out like a—"

"Like a Cyclops. I see. My mom called it a Popeye." And with the memory of a simple egg dish, she felt the connection to Tony spin and gain strength again.

He glanced up, a half smile kicking into his one cheek. "Cyclops appealed to the bloodthirsty little boy in me. Just like Kolby and the caterpillar and snake pasta."

To hell with distance and waiting for him to reach out, she covered his hand with hers. "Your mother sounds wonderful."

He nodded briefly. "I believe she was."

"Believe?"

"I have very few memories of her before she...died." He turned his hand over and stroked hers with his thumb. "The beach. A blanket. Food."

"Scents do tend to anchor our memories more firmly."

More shadows drifted through his eyes, darker this time, like storm clouds. *Died* seemed such a benign word to describe the assassination of a young mother, killed because she'd married a king. A vein pulsed visibly in Tony's temple, faster by the second. He'd dealt with such devastating circumstances in life honorably, while her husband had turned to stealing and finally, to taking the ultimate coward's way out.

She held herself very still, unthreatening. Her heart ached for him on a whole new and intense level. "What do you remember about when she died? About leaving San Rinaldo?"

"Not much really." He stayed focused on their connected hands, tracing the veins on her wrist with exaggerated concentration. "I was only five."

So he'd told her before. But she wasn't buying his nonchalance. "Traumatic events seem to stick more firmly in our memory. I recall a car accident when I couldn't have been more than two." She wouldn't back down now, not when she was so close to understanding the man behind the smiles and bold gestures. "I still remember the bright red of the Volkswagen bug."

"You probably saw pictures of the car later," he said dismissively, then looked up sharply, aggressively full of bravado. The storm clouds churned faster with each throb of the vein on his temple. He stroked up her arm with unmistakable sensual intent. "How much longer are you going to wait before you ask me to kiss you again? Because right now, I'm so on fire for you, I want to test out the sturdiness of that table."

"Tony, can you even hear yourself?" she asked, frustrated and even a bit insulted by the way he was jerking her around. "One minute you're Prince Romance and Restraint, the next you're ignoring me over dinner. Then you're spilling your guts. Now, you proposition me—and not too suavely, I might add. Quite frankly, you're giving me emotional whiplash."

His arms twitched, thick roped muscles bulging against his sleeves with restrained power. "Make no mistake, I have wanted you every second of every day. It's all I can do not to haul you against me right now and to hell with the dozens of people that might walk in. But today on the water and tonight here, I'm just not sure this crazy life of mine is good enough for you."

Her body burned in response to his words even as her mind blared a warning. Tony had felt the increasing connection too, and it scared him. So he'd tried to run her off with the crude offer of sex on the table.

Well too damn bad for him, she wasn't backing down. She'd wanted this, *him,* for too long to turn away.

Ten

He'd wanted Shannon back in his bed, but somewhere between making a sandwich and talking about eggs, she'd peeled away walls, exposing thoughts and memories that were better forgotten. They distracted. Hurt. Served no damn purpose.

Anger grated his raw insides. "So? What'll it be? Sex here or in your room?"

She didn't flinch and she didn't leave. Her soft hand stayed on top of his as she looked at him with sad eyes behind her glasses. "Is that what this week has been about?"

He let his gaze linger on the vee of her frothy nightgown set. Lace along the neckline traced into the curve of her breasts the way his hands ached to explore. "I've been clear from the start about what I want."

"Are you so sure about that?"

"What the hell is that supposed to mean?" he snapped.

Sliding from her chair, she circled the table toward him, her heels clicking against the tile. She stopped beside him, the hem of her nightgown set swirling against his leg. "Don't confuse me with your mother."

"Good God, there's not a chance of that." He toppled her into his lap and lowered his head, determined to prove it to her.

"Wait." She stopped him with a hand flattened to his chest just above the two closed buttons. Her palm cooled his overheated skin, calming and stirring, but then she'd always been a mix of contradictions. "You suffered a horrible trauma as a child. No one should lose a parent, especially in such an awful way. I wish you could have been spared that."

"I wish my *mother* had been spared." His hands clenched in her robe, his fists against her back.

"And I can't help but wonder if you helping me—a mother with a young child—is a way to put her ghost to rest. Putting your own ghosts to rest in the process."

Given the crap that had shaken down in his past, he'd done a fine job turning his life around. Frustration poured acid on his burning gut. "You've spent a lot of time thinking about this."

"What you told me this afternoon and tonight brought things into focus."

"Well, thanks for the psychoanalysis." His words came out harsh, but right now he needed her to walk away. "I would offer to pay you for the services, but I wouldn't want to start another fight."

"Sounds to me like you're spoiling for one now." Her eyes softened with more of that concern that grated along his insides. "I'm sorry if I overstepped and hit a nerve."

A nerve? She'd performed a root canal on his emotions. His brain echoed with the retort of gunfire stuttering, aimed at him, his brothers. His mother. He searched for what to say to shut down this conversation, but he wasn't sure of anything other than his need for a serious, body-draining jog on the beach. Problem was? The beach circled right back around to this place.

Easing from his lap, she stood and he tamped down the swift kick of disappointment. Except she didn't leave. She extended her hand and linked her fingers with his.

Just a simple connection, but since he was raw to the core, her touch fired deep.

"Shannon," he said between teeth clenched tight with restraint, "I'm about a second from snapping here. So unless you want me buried heart deep inside you in the next two minutes, you need to go back to your room."

Her hold stayed firm, cool and steady.

"Shannon, damn it all, you don't know what you're doing. You don't want any part of the mood I'm in." Her probing may have brought on the mood, but he wouldn't let it contaminate her.

Angling down with slow precision, she pressed her lips to his. Not moving. Only their mouths and hands linked.

He wanted—needed—to move her away gently. But his fingers curled around the softness of her arm.

"Shanny," he whispered against her mouth, "tell me to leave."

"Not a chance. I only have one question."

"Go ahead." He braced himself for another emotional root canal.

She brought his hand to her chest, pressing his palm against her breast. "Do you have a condom?"

Relief splashed over him like a tidal wave. "Hell, yes, I have one, two in fact, in my wallet. Because even when we're not talking, I know the way we are together could combust at any second. And I will always, always make sure you're protected and safe."

Standing, he scooped her into his arms. Purring her approval, she hooked her hands behind his neck and tipped her face for a full kiss. The soft cushion of her breasts against his chest sent his libido into overdrive. He throbbed against the sweet curve of her hip. At the sweep of tongue, the taste of caramel and *her,* he fought the urge to follow through on the impulse to have her here, now, on the table.

He sketched his mouth along her jaw, down to her collarbone, the scent of her lavender body wash reminding him of shared showers at his place. "We need to go upstairs."

"The pantry is closer." She nipped his bottom lip. "And empty. We can lock the door. I need you now."

"Are you su—?"

"Don't even say it." She dipped her hands into the neckline of his loose shirt, her fingernails sinking insistently deep. "I want you. No waiting."

Her words closed down arguments and rational thought. He made a sure-footed beeline across the tiled floor toward the pantry. Shannon nuzzled his neck, kissed along his jaw, all the while murmuring disjointed words of need that stoked him higher—made his feet move faster. As he walked, her silky blond hair and whispery robe trailed, her sexy little heels dangling from her toes.

Dipping at the door, he flipped the handle and shouldered inside the pantry, a food storage area the size of a small bedroom. The scent of hanging dried herbs coated the air, the smell earthy. He slid her glasses from her face and set them aside on a shelf next to rows of bottled water.

As the door eased closed, the space darkened and his

other senses increased. She reached for the light switch and he clasped her wrist, stopping her.

"I don't need light to see you. Your beautiful body is fired into my memory." His fingers crawled up her leg, bunching the frothy gown along her soft thigh, farther still to just under the curve of her buttocks. "Just the feel of you is about more than my willpower can take."

"I don't want your willpower. I'm fed up with your restraint. Give me the uninhibited old Tony back." Her husky voice filled the room with unmistakable desire.

Pressing her hips closer, he tasted down her neck, charting his way to her breasts. An easy swipe cleared the fabric from her shoulders and he found a taut nipple. Damn straight he didn't need light. He knew her body, knew just how to lave and tease the taut peak until she tore at his shirt with frantic hands.

His buttons popped and cool air blanketed his back, warm Shannon writhing against his front. Hooking a finger along the rim of her bikini panties, he stroked her silky smooth stomach. Tugging lightly, he started the scrap of fabric downward until she shimmied them the rest of the way off.

Stepping closer, the silky gown bunched between them, she flattened her hand to the fly of his jeans. He went harder against the pleasure of her touch. Shannon. Just Shannon.

She unzipped his pants and freed his arousal. Clasping him in her fist, she stroked once, and again, her thumb working over his head with each glide. His eyes slammed shut.

Her other hand slipped into his back pocket and pulled out his wallet. A light crackle sounded as she tore into the packet. Her deft fingers rolled the sheath down the length of him with torturous precision.

"Now," she demanded softly against his neck. "Here. On the stepstool or against the door, I don't care as long as you're inside me."

Gnawing need chewed through the last of his restraint. She wanted this. He craved her. No more waiting. Tony backed her against the solid panel of the door, her fingernails digging into his shoulders, his back, lower as she tucked her hand inside his jeans and boxers.

Arching, urging, she hooked her leg around his, opening for him. Her shoe clattered to the floor but she didn't seem to notice or care. He nudged at her core, so damp and ready for him. He throbbed—and thrust.

Velvet heat clamped around him, drew him deeper, sent sparks shooting behind his eyelids. In the darkened room, the pure essence of Shannon went beyond anything he'd experienced. And the importance of that expanded inside him, threatening to drive him to his knees.

So he focused on her, searching with his hands and mouth, moving inside and stroking outside to make sure she was every bit as encompassed by the mind-numbing ecstasy. She rocked faster against him. Her sighs came quicker, her moans of pleasure higher and louder until he captured the sound, kissing her and thrusting with his tongue and body. He explored the soft inside of her mouth, savoring the soft clamp of her gripping him with spasms he knew signaled her approaching orgasm.

Teeth gritted, he held back his own finish. Her face pressed to his neck. Her chants of *yes, yes, yes* synced with his pulse and pounding. Still, he held back, determined to take her there once more. She bowed away from the door, into him, again and again until her teeth sunk into his shoulder on a stifled cry of pleasure.

The scent of her, of slick sex and *them* mixed with the already earthy air.

Finally—*finally*—he could let go. The wave of pleasure pulsing through him built higher, roaring louder in his ears. He'd been too long without her. The wave crested. Release crashed over him. Rippling through him. Shifting the ground under his feet until his forehead thumped against the door.

Hauling her against his chest, heart still galloping, as they both came back down to earth in the pantry.

The pantry, for God's sake?

His chances of staying away from Shannon again were slim. That path didn't work for either of them. But if they were going to be together, he would make sure their next encounter was total fantasy material.

Sun glinting along the crystal clear pool, Shannon tugged Kolby's T-shirt over his head and slid his feet into tiny Italian leather sandals. She'd spent the morning splashing with her son and Tony's sister, and she wasn't close to working off pent-up energy. Even the soothing ripple of the heated waters down the fountain rock wall hadn't stilled the jangling inside her.

After making love in the pantry, she and Tony had locked themselves in her room where he'd made intense and thorough love to her. Her skin remembered the rasp of his beard against her breasts, her stomach, the insides of her thighs. How could she still crave even more from him? She should be in search of a good nap rather than wondering when she could get Tony alone again.

Of course she would have to find him first.

He'd left via her balcony just as the morning sun peeked over the horizon. Now that big orange glow was directly overhead and no word from him. She deflated her son's water wings. The hissing air and the maternal ritual reminded her of Tony's revelations just before they'd ended up in the closet.

Could he be avoiding her to dodge talking further? He'd made no secret of using sex to skirt the painful topic. She couldn't even blame him when she'd been guilty of the same during their affair. What did this do to their deadline to return home?

Kolby yanked the hem of her cover-up. "Want another movie."

"We'll see, sweetie." Kolby was entranced by the large home theater, but then what child wouldn't be?

Tony's half sister shaded her eyes in the lounger next to them, an open paperback in her other hand. "I can take him in if you want to stay outside. Truly, I don't mind." She toyed with her silver shell necklace, straightening the conch charm.

"But you're reading. And aren't you leaving this afternoon? I don't want to keep you from your packing."

"Do you honestly think any guest of Enrique Medina is bothered by packing their own suitcases? Get real." She snorted lightly. "I have plenty of time. Besides, I've been wanting to check out the new Disney movie for my library's collection."

She'd learned Eloisa was a librarian, which explained the satchel of books she'd brought along. Her husband was an architect who specialized in restoring historic landmarks. They were an unpretentious couple caught up in a maelstrom. "What if the screening room doesn't have the movie you w—" She stopped short. "Of course they have whatever you're looking for on file."

"A bit intimidating, isn't it?" Eloisa pulled on her wraparound cover-up, tugging her silver necklace out so the conch charm was visible. "I didn't grow up with all of this and I suspect you didn't, either."

Shannon rubbed her arms, shivering in spite of the eighty-degree day. "How do you keep from letting it overwhelm you?"

"I wish I could offer you reassurance or answers, but honestly I'm still figuring out how to deal with all of this myself. I had only begun to get to know my birth father a few months ago." She looked back at the mission-style mansion, her eyebrows pinching together. "Now the whole royal angle has gone public. They haven't figured out about me. Yet. That's why we're here this week, to talk with Enrique and his attorneys, to set up some preemptive strikes."

"I'm sorry."

Thank God Eloisa had the support of her husband. And Tony had been there for her. Who was there for him? Even his brothers hadn't shown up beyond sterile conference calls.

"You have nothing to apologize for, Shannon. I'm only saying it's okay to feel overwhelmed. Cut yourself some slack and do what you can to stay level. Let me watch a movie with your son while you swim or enjoy a bubble bath or take a nap. It's okay."

Indecision warred inside her. These past couple of weeks she'd had more help with Kolby than since he was born. Guilt tweaked her maternal instincts.

"Please, Mama?" Kolby sidled closer to Eloisa. "I like Leesa."

Ah, and just like that, her maternal guilt worried in another direction, making her fret that she hadn't given her son enough play dates or socialization. Funny how a mother worried no matter what.

Shannon nodded to Tony's sister. "If you're absolutely sure."

"He's a cutie, and I'm guessing he will be asleep before

the halfway point. Enjoy the pool a while longer. It'll be good practice for me to spend time with him." She smiled whimsically as she ruffled his damp hair. "Jonah and I are hoping to have a few of our own someday."

"Thank you. I accept gratefully." Shannon remembered well what it felt like to be young and in love and hopeful for the future. She couldn't bring herself to regret Nolan since he'd given her Kolby. "I hope we'll have the chance to speak again before you leave this afternoon?"

"Don't worry." Eloisa winked. "I imagine we'll see each other again."

With a smile, Shannon hugged her little boy close, inhaling his baby fresh scent with a hint of chlorine.

He squirmed, his cheeks puffed with a wide smile. "Wanna go."

She pressed a quick kiss to his forehead. "Be good for Mrs. Landis."

Eloisa took his hand. "We'll be fine."

Kolby waved over his shoulder without a backward glance.

Too restless for a bath or nap, she eyed the pool and whipped off her cover-up. Laps sounded like the wisest option. Diving in, she stared through the chlorinated depths until her eyes burned, forcing her to squeeze them shut. She lost herself in the rhythm of slicing her arms through the heated water, no responsibilities, no outside world. Just the *thump, thump, thump* of her heart mingling with the roar of the water passing over her ears.

Five laps later, she flipped underwater and resurfaced face up for a backstroke. She opened her eyes and, oh my, the view had changed. Tony stood by the waterfall in black board shorts.

Whoa. Her stomach lurched into a swan dive. Tony's bronzed chest sprinkled with hair brought memories of their night together, senses on overload from the darkened herb-scented pantry, later in the brightly lighted luxury of her bedroom. Who would have thought dried oregano and rosemary could be aphrodisiacs?

His eyes hooked on her crocheted two piece with thorough and unmistakable admiration. He knew every inch of her body and made his appreciation clear whether she wore high-end garb or her simple black waitress uniform, wilted from a full shift. God, how he was working his way into her heart as well as her life.

She swam toward the edge with wide lazy strokes. "Is Kolby okay?"

"Enjoying the movie and popcorn." He knelt by the edge, his elbow on one knee drawing her eye to the nautical compass tattooed on his bicep. "Although with the way his head is drooping, chances are he'll be asleep anytime now."

"Thank you for checking on him." She resisted the urge to ask Tony what *he*'d been doing since he left her early this morning.

"Not a problem." His fingers played through the water in front of her without touching but so close the swirls caressed her breasts. "I said I intended to romance you and I got sidetracked. I apologize for that. The woman I'm with should be treated like a princess."

His *princess?* Shock loosened her hold on the edge of the pool. Tony caught her arm quickly and eased her from the water to sit next to him. His gaze swept her from soaking wet hair to dripping toes. Appreciation smoked, darkening his eyes to molten heat she recognized well.

He tipped her chin with a knuckle scarred from handling sailing lines. "Are you ready to be royally romanced?"

Eleven

A five-minute walk later, Tony flattened his palm to Shannon's back and guided her down the stone path leading from the mansion to the greenhouse. Her skin, warmed from the sun, heated through her thin cover-up. Soon, he hoped to see and feel every inch of her without barriers.

He'd spent the morning arranging a romantic backdrop for their next encounter. Finding privacy was easier said than done on this island, but he was persistent and creative. Anticipation ramped inside him.

He was going to make things right with her. She deserved to be treated like a princess, and he had the resources to follow through. His mind leaped ahead to all the ways he could romance her back on the mainland now that he understood her better—once he fulfilled the remaining weeks he'd promised his father.

A kink started in his neck.

Squeezing his hand lightly, she followed him along the

rocky path, the mansion smaller on the horizon. Few trees stood between them and the glass building ahead. Early on, Enrique had cleared away foliage for security purposes.

"Where are we going?"

"You'll see soon."

Farther from shore, a sprawling oak had been saved. The mammoth trunk declared it well over a hundred years old. As a kid, he'd begged to keep this one for climbing. His father had gruffly agreed. The memory kicked over him, itchy and ill timed.

He brushed aside a branch, releasing a flock of butterflies soaring toward the conservatory, complete with two wings branching off the main structure. "This is the greenhouse I told you about. It also has a café style room."

Enrique had done his damnedest to give his sons a "normal" childhood, as much as he could while never letting them off the island. Tony had undergone some serious culture shock after he'd left. At least working on a shrimper had given him time to absorb the mainland in small bites. Back then, he'd even opted to rent a sailboat for a home rather than an apartment.

As they walked past a glass gazebo, Shannon tipped her face to his. Sunlight streaked through the trees, bathing her face. "Is that why the movie room has more of a theater feel?"

Nodding, he continued, "There's a deli at the ferry station and an ice cream parlor at the creamery. I thought we could take Kolby there."

He hoped she heard his intent to try with her son as well, to give this relationship a real chance at working.

"Kolby likes strawberry flavored best," she said simply.

"I'll remember that," he assured her. And he meant it.

"We also have a small dental clinic. And of course there's the chapel."

"They've thought of everything." Her mouth oohed over a birdbath with doves drinking along the edge.

"My father always said a monarch's job was to see to the needs of his people. This island became his minikingdom. Because of the isolation, he needed to make accommodations, try to create a sense of normalcy." Clouds whispered overhead and Tony guided her faster through the garden. "He's started a new round of renovations. A number of his staff members have died of old age. That presents a new set of challenges as he replaces them with employees who aren't on the run, people who have options."

"Like Alys."

"Exactly," he said, just as the skies opened up with an afternoon shower. "Now, may I take you to lunch? I know this great little out-of-the-way place with kick-ass fresh flowers."

"Lead on." Shannon tugged up the hood on her cover-up and raced alongside him.

As the rain pelted faster, he charged up the stone steps leading to the conservatory entrance. Tony threw open the double doors, startling a sparrow into flight around the high glass ceiling in the otherwise deserted building. A quick glance around assured him that yes, everything was exactly as he'd ordered.

"Ohmigod, Tony!" Shannon gasped, taking in the floral feast for her eyes as well as her nose. "This is breathtaking."

Flipping the hood from her head, she plunged deeper into the spacious greenhouse where a riot of scents and colors waited. Classical music piped lowly from hidden speakers. Ferns dangled overhead. Unlike crowded nurseries she'd visited in the past, this space sprawled more like an indoor floral park.

An Italian marble fountain trickled below a skylight, water spilling softly from a carved snake's mouth as it curled around some reclining Roman god. Wrought iron screens sported hydrangeas and morning glories twining throughout, benches in front for reading or meditation. Potted palms and cacti added height to the interior landscape. Tiered racks of florist's buckets with cut flowers stretched along a far wall. She spun under the skylight, immersing herself in the thick perfume, sunbeams and Debussy's *Nocturnes*.

While she could understand Tony's point about not wanting to be isolated here indefinitely, she appreciated the allure of the magical retreat Enrique had created. Even the rain *tap, tap, tapping* overhead offered nature's lyrical accent to the soft music.

Slowing her spin, she found Tony staring at her with undeniable arousal. Tony, and only Tony because the space appeared otherwise deserted. Her skin prickled with awareness at the muscular display of him in nothing but board shorts and deck shoes.

"Are we alone?" she asked.

"Completely," he answered, gesturing toward a little round table set for two, with wine and finger foods. "Help yourself. There are stuffed mussels, fried squid, vegetable skewers, cold olives and cheese."

She strode past him, without touching but so close a magnetic field seemed to activate, urging her to seal her body to his.

"It's been so wonderful here indulging in grown-up food after so many meals of chicken nuggets and pizza." She broke off a corner of ripe white cheese and popped it in her mouth.

"Then you're going to love the beverage selection." Tony scooped up a bottle from the middle of the table. "Red wine from Basque country or sherry from southern Spain?"

"Red, please. But can we wait a moment on the food? I want to see everything here first."

"I was hoping you would say that." He passed her a crystal glass, half full.

She sipped, staring at him over the rim. "Perfect."

"And there's still more." His fingers linked with hers, he led her past an iron screen to a secluded corner.

Vines grew tangled and dense over the windows, the sun through the glass roof muted by rivulets of rain. A chaise longue was tucked in a corner. Flower petals speckled the furniture and floor. Everything was so perfect, so beautiful, it brought tears to her eyes. God, it still scared her how much she wanted to trust her feelings, trust the signals coming from Tony.

To hide her eyes until she could regain control, she rushed to the crystal vase of mixed flowers on the end table and buried her face in the bouquet. "What a unique blend of fragrances."

"It's a specially ordered arrangement. Each flower was selected for you because of its meaning."

Touched by the detailed thought he'd put into the encounter, she pivoted to face him. "You told me once you wanted to wrap me in flowers."

"That's the idea here." His arms banded around her waist. "And I was careful to make sure there will be no thorns. Only pleasure."

If only life could be that simple. With their time here running out, she couldn't resist.

"You're sure we won't be interrupted?" She set her wine glass on the end table and linked her fingers behind his neck. "No surveillance cameras or telephoto lenses?"

"Completely certain. There are security cameras outside, but none inside. I've given the staff the afternoon off and our guards are not Peeping Toms. We are totally and completely alone." He anchored her against him, the rigid length of his arousal pressing into her stomach with a hefty promise.

"You prepared for this." And she wanted this, wanted him. But… "I'm not sure I like being so predictable."

"You are anything but predictable. I've never met a more confusing person in my life." He tugged a damp lock of her hair. "Any more questions?"

She inhaled deeply, letting the scents fill her with courage. "Who can take off faster the other person's clothes?"

"Now there's a challenge I can't resist." He bunched her cover-up in his hands and peeled the soft cotton over her head.

Shaking her hair free, she leaned into him just as he slanted his mouth over hers. His fingers made fast work of the ties to her bathing suit top. The crocheted triangles fell away, baring her to the steamy greenhouse air.

She nipped his ear where a single dot-shaped scar stayed from a healed-over piercing. A teenage rebellion, he'd told her once. She could envision him on a Spanish galleon, a swarthy and buffed pirate king.

For a moment, for *this* moment, she let herself indulge in foolish fantasies, no fears. She would allow the experience to sweep her away as smoothly as she brushed off his board shorts. She pushed aside the sterner responsible voice inside her that insisted she remember past mistakes and tread cautiously.

"It's been too damn long." He thumbed off her swimsuit bottom.

"Uh, hello?" She kicked the last fabric barrier away and

prayed other barriers could be as easily discarded. "It's been less than eight hours since you left my room."

"Too long."

She played her fingers along the cut of his sculpted chest, down the flat plane of his washboard stomach. Pressing her lips to his shoulder, she kissed her way toward his arm until she grazed the different texture of his tattooed flesh—inked with a black nautical compass. "I've always wanted to ask why you chose this particular tattoo."

His muscles bunched and twitched. "It symbolizes being able to find my way home."

"There's still so much I don't know about you." Concerns trickled through her like the rain trying to find its way inside.

"Hey, we're here to escape. All that can wait." He slipped her glasses from her face and placed them on the end table.

Parting through the floral arrangement to the middle, he slipped out an orchid and pinched off the flower. He trailed the bloom along her nose, her cheekbones and jaw in a silky scented swirl. "For magnificence."

Her knees went wobbly and she sat on the edge of the chaise, tapestry fabric rough on the backs on her thighs, rose-petal smooth. He tucked the orchid behind her ear, easing her back until she reclined.

Returning to the vase, he tugged free a long stalk with indigo buds and explored the length of her arm, then one finger at a time. Then over her stomach to her other hand and back up again in a shivery path that left her breathless.

"Blue salvia," he said, "because I think of you night and day."

His words stirred her as much as the glide of the flower

over her shoulder. Then he placed it on the tiny pillow under her head.

A pearly calla lily chosen next, he traced her collarbone before lightly dipping between her breasts.

"Shannon," he declared hoarsely, "I chose this lily because you are a majestic beauty."

Detouring, he sketched the underside of her breast and looped round again and again, each circle smaller until he teased the dusky tip. Her body pulled tight and tingly. Her back arched into the sweet sensation and he transferred his attention to her other breast, repeating the delicious pattern.

Reaching for him, she clutched his shoulders, aching to urge him closer. "Tony…"

Gently, he clasped her wrists and tucked them at her sides. "No touching or I'll stop."

"Really?"

"Probably not, because I can't resist you." He left the lily in her open palm. "But how about you play along anyway? I guarantee you'll like the results."

Dark eyes glinting with an inner light, Tony eased free… "A coral rose for passion."

His words raspy, his face intense, he skimmed the bud across her stomach, lower. Lower still. Her head fell back, her eyes closed as she wondered just how far he would dare go.

The silky teasing continued from her hip inward, daring more and even more. A husky moan escaped between her clenched lips.

Still, he continued until the rose caressed…oh my. Her knee draped to the side giving him, giving the flower, fuller access as he teased her. Gooseflesh sprinkled her skin. Her body focused on the feelings and perfumes stoking desire higher.

A warm breath steamed over her stomach with only a second's warning before his mouth replaced the flower. Her fingers twitched into a fist, crushing the lily and releasing a fresh burst of perfume. A flick of his tongue, alternated with gentle suckles, caressed and coaxed her toward completion.

Her head thrashed as she chased her release. He took her to the brink, then retreated, drawing out the pleasure until the pressure inside her swelled and throbbed...

And bloomed.

A cry of pleasure burst free and she didn't bother holding it back. She rode the sensation, gasping in floral-tinged breaths.

His bold hands stroked upward as he slid over her, blanketing her with his hard, honed body. She hooked a languid leg over his hip. Her arm draped his shoulders as she drew him toward her, encouraging him to press inside.

The smell of crushed flowers clung to his skin as she kissed her way along his chest, back up his neck. He filled her, stretched her, moved inside her. She was surprised to feel desire rising again to a fevered pitch. Writhing, she lost herself in the barrage of sensations. The bristle of his chest hair against her breasts. The silky softness of flower petals against her back.

And the scents—she gasped in the perfect blend of musk and sex and earthy greenhouse. She raked his back, broad and strong and yet so surprisingly gentle, too.

He was working his way not only into her body but into her heart. When had she ever stood a chance at resisting him? As much as she tried to tell herself it was only physical, only an affair, she knew this man had come to mean so much more to her. He reached her in ways no one ever had before.

She grappled at the hard planes of his back, completion so close all over again.

"Let go and I'll catch you," he vowed against her ear and she believed him.

For the first time in so long, she totally trusted.

The magnitude exploded inside her, blasting through barriers. Pleasure filled every niche. Muscles knotted in Tony's back as he tensed over her and growled his own hoarse completion against her ear.

Staring up at the rain-splattered skylight, tears burning her eyes again, she held Tony close. She felt utterly bare and unable to hide any longer. She'd trusted him with her body.

Now the time had come to trust him with her secrets.

Twelve

Tony watched Shannon on his iPhone as she talked to Kolby. She'd assured him that she wanted to stay longer in their greenhouse getaway, once she checked on her son.

Raindrops pattered slowly on the skylight, the afternoon shower coming to an end. Sunshine refracted off the moisture, casting prisms throughout the indoor garden.

He had Shannon back in his bed and in his life and he intended to do anything it took to keep her there. The chemistry between them, the connection—it was one of a kind. The way she'd calmly handled his bizarre family set-up, keeping her down-to-earth ways in the face of so much wealth... Finally, he'd found a woman he could trust, a woman he could spend his life with. Coming back to the island had been a good thing after all, since it had made him realize how unaffected she was by the trappings. In a compass, she would be the magnet, a grounding center.

And he owed her so much better than he'd delivered thus

far. He'd wrecked Shannon's life. It was up to him to fix it. Here, alone with her in the bright light of day, he couldn't avoid the truth.

They would get married.

The decision settled inside him with a clean fit, so much so he wondered why he hadn't decided so resolutely before now. His feelings for her ran deep. He knew she cared for him, too. And marrying each other would solve her problems.

They were making progress. He could tell she'd been swayed by the flowers, the ambience.

A plan formed in his mind. Later tonight he would take her to the chapel, lit with candles, and he would propose, while the lovemaking they'd shared here was still fresh in her memory.

Now he just had to figure out the best way to persuade her to say yes.

Thumbing the off button, she disconnected her call. "The nanny says Kolby has only just woken up and she's feeding him a snack." She passed his phone to him and curled against his side on the chaise. "Thanks for not teasing me about being overprotective. I can't help but worry when I'm not with him."

"I would too, if he was mine," he said. Then her surprised expression prompted him to continue, "Why do you look shocked?"

"No offense meant." She smoothed a hand along his chest. "It's just obvious you and he haven't connected."

Something he would need to rectify in order to be a part of Shannon's life. "I will never let you or him down the way his father did."

She winced and he could feel her drawing back into herself. He wanted all barriers gone between them as fully as they'd tossed aside their clothes.

"Hey, Shannon, stay with me here." He cupped her bare hip. "I asked you before if your husband hit you and you said no. Did you lie about that?"

Sitting up abruptly, she gathered her swimsuit off the floor.

"Let's get dressed and then we can talk." She yanked on the suit bottom briskly.

Waiting, he slid on his board shorts. She tied the bikini strings behind her neck with exaggerated effort, all the while staring at the floor. A curtain of tousled blond locks covered her face. Just when he'd begun to give up on getting an answer, she straightened, shaking her hair back over her shoulders.

"I was telling the truth when I said Nolan never laid a hand on me. But there are things I need to explain in order for you to understand why it's so difficult for me to accept help." Determination creased her face. "Nolan was always a driven man. His perfectionism made him successful in business. And I'd been brought up to believe marriage is forever. How could I leave a man because he didn't like the way I hung clothes in the closet?"

He forced his hands to stay loose on his knees, keeping his body language as unthreatening as possible when he already sensed he would want to beat the hell out of Nolan Crawford by the end of this conversation—if he wasn't already dead.

Plucking a flower petal from her hair, she rubbed the coral-colored patch between two fingers. "Do you know how many people laughed at me because I was upset that he didn't want me to work? He said he wanted us to have more time together. Somehow any plans I made with others were disrupted. After a while I lost contact with my friends."

The picture of isolation came together in his head with startling clarity. He understood the claustrophobic feeling of being cut off from the rest of the world. Although he couldn't help but think his father's need to protect his children differed from an obsessive—abusive—husband dominating his wife. Rage simmered, ready to boil.

She scooped her cover-up from the floor and clutched it to her stomach. "Then I got pregnant. Splitting up became more complicated."

Hating like hell the helpless feeling, he passed her glasses back to her. It was damn little, but all he could see her accepting from him right now.

With a wobbly smile, she slid them on her face and seemed to take strength from them. "When Kolby was about thirteen months old, he spiked a scary high fever while I was alone with him. Nolan had always gone with us to pediatric check-ups. At the ER, I was a mess trying to give the insurance information. I had no idea what to tell them, because Nolan had insisted I not 'worry' about such things as medical finances. That day triggered something in me. I needed to take care of my son."

He took her too-cold hand and rubbed it between his.

"Looking back now I see the signs were there. Nolan's computer and cell phone were password protected. He considered it an invasion of privacy if I asked who he was speaking to. I thought he was cheating. I never considered..."

He squeezed her hand in silent encouragement.

"So I decided to learn more about the finances, because if I needed to leave him, I had to make sure my son's future was protected and not spirited away to some Cayman account." She fidgeted, her fingers landing on the blue salvia—*I think of you often* took on a darker meaning. "I was lucky enough to figure out his computer password."

"*You* discovered the Ponzi scheme?" Good God,

what kind of strength would it take to turn in her own husband?

"It was the hardest thing I've ever done, but I handed over the evidence to the police. He'd stolen so much from so many people, I couldn't stay silent. His parents posted bail, and I wasn't given warning." She spun the stem between her thumb and forefinger. "When he walked back into the house, he had a gun."

Shock nailed him harder than a sail boom to the gut.

"My God, Shannon. I knew he'd committed suicide but I had no idea you were there. I'm so damn sorry."

"That's not all, though. For once the media didn't uncover everything." She drew herself up straight. "Nolan said he was going to kill me, then Kolby and then himself."

Her words iced the perspiration on his brow. This was so much worse than he'd foreseen. He cupped an arm around her shoulders and pulled her close. She trembled and kept twirling the flower, but she didn't stop speaking.

"His parents pulled up in the driveway." A shuddering sigh racked her body, her profile pained. "He realized he wouldn't have time to carry out his original plan. Thank God he locked himself in his office before he pulled the trigger and killed himself."

"Shannon." Horror threatened to steal his breath, but for her, he would hold steady. "I don't even know what to say to fix the hell you were put through."

"I didn't tell his parents what he'd planned. They'd lost their son and he'd been labeled a criminal." She held up the blue salvia. "I couldn't see causing them more grief when they thought of him."

Her eyes were filled with tears and regret. Tony kissed her forehead, then pulled her against his chest. "You were generous to the memory of a man who didn't deserve it."

"I didn't do it for him. No matter what, he's the father

of my child." She pressed her cheek harder against him and hugged him tightly. "Kolby will have to live with the knowledge that his dad was a crook, but I'll be damned before I'll let my son know his own father tried to kill him."

"You've fought hard for your son." He stroked her back. "You're a good mother and a strong woman."

She reminded him of a distant memory, of his own mother wrapping him in a silver blanket as they left San Rinaldo and telling him the shield would keep him safe. She'd been right. If only he could have protected her, as well.

Easing away, Shannon scrubbed her damp cheeks. "Thank God for Vernon. I'd sold off everything to pay Nolan's debts, even my piano and my oboe. The first waitressing job I landed in Louisiana didn't cover expenses. We were running out of options when Vernon hired me. Everyone else treated me like a pariah. Even Nolan's parents didn't want anything to do with either of us. So many people insisted I must have known what he was doing. That I must have tucked away money for myself. The gossip and the rumors were hell."

Realization, understanding spewed inside him like the abrupt shower of the sprinklers misting over the potted plants. He'd finally found a woman he could trust enough to propose marriage.

Only to find a husband was likely the last thing she ever wanted again.

Three hours later, Shannon sat on the floor in her suite with Kolby, rolling wooden trains along a ridged track. An ocean breeze spiraled through the open balcony door. She craved the peace of that boundless horizon. Never again would she allow herself to be hedged in as she'd been in her marriage.

After she'd finished dredging up her past, she'd needed to see her son. Tony had been understanding, although she could sense he wanted to talk longer. Once she'd returned to her suite, she'd showered and changed—and had been with her son ever since.

The past twenty-four hours had been emotionally charged on so many levels. Tony had been supportive and understanding, while giving her space. He'd also been a tender—thorough—lover.

Could she risk giving their relationship another try once they returned to the mainland? Was it possible for her to be a part of a normal couple?

A tug on her shirt yanked her attention back to the moment. Kolby looked up at her with wide blue eyes. "I'm hungry."

"Of course, sweetie. We'll go down to the kitchen and see what we can find." Hopefully the cook—the *chef*—wouldn't object since he must be right in the middle of supper prep. "We just need to clean up the toys first."

As she reached for the train set's storage bin, she heard a throat clear behind her and jerked around to find her on-again lover standing in the balcony doorway.

Her stomach fluttered with awareness, and she pressed her sweaty palms to her jeans. "How long have you been there?"

"Not long." Tony had showered and changed as well, wearing khakis and a button-down. "I can make his snack."

Whoa, Tony was seeking time with her son? That signaled a definite shift in their relationship. Although she'd seen him make his own breakfast in the past, she couldn't miss the significance of this moment and his efforts to try.

Turning him away would mean taking a step back. "Are you sure?"

Because God knows, she still had a boatload of fears.

"Positive," he said, his voice as steady as the man.

"Okay then." She pressed a hand over her stomach full of butterflies. "I'll just clean up here—"

"We've got it, don't we, pal?"

Kolby eyed him warily but he didn't turn away, probably because Tony kept his distance. He wasn't pushing. Maybe they'd both learned a lot these past couple of weeks.

"Okay, then." She stood, looking around the room, unsure what to do next. "I'll just, uh…"

Tony touched her hand lightly. "You mentioned selling your piano and I couldn't miss the regret in your voice. There's a Steinway Grand in the east wing. Alys or one of the guards can show you where if you would like to play."

Would she? Her fingers twitched. She'd closed off so much of her old life, including the good parts. Her music had been a beautiful bright spot in those solitary years of her life with Nolan. How kind of Tony to see beyond the surface of the harrowing final moments that had tainted her whole marriage. In the same way he'd chosen flowers based on facets of her personality, he'd detected the creativity she'd all but forgotten, honoring it in a small, simple offer.

Nodding her head was tougher than she thought. Her body went a little jerky before she could manage a response. "I would like that. Thank you for thinking of it and for spending time with Kolby."

He was a man who saw beyond her material needs…a man to treasure.

Her throat clogging with emotion, she backed from the room, watching the tableau of Tony with her son. Antonio Medina, a prince and billionaire, knelt on the floor with Kolby, cleaning up a wooden train set.

Tony chunked the caboose in the bin. "Has your mom ever cooked you a Cyclops?"

"What's a cycle-ops?" His face was intent with interest.

"The sooner we clean up the trains, the sooner I can show you."

She pressed a hand to her swelling heart. Tony was handling Kolby with ease. Her son would be fine.

After getting directions from Alys, Shannon found the east wing and finally the music room. What a simple way to describe such an awe-inspiring space. More of a circular ballroom, wooden floors stretched across, with a coffered ceiling that added texture as well as sound control. Crystal chandeliers and sconces glittered in the late afternoon sun.

And the instruments… Her feet drew her deeper into the room, closer to the gold gilded harp and a Steinway grand piano. She stroked the ivory keys reverently, then zipped through a scale. Pure magic.

She perched on the bench, her hands poised. Unease skittered up her spine like a double-timed scale, a sense of being watched. Pivoting around, she searched the expansive room….

Seated in a tapestry wingback, Enrique Medina stared back at her from beside a stained glass window. Even with his ill health, the deposed monarch radiated power and charisma. His dogs asleep on either side, he wore a simple dark suit with an ascot, perfectly creased although loose fitting. He'd lost even more weight since her arrival.

Enrique thumbed a gold pocket watch absently. "Do not mind me."

Had Tony sent her to this room on purpose, knowing his father would be here? She didn't think so, given the stilted relationship between the two men. "I don't want to disturb you."

"Not at all. We have not had a chance to speak alone, you and I," he said with a hint of an accent.

The musicality was pleasing to the ear. Every now and then, a lilt in certain words reminded her of how Tony spoke, small habits that she hadn't discerned as being raised with a foreign language. But she could hear the similarity more clearly when listening to his father.

While she'd seen the king daily during her two weeks on the island, those encounters had been mostly during meals. He'd spent the majority of his time with his daughter. But since Eloisa and her husband had left this afternoon, Enrique must be at loose ends. Shannon envied them that connection, and missed her own parents all the more. How much different her life might have been if they hadn't died. Her mother had shared a love of music.

She stroked the keyboard longingly. "Who plays the piano?"

"My sons took lessons as a part of the curriculum outlined by their tutors."

"Of course, I should have realized," she said. "Tony can play?"

Laughter rattled around inside his chest. "That would be a stretch. My youngest son can read music, but he did not enjoy sitting still. Antonio rushed through lessons so he could go outside."

"I can picture that."

"You know him well then." His sharp brown eyes took in everything. "Now my middle boy, Duarte, is more disciplined, quite the martial arts expert. But with music?" Enrique waved dismissively. "He performs like a robot."

Her curiosity tweaked for more details on Tony's family. Over the past couple of weeks, their relationship had deepened, and she needed more insights to still the fears churning her gut. "And your oldest son, Carlos? How did he fare with the piano lessons?"

A dark shadow crossed Enrique's face before he schooled his regal features again. "He had a gift. He's a surgeon now, using that touch in other ways."

"I can see how the two careers could tap into the same skill," she said, brushing her fingers over the gleaming keys.

Perhaps she could try again to find a career that tapped into her love of music. What a gift it would be to bring joy deeper into her life again.

Enrique tucked one hand into his pocket. "Do you have feelings for my son?"

His blunt question blindsided her, but she should have realized this cunning man never chatted just for conversation's sake. "That is a personal question."

"And I may not have time to wait around for you to feel comfortable answering."

"You're playing the death card? That's a bit cold, don't you think, sir?"

He laughed, hard and full-out like Tony did—or like he used to. "You have a spine. Good. You are a fine match for my stubborn youngest."

Her irritation over his probing questions eased. What parent didn't want to see their children settled and happy? "I appreciate your opening your home to me and my son and giving us a chance to get to know you."

"Diplomatically said, my dear. You are wise to proceed thoughtfully. Regrets are a terrible thing," he said somberly. "I should have sent my family out of San Rinaldo sooner. I waited too long and Beatriz paid the price."

The darker turn of the conversation stilled her. She'd wanted more insights into Tony's life, yet this was going so much deeper than she had anticipated.

Enrique continued, "It was such chaos that day when the coup began. We had planned for my family to take one escape route and I would use another." His jaw flexed sharply in his gaunt face. "I made it out, and the rebels found my family. Carlos was injured trying to save his mother."

The picture of violence and terror he painted sounded like something from a movie, so unreal, yet they'd lived it. "Tony and your other sons witnessed the attack on their mother?"

"Antonio had nightmares for a year, and then he became obsessed with the beach and surfing. From that day on, he lived to leave the island."

She'd known the bare bones details of their escape. But the horror they'd lived through, the massive losses rolled over her with a new vividness. Tony's need to help her had more to do with caring than control. He didn't want to isolate her or smother her by managing everything the way her husband had. Tony tried to help her because he'd failed to save someone else he cared about.

Somehow, knowing this made it easier for her to open her heart. To take a chance beyond their weeks here.

Without question, he would have to understand her need for independence, but she also had to appreciate how he'd been hurt, how those hurts had shaped him. And as Antonio Medina and Tony Castillo merged in her mind, she couldn't ignore the truth any longer.

She loved him.

Approaching footsteps startled her, drawing her focus from the past and toward the arched entry. Tony stepped into view just when her defenses were at their lowest. No doubt her heart was in her eyes. She started toward him, only to realize *his* eyes held no tender feelings.

The harsh angles of his face blared a forewarning before he announced, "There's been a security breach."

Thirteen

Shock jolted through Shannon, followed closely by fear. "A security breach? Where's Kolby?"

She shot to her feet and ran across the music room to Tony. The ailing king reached for his cane, his dogs waking instantly, beating her there by a footstep. Enrique steadied himself with a hand against the wall, but he was up and moving. "What happened?"

"Kolby is fine. No one has been hurt, but we have taken another hit in the media."

Enrique asked, "Have they located the island?"

"No," Tony said as Alys slid into view behind him. "It happened at the airport when Eloisa and Jonah's flight landed in South Carolina. The press was waiting, along with crowds of everyday people wanting a picture to sell for an easy buck."

Shannon's stomach lurched at another assault in the

news. "Could the frenzy have to do with the Landis family connections?"

"No," Tony said curtly. "The questions were all about their vacation with Eloisa's father the king."

Alys angled past Tony with a wheelchair. "Your Majesty, I'll take you to your office so you can speak to security directly."

The king dropped into the wheelchair heavily. "Thank you, Alys." His dogs loped into place alongside him. "I am ready."

Nerves jangled, Shannon started to follow, but Tony extended a hand to stop her.

"We need to talk."

His chilly voice stilled her feet faster than any arm across the entranceway. Had he been holding back because of concerns for his father's health? "What's wrong? What haven't you told me?"

She stepped closer for comfort. He crossed his arms over his chest.

"The leak came from this house. There was a call placed from here this afternoon—at just the right time—to an unlisted cell number."

"Here? But your father's security has been top notch." No wonder he was so concerned.

Tony unclipped his iPhone from his waistband. "We have security footage of the call being made."

Thumbing the controls, he filled the screen with a still image of a woman on the phone, a woman in a white swimsuit cover-up, hood pulled over her head.

A cover-up just like hers? "I don't understand. You think this is *me?* Why would I tip off the media?"

His mouth stayed tight-lipped and closed, and his eyes... Oh God, she recognized well that condemning look from the days following Nolan's arrest and then his death.

Steady. Steady. She reminded herself Tony wasn't Nolan or the other people who'd betrayed her, and he had good reasons to be wary. She drew in a shuddering breath.

"I understand that Enrique brought you up to be unusually cautious about the people in your life. And he had cause after what happened to your mother." Thoughts of Tony as a small child watching his mother's murder brushed sympathy over her own hurt. "But you have to see there's nothing about me that would hint at this kind of behavior."

"I know you would do anything to secure your son's future. Whoever sold this information received a hefty payoff." He stared back at her with cold eyes and unswerving surety.

In a sense he was right. She would do anything for Kolby. But again, Tony had made a mistake. He'd offered her money before, assuming that would equate security to her. She had deeper values she wanted to relay to her son, like the importance of earning a living honorably. Tony had needed to prove that himself in leaving the island. Why was it so difficult to understand she felt the same way?

Her sympathy for him could only stretch so far.

"You actually believe I betrayed you? That I placed everyone here at risk for a few dollars?" Anger frothed higher and higher inside her. "I never wanted any of this. My son and I can get by just fine without you and your movie theater." She swatted his arm. "Answer me, damn you."

"I don't know what to think." He pinched the bridge of his nose. "Tell me it was an accident. You called a friend just to shoot the breeze because you were homesick and that friend sold you out."

Except as she'd already told him and he must remember, she didn't have friends, not anymore. Apparently she didn't even have Tony. "I'm not going to defend myself to you. Either you trust me or you don't."

He gripped her shoulders, his touch careful, his eyes more tumultuous. "I want a future with you. God, Shannon, I was going to ask you to marry me later tonight. I planned to take you back to the chapel, go inside this time and propose."

Her heart squeezed tight at the image he painted. If this security nightmare hadn't occurred, she would have been swept off her feet. She would have been celebrating her engagement with him tonight, because by God, she would have said yes. Now, that wasn't possible.

"You honestly thought we could get married when you have so little faith in me?" The betrayal burned deep. And hadn't she sworn she'd never again put herself in a position to feel that sting from someone she cared about? "You should have included some azaleas in the bouquet you chose for us. I hear they mean fragile passion."

She shrugged free of his too tempting touch. The hole inside her widened, ached.

"Damn it all, Shannon, we're talking." He started toward her.

"Stop." She held up a hand. "Don't come near me. Not now. Not ever."

"Where are you going?" He kept his distance this time. "I need to know you're safe."

"Has the new security system been installed at my apartment?"

His mouth tight, he nodded. "But we're still working on the restraining orders. Given the renewed frenzy because of Eloisa's identity—"

"The new locks and alarms will do for now."

"Damn it, Shannon—"

"I have to find Alys so she can make the arrangements."

She held her chin high. Pride and her child were all she had left now that her heart was shattered to pieces. "Kolby and I are returning to Texas."

"Where are Shannon and her son?"

His father's question hammered Tony's already pounding head. In his father's study, he poured himself three fingers of cognac, bypassing the Basque wine and the memories it evoked. Shannon wrapped around him, the scent of lilies in her hair. "You know full well where she is. Nothing slips past you here."

They'd spent the past two hours assessing the repercussions of the leak. The media feeding frenzy had been rekindled with fresh fuel about Eloisa's connection to the family. Inevitable, yet still frustrating. It gnawed at his gut to think Shannon had something to do with this, although he reassured himself it must have been an accident.

And if she'd simply slipped up and made a mistake, he could forgive her. She hadn't lived the Medina way since the cradle. Remembering all the intricacies involved in maintaining such a high level of security was difficult. If she would just admit what happened, they could move on.

His father rolled back from the computer desk, his large dogs tracking his every move from in front of the fireplace. "Apparently I do not know everything happening under my roof, because somebody placed a call putting Eloisa's flight at risk. I trusted someone I shouldn't have."

"You trusted me and my judgment." He scratched his tightening rib cage.

His father snorted with impatience. "Do not be an impulsive jackass. Think with your brain and not your heart."

"Like you've always done?" Tony snapped, his patience for his father's cryptic games growing short. "No thank you."

Once he finished his one-month obligation, he wouldn't set foot on this godforsaken island again. If memories of his life here before were unhappy, now they were gut-wrenching. His father should come to the mainland anyway for medical treatment. Even Enrique's deep coffers couldn't outfit the island with unlimited hospital options.

Enrique poured himself a drink and downed it swiftly. "I let my heart guide me when I left San Rinaldo. I was so terrified something would happen to my wife and sons that I did not think through our escape plan properly."

Invincible Enrique was admitting a mistake? Tony let that settle inside him for a second before speaking.

"You set yourself up as a diversion. Sounds pretty self-less to me." He'd never doubted his father's bravery or cool head.

"I did not think it through." He refilled his glass and stared into the amber liquid, signs of regret etched deep in his forehead. Illness had never made the king appear weak, but at this moment, the ghosts of an old past showed a vulnerability Tony had never seen before. "If I had, I would have taken into account the way Carlos would react if things went to hell. I arrogantly considered my plan foolproof. Again, I thought with my emotions and those assassins knew exactly how to target my weakness."

Tony set aside his glass without touching a drop. Empathy for his father seared him more fully than alcohol. Understanding how it felt to have his feelings ripped up through his throat because of a woman gave him insights to his father he'd never expected. "You did your best at the time."

Could he say the same when it came to Shannon?

"I tried to make that right with this island. I did everything in my power to create a safe haven for my sons."

"But we all three left the protection of this place."

"That doesn't matter to me. My only goal was keeping you safe until adulthood. By the time you departed, you took with you the skills to protect yourself, to make your way in the world. That never would have been possible if you'd grown up with obligations to a kingdom. For that, I'm proud."

Enrique's simply spoken words enveloped him. Even though his father wasn't telling him anything he didn't already know, something different took root in him. An understanding. Just as his mother had made the silver security blanket as a "shield," to make him feel protected, his father had been doing the same. His methods may not have been perfect, but their situation had been far from normal. They'd all been scrambling to patch together their lives.

Some of his understanding must have shown on his face, because his father smiled approvingly.

"Now, son, think about Shannon logically rather than acting like a love-sick boy."

Love-sick boy? Now that stung more than a little. And the reason? Because it was true. He did love her, and that had clouded his thinking.

He loved her. And he'd let his gut drive his conclusions rather than logic. He forced his slugging heart to slow and collected what he knew about Shannon. "She's a naturally cautious woman who wouldn't do anything to place her son at risk. If she had a call to make, she would check with you or I to make sure the call was safe. She wouldn't have relied on anyone else's word when it comes to Kolby."

"What conclusion does that lead you to?"

"We never saw the caller's face. I made an assumption

based on a female in a bathing suit cover-up. The caller must have been someone with detailed knowledge of our security systems in order to keep her face shielded. A woman of similar build. A person with something to gain and little loyalty to the Medinas..." His brain settled on... "Alys?"

"I would bet money on it." The thunderous anger Enrique now revealed didn't bode well for the assistant who'd used her family connections to take advantage of an ailing king with an aging staff. "She was even the one to order Shannon's clothes. It would be easy to make sure she had the right garb...."

Shannon had done nothing wrong.

"God, I wonder if Alys could have even been responsible for tipping off the Global Intruder about that photo of Duarte when it first ran, before he was identified." The magnitude of how badly he'd screwed up threatened to kick his knees out from under him. He braced a hand on his father's shoulder, touching his dad for the first time in fourteen years. "Where the hell is Alys?"

Enrique swallowed hard. He clapped his hand over Tony's for a charged second before clearing his throat.

"Leave Alys to me." His royal roots showed through again as he assumed command. "Don't you have a more pressing engagement?"

Tony checked his watch. He had five minutes until the ferry pulled away for the airstrip. No doubt his father would secure the proof of Alys's deception soon, but Shannon needed—hell, she deserved—to know that he'd trusted in her innocence without evidence.

He had a narrow, five-minute window to prove just how much he loved and trusted her.

* * *

The ferry horn wailed, signaling they were disconnecting from the dock. The crew was stationed at their posts, lost in the ritual of work.

Kolby on her hip, Shannon looked at the exotic island for the last time. This was hard, so much harder than she'd expected. How would she ever survive going back to Galveston where even more memories of Tony waited? She couldn't. She would have to start over somewhere new and totally different.

Except there was no place she could run now that would be free of Medina reminders. The grocery store aisles would sport gossip rags. Channel surfing could prove hazardous. And she didn't even want to think of how often she would be confronted with Tony's face peering back at her from an internet headline, reminding her of how little faith he'd had in her. As much as she wanted to say to hell with it all and accept whatever he offered, she wouldn't settle for half measures ever again.

Tears blurred the exotic shoreline, sea oats dotting the last bit of sand as they pulled away. She squeezed her eyes closed, tears cool on her heated cheeks.

"Mommy?" Kolby patted her face.

She scavenged a wobbly smile and focused on his precious face. "I'm okay, sweetie. Everything's going to be fine. Let's look for a dolphin."

"Nu-uh," he said. "Why's Tony running? Can he come wif us, pretty pwease?"

What? She followed the path of her son's pointing finger....

Tony sprinted down the dock, his mouth moving but his words swallowed up by the roar of the engines and churning water behind the ferry. Her heart pumped in time with his long-legged strides. She almost didn't dare hope, but then Tony had always delivered the unexpected.

Lowering Kolby to the deck with one arm, she leaned over the rail, straining to hear what he said. Still, the wind whipped his words as the ferry inched away. Disappointment pinched as she realized she would have to wait for the ferry to travel back again to speak to him. So silly to be impatient, but her heart had broken a lifetime's worth in one day.

Just as she'd resigned herself to waiting, Tony didn't stop running. Oh my God, he couldn't actually be planning to—

Jump.

Her heart lodged in her throat for an expanded second as he was airborne. Then he landed on deck with the surefooted ease of an experienced boater. Tony strode toward her with even, determined steps, the crew parting to make way.

He extended his hand, his fist closed around a clump of sea oats, still dripping from where he'd yanked them up. "You'll have to use your imagination here because I didn't have much time." He passed her one stalk. "Imagine this is a purple hyacinth, the 'forgive me' flower. I hope you will accept it, along with my apology."

"Go ahead. I'm listening." Although she didn't take his pretend hyacinth. He had a bit more talking to do after what he'd put her through.

Kolby patted his leg for attention. Winking down at the boy, Tony passed him one of the sea oats, which her son promptly waved like a flag. With Kolby settled, Tony shifted his attention back to Shannon.

"I've been an idiot," he said. Sea spray dampened his hair, increasing the rebellious curls. "I should have known you wouldn't do anything to put Kolby or my family at risk.

And if you'd done so inadvertently, you would have been upfront about it." He told her all the things she'd hoped to hear earlier.

While she appreciated the romanticism of his gesture, a part of her still ached that he'd needed proof. Trust was such a fragile thing, but crucial in any relationship.

"What brought about this sudden insight to my character? Did you find some new surveillance tape that proves my innocence?"

"I spoke to my father. He challenged me, made me think with my head instead of my scared-as-hell heart. And thank God he did, because once I looked deeper I realized Alys must have made the call. I can't help but wonder if she's the one who made the initial leak to the press. We don't have proof yet, but we'll find it."

Alys? Shannon mulled over that possibility, remembering the way the assistant had stared at Tony with such hunger. She'd sensed the woman wanted to be a Medina. Perhaps Alys had also wanted all the public princess perks to go with it rather than a life spent in hiding.

Tony extended his hand with the sea oats again, tickling them across Kolby's chin lightly before locking eyes with Shannon. "But none of that matters if you don't trust me."

Touching the cottony white tops of the sea oats, she weighed her words carefully. This moment could define the rest of her life. "I realize the way you've grown up has left marks on you...what happened with your mother... living in seclusion here. But I can't always worry when that's going to make you push me away again just because you're afraid I'll betray you."

Her fingers closed around his. "I've had so many people turn away from me. I can't—I won't—spend my life proving myself to you."

"And I don't expect you to." He clasped both hands around hers, his skin callused and tough, a little rough around the edges like her impetuous lover. "You're absolutely right. I was wrong. What I feel for you, it's scary stuff. But the thought of losing you is a helluva lot scarier than any alternative."

"What exactly are you saying?" She needed him to spell it out, every word, every promise.

"My life is complicated and comes with a lot more cons than pros. There's nothing to stop Alys from spilling everything she knows, and if so, it's really going to hit the fan. A life with me won't be easy. To the world, I am a Medina. And I hope you will consent to be a Medina, too."

He knelt in front of her with those sea oats—officially now her favorite plant.

"Shannon, will you be my bride? Let me be your husband and a father to Kolby." He paused to ruffle the boy's hair, eliciting a giant smile from her son. "As well as any other children we may have together. I can't promise I won't be a jackass again. I can almost guarantee that I will. But I vow to stick with it, stick with us, because you mean too much to me for me to ever mess this up again."

Sinking to her knees, she fell into his arms, her son enclosed in the circle. "Yes, I'll marry you and build a family and future with you. Tony Castillo, Antonio Medina, and any other name you go by, I love you, too. You've stolen my heart for life."

"Thank God." He gathered her closer, his arms trembling just a hint.

She lost track of how long they knelt that way until Kolby squirmed between them, and she heard the crew applauding and cheering. Together, she and Tony stood as the ferry captain shouted orders to turn the boat around.

Standing at the deck with Tony, she stared at the approaching island, a place she knew they would visit over the years. She clasped his arm, her cheek against his compass tattoo. Tony rested his chin on her head.

His breath caressed her hair. "The legend about the compass is true. I've found my way home."

Surprised, she glanced up at him. "Back to the island?"

Shaking his head, he tucked a knuckle under her chin and brushed a kiss across her mouth. "Ah, Shanny, *you* are my home."

* * * * *

LET'S TALK
Romance

For exclusive extracts, competitions and special offers, find us online:

- **f** MillsandBoon
- **𝕏** @MillsandBoon
- **◎** @MillsandBoonUK
- **♪** @MillsandBoonUK

Get in touch on 01413 063 232

MILLS & BOON

THE HEART OF ROMANCE

A ROMANCE FOR EVERY READER

MODERN

Prepare to be swept off your feet by sophisticated, sexy and seductive heroes, in some of the world's most glamourous and romantic locations, where power and passion collide.

HISTORICAL

Escape with historical heroes from time gone by. Whether your passion is for wicked Regency Rakes, muscled Vikings or rugged Highlanders, awaken the romance of the past.

MEDICAL

Set your pulse racing with dedicated, delectable doctors in the high-pressure world of medicine, where emotions run high and passion, comfort and love are the best medicine.

True Love

Celebrate true love with tender stories of heartfelt romance, from the rush of falling in love to the joy a new baby can bring, and a focus on the emotional heart of a relationship.

Desire

Indulge in secrets and scandal, intense drama and sizzling hot action with heroes who have it all: wealth, status, good looks…everything but the right woman.

HEROES

The excitement of a gripping thriller, with intense romance at its heart. Resourceful, true-to-life women and strong, fearless men face danger and desire - a killer combination!

To see which titles are coming soon, please visit

millsandboon.co.uk/nextmonth

JOIN US ON SOCIAL MEDIA!

Stay up to date with our latest releases, author news and gossip, special offers and discounts, and all the behind-the-scenes action from Mills & Boon...

 @millsandboon

 @millsandboonuk

 facebook.com/millsandboon

 @millsandboonuk

It might just be true love...

MILLS & BOON
A ROMANCE FOR EVERY READER

- **FREE** delivery direct to your door
- **EXCLUSIVE** offers every month
- **SAVE** up to 30% on pre-paid subscritions

SUBSCRIBE AND SAVE

millsandboon.co.uk/Subscribe

GET YOUR ROMANCE FIX!

Get the latest romance news,
exclusive author interviews, story
extracts and much more!

MILLS & BOON
True Love
Romance from the Heart

Celebrate true love with tender stories of
heartfelt romance, from the rush of falling in love
to the joy a new baby can bring, and a focus on the
emotional heart of a relationship.

MILLS & BOON

HEROES

At Your Service

Experience all the excitement of a gripping thriller, with an intense romance at its heart. Resourceful, true-to-life women and strong, fearless men face danger and desire – a killer combination!